The
Fallout

ALSO BY MARGARET SCOTT

Between You and Me

The
Fallout

To Bridget
Wishing you a speedy
recovery
All the best
Margaret
xx

Margaret Scott

POOLBEG

Published 2016
by Poolbeg Press Ltd
123 Grange Hill, Baldoyle
Dublin 13, Ireland
www.poolbeg.com

© Margaret Scott 2016

Copyright for editing, typesetting, layout, design, ebook
© Poolbeg Press Ltd

The moral right of the author has been asserted.

A catalogue record for this book is available from the British Library.

ISBN 978-1-78199-955-4

Printed and bound by CPI Group (UK) Ltd, Coydon, CR0 4YY

www.poolbeg.com

About the Author

Margaret Scott lives in Kildare with her husband Keith Darcy, two little girls Isabelle & Emily, one-year-old Michael and an assortment of pets. An accountant by day, her first book *Between You and Me* was published by Poolbeg Press in 2013 and enjoyed several weeks in the ROI top ten Bestsellers List.

Acknowledgements

The biggest risk of writing a book like this is that readers will think that the characters and situations are either based on somewhere I've worked myself, or on someone I've worked with, or worse still that it's about them personally. To all my lovely colleagues and friends over the years, let me assure you this is not true. To all the ones that weren't so lovely – you can also relax – you're not in it either.

On a more serious note, when researching the workplace conflict for this book I did actually speak to several people who shared their experiences with me about what they went through in the years of the recession and how the pressure they were under affected them on both a private and a professional level. You know who you are, I am humbly grateful for your story and may you continue to rise above what you went through.

Other people who unwittingly contributed to this book were authors whose work I used extensively for research, so thank you to Senator Shane Ross for *The Bankers*, Dearbhail McDonald for *Bust* (and a very generous offer to help in any way she could), Pat Leahy for *Showtime*, Frank McDonald and Kathy Sheridan *The Builders* and last but not least a huge thanks to Conor McCabe whose *Sins of the Father* gave me a huge insight into how the whole mess started many, many years ago. And a special thank-you, Joe Curtis, for pointing me towards most of these sources!

This book was born out of an almost Phoenix-type moment, quite literally from the ashes of one-that-didn't-work-out, and I would like to thank everyone who encouraged me to keep going, in particular Alan Bennett of Headstuff.org who, possibly to just stop me whining, asked me what I wanted to write, then said simply "Now go do it" and fellow Poolbeg author Caroline Finnerty who listened to more crying than was either fair or reasonable without either changing her phone number or entering a witness protection programme. In fact, over the last few years I have had the good fortune to get to know so many other authors, especially my lovely original stable-mates at Poolbeg – Claire Allan, Caroline Grace Cassidy, Shirley Benton Bailey, Maria Murphy and the aforementioned Ms Finnerty – each one of you have been both an inspiration and a support. Thank you.

Also thank you to Margaret Bonass Madden of BleachHouseLibrary.ie for including me in her Irish Fiction Fortnight this year and for introducing me to Poppy Peacock of PoppyPeacockPens.com who included me on her Round the Wold Book Tour. Both ladies gave me my first opportunities to talk about *The Fallout* and only then did I start to believe that this book was about to become a reality. And I also have to say a massive thank-you to Andrea Mara whose blog OfficeMum.ie has been a constant source of inspiration for this book and I have every faith that Andrea will be joining me on the shelves herself in no time.

As someone who is driven to create, it is very hard to imagine that the giants that have gone before you ever had a moment of self-doubt, or produced anything that was less than successful. For this reason, Jarlath Regan's *An Irishman Abroad* podcast has been a constant source of inspiration and reassurance – so thank you, Jarlath, and keep recording – I have to write another one ...

The plot for *The Fallout* took on a few more twists and turns than was originally planned and many of these were dreamed up while plodding around the Naas highways and byways in the company of Brendan's Running Club, a super group of people led by the inspirational and encouraging Brendan Loughlin. I don't think this book is as wild as you'd like, Brendan, but hopefully the running bits pass the technical test. And of course, my other go-to place for inspiration is still Alice's Restaurant, Naas, where the lovely Eibhlinn Ní Chearbhaill puts up with me for long hours and always manages to supply a fresh cuppa at exactly the right time.

My gorgeous baby Michael is over a year now but when he just a few weeks old he was diagnosed with a mild form of reflux. When I went to research his ailment I stumbled across Surviving Reflux Ireland, a group of ladies who were dealing with reflux and reflux-related issues on a scale that I just couldn't comprehend. When, almost a year later, I decided to incorporate this dreadful affliction into the story, they were hugely helpful when it came to research, in particular Cherie Bacon (author of *The Reflux Bible*) who despite already having so much on her plate gave freely and generously of her time to assist me with portraying the nightmare that raising a small baby with reflux can be.

Whilst on the subject of other mothers, I couldn't not thank the Q107 Rollercoaster Mammies again for being an unfailing support for the last few years. Also all my other friends without whom life would be a very dull place – in no particular order: Mairead, Sabrina, Tracey, Áine, Sonia, Jane, Órla, Eilish, the Ballycane School Mammies, and all my lovely colleagues in HRI. Also a special thanks to Liam, MJ and Bob in IT Monkey for putting up with my constant IT and website questions. I also owe a huge debt of gratitude to two ladies in particular who helped change the way I think and ensured I made it to the end of writing this with some level of sanity remaining – so Evelyn Burke and Kathleen Lambe, thank you. (And Kathleen, here's to our road trips full of your fascinating, inspiring stories – we'll have a laugh if nothing else x)

There is one particular person who was a constant source of support during the writing of this book and so thank you, Anne Marie Malone. I'm quite sure I drove you mental over the last year and even surer that I'll continue to do so for a long time yet. But sure that's what friends are for x.

Another person I'm sure I put through the wringer was my agent Ger Nichol who has stuck by me quite literally through thick and thin, and of course Paula Campbell of Poolbeg Press whose greatest gift to me was the time to finish this book properly. And as always thanks to my editor Gaye Shortland – no one appreciates more than me how complex a task it was to pull this book together so thank you for keeping me on the straight and narrow whilst we did so.

And last but not least, my wonderful family, especially my husband and best friend Keith and my three beautiful children, Isabelle, Emily and Michael – every day with you guys is a day well lived and you are a constant source of inspiration, joy and pride.

*For every Mary, Kate, Olivia and Leona worldwide who goes
to work every day and just tries to get the balance right.*

There is a special place reserved in hell for
women who don't help other women.
Madeleine Albright, Former US Secretary of State,
on women in the workplace.

People are sitting down, I know, and asking
'how can we all share this burden of adjustment?'
An Taoiseach Brian Cowen, 4 February 2009

fallout
[fôl out]

NOUN
noun: **fallout** · noun: **fall-out**

1. radioactive particles that are carried into the atmosphere after a nuclear explosion or accident and gradually fall back as dust or in precipitation.

• airborne substances resulting from an industrial process or accident:

"acid fallout from power stations"

2. the adverse side effects or results of a situation:

"almost as dramatic as the financial scale of the mess is the growing political fallout"

synonyms: repercussion(s) · reverberation(s) · aftermath · effect(s) · consequence(s)

Powered by OxfordDictionaries · © Oxford University Press

1

Thursday October 31st 2011

THE DAY OF . . .

There's a lot to be said for a boring day at the office. Excitement rarely leads to anything that doesn't cause some amount of stress to someone. So sitting in an office wishing something exciting would happen isn't always the best plan.

They say that, don't they? "Be careful what you wish for ..." But people never are careful really, are they? They wish and they plan and they scheme and they never really consider the full effects of what might happen if it all came to pass.

The letters arrived on a Thursday morning. Granted, it wasn't exactly any old ordinary Thursday morning but, having said that, lots of letters arrived, as they always did. It was a busy office and, well, when people talk about paperless offices and how the advent of email has replaced the stamp, it's not true really, is it?

Bad news still always arrives by post.

Of course it does, because, well, the impact of opening an email just isn't the same, is it? And sometimes the sender wants impact. Wants the envelope to be turned over in someone's hand, wants them to hesitate before opening it. Wants the thumb they use to slide under the seal to be shaking. It must be disappointing for these people not to actually *be* there to hear the intake of breath when the envelope is finally open and the letter eased out enough to read the stark print of

3

the headed notepaper. To see their jaws clench as they hope that it's not what they think.

To watch their world fall around their feet as the pages of the letter are unfolded and the full impact absorbed.

Yes, sometimes people know exactly what they're wishing for and wish it anyway.

But back to the letters. No, they weren't the only letters that morning, but they were the only registered ones. And even that wasn't what made them stand out, the fact that Jacinta had to sign for two registered letters. After all, registered letters weren't that unusual in the Dublin branch of the Deutsche Kommerzielle Bank, but to get two thick cream envelopes, both identical bar the addressee, in the one morning?

That was unusual.

Jacinta Fitzmaurice knew that there was a way to handle this. She knew because at sixty-four years of age she'd seen it all. She knew that she could flap and speculate and make a song and dance about the origin and intent of the two identical envelopes or she could be discreet. Had her assistant Alice signed for them, she'd have run into the department, shrieking, "*Get this, one for everyone in the audience!*" and handed them over in full view to the two people concerned:

Geraldine Lyttle, HR Manager
Declan Donovan, Finance Director

They just didn't make secretaries like they used to, Jacinta thought on a now daily basis. No sense of propriety. Back ten years ago when the Dublin headquarters of the Deutsche Kommerzielle Bank was in Merrion Square, Alice would not have lasted ten seconds. But people of any calibre were so hard to get these days. Young people didn't want to go to secretarial college and most thought typing with two fingers was all you needed to know in the modern world. Actually the only good thing Alice Conway *had* going for her was that text-speak had managed to pass her by. She didn't know that you could abbreviate words and so didn't. Whereas the lassie they'd had before her?

'Encl pls find ...'

It had been the straw that broke Jacinta's back.

"Could you not train her?" Geraldine from Human Resources had sighed, not welcoming the thought of heading back down the recruitment road.

"The reason I don't have a dog is that I'm too long in the tooth to waste any time training dumb animals," growled Jacinta and within hours Mandii-with-two-i's had left the building with her P45 firmly in the back pocket of her hipster flares.

Yes, Alice had been something of an improvement. But she still had a way to go. Like now. Feeling her assistant lean over her shoulder to see whose names were on the two identical envelopes, Jacinta turned them swiftly over and to one side, continuing with Declan's dictation as if they were something of nothing.

"Are you not going to ..." Alice started but then hesitated, wondering should she finish her sentence. She didn't mind admitting she was half afraid of Jacinta, fully afraid if the truth were known.

The decision was taken from her hands as Jacinta's rich baritone, like a rumble of southside Dublin thunder, cut across her. "Never you mind what I'm going to do. Why don't you get focused and try to get to the end of that filing?"

Alice blushed and scuttled back to the job that she had, as usual, abandoned for something more interesting. Alice had the staying power of used Sellotape. She moved from task to task the same way she moved from diet to diet, sticking with nothing to completion, making sure that her to-do list was as ever-increasing as her waistline.

Someday Jacinta was going to growl at her so deeply that she would simply combust into a million ditzy pieces and be no more.

But for now Jacinta had bigger problems. Looking across the open-plan office, she saw the bent heads working away. Each focused on their own project, no one any the wiser about the bombshells that lay, face down, on her desk.

Beyond the open-plan area were three open office doors. Her boss, Declan Donegan, was in his airy corner office on the phone. She could hear him shout in broken English from where she was sitting. He must be on to Frankfurt again. Despite the fact that Group Director Dyrk Janssens had perfect English, Declan still felt he had to be helpful by barking loudly and slowly in Basil Fawlty pidgin English. Jacinta sighed, she'd worked for Declan for enough years now to realise that what was in this envelope was going to annoy him. Enough time to know that she should wait until after his eleven o'clock coffee before approaching him.

And he would have to be approached first, much and all as she wanted to forewarn the other parties. Declan would have to be first.

Propriety.

Beside Declan's room was Leona's.

Jacinta sighed. It seemed such a shame, this whole mess. Some people were just their own worst enemy.

Her eye wandered to the next door, this one closed. It was hard to know how Geraldine was going to take this. While she moaned about the horrendous monotony of the quarterly appraisals, she was still not likely to appreciate the excitement or the trauma that was undoubtedly marching across the horizon towards her. Geraldine had tried to warn anyone that would listen that this was where it would all end up. Finding anyone who'd listen had been the problem. That would be of no consequence now, Jacinta knew. They'd deny that she'd said anything. They would attempt to implicate poor law-abiding Geraldine in this whole sorry mess. Declan would fling around phrases like 'belt and braces' and 'damage limitation' as he did in even the most minor situations and the entire board would wear solemn faces as they focused on who to punish for this.

Jacinta knew exactly who that was going to be.

She knew everything that went on in this office. Oh, they thought they had their secrets alright, but they didn't. She was no fool. She'd learnt her trade in the era of the switchboard, where you could listen in on every call and every letter went through the typing pool which she ran like a galley ship. Nothing had changed. They might think their emails and their conversations were private, but she didn't have to listen in on their calls to know what was in their heads.

Looking back at the desks in the open-plan area she knew already how certain people would react to this news. One, she was pretty certain, knew this was coming and would try to look surprised. The other would be hand-wringing in mock support but inside would be swelling with smugness, and would revel in the trauma and torment of their superior.

Her eyes lingered briefly on the one empty desk that sat at the edge of the room.

"What have you done?" she whispered to herself before sighing deeply.

No, Jacinta was no fool. Or was she?

She looked at the upturned envelopes and sighed again. She

probably should have done more at the time. Tried to talk to them. Not to take sides but to show them that they were fighting the wrong battle. That this was what the powers that be wanted. Would they have listened to her? Probably not. But it might have stopped it coming to this.

Letters.

Be careful what you put in print. That's something else they say. Be careful what you put in print. It's there forever once it's written down. There's never any going back. If you wanted to go back, that is. Sometimes, even if you could go back and do it differently, you still wouldn't want to. Because you did what you thought was right at the time.

Right for you, that is.

What you thought you needed to do to survive.

That's all most people are trying to do really, isn't it?

Survive.

Do the best they can.

For themselves.

She reached for the letter opener.

PART ONE

Touching Base
colloq. (orig. *U.S.*). *to touch base* : to meet with or talk to a person (esp. only briefly); to make brief contact; also in extended use. Freq. with *with*.

ALICE

I don't know what you're talking about. I never noticed anything going on. Especially not the kind of thing you're talking about. Seriously, sure I just mind my own business, get my work done. I didn't care what was going on between any of them. I just kept my head down. I don't want to know really, it's none of my business. I get on with everyone. Well, okay, I'm a bit wary of Leona but I wouldn't be the only one there. She can be very grumpy, a bit of a bully really if you ask me. Sorry, bully is the wrong word, I think – I just mean that, well, she likes things her way – that's all – but that's okay, isn't it? Like, she's grand really ... Can you take that bit out? The bully bit, I mean. I shouldn't have said anything, sure it all has nothing to do with me. I never saw anything. Honestly. I just do my work. Like I said, she's grand really ... You'll take it out, won't you?

Extract from interview with Alice Conway
Recorded 11 November 2011
10.08am

OLIVIA

I've been told to start writing all of this down, that it's one of the first things people are advised to do in these situations. And that really I should have started before now.

Well, I'm going to be honest here – up to now it's the last thing I'd have wanted to be doing. Sure all I wanted was just to forget it all. The whole thing was a kind of living hell that no one else really understood and the last thing I wanted was to relive the nightmare by writing it down.

In fact, lately, when I got to the end of each day all I wanted to do was forget that day had ever happened. Only ahead of me then was the night, and that was never any better. In fact, it was usually worse. Because at night came the flashbacks and no matter how hard I tried to forget, it was no use. I was re-living every single incident.

So no, I haven't been writing it down, but I'm going to start now. It's never too late apparently ...

So here goes. I'm Olivia. Sharpe is my married name. I was originally Olivia McDonald, but then I married Danny Sharpe. We'd met in a nightclub in town exactly two years previously after one of the Meath/Dublin matches.

Danny was from Enfield, County Meath, you see, and I was a Dub. Not a big enough fan for my dad to give me his spare ticket to

13

the match though – he knew I wasn't that big into sport. He was mad for the Dublin matches himself, never missed one. Between going to Dublin matches and keeping up with Liverpool in the soccer he was kept well busy. So he'd been on The Hill that day with some friend of his from the local. I was happy enough to just watch it on the telly with my mam then head out with the girls when it was over. The match nights were always good craic, a great night to meet someone. We went to Coppers: it was the only spot to be after a match, especially after a Dublin match.

That one wasn't such a good one for Dublin though. Meath won 1-14 to Dublin's 0-12. Now, as I said, it didn't make too much difference to me but I always wondered was that why Dad was never that fond of Danny – because of the night we met, like. I don't know would it have been worse or better if I'd met a Kildare man. They knocked us out in '98 and went on to the Final. The only good to ever come out of Kildare was Ruby Walsh and Charlie McCreevy, my dad always said, so maybe not. Maybe a Meath man was the lesser of two evils.

Anyhow, we met that night in Coppers and sure Danny was in great form. I'd seen him earlier bopping away to some extended remix of Fat Boy Slim and sure I thought to myself I'd have a few more Bacardi Breezers and hang on till he wore himself out. And sure as eggs are eggs we were bumping and grinding to some awful Westlife number before the hour had passed.

I can't remember if it was a slow set or not, I'm not sure that there even were slow sets in clubs then. I used to love an ould slow set back in the day. I think it's crazy that they don't do them anymore. But then that whole scene has changed completely, I'd say – not that I really know as I haven't been in a club in years. I don't go out much at all really as Danny says that drink is so expensive I'm better off having a few of the girls over while he nips out for the late few in Donegan's, our local. He still goes to the odd club after the matches but I'm happy enough to stay at home. Getting a baby-sitter is still next to impossible. Me mam has the kids all day, so she's hardly going to want them again in the evenings so we'd actually have to pay someone. So Danny's right really – it's cheaper if it's just one of us goes out.

Anyhow, I guess I should be sticking to the point – that was all before I started in DKB. When I met Danny I was still in Bank of Ireland where I'd been since I'd left school in '97. I heard lately that Brian Goggin went straight to Bank of Ireland from school too, and there he was, CEO at the top of the heap in 2004. I often wonder now if that could have happened to me, if I should have stayed there. Imagine. Though, actually, maybe now Goggin wishes he'd bailed after four years too …

I was one of the few girls in my class who didn't go straight on to college. The bleak years of the eighties were still fresh in a lot of people's minds and I guess they thought that there was nothing out there for people our age so why not go spend four years drinking your way through an Arts Degree? And then there were the few that went to train as teachers, the nurses, the corporation workers – they were the clever ones really. Oh, they might be throwing their toys out of the pram these days with the odd strike but, let's face it, they have it okay.

If I knew back then what I know now I might have joined the corporation too.

But I didn't, did I?

Anyhow, while everyone else was reviewing prospectuses for college, I was sitting with Dad going over my options. Emigration was one option we discussed but I didn't want to go. Family was important to me even back then and being on my own in some suburb of London or Liverpool just didn't appeal. Actually, given that the IRA had just bombed both Manchester and Canary Wharf earlier that year, I'm not so sure I'd have been wanted over there anyway. So that just left farther afield. Some of my cousins had emigrated – a few to America and one or two were in Australia.

But I wanted to stay.

So Dad's advice was to get a job. He wasn't against college but he felt that the clever thing to do would be to get a job that provided the training.

"If you want to stay you need to get a job – and get one where they'll pay for any training you need. This country is a mess, but it's starting to improve and you need to be in a boat that'll rise with it."

So I did. Okay, so the pay starting off wasn't great, but they paid for me to study the ACCA professional accountancy qualification and by the time I came out the far end I'd been promoted three times and had work experience to back up the qualification.

Again some of the girls did accountancy in college but sure they came out the far end without even knowing how to do the basics, like pull together a bank rec or a VAT return. All the 'ologies' in the world aren't worth a curse without the experience.

Then again, some of them in the bank thought I was mad to be bothering my arse with all that studying, but I didn't want to work on foreign exchange forever like them, with the highlight of your day cashing up a tray every evening before bolting out the door at five o'clock. Mind you, back then branch banking was better than it is now. The girls now are under some pressure these days – huge queues, customers more frustrated than the staff, and maybe only two counters open? It's shocking. I've heard some awful stories, virtual assaults from angry customers. It must be so stressful.

Anyhow, I didn't mind the studying too much and I'll never forget the night of my graduation. There we were, sitting in the National Concert Hall, my dad in his suit, his grimy work clothes left abandoned in our little house in Coolock. When I met up with my parents after receiving my cert there were actually tears in my dad's eyes and he squeezed my shoulder like I was eight again.

"You're going to be alright, Livvy," he said. "There's none of them can stop you now!"

And back then I really believed him.

Poor Da.

All he ever wanted was the best for me.

Chapter 1

KATE

SEPTEMBER 2011

"And then it went up to 36.4, which I know isn't high, but it's still going in the wrong direction, so I rang my mother and she said to put a bit of butter on his nose, now I ask you, what exactly is that meant to mean, so I told her about the temperature and she said that those fancy digital thermometers are too advanced and in her day you just knew by the feel of the child so I hung up on her and took the temperature again and it had gone up to 36.5 so with the rate it was climbing I rang Dr Tuttle but his receptionist said he'd no appointments free and sure I know that if I could just have spoken to him myself he'd have seen me but she was very unhelpful so then I'd to wait until after six and go into that D-Doc business and I hate doing that because they don't know Ralphie's history and sure they're only looking at symptoms in isolation but we went anyway and they said just to observe him, now I mean what do they think I had been doing for the four hours previous so anyhow I told them that there was no way I was paying another sixty-five euro if I had to come in again and get the antibiotic I should have got the first time and so here we are today, I wouldn't have come at all only he's been looking forward to it so much and now I don't know whether I should have brought him at all cos I think he looks a bit flushed, do you think he looks flushed?"

Kate O'Brien looked at her neighbour Patricia sitting opposite her and started to rub her temples. She wasn't sure what was giving her the headache – the persistent droning or the fact that she herself, in sympathy with Patricia, had not taken a single breath during the first half of that monologue. At that point, her mind had started to wander and she'd spent the rest of the time trying to formulate a plan of escape but the best she'd been able to come up with was a lie about remembering the iron was left plugged in back in her house across the cul-de-sac. As a result she had only a vague idea of what the woman was talking about and, worse still, from the expectant look on Patricia's face, it would appear that she'd been asked a question that necessitated some kind of reply.

"Oh absolutely …" she murmured in what she hoped was an 'I've-been-listening-and-yes-you're-so-right' kind of way.

"You think?"

Patricia now looked excited so Kate relaxed – obviously agreement had been right response.

"Oh yes, absolutely. Without a shadow of a doubt."

And with that Patricia was gone. Kate heaved a sigh of relief and looked around to ascertain what the chances of a fresh cup of coffee were. She decided that self-service was the way to go and was just filling the kettle when she felt a hand on her arm.

"Did you just tell Patricia McGonagle that her child is flushed?"

Kate turned to see another neighbour, Lynn Nash, beside her.

"Oh! Did I? Oh well, it's a four-year-old's birthday party, there's a bouncy castle, fizzy drinks and sugary treats – they're *all* flushed. And do you know what? I'm feeling flushed myself after the last ten minutes listening to her."

Lynn snorted. "You have a point. I believe she now has our lovely host Helen looking for a thermometer for her on your recommendation. With any luck little Ralphie's temperature has gone through the roof and she can feck off back to the doctor's for the afternoon. But look, the good news is you've escaped, so now you can come and sit with us when you've that coffee made and tell everyone your news."

"Oh God, Lynn, I don't think I'm up to that just yet."

"Kate, you're being ridiculous! You'll have to tell them sometime and, for goodness' sake, it's good news! What are you so afraid of?"

"They're going to think I'm nuts!"

"Why? Because they're all stay-at-home mothers? I think you're forgetting that so am I, and I don't think you're nuts at all."

"No, because you're normal and well-adjusted and –"

"Look, Kate, you're being far too sensitive. Sure when I said I was expecting my fifth child the same crowd all thought I was nuts too. Don't be worrying about what other people are saying, it's nothing to do with them. Go on in! There are rumours that my Charlie has poo oozing up his back so I'll follow you when same has been either confirmed or denied …"

Kate nodded. She knew that Lynn was right. Taking a peek out the window she could see her almost-three-year-old daughter Jess bouncing on the giant inflatable castle and she hoped six-month-old David was still passed out in his buggy in the hall. She had a sudden sense of butterflies in her stomach and for a second she wondered if it could be a bout of nerves. The nearer and nearer Monday came, the more she checked herself for nerves, but as yet there was no sign. Excitement more like. Because she was fine. She was good with this. Or at least she would be after she'd broken the news …

Picking up her coffee, she made her way back to the sitting room where the rest of the mothers were sitting.

"So are we doing the play centre as usual on Thursday?" asked Siobhán, a neighbour from two doors down.

It was one good thing that had come out of the last couple of years: she'd got to know her neighbours who, up to the first day of her first maternity leave, had all been strangers to her despite having moved to the quiet little cul-de-sac in Saggart some years previously.

"Thursday doesn't suit me – could we do Wednesday?" asked Anna, Patricia's sister-in-law from another housing estate just down the road.

"Wednesday's fine with me – what about you, Kate?"

For the second time in twenty minutes Kate had that awful feeling that she'd just been asked a question that she'd no idea how to answer.

It was now or never.

"Ehm, me?" she stuttered. "Don't worry about me – I'm not around this week or, ehm, any week for that matter."

The four women in the room looked at her.

Lynn, where are you??

19

She could feel her body tensing, practically certain who would speak first.

"What do you mean?" asked Siobhán.

Yep, she was right. It was always going to be Siobhán.

"Well, I'm eh, going back to work actually."

"Work?"

As predicted, if she'd said that she was going into prison there would have been less of a reaction.

"Yes, work. I'm going back. I got a job." Kate looked at the four open mouths in front of her. "So, eh, go me!" she finished lamely with a forced smile.

"You're going back to work?" Siobhán repeated.

"I am."

"Part-time?"

"Full-time."

There was silence again.

"But Michael's job is okay, isn't it?" Anna was struggling to make sense of the announcement.

"Oh yes, he's fine luckily enough. It got pretty hairy a few years back but thankfully they seem to be riding the storm."

"So what on earth are you doing so?" Siobhán was flabbergasted.

"Well, it was always the plan to go back."

"But what about the children?"

"They're starting in Happy Hands on Monday morning – they've already been in for a few half-days actually. Jess, ehm, actually seems to like it and sure, in fairness, David isn't aware where he is half the time." She could feel a defensive tone creeping into her voice and she hated herself for it. But the interrogation she was getting at the moment was no less than she'd expected.

"A *crèche*."

"Well, yes, I haven't much of an alternative really, but sure they'll love the company and there's one or two from ballet there so Jess will settle in just fine."

"But a crèche," Siobhán repeated. "Surely that'll cost you a fortune? It'll hardly be worth your while once you've paid them."

Kate felt herself bristle.

"Well, Siobhán, I'm a qualified accountant so it's not like I'll be on minimum wage."

"But still, I can't believe you're going back – I mean, you hardly need the money – why on earth would you put yourself through all that?"

"Because I've done what I set out to do. David is at the age when most working mothers go back, I've been at home for almost three years and if I want to go back, which I do and always have done, then it's not going to get any easier the longer I leave it."

"Oh, I think you're lucky." Patricia was back, armed with Jacinta's digital thermometer. "I'd love to have a little job, just a few hours a week mind you, like obviously I'd have to be home by two to pick up the boys and then it'd have to be only term time like but you know a few hours a week just for a few bob of my own would be lovely, not sure what I'd do mind you but I do all that work for the animal sanctuary so I'm sure that'd count for something like I organise their fundraising so maybe a job in marketing or event management or doing the twitters and stuff for them though I'd have to do a course in that as I don't even know how to use Facebook and my sister won't show me for some reason …"

Patricia's voice trailed off as if she'd just become aware of the deathly silence in the room.

"Well, congratulations, Kate! I think it's super!" came a voice of reason from the door.

"Why, thank you, Lynn!" Kate turned to her friend. "It is what I want, in fact it's what I've wanted to do for some time. I'm not cut out to be at home. I'd like to give this a go."

"Well, that's good, isn't it? At least you'll be able to have a cup of tea in peace for starters." Lynn looked almost wistfully at Kate. "So come on, tell us all about this new job!"

Kate smiled a thank-you to Lynn. Of course her friend knew all about the job – she was the first person she'd confided in about her plan to go back to work and she'd been very supportive.

Lynn and herself were unlikely friends but, living next door to each other and with two children the same age, it was a case of opposites meeting on some kind of suburban common ground and they just seemed to click. In Kate's eyes, Lynn was one of those Super Mothers that people talked about in low hushed tones at school walls. The type that shouldn't really exist at all. She had five children ranging in ages from fourteen down to eight months including a particularly challenging eight-year-old, and her day was a carefully calculated series of car outings. To school, to the shops, to afterschool activities, and in between them all she managed to keep a clean house and a smile on her face. Her husband travelled a lot with work and it caused her great amusement when Kate complained about Michael being late home. There were whole weeks when Lynn's husband was away. Whole weeks where she didn't get to leave her house unaccompanied by a child and Kate honestly did not know how she coped. And yet here was Lynn beside her now, her slim figure in a pair of skinny jeans and the last of her tan from their camping holiday in France visible under her crisp white shirt.

Yes, white shirt. Kate had thought she was doing well to apply a full face of make-up before the party but Lynn, the bitch, always had to go a step further ...

But yet despite their differences, good friends they were, and Kate was glad her friend had her back on this occasion.

"It's in a bank, actually – in town," she answered Lynn.

"A bank?" said Siobhán. "Are you mad? Sure they're crashing right, left and centre."

Siobhán could be so overwhelmingly negative when she wanted.

"Well, obviously this one isn't," said Kate, trying hard to control the annoyance in her tone, "and, as it's a German merchant bank, then the chances of it going under are probably very slim."

"What's being a merchant bank got to do with anything?" Siobhán wasn't letting this go.

"Well, it just means that they wouldn't have had the exposure to things like sub-prime mortgages and man-on-the-street loan defaulters that maybe some of our own banks would have had. And I'm not stupid, I've researched them pretty thoroughly and they appear to have a reputation for being quite conservative."

"Oh but still, all that stress?"

"Well, I'm not sure it will be all that stressful actually. I've deliberately not taken on anything too senior. In fact, the role is a much lesser one than I had in my old job, but I'm fine with that. I don't want any stress or pressure myself. I just want to do my job and come home."

Kate was getting really annoyed at having to explain herself.

"Well, that'll be a feat in itself." Siobhán was impervious to the annoyance, it would seem. "In town, did you say? So you're going to have a commute too?"

"It's not going to be too bad. I'm going to drive down to Citywest and get the Luas in – sure that'll take me nearly to the door."

"Oh? Where in town is it?"

"Down in the IFSC – you know, down in the docks."

"All the way down there? You don't do things by halves, do you?"

"It'll be grand."

"Grand? I wouldn't be so sure. Not sure 'grand' and 'the Luas' exactly go hand in hand." Siobhán did an exaggerated shudder. "Rather you than me travelling in and out with all those junkies in the hoodies."

Kate rolled her eyes. "Not everyone in a hoodie is a junkie, Siobhán."

"I'm telling you, avoid anyone in a hoodie on those journeys."

"It will be grand," Kate repeated. "In fact, it'll be more than grand – it'll be great. And sure if it's not, I can leave. But, to be honest, I've looked into this for quite some time, and I'm pretty sure this is the going to be the answer to all my prayers."

There was silence again and Kate knew they all thought she was crazy. Probably even Lynn thought she was a bit mad, and if the truth were known they were probably all even more correct than they ever could have guessed ...

But this was going to solve that.

This was the answer.

Chapter 2

MARY

"To Toni!"

"*To Toni!*" came the rousing cheer.

"Actually to Toni and Arthur!" someone called.

"Never mind Arthur, it's our Toni we care about!" called another voice and the champagne glasses clinked again to another toast.

Mary Lawlor smiled and looked around. Now this was her kind of hen night. A private room in the beautiful Mount Ainsley period house. Through the floor-length sash windows she could see rolling parkland stretching off into the autumn evening and inside the room was the muffled sound of pure luxury: thick damask tablecloth, heavy monogrammed cutlery and the soft clunk of weighty crystal glasses.

Not a plastic willy in sight.

It was exactly the kind of hen night she would have chosen for herself, so, as hosting her own was never going to happen, she was going to savour every moment of this one.

"You're not starting to lag on me, are you?"

Mary turned to see Toni taking a seat next to her.

"Indeed and I am not – I'm simply letting that chocolate fondant settle before I throw too much more wine in on top of it."

"Ah, good." Toni sat back in her chair.

She was the only one of Mary's school friends who hadn't changed a jot since sixth year. Her face was as fresh and dewy as it used to be after one of their camogie matches, and her figure as lithe and supple. She still wore her hair short, in the kind of cut that only looked this amazing on people with excellent bone structure and, in fact, it actually seemed to suit her more now than it had done twenty years ago.

Toni was definitely one of those few women whose beauty could truly be called 'timeless'.

Mary shook her head and smiled. This was all a bit deep for an early Saturday evening.

"What are you smiling at?" Toni asked.

"Nothing. Nothing important. I'm just thinking that you haven't changed a bit really. Not in all the time I've known you."

"Well, you haven't changed much either, you know," Tony chided gently. "Though you're slimmer and your hair is definitely nicer without that pudding-bowl cut."

"Oh stop! My mother has a lot to answer for! And then I let her stick a flower in it for my Deb's …"

The two women squealed with laughter.

"How is your mother?" Toni asked.

Mary rolled her eyes. "To be honest, I haven't seen her in about two weeks and that suits me absolutely fine. I've been up to my absolute tonsils in work and I can do without her histrionics on top of all that."

"Oh dear – how is work?"

Mary reached for her wineglass. "It's been a nightmare, and God only knows what's going to happen now …"

"Oh no – what happened?"

"Olivia walked out yesterday."

"*What?*"

"Yep, she's gone – or at least her parting remarks certainly implied she was …"

"And she just walked out? Without giving any notice?"

"Yes," Mary sighed. "To be honest, it was only a matter of time and no one was ever going to do a whole lot to stop her."

"No way!"

"Well, let's just say that this probably suits Leona better in the long run."

"Christ, that's awful. She must have been pretty pissed off about something all the same, you know, to just walk out like that – I mean, I met her a few times, didn't I? She never struck me as being someone who was in any way impulsive. In fact, I would have thought she was cautious enough. Wasn't she the one with the penny-pinching husband? It's a pretty big deal to walk out on a good job these days ..."

Mary didn't answer – instead she traced the condensation down the side of her glass. "Yes," she said eventually. "Yes, it's a pretty big deal alright. But there you go," she shrugged, "enough about my work – how's hospital administration these days? You must surely have your own fair share of headaches?"

Toni laughed. "Oh Christ, sure you're sick of listening to me! It seems now that those junior doctors are definitely going to strike – I had two people again this week whining about the bloody pension levy that is now almost three years old. And of course there's still no sign of them lifting that recruitment embargo so, any gaps I have, I'm still not allowed to fill. Did I tell you Betty Whatshername is out sick again? She's like a one-woman episode of *Casualty* – I swear to God, if she was a dog I'd have her put down, she's sick that often."

"Oh Toni, I don't envy you. It's very frustrating when someone won't pull their weight..." Mary knew only too bloody well just how frustrating but she remembered that now really wasn't the time or the place. Instead, she raised her glass to her friend. "Let's drink to stress-free work lives!"

"What a super toast – to stress-free work!"

They clinked glasses and each took a long slow gulp of the delicious icy-cold Pinot Grigio.

"And to you getting some kind of life for yourself." Toni spoke cautiously and it was obvious she was afraid to catch Mary's eye as she picked her words.

"Now, Toni, don't start. You are like the proverbial reformed smoker – you used to be fairly married to your job at one stage too." There was a slight warning edge to Mary's tone but this was Toni she was talking to. They knew each other far too long to be worried that one might offend the other.

"Yes, yes, I was. You know I clawed my way up in that bloody hospital by the fingernails, Mary. And I've got my promotions and my pay increases – well, now it looks like they'll take all those back eventually – but still, I got there. And now I don't work the same kind of ridiculous hours. I do my job and go home and I have a life outside work…" She trailed off.

"And I don't?" Mary all but snapped. "Just say what you really mean, Toni. You have Arthur and I have no one."

"It's nothing to do with having Arthur – I was perfectly happy when I was single and well you know that. I just worry about you, Mary. That's all. I want you to have everything. You deserve it. And that ungrateful shower are just working you into an early grave. I wouldn't bring it up at all only you look exhausted."

Mary nodded. "I'm not going to lie – this week was particularly taxing but it will get better. There's a new system going in, Leona has plans …"

"I've been hearing this for well over a year now, Mary. That's all I'm saying."

"But –"

"But nothing, and now you're telling me that a key member of staff has just walked out? Rats and sinking ship spring to mind."

"I know what it looks like, Toni, I really do. But honestly? I think it'll get better now. I know that sounds mad, but I really do."

Toni looked at her friend and was surprised at the look of positivity on her face. Something she hadn't seen in some time.

"I can't see how," she sighed, "but you're a big girl now."

"Gee, thanks!" Mary slapped her on the wrist playfully. "I'm not that big! And come on, there's really no need to be so worried about me – my life isn't that bad – in fact, it's pretty much the way I want it."

Toni risked going for the jugular. "It'd be nice if you had a man in your life though."

"Toni Culloty – only you – and I mean *only you* would get away with saying that to me!" Mary looked at her friend in mock horror. "And anyway, Miss Smug Nearly-Married – I have a man in my life and well you know it."

"Mary, a twice-a-year bonk-fest doesn't count."

"It counts if it's all I want, Toni, and for your information, it's generally more than twice a year."

"You deserve more."

"Oh for goodness sake, who says I want more?" Mary was trying really hard not to lose her temper. "I've never been one of those girls whose biological clock was reverberating in their ears and I never will be. I've no interest in having children and I've no interest in being at someone's beck and call. I love my life, Toni, and it's unfair of you to say that's not good enough."

"Okay, okay, I'm sorry – but you can't give out to me tonight – it's my night and I'm allowed say stupid things!"

She looked so downcast that Mary had to smile.

"Right, you're forgiven, if only for the distinct lack of willy-straws and L-plates at this shindig – now that is something I would never have forgiven you for."

"Cheers, buddy! Now let me tell you again about my dress …"

Mary and Toni clinked glasses and equilibrium was restored.

Chapter 3

ROB

Rob Gallagher looked at the clock in his car again. At almost 7am, he knew he had plenty of time but still he worried as he always did. And he berated himself as he always did that this whole trip was stupid, an indulgence, and that really he needed to grow up. But then it was even darker this week than last so he knew that realistically these indulgences would have to stop soon.

For some reason that made him feel almost relieved.

Because this really was all so stupid.

On each side of the deserted motorway, the high banks acted like blinkers. He could have been on any of the big fancy roads that now spanned the country, making life so much easier but still meaning that long journeys looked all the same. He watched for the sign for Junction 12, always afraid that he'd shoot by it and waste even more precious time. He rounded the bend and, seeing the sign for the racecourse, flicked on his indicator.

The mist hung low over the early-morning plains in horizontal bands that hovered feet from the ground. Later they would rise and vanish and the day would be warm and bright but, for now, the watery sun could do nothing but add to the unreality of the dawn. The Curragh was like that, though – it seemed to exist in a weather system and time zone all of its own. Even as a child coming here, it had held an otherworldly quality that had made him think he'd never tire of visiting it.

The innocence of youth.

He drove slowly up the hill towards the car park, rolling down his window and pulling the cold, damp air into his lungs, his eyes wildly, greedily drinking in the sight before him. In every direction the Curragh rolled flat, green, familiar, already dotted with the sight of early-morning strings of horses. He glanced at his watch and started to speed up. He'd better hurry. Blue mightn't wait.

"Hope you brought a torch," was the gruff greeting from the older man when Rob finally parked and hopped out of his car.

"The mornings are getting darker alright." Rob looked at the sky as he took his hat and whip out of the boot of the car. "But you only need to see the few feet in front ... sure by the time we get them out it'll be grand."

"Grand, he says!" the old man snorted. "Well, stay bloody grand because, I'm telling you, if you get yourself killed I'll be throwing your body in the nearest furze and making like I never saw you."

"Jesus, Blue, I never managed to kill myself in the last fifteen years – why would I be starting now?"

"I'm just saying, is all. Your da has enough to be –"

"Right, let's get them out." Rob had already moved to the back of the horsebox and was unclipping the latches on the back ramp.

Within minutes the horses were backing down noisily from the box, their feet scrabbling to keep balance on the ramp. The chestnut filly looked warily at Rob as Blue handed over the reins.

"So what's the deal with this one?"

"He has her in for Punchestown next month. She's good, but hard work. Don't let her off on you now – keep a check on her or she'll be gone."

"I will. Punchestown, eh? The novice handicap."

"Yeah, well, what he really wanted to aim for was Cheltenham but sure he can't look that far ahead, can he? Not with all that hanging –"

"Hey! Stand and behave!" Rob gave the reins a tug in an effort to stop the filly from wheeling around him in circles. When this didn't work he bounded up and within seconds was astride. Rob might have been slight but he was tall and strong and his long legs gripped her barrel of a stomach and she soon started to behave. Once he had her under control, he tightened the girths and adjusted the stirrups.

"I'm warning you now, be careful – no messing – keep her nice and steady!" Blue called as he mounted the second horse.

But Rob had moved off, his eyes already on the mouth of the gallop, then tracing its course off into the distance.

The filly too had seen where they were going, and by the time they reached the start of the gallop she had started bouncing and skipping on the spot. Rob was very definitely the boss though and managed to keep her in check until her hooves were safely on the brink of the chippings track.

And then in three huge, bounding strides they were off.

As she surged forward under him Rob laughed aloud. "Jesus, the bould Blue wasn't joking about you, was he, missy?"

He dug his heels down and pulled his elbows close to his sides.

"You wait there now," he muttered, "until I tell you when."

She pulled against him but only momentarily, conceding defeat within strides. Feeling her come back to him, he released his hold slightly and she relaxed further, settling into a steady, rhythmic stride.

"Right-ho, lady, now let's see what you can do." He slipped his reins another inch and when nothing happened, let the horse have two clips on her flank with his whip, and that was all the encouragement she needed. In one glorious surge forwards, they were off.

The gear change was instantaneous, the wind in his face starting to whip tears from his eyes as he crouched down over her neck.

He could see two other riders ahead and as he steamed past them he called, "Sorry, lads, can't hold her!"

"Stop bleedin' drivin' her then!" one of them shouted back, but he was long gone.

Every muscle strained, foam spilling back from her mouth onto her neck, her hooves barely clipping the all-weather surface. With every stride the ground flashed beneath them but Rob was in another place, another time. Crouched so low that the chestnut mane stung his cheeks, he urged her on and on like someone possessed.

And then they were nearing the end. Just as he started to worry about how he was going to pull her up, the filly started to slow in long, grateful strides, her slick sides heaving.

It took five minutes for Blue to gambol up alongside them.

"Sorry, boss, she got away from me," Rob called over his shoulder.

"I could see that alright," the older man answered drily. "Good job she was due a workout. You okay?"

Rob nodded. "Yep. I'm telling you, though, you don't be long losing the fitness."

"That's true." Blue reached into his pocket, took out a pack of cigarettes and drew one out. "Well, you're gone how long now? Six months? A year?"

Rob put his hand out for a cigarette. Blue raised one eyebrow before throwing him one and then precariously bringing his horse alongside the filly to light it.

"Something like that alright." Rob drew deeply on his first drag from the cigarette in the manner of someone who hasn't had one for some time.

"He's in an awful way, Rob."

"I'm sure he is." He blew the smoke back out into the crisp air and watched it disappear.

"Would you not come back?"

"I've been back. Sure wasn't I back at the weekend?"

"I'm sure you were ..."

"I was!"

Blue sighed. "Look, Rob, if you don't come back –"

"If you mean for good, Blue, then you need to know that I'm not coming back. I've no interest. That life is not for me."

"But he's your da ..."

"If I go back, that'll be it, Blue. Everything else, gone."

The old man knew this conversation was going nowhere so he was quiet for a minute, sucking on the last of his cigarette before continuing.

"So the job is going well then?"

"It's going grand. It's a job. A career. It doesn't mean pulling a box to Ballinrobe at 6am on a Saturday morning and being at the beck and call of total wankers that send you up shit creek without a paddle and then don't even have the decency to pay their fucking training bills."

"True. If it's any consolation, they say Bailey is heading for NAMA – good enough for the fucker."

"It won't cost him a thought, Blue – that bad bastard has it all well hidden by now."

"S'pose." There was silence, so he continued, "He misses you though, Rob. You'll come down sometime soon, won't you? Before the case comes up?"

Rob looked at his watch and flicked the last of his cigarette down onto the sandy gallop.

"We'd better head back. The other crowd think I've a dentist appointment."

The old man sighed.

"Right, so. Now, we're taking it easy on the way back. I mean it now, stay upsides of me, no monkey business!'

"I will, I promise – and Blue – thanks, thanks a million for this – I miss this bit of it."

"Ah sure, don't I owe you, after getting me out of a hole with the Revenue that time? Who'd have thought it, our tall stringy Rob, an accountant in a bank up in the Big Smoke!" He laughed, "I remember when I worked for your da, and you with your little swagger, strutting over to your little white pony ..."

But Rob was gone. Steadier this time but gone off ahead all the same. Without a single glance behind.

Chapter 4

KATE

Kate looked around her at her fellow passengers on the Luas. Siobhán had warned her yet again about the Luas but so far it was working out pretty well. Lots of people like her, sitting clutching travel cups, their work bags clamped firmly between their ankles. She'd expected it to smell but it didn't. The DART had been smelly. She had bad memories of the DART, from when she'd worked in town before. Especially all those mornings where she'd get stuck under someone's armpit from Pearse Street to Blackrock on a daily basis, while on secondment to a client on the southside. Not being tactile at the best of times, that hadn't been a good situation. Not as bad, mind you, as the day the smiling man had noticed her protruding bump through her rain mac and without a second's warning had made a lunge for it, as if a big cheesy grin was all he needed to gain access to her person. He'd been lucky to escape with a swift step back and a glare to end all glares.

Would you grab my arse as quick? she had wanted to shout at him.

But that was a few years ago. She was a mother now, slower to blow a fuse at stuff she could do nothing about.

James's Hospital.

The carriage glided down the steep hill. She had to admit this commuting to work was alright really. She had her phone to flick through Facebook or Twitter, she'd a book in her bag and she had time to think.

Once word had got out that she was returning to work, the most common question people had asked her was if she was dreading going back, looking at her with big sympathetic eyes as if she was heading back to the Somme instead of back to work after one rather protracted maternity leave.

"Dreading it, are you?" was the most commonly asked question.

How do you respond to a question like that?

"No, I'm not actually," made her sound like a heartless mother, but if she lied and said 'Yes, dreading it,' then it just encouraged an onslaught of sympathy that she neither needed nor deserved.

But that was not surprising really. There was something about becoming a mother that meant you were open season for people to say quite literally whatever they wanted. Announcing she was pregnant with David had for some reason led to all sorts of questions.

"Oh, was it planned?" was the most common.

Was it planned?

That was like something a prosecutor would ask you in the dock. "So, Mrs O'Brien. On the night of May 16th 2013, did you or did you not have sex with your husband with the express intention of conceiving?"

"I did not, Your Honour."

"But, Mrs O'Brien, you knew that it was Day 14 and that there were already signs of ovulation and that conception was possible."

"I did, Your Honour."

"So why then did you proceed with said act?"

"Well, Your Honour, Michael Fassbender was on the *Late Late* and I was in the mood, an occurrence which might not have happened again for quite some time. Me being in the mood, that is, though it's unlikely Fassbender is a mad man for the *Late Late* either."

And that was just the start of it.

Oh, you're big!

You're very neat.

You're carrying to the front.

You're all to the back.

Or her absolute least favourite of all: *Oh, you've dropped.*

You've dropped? Like what the hell was that supposed to mean?

In an era where you were supposed to say to someone, 'Oh, have you done something with your hair?' rather than scream 'Oh my God, you've lost four stone!' how was it okay to say 'Oh, your big fat pregnant stomach has sagged three inches lower than last week'?

You've dropped.

When she'd bemoaned this one to Lynn, she had suggested she simply say: "Thanks. While we're on the subject, did you ever consider wearing a better-fitting bra yourself?"

But then Lynn was quick like that.

Anyway, what was she getting so riled about it all now for? People meant well. They felt they had to be saying something, that was all. It was an improvement on Scarlett O'Hara's time when you went into 'confinement' for months before you had the baby lest anyone see you in such a delicate condition. Or was it?

Or a better question – was it possible that it was just her that hated her ever-burgeoning figure to be a constant source of conversation? Take her friend Danielle, for example – the pee was barely cold on the stick before she had it on Facebook. And on it went. Every stretch mark, every belch of heart burn, her bump from every angle for a full 40.5 weeks.

Oh, because Danielle had also gone over. And her 594 Facebook friends had felt every second of it.

"**Still no sign.**"

"**Demanding answers tomorrow.**"

"**Had a twinge, I'm on my way.**"

"**Can you believe they're sending me home??**"

For twelve days straight. Well, eleven days really if you didn't count the rather protracted labour that they'd all been privy to also. How anyone could still update their Facebook page at every centimetre of dilation was beyond Kate. Seriously like. She hadn't even known where her phone was for Jessica's birth …

She hadn't even known where *she* was for Jessica's birth.

She really needed not to be thinking about Jessica's birth.

Not today.

The Four Courts

Smithfield

Jervis

And on the Luas glided through the bustling city.

Connolly
Busáras
Spencer Dock

Wait – Spencer Dock – that was her stop! She lunged into the queue that was rapidly departing the carriage and, before she stepped down, she made sure her bag was shut and her phone in an inside pocket.

Apparently you couldn't be too careful these days. Dublin was a hotbed of crime and, according to Siobhán, if she made it as far as the International Financial Services Centre at all without being raped and pillaged it'd be an awfully good start to the day. But then ever since she'd told Siobhán last Saturday that she was going to go back to work it had just been one dire warning after another.

"Oh, it's no joke working full time with children. Sure I'd love to be working but it just wouldn't be feasible …"

Blah, blah, blah!

So getting mugged had to be avoided – she'd hate to prove Siobhán right on her very first day. In fact, she'd hate to prove Siobhán right about anything.

Because Kate O'Brien knew what the correct answer was to the 'Are you dreading going back?' question.

As she stepped off the Luas on that first morning she looked at the glistening water of Dublin Bay, and the lights bouncing off the acres of glass rooftops that stretched before her.

Not a child in sight.

"Dreading it? I can't bloody wait!"

Chapter 5

LEONA

"Oh, I don't know ... I was thinking Tutti Frutti maybe ..." Alice was sitting on the edge of the legal junior Arianne's desk and gazing at her nails with a level of concentration that she reserved only for non-work-related issues. She was very pretty – slightly plump, but with a riot of blonde curls and the biggest, bluest eyes that seemed to be permanently wide and shocked at something or other.

"Oh, you mean Shellac? Yeah, I used to get that – it's shite on your nails though ..." Now Arianne also was gazing at her own fingernails with great intent. She too was quite striking, but mostly because she wore a vast amount of carefully applied make-up every day. An endless source of information on what primer, highlighter and contourer everyone of every skin type should be wearing, she seemed to spend her weekends standing at the MAC counter in Brown Thomas. When not in BT's she spent her time on Instagram following every beauty blogger that had ever strung a sentence together and appeared to have endless disposable income to spend on any product they suggested.

So engrossed were they both in their nails that neither girl noticed that from her desk at the far side of the room Jacinta had them both fixed in a steely gaze.

"Oh no – really? Oh God, maybe I won't get them done so." Alice's face crumpled in disappointment.

"Oh look, it could just be mine – sure Olivia used to get them done all the time and had no issues with it."

"Mmmm, true." Now Alice was confused. She could never make a decision on her own so tended to hop and jump from person to person, asking as many opinions as possible before she committed to any action. "I'll ask her when she comes in. Funny she's not in yet – though, actually, neither is Rob."

"Rob has the dentist this morning," said Arianne.

"Oh. Olivia must be just running late. Probably one of the kids."

"She's not running late!" called Cian, one of the two younger men who worked in the Strategy Department over by the floor-to-ceiling windows that looked out over Dublin bay.

"What do you mean? Where is she so?"

"She's not coming in. She's gone." Cian stretched his arms out and yawned, almost as if this was old news and he was already bored.

"What do you mean 'gone' – gone on holidays, like? I don't remember her mentioning anything about holidays?"

"No – gone. Walked out, left, gone." Cian was being deliberately vague now, enjoying the look of confusion and shock that was spreading over Alice's cherubic face.

"But she couldn't be gone!" Alice looked around the big open-plan office with a wide-eyed suspicious look, almost as if Olivia might jump out from behind a desk and shout 'Gotcha!' and she'd be made a fool of yet again. Alice was quite often the butt of the jokes of the younger men in the office but it didn't stop her having a very obvious soft spot for Rob, Cian's strategy colleague.

But no, he was right – Olivia was nowhere to be seen. There were surprisingly few staff in actually, which was unusual for ten past eight on a Monday morning. There was no sign of Mary, for example, who was usually in first and, as for Leona, well, her door was closed so it was hard to tell if she was inside or not but it didn't appear so.

"Well, she is," said Cian. "Unless of course she takes back all the abuse she screamed around this place on Friday evening."

"She did what?" Now Alice was open-mouthed with shock, "What did she –"

"Right, that's enough, Alice." Even in her expensively cut pencil skirt, Jacinta seemed to get from the far side of the room in two steps in order to cut across the questioning. "I believe you are actually meant to start work at eight? Not come in here to stand around talking idle gossip with *junior* –" she paused to put the maximum inflection on the word '*junior*', "members of staff."

Alice scuttled back to her desk and Jacinta shot Cian a warning glare.

"And as for you, Cian, you really should be careful about the kind of gossip you spread around."

"Eh, it's not gossip, Jacinta. I was here, remember?"

"It most certainly *is* gossip and it has nothing to do with you. What happened on Friday should stay between these four walls and not be repeated idly to any airhead that walks your way."

"Eh Jacinta, I know you think you run this place, but in actual fact you are not in charge of me so why don't you toddle off there and do a bit of typing?" Cian was very proud of the fact that he could be a condescending little prick when he wanted to be.

But when Jacinta leaned in towards him, without even realising it he leaned back quickly.

"I may not be your boss as you so rightly point out, Mr Casey," she hissed, "but I do have the ear of your boss's boss so maybe bear that in mind when you are speaking to me."

"Oh whatever! I was only telling Alice that Olivia wasn't coming in, that's all."

"Well, just make sure that that *is* all. There were serious things said in here on Friday, and they're not for everyone's ears – especially not that little fool," Alice shifted uncomfortably in her seat at Jacinta's words but Jacinta carried on regardless, not caring one jot who could hear her, "who's likely to be standing on the roof of the Harbourmaster pub telling the whole IFSC by lunchtime. How do you think that'd make us look? This is a one-hundred-year-old bank and we have a reputation to uphold and, if it's the last thing I do, I shall ensure that this is done. Do you hear me?"

"Oh relax, sure I told her nothing." Cian turned back around to his PC in a huff.

"Well, keep it that way," was Jacinta's parting shot before she strode back to her desk in the corner.

"Jesus, the women in here really need to take a chill pill," Cian muttered before looking up, rolling his eyes "And sure here's another one ..."

Mary crossed the room, throwing a glance at Olivia's empty desk before flinging her bag under her own and sitting down.

"Morning, Mary!" called Cian across the room to her.

Mary looked at him. "Morning, Cian," she answered in a voice that said clearly, 'You don't normally say anything to me in the morning – I know exactly what you're up to."

"Sure at least *you're* here, eh?" he continued with a smirk on his face.

She didn't even answer this, instead continuing to take off her suit jacket. She placed it carefully over the back of her chair, just as she always did.

"Oh, all picture no sound, that's a good idea, Mary, me ould pal, least said and all that …"

There was a loud bang then and Cian leapt in his chair before turning to see the diminutive form of the senior finance manager, Leona Blake, standing at Olivia's desk, dark-green eyes fixed in a steely gaze, her sharp cheekbones appearing more pronounced than normal with the set of her pointed jaw. The bang had apparently come from a large file which she seemed to have placed, with more violence than was necessary, on the desk.

"Cian, my office now if that's okay."

Mary smirked at Cian as he grudgingly dragged back his chair and followed Leona into her office. That would soften his cough for him, cheeky brat, she thought.

"Shut the door, please," said Leona as she took her seat. She waited until the door was shut and he had sat down before continuing. "Now, where do I start? Right, well, I wanted to call you both in to let you know there's been some changes in personnel, but I believe Robert won't be in for another while and, from what I hear, this conversation can't wait for much longer. It would seem that it's only going to be a matter of time before even the dogs on the street know that Olivia has left –" She looked directly at Cian as she spoke and it was obvious that she'd heard every word of the exchange between himself and Jacinta in the main open-plan area some minutes previously, "so I can apparently skip that bit."

Cian did not even so much as squirm in his seat.

"So yes, the fact that Olivia will not be working here any longer leaves us with a very big gap to fill. Obviously we were not exactly expecting her to leave so we have no one lined up for her position or to even take over her duties." She paused before continuing, "So the bad news is that it is I who will fill the role of your direct line manager for the foreseeable future."

Cian paled slightly but even he wasn't brave enough to do so much as flinch.

"I know we haven't worked together much in the past and I have to admit to knowing very little about either you or Rob, but I have both your appraisals here which obviously Olivia had been working on as they're tabled for the next week or two. So we're going to get well acquainted with each other over the next few weeks. I'd imagine that could go either way. But anyhow, like it or not, this is the situation we've been dealt, and now we have to cope with it as best we can. Have you any suggestions, or questions?"

"What about the grade reviews?" asked Cian.

"Yes, I believe Olivia had identified that there was scope to make one of you into a Grade 2, but this, shall I say, recent turn of events has obviously set this situation back somewhat."

"So no promotions?"

"That's not what I said, Cian. I intend to have a good look at the Strategy Department in time and see what its personnel needs are. However, this is something that cannot be rushed and, with the upcoming Institution-wide system change, this is not something that can be rushed into now. The Grade 2 position for the Strategy Department was obviously sanctioned at board level and I can't see how that won't still be part of the strategy plan, but, as I said earlier, I'm not completely up to speed with either this department and its workings or you guys and your capabilities, so it seems prudent to let it sit for a short while until we see what's what."

Cian nodded though it was plain to see that he was not happy with the answer.

"So that's it really. I just wanted to let you know that there'd been a change – oh, and also to remind you that this is a sensitive topic. Now, obviously there will be a number of stories doing the rounds but, really, none of that is anyone's business and there will be severe repercussions should any of us on the inside be caught giving our tuppence-worth. But then, I'm quite sure I don't need to tell you guys that. Anyway, from what I hear, the Strategy Department is far, far too busy these days to have any time for idle gossip."

Cian looked at her and sighed.

He was right: the women around here really needed to relax.

Chapter 6

KATE

Threading her way through the crowds on the street, Kate was amazed at how different Dublin looked in daylight. She hadn't actually been right into the city since her cousin Vicky's hen night and that was at least four years ago or 'pre-children' as she automatically classed that time of her life.

But the thing was, some days Kate O'Brien couldn't remember what her life was like before the children, and then some days it was the only thing she could think about. Michael never found it hard to tell which kind of day it had been for her when he got through the door at six o'clock. Actually he could usually predict from the response to his 'I'm on my way home, is there anything you need from the shop?' phone call – which was good, as it gave him enough time to prepare for his reception. If the answer was a frosty 'You mean you're only leaving now?' he knew not to dawdle, if it was a breezy 'We're grand' he could exhale and slow down enough to catch the sports news on the George Hook show before turning into the driveway towards the madness.

Kate often wondered how she'd missed out on that particular mothering gene. The one that meant you didn't want to fire one or both of them through an upstairs window by seven o'clock in the evening. The one where you didn't actually have to close your eyes and count to ten if someone asked you for another drink of juice. The one where a call of "Mammy? Are you in there?" through the bathroom door didn't make your head sink in your hands and the sight of the toilet cleaner on the shelf seem more appetising than the now-lukewarm can of Diet Coke that you'd been clinging to all afternoon.

"Mammy's Little Helpers," Michael called the stock of silver cans in the bottom of the fridge.

Hilarious he was.

So bearing in mind this missing mothering gene, how was it that Kate O'Brien had ever found herself in the role of stay-at-home mother? Well, it was funny really, now that she thought about it. But at one stage it was what she thought she wanted. When pregnant with Jess they had taken the decision that she'd leave once she was eight months pregnant. Well, actually, Kate had made the decision – Michael had said it was up to her.

He'd said it was up to her, yet he'd looked a bit worried at the time. He knew she loved her job and she had never really been any good with change. Michael had always said that. Said that she was like that little old man in the *Shawshank Redemption*, who killed himself when they let him *out* of prison.

"You're no good with change," he'd say, "and you're even worse with good change."

Whatever.

Well, anyway, here she was. She'd given it her best shot and it was time for more change.

And this wasn't just any old change.

This *was* good change.

Speaking of change, as she waited for the tram to slide on so she could cross the road, she realised that she'd never really been down this part of town before. Her old office had been in a huge building down at the Grand Canal, between Baggot Street and Leeson Street. All the big companies had been down in that area then and the redevelopment of the Dublin docklands had been very much something she'd only heard of. So when she realised that the giant shiny building in front of her, made almost completely from a kind of green glass, was to be her new home, she felt herself almost quiver with excitement. Everything looked so shiny and new and so, so professional.

She stepped off the footpath and at the feel of the dirty cobbles beneath her feet she was glad that she was wearing a pair of sensible courts. In fact, last night when she was laying out her clothes for today, she'd considered wearing runners and carrying a pair of heels in her bag like she used to do when she worked in town before – that had been all the rage a few years ago. But she wasn't sure what the rage was these days and she didn't want to look stupid. No, instead she very definitely wanted to fit in with the teeming hordes of working women that were pounding the streets towards their offices.

IFSC HOUSE

Her office.

This beautiful big building was *her* office.

She was almost one of them again.

The relief.

She stepped up confidently to the door and pressed the buzzer.

"Yes, hello?" came the deep-voiced reply through the intercom system.

"It's Kate, Kate O'Brien. I start work with you today. I'm a bit –"

"Push the door, please."

"– early," Kate finished. She heard the soft click of the door so did as she was bid and pushed it open.

Chapter 7

GERALDINE

As Geraldine reread the email on her screen again, hoping against hope that she'd misunderstood, that she'd read it wrong the first time, her phone buzzed.

"Geraldine, that new girl is at the front door. Just to let you know – oh, and welcome back." There was something about Jacinta's tone that was definitely more 'Thank God you're back' than 'Welcome back'.

"The new girl? Oh yes, Kate O'Brien." Geraldine sighed. "Great."

"I'll keep her in reception until you come out?"

"Yes. And Jacinta? Come in to me first, will you? I need someone I can trust to tell me exactly what the hell went on here on Friday afternoon."

"Oh, I can tell you alright. I'll be in as soon as I've explained to Declan that the phrase 'drinking the Kool-Aid' is not something he should put in board papers." Jacinta hung up.

Geraldine Lyttle smiled for a second then, before looking out the window of her office and sighing again. Even though her view was of a pleasant October morning in Dublin, she suddenly wished with all her heart she was back in her by-now-damp holiday home in Dunmore East. She'd only packed it up for the winter yesterday and already she felt like getting in her car, speeding down the N11 and shutting its rickety door behind her.

Could she not turn her back for two minutes?

Okay, it had been longer than two minutes – but to come back from a week's annual leave to encounter the chaos she had found beggared belief. Olivia was gone? Had walked out? Geraldine had warned them, she'd *warned* them that the situation was reaching boiling point. But why would anyone ever listen to her?

Geraldine had been with DKB for almost twenty years now. Herself and Jacinta were part of the crew that had come from Merrion Square when the bank's Dublin HQ had decided to avail of the flash new possibilities (and tax breaks, no doubt) down on the quays. Like Jacinta she often thought back to the Merrion Square days with longing. Everything had seemed so much simpler then. She went to work every day, she did her job, and she went home from work. There was no stress, no second-guessing herself, no trying to convince anyone to do the right thing. She had seen many changes over the years, both in terms of staff and systems, but the last three or four years and in particular the stress of the last eighteen months had ground her down completely.

It just wasn't possible. None of what they were trying was possible. Some kind of calamity had been rumbling down the line for months and, boy, had it landed now!

She was just too old for this. It wasn't how she'd expected the last few years of her working career to end up. Especially when it wasn't even such a large bank. It had less than a hundred employees spread across its various departments and for years she'd really, really loved her job.

She sighed. Maybe it was time to think about retiring. Or a career change. But what could she do? She'd often thought she might like to be a piano teacher, though it was hard to tell if there would be much call for scales and arpeggios in Dunmore East.

One thing for sure, she was not paid enough for this level of stress. What sort of fools were they? You just couldn't get away with this kind of thing these days. Yes, they had their reasons and she wasn't saying that there wasn't fault on both sides but there was a way to do these things. There was a correct procedure and not to follow this could mean serious repercussions.

How had this previously uneventful department become so dysfunctional? They weren't one of the 'toxic' banks – in fact, they were barely affected at all by the banking crisis, not having succumbed to sub-prime lending or overextending themselves on the capital front. But yet, when the tide had started to turn in 2008 and 2009, head office in Frankfurt had started to panic. It wasn't so much that they let people go – they did but not in the same numbers as other companies – but what was worse was that they put a freeze on hiring for all the positions they had vacant. Positions they really should have filled months previously but, because Geraldine and some of senior management had spent so much time putting a whole new organizational structure together to cope with the increase in workload, they missed the boat and overnight it was cancelled – or, as Frankfurt called it, "put on indefinite hold".

There was no avoiding the fact that head office were deeply embarrassed when the Troika arrived in Ireland to bail out the country. They wanted, above everything else, to be seen to handle their own affairs properly. They wanted to make it clear that they weren't spending anything they shouldn't and could run a streamlined, profitable ship.

But at what cost? She would never forget that evening that the news of the cancellation had come through. Geraldine had called a meeting with Declan and Frank Newcombe who was Head of Risk. She'd explained to them that they were in a bind – that they weren't going to be hiring. Declan in particular was incensed. He was at that stage doing far more lower-level work than he should have been and he'd been campaigning for a second-in-command for a long time. After much to-ing and fro-ing, and some fortunate support from Group Finance, the directors had conceded to offering a pay increase to Leona, then a senior accountant on the team, to step up to Finance Manager. And at first she'd said no. Geraldine hadn't been surprised really. Leona was quiet and had a young child, the job was going to be demanding time-wise and worse still would require her to take over all the people management of the team from Declan, a job which was not for the fainthearted.

But then, the following Monday, Leona had called a meeting with both Geraldine and Declan and told them that she'd changed her mind. That she would take the position if it was still going. Geraldine would always remember feeling that there was more to the change of mind than met the eye.

But they hadn't wasted any time questioning Leona's motives and within days she'd transformed from the 'pretty, clever girl in accounts' to someone who was feared by the entire team.

So that was one problem solved. The other gaps they'd tried to deal with in time but they never did manage to persuade Frankfurt to sanction a new strategy specialist and it had taken two years to get Rob and Cian instead.

But still, she would always pinpoint that evening as being the time when everything started to go downhill.

And it wasn't that the staff they had weren't second to none. She prided herself on the fact that, over the years, anyone they'd taken on board had been of good calibre. Okay, there were one or two secretarial disasters but, frankly, she doubted that Jacinta was ever going to be happy with anyone in that section.

But in the rest of the group? Mary, for example, was a gem. She worked hard, she was interested in her job and she seemed to understand that times had changed. Okay, she was no barrel of laughs and she didn't appear to have a massive social life outside of work, but Geraldine failed to see how that was a bad thing. If she had a building full of Cian Caseys or, worse still, Arianne Phillipses, she'd be in worse trouble.

Yes, they were blessed with good people. From relative newcomers like the handsome Rob Kinirons, whose mop of dark curly hair reminded her so much of her own son, to the old stock like Jacinta Fitzmaurice.

Where would she be without Jacinta? Jacinta was the only one she could trust to fill her in on how the lid had finally blown on this long-simmering situation.

Geraldine sighed.

Why had no one listened to her?

Chapter 8

KATE

However impressive the building had been from the outside, it was even more amazing inside. IFSC House housed a number of companies so when Kate stepped inside the front door she had to take a lift to the sixth floor where DKB had their offices. When she then stepped out of the lift it was into a huge glass atrium with a reception desk at one end that in turn backed onto a large open-plan office beyond. Floor-to-ceiling windows seemed to wrap the south wall on every floor and through them was the beautiful sight of the sun streaming onto the mouth of the River Liffey. It was all very tastefully done, in creams and mahogany with a beautifully laid marble floor. And there were real live people to be seen. Not like normal banks these days that hid their staff behind giant screens lest they be required to help someone. Many's the time Kate had wondered lately about the rise in the double-door system – where you had to buzz to get into a kind of glass box, wiggle your buggy around to let others in behind you, wait for that door to close and then buzz again for everyone to shuffle out the next door. And for what? Sure even if you were a bank robber it's unlikely you'd find anyone to tackle inside anyway?

No, the Deutsche Kommerzielle Bank required no such system as it didn't deal with walk-in customers at all. All its dealings were with other banks and big companies, the kind of people that didn't cash cheques or make lodgements or have any small-fry cash requirements.

Kate's years as a bank auditor had seen her visit all sorts of premises. And, as such, she was used to walking into a bank to a less than warm reception. So it wasn't that she was nervous on this first day at DKB, but she still wanted to create a good impression. Start as you mean to go on, that kind of thing. She walked over to the reception desk and held out her hand to the lady who sat behind it. "Good morning," she said, smiling brightly. "Kate O'Brien. I was told to ask for Geraldine."

"Yes, good morning, Kate. Welcome to Deutsche Kommerzielle Bank. If you'd like to take a seat? Geraldine is expecting you."

She had the most glorious voice that Kate had ever heard. Deeply gravelly, almost like that of an aging movie star. It went with her sleek bobbed hair that was blow-dried into a golden set, not a hair out of place.

Kate turned and sat in the plush chairs provided. There was a selection of magazines on the little table in front of her. As she looked down at them she realised that it had been two years since she'd seen a magazine that didn't include the latest celebrity wedding or diet tips. She used to buy the *Financial Times* every morning from a little newspaper stand on Baggot Street. Every morning without fail since the time one of her college lecturers had told her that people who read only the television supplement of the weekend papers got jobs accordingly. Not that she'd ever read it from cover to cover, but even walking down Baggot Street with its soft peach-coloured pages folded under her arm had made her feel successful, had focused her mind on the job in hand. She'd kept one actually, the one she'd bought the morning after the Twin Towers tragedy in New York. She remembered going to work that morning, clutching her paper while the uncertainty that the world was facing seemed so, so frightening. But it had all returned to normal eventually.

Everything always did, didn't it?

She was here now, wasn't she? Back where she belonged. Just as she wondered whether *Forbes* or *The Economist* would look the most impressive to be observed flicking through, she heard a voice she recognised above her head.

"Kate, so glad to see you – welcome to DKB."

Kate looked up to see Geraldine Lyttle, the lady who had interviewed her in the meeting rooms of the Shelbourne Hotel some three weeks previously.

"Geraldine, hi, lovely to see you again too." She smiled warmly as she stood.

"If you just come with me first to my office, we can run through a few bits and pieces and then I'll introduce you to the team."

Kate nodded and followed her through the door that led from reception to the big open-plan office beyond. As they walked through the room, she could feel every eye on her but she tried to just look straight ahead.

They wouldn't be strangers soon.

Patience.

Geraldine's office was on the far side of the room. Kate followed her in and Geraldine held the door open as she gestured to Kate to take a seat before closing the door and sitting in her own seat opposite.

"Right, Kate, first of all let me again say you're very welcome to the bank. We were very happy when you accepted our offer and are really excited to have you join our team but – ehm – since our last meeting a key member of our staff has left. And, well, it's put everyone under a bit of extra pressure."

She seemed to shift uncomfortably and for the first time Kate noticed that she looked a shade paler than she had before, tenser. She felt she had to say something.

"Oh, I'm sorry to hear that. I take it you weren't expecting it – I mean, it's only two weeks since we met."

"No, no. We weren't." Geraldine seemed to hesitate before continuing. "But there you go, these things happen. We'll be in a bit of a bind for a while, but nothing we can't cope with." She smiled brightly again, but then her smile seemed to falter. "The thing is, with all the upheaval, I only got to tell the others earlier this morning that you were starting today. I was on a week's annual leave and had assumed the team would have been told in my absence but then, you know how it is ..."

"Earlier this morning?" Kate looked at her watch and, without thinking, said, "It's not even nine o'clock yet."

"Oh," Geraldine smiled at the look of shock on her face, "they start early here – the girls can be in any time from seven and reception opens at half eight. Well, if there are meetings scheduled they might even be in earlier."

Earlier? Kate felt a cold sense of unease in her gut as she decided against asking what time they went home.

"But I don't doubt that they'll be delighted with any help they can get, once they get used to the idea."

The bright smile that Kate now knew to associate with a forced attempt at jollity was back.

Great.

"So, we've a few things we need to go through first – do you have your contract with you?"

Kate nodded.

"Perfect." Geraldine seemed to have composed herself. "And I have a key fob and your handbook. Then I can introduce you to the team."

Chapter 9

ALICE

Ping! Alice Conway looked up from her filing at her screen. A new email. Obviously it could wait but there was nothing Alice loved more than a distraction. She looked sidelong to see if Jacinta would notice if she stopped briefly to see what it was about but Jacinta was also staring intently at her screen so she decided to sneak a peek.

Turned out, it was a good job she did. Geraldine wanted a meeting with her. A brief meeting, straight away in Meeting Room 7, and she requested that she be "discreet".

Whatever could that be about?

Alice really had no idea. Had something happened? Was there an event she'd forgotten about? This was not beyond the realms of possibility given that she prided herself on living mostly in a little world of her own and found it served her well in an environment like DKB. The others just took everything so seriously. So, *so* seriously. Like it wasn't that any of them were brain surgeons. Alice was a big fan of *Grey's Anatomy* and she could understand how those guys would be stressed – like, one casual slip of a scalpel generally meant curtains for whatever patient was on the table. Now, frankly, she did feel on occasion that if they spent less time rolling around in the on-call room with each other then maybe less dying would happen but then a certain amount of sad was good. Alice loved a good sob-fest in fairness. When she wasn't watching *Grey's* she was scrolling down through the listings for other tearjerkers like *One Born Every Minute* or *Secret Millionaire* – anything really for an ould bawl. So much so that she was usually fairly disappointed in the episodes where someone didn't die and leave a paraplegic only child behind, and those episodes where everybody just recuperated nicely with no goose-bumpy *Snow Patrol* music just annoyed her.

Like the way this place annoyed her sometimes. It was just a bank. No one was going to die if everyone decided '*Woohoo* – let's not stay till midnight tonight!' It wasn't exactly life or death, was it? They'd give you a pain to be honest. Okay, she could understand how the ones up at the top might have the odd sleepless night alright but Jacinta – she really didn't get Jacinta. Surely the reason anyone became a secretary was to avoid all that stress and hassle? But no, Jacinta had an inflated sense of secretarial importance and was obsessed with stupid stuff like punching holes in paper.

Punching holes for the love of God! How could that be such a big deal? The first morning when Jacinta had sat her down and shown her how to crease each page in the centre to ensure that the paper punch was positioned correctly – well, to be honest, she'd thought someone was having a laugh. And the stapler, having to line up your corners *precisely* before stapling a sheaf of pages – come *on*!

And that was before the endless lectures on the right way to answer the phone – within three rings or you're dead – and the correct way to phrase an email or set out a letter – seriously, it was all a bit mad.

The money was good though, she had to say that for the place. Her friend Stacey was a secretary in a legal firm and the money was awfully poor, and her boss was a complete asshole. And the mess! Piles and piles of dusty old files. At least here they weren't too bad. Yes, Jacinta was fussy but she was alright, like.

There was, however, another positive and that was Rob Kinirons.

Alice thought Rob was just lovely. He was kind and handsome and such great fun and she didn't think she was imagining that he seemed to like her too. Well, okay, maybe that was stretching it, but he definitely was nicer to her than that sneery Cian.

She wondered did she need to tell Jacinta that she was leaving her desk? The email had said to be discreet but surely Geraldine didn't mean for her not to even tell Jacinta? Sure there was nothing Jacinta didn't know. Anyhow, before she got a chance to ask her Jacinta herself had left her own seat and gone out the door.

Alice shrugged. She could ask Geraldine what the protocol was. Actually that was a good word, she thought, suddenly proud of herself – *protocol* – maybe Jacinta was starting to rub off on her after all.

She pushed open the door to Meeting Room 7 and jumped when she saw Jacinta already sitting opposite Geraldine. Her first thought was that she'd walked into the wrong room but then with a sinking heart she realised that she hadn't and that this meeting clearly included Jacinta. Then to make matters worse, out of the corner of her eye she spotted someone else. Cian – and beside him was Mary.

She was dead.

With a sickening feeling in her stomach, she wondered was it her filing yesterday. She'd been in a hurry, she'd taken a guess instead of folding the page midway like she'd been told to. But it was only nine sheets – surely they wouldn't be all here if it was just for filing?

But Jesus, Mary and Holy Saint Joseph – if it wasn't the filing, then what *had* she done?

"Ah, Alice," said Geraldine pleasantly, "take a seat there."

"What – I mean – I don't know …" Alice could hardly get the words out, the room was starting to spin and all she could think about was trying to retrace her steps over the last few days, racking her brain to think of what she could possibly have done wrong to necessitate such a meeting.

"Alice."

"Alice!"

She realised that Jacinta was calling her and looked at her, anguish written all over her face.

"Will you just sit down? Geraldine wants to say something quickly to you all and you are delaying her!"

You all?

Oh. It wasn't just her then. That was fine.

She sat quickly and Geraldine wasted no time in getting started.

"Look. I've called you all in for a quick chat because, well, I thought it best if we discussed the protocol of what we should and shouldn't be saying publicly around here regarding disputes or disagreements in the office."

Alice smiled. *Protocol.* She was using her word. Wait, what disagreements?

Geraldine looked at them in turn.

"So, as you all know, there isn't really any policy or directive for this kind of thing – it's something we've been looking at, but, you know, it's a hard one to put into words."

Alice was relieved to see that she was no longer the only one looking at Geraldine blankly.

"So, I think for now we'll just leave it at the fact that any disagreements or disputes or conversations that might get a little bit heated – as these things can get – without any one individual being actually in the wrong but, you know, things can get out of hand very quickly when people are tired or emotional."

Cian shifted in his chair and Mary rolled her eyes.

"And bearing in mind that we have a new person that started only this morning, we feel that now is as good a time as any to start some new procedures so that, going forward, this kind of thing can be kept, well ..." She drifted off.

"With respect, Geraldine," Cian raised his hand, "I have no clue what you are talking about."

Geraldine blushed but before she could open her mouth to answer Jacinta had interrupted with a growl.

"What Geraldine is saying," she said quietly but with a menacing tone that could not be ignored, "is that there will be serious repercussions if anyone else is caught gossiping about the row here on Friday with anyone, especially the new girl. Is that understood?"

"*Ah!*"

Everyone's shoulders relaxed slightly as it dawned on them what this was really all about.

"Right? Now get back to work," Jacinta finished and so they did.

Chapter 10

KATE

Meeting the team that morning had gone by in a bit of a blur. Kate smiled at them all one by one but knew that, with each new face she met, she'd already forgotten the name of whatever face went before it. It even felt funny to be in the office for the first time as an employee – even her interview had been held off-site but Michael had said that was pretty normal practice these days. Eh, yeah, if you're recruiting a spy, Kate had thought. But then this was a bank. She'd heard that banks had their Christmas parties under other non-banking company names these days lest they be doused in bounced cheques from protestors. It was all a bit ridiculous really – it was hardly the type of people who went to Christmas parties that had caused the economy to dive-bomb. The 'Big Gerry from the post-room' sort wasn't in on any infamous bail-out meetings, stroking his mongrel Keano with glee at the heist he was about to pull off. As for the 'Mousy Margaret' types that manned Foreign Exchange with a look of pinched envy in their eyes that they weren't 'heading anywhere nice', well, they were hardly the ones that sanctioned ridiculous loans to buy shares in the bank in which they worked.

Why deprive the poor Gerrys and Margarets of the chance to get out the glad rags, drink warm wine and shuffle from foot to foot to the raucous strains of 'Dancing Queen'?

But then she was hoping that there wouldn't be too many Gerrys or Margarets in her shiny new job and so far so good.

58

She was put sitting at a desk next to that of a girl called Mary, who it would appear she'd be working closely with. It was hard to put an age on Mary. She was definitely older than Kate but it might have been by as little as a year or two or as much as five years. And she didn't look like the type that would be divulging her age any time soon. She seemed nice enough though and smiled at Kate when introduced, even though she clearly hadn't been expecting her.

After the endless stream of introductions, she was then told to read over her manual and that Mary would be with her with some work soon. Just after that everyone had vanished to some weekly meeting or other and by the time they'd all returned she'd practically read the manual from cover to cover.

And there lay the problem.

At that stage it was almost eleven o'clock and she was starting to get bored. There were about twenty other people in the room in various groupings of desks. Across from her were two younger guys and an empty desk and she'd a vague recollection of that grouping being the Strategy section, and off to her right were the girls from Legal, one of whom seemed to be wearing more make-up than the rest of the women put together. Further down the room was the Tax section and she thought that the rather serious-looking people in the very far corner were the Risk Department.

Despite all these people it was a very quiet office though.

Then, at eleven o'clock, she saw Mary take a mug from her drawer and leave her desk and with that her stomach gave a giant rumble.

No one had come near her since Geraldine had shown her to her desk. She was dying for a coffee herself but she didn't even know where the kitchen was, not to mention the toilet. Just as she wondered if she should get up from her desk and go exploring there was a voice behind her.

"Has anyone shown you where the staff kitchen is?"

She looked up. It was one of the younger lads who sat across from her in the Strategy Department. For the life of her she couldn't recall what name Geraldine had used when introducing anyone on that side of the room. But he was the friendlier of the two, the one with the shock of curly dark hair and the smiley eyes.

"Oh. Ehm, no, they haven't," she said, blushing. More out of embarrassment that she'd been left in this situation than the fact that there was a good-looking young lad talking to her. Well, actually, he probably wasn't even all that good-looking, but he had nice hair, he was friendly and he was about to tell her where she could get a cup of coffee.

"Well, I'm going for a coffee now. I'm sure you'd like one. Come on and I'll show you around."

Kate followed him gratefully out of the room and down the corridor to a little tea room. There was Mary sitting at one of the small tables and when she saw Kate and her guide her hand went to her mouth in horror.

"Oh Kate, gosh, I never thought to ask you would you like a coffee. Sorry, it's just been the morning from hell and –"

"That's fine, Mary, someone is looking after me now." Kate smiled but she couldn't help the frosty tinge in her voice.

"Ah Rob, you're after showing me up good and proper," Mary said and it was hard to tell if her embarrassment was genuine. "Good job we have one gentleman around the place."

Kate said nothing. The nice boy now-known-as-Rob was showing her where the cups were and how to work the rather complicated-looking coffee machine. He then led her over to a table near where Mary was sitting and they sat down.

"So how's your first morning going?" he asked.

"Pretty quiet so far," Kate said, "but I should probably enjoy that while it lasts."

"Oh, you definitely should," said Mary, rolling her eyes. "We'll only be this nice to you on the first day." She was clearly trying to make up for her earlier neglect so Kate decided to forgive her and smile back.

"Now, Mary," said Rob, "don't put her off yet. She's entitled to at least one day without pressure."

"Actually, Mary," Kate turned to look at her, "Geraldine did say that you'd be along with a few bits you needed doing."

"Oh, I've no doubt she did," Mary rolled her eyes again, "but as I wasn't aware you were coming until this morning, I've nothing, well, *nice*, to give you. Things are not always as simple as Geraldine sees them."

"Of course, always a pain when a new person starts. I remember it well." Kate was almost annoyed with herself for feeling the need to clarify that she too was often in Mary's position and hadn't always been the most junior person on the team.

"Where did you work before, Kate?" Rob asked as he handed her a packet of chocolate biscuits.

"TG & P," replied Kate. "I was in their Banking Department for a long time."

"Oh great. We love auditors here, don't we, Mary?"

Mary sniffed. "You might, Rob. I certainly can do without them."

"And you left there to see what the other side of the coin was like?" he continued.

"No, I left almost three years ago, decided to take some time off while the kids were smaller –"

"Oh wow – kiddies – how lovely!" Mary beamed but Kate got the distinct impression that her smile wasn't quite meeting her eyes.

"Have you any yourself?" she asked without thinking.

"Eh, no," Mary answered shortly. "Now if you'll excuse me, I'm up to my tonsils out there." With that she scraped back her chair and, after putting her mug in the dishwasher, left the room.

Kate looked at Rob but he just looked away and it was clear that he had no interest in clarifying Mary's family situation any further. She didn't get too far when she then tried to talk to him about his family either, so at that point she gave up. At least she got her coffee.

By the time half past four came, Kate had turned her thoughts to going home. She was half tempted to go online to check the traffic reports though there was a rather lengthy policy in the handbook that precluded pretty much any personal internet usage. There was a loophole that allowed limited usage in the event of an emergency but she wasn't sure if boredom and commuting-anxiety qualified.

The day had gone by so slowly. The only bit of excitement had been when a strikingly attractive girl called Leona had swept through the open-plan section and towards what seemed to be her own office, and everyone had quite literally cowered or at least lowered their heads so far into their work that they became practically invisible behind their partitions. Kate would have found their discomfort even funnier had this scary lady not stopped as she went past Kate's desk when she spotted the new face. She'd opened her mouth as if to say something but then shut it again and was gone as quickly as she'd appeared.

And that was about as exciting as the day got.

Just as she'd decided to risk using the internet anyway there was a voice at her shoulder.

"Right, well, better late than never, eh?"

She looked up to see Mary standing over her with two lever-arch files and a sheaf of loose papers.

"I beg your pardon?" said Kate.

"You wanted something to do. Now these are your purchases invoices – nothing too complicated to start you off – you'll be well able to process them all by the morning."

Kate looked from her face to the tiny clock in the corner of her computer screen.

4.37pm

For *fuck's* sake.

ROB

Look, I know what you're going to ask me. But if you're wondering did I try to influence anyone, then no, of course I didn't. And do you know what? Looking back, maybe I should have.

And I wasn't there that Friday evening. I wasn't lying to Blue. I'd gone home to Tipp. It was my sister's thirtieth – my sister Claire, she's the one next to me. And I knew that Dad wouldn't be there. That's why I went – how bad is that? I picked an occasion that I knew he'd stay away from. There weren't many of the older relations there in fairness, but with seven of us kids and assorted friends sure the pub was nearly packed. Yep, seven of us – me and six girls. So poor Claire was born just the year before me which just ensured that she didn't get a look-in as the golden-haired boy arrived just before her first birthday. Poor Claire.

My mam was there though – she's like that, Mam. She wouldn't see any reason why she shouldn't be there, making sure we all behaved. I'd say she felt there was enough shame on the family without us running riot in the local.

So no, I wasn't in DKB for the big row. So I'd no idea that Olivia had walked out until Cian texted me just after six. He thought it was a howl. I couldn't believe it actually. Olivia was alright. A bit intense and you wouldn't get much of a

63

laugh out of her, but she knew her stuff.

She was alright.

So yes, Cian texted me and, to be honest, I just thought it was a spat. You know women, they get a bit emotional. Claire got emotional that night too, when her and Paulie didn't hook up. I'm not sure why – I think he just felt uncomfortable with my mam and all there. It's one thing doing the biz up in town where you can forget ye knew each other as toddlers but sure if he'd snogged her that night me mam would have clipped him round the ear first and then made them get married.

Wait, where was I? Oh yes, Claire got emotional – but sure look, she was turning thirty. She thought it was an omen. No snog on her thirtieth might mean she'd be single forever – you know, that kind of thing.

Look, all I'm saying is that I have six sisters. I've seen emotional women. And Olivia, well, she was up there with the best of them. She'd thrown her toys out of the pram, but I never expected that she wouldn't be back. I don't know what I expected really.

What do you mean 'and Leona'?

'And Leona' what?

I can't believe you're even asking me that.

Of course that was never my plan. I didn't expect what happened either. But it happened. What can I say? It happened.

Extract from interview with Robert Kinirons
Recorded 12 November 2011
2.15pm

Chapter 11

MARY

When Mary left the office, for some reason it seemed later than normal. She peered in the door at the clock in her car, but no, it was only eight thirty. It must be just the low-hanging clouds, she decided, refusing to think that the evenings might be drawing in and that the days of going to work in the dark and returning home in the dark might soon be approaching.

There was still enough September evening light now to go for a run when she got home. It would clear her head after that long day and almost as importantly help keep her in a Size 10. Who'd have thought that after hitting forty, weight would be so easy put on, and so damn hard to keep at bay?

She slipped off her black high heels and put on her Todd's driving shoes. Placing the high heels into the cloth bag on the floor in front of the passenger seat, she hung her jacket on the hanger inside the passenger door. Each movement was precise. She wasn't in a hurry.

Mary Lawlor was never in a hurry.

Not only was she never in a hurry, but she failed to understand people who did have to hurry. It clearly denoted that something had gone wrong in their preparations and that was not something to be proud of. It wasn't that hard to make a proper plan of your day and to stick to it. Of course things happened that weren't part of the original plan, but if you handled them correctly, it didn't mean that the original plan had to change.

Like this morning, for example.

How had Geraldine possibly thought that this morning was the morning to spring a new girl on her? She'd obviously known for some time that Kate was coming – she should have told them before she'd gone on holidays. Did Geraldine think that Mary went into work and achieved the gargantuan amount of work that she did by flying by the seat of her pants every day? Why would it not be obvious that training a new person had to be factored into a day like hers?

Why did everyone assume that she would just 'make time'? Well, they were going to have to stop assuming.

She knew that Kate had not been impressed when she'd eventually given her something to do, but it had honestly taken that long for her to get around to it. No one ever minded handing *her* something to do at half four so what was the big deal? And anyway, she'd *plenty* of time to get it done – it wasn't needed until eleven o'clock tomorrow morning. Couldn't she come in early and finish it if leaving at five o'clock had been such a life-threatening event?

Plus, it was far better that she find out on her first day that five o'clock in DKB was just a number. That it was just a number in most jobs of this calibre these days. That it would be a rare day that it actually signalled the time you left the building and went home.

Mary exhaled deeply. She was not letting this stress her out. She'd had months of that kind of stress and had hoped that, given the events of last Friday, it was all behind her.

This new girl would have to learn. Mary would be no scapegoat for anyone.

Never again.

She might run along the pier tonight. With any luck the change of scenery might be what she needed to get her running mojo back. If she parked in the church carpark and ran down past the DART Station and back it'd be a nice 5k.

Just as the plan formulated itself in her head and she could practically smell the salty tang of the sea breeze, her phone rang.

She looked at her hands-free display.

Dympna.

Her finger hovered over the 'accept' button. Her sister was the last person she wanted to hear from right now, but if she didn't answer it meant she'd just ring her later.

"Hi," she sighed, finally giving in and answering. She sat back in her seat then and prepared herself.

"Hi. Where are you?"

"I'm fine thanks, how are you?"

"No, I said where – oh, you're being smart. Well, if you're finished being funny ..."

"I'm finished. So tell me what you want."

"Who said I wanted anything? All I wanted to know was where you were."

"Ah but why?"

This was the usual formation of their telephone conversations. Dympna would demand to know Mary's whereabouts and Mary would refuse to tell her.

"Well, are you in work or at home?"

"As it's clear that I have you on hands-free, I think it's safe to say neither. Now could you just get to the point? I'm about to get onto busy roads."

"Can you call up to Mammy on the way home then?"

Mary's eyes flickered shut for a nanosecond. Exactly the words she was dreading.

"Why?"

"She's up the walls about Daddy. She's insistent that there's something wrong with him."

"Wrong? What kind of wrong? He looked fine to me on Sunday."

"Well, she thinks his mind is going. She's convinced he has Alzheimer's. She says he doesn't listen to a word she says and then forgets half of it."

"Ah, Dee, none of us listen to a word she says and then we forget most of it. Or at least try to."

"Well, she's just phoned me in bits so I think you should call in."

"So she just phoned *you*, but *I* should call in?"

"Well, *I* can hardly go with a house full of children, can I?" Mary felt her hands grip the steering wheel tighter.

"Sorry, I assumed Phil was there."

"Well, he is, but that's not the point – they need baths and stories and you know what Elsa is like to get to bed. And Drew is now afraid of the dark ever since that horrible little child next door told him about the man in the van and ..."

Mary tuned out. She knew from experience that any stories involving her nieces and nephews and their bedtime proclivities could go on for some time.

"Mary?"

"What?"

"It's so obvious that you're not listening to me."

"Ah Jesus, Dympna, give me a break. It's been a long day."

"We've all had a long day, Mary. Oh! By the way, did you know Stephen is moving back in?"

"Stephen? As in our brother Stephen? Moving back in where? Home?"

"Apparently so."

"Oh, for God's sake – what's that all about?"

"Well, apparently his bonus fell through and as a result so did whatever house he was buying and he has his own apartment let and sure it'd be madness to kick out good tenants and take that back himself."

"So he's back to sponge off Mammy and Daddy. Great."

"It would seem so. I suppose if he's in a bind ..."

"He's not in a bloody bind, Dee. If he stopped drinking his wages every weekend as is so clearly evident from his Facebook page then he could afford to rent somewhere like everyone else."

"I guess you're right."

"I bloody know I'm right."

"So you'll go then."

"Go where?"

"To Mammy's tonight – you could warn her about Stephen when you're there."

"Nice try but I didn't say that I'd go. I don't see why anyone should go. That woman is daft, Dee, you know that and I know that. She has far too much time on her hands. She spends all day deciding what ailments she has, and now, when she should be clinically dead with all she thinks is wrong with herself, she's moved onto someone else. The only thing wrong with Dad is that she has him driven fucking demented with her goings-on. And I know how he feels!"

"Well, they're not going to be around forever, you know."

"Eh, I could say the same thing to you, *you know*!"

"Oh, come on, Mary – it's easy for you – you know I've the kids, and Phil is working such stupid hours and I can't begrudge him a game of golf on Saturdays and sometimes I think if I bring them with me that they're just wearing Mammy out. It's easier for you."

"Course it is – sure I only work seventeen-hour days!"

"Well, go tomorrow then. I'm sure she'll last till then."

"I can't go tomorrow, it doesn't suit."

"Why not? What could you possibly have on?"

"I said it doesn't suit."

"Well, come on, you can't have it every way! Just pop down for ten minutes and then go back to your Sky box or whatever else you have lined up."

"I was going for a run actually."

"Oh, for God's sake, you're like a rake. Missing one night is not going to do you any harm, is it? You're the only one that can talk sense into her. And you know Daddy would love to see you ..."

And that was the killer blow. And well Dympna knew it.

"Oh right! I'll go then. But for God's sake, Dee, that means I'm done with these stupid errands for at least a bloody month!"

"You know I'd go if I could ..."

But Mary hung up. She was so annoyed. She would go alright, but she was going to swing in home first and change into her running gear and find somewhere to grab a few kilometres afterwards no matter how dark it was.

She was sick to the back teeth of being pushed around.

It had to stop.

Barely twelve months before Mary had gone to her dentist as she was repeatedly waking at night with a piercing pain in her jaw. At first she'd tried to ignore it – there couldn't possibly be anything wrong with her teeth. She attended Dr Harvey religiously every six months and a hygienist every three. But after several weeks of this pain getting steadily worse she booked some precious time off for an appointment.

And she'd been right. There was nothing wrong with her teeth. They were flawless, as always. She was stunned, however, when her dentist then turned and informed her that he thought the cause of her pain was stress.

"But that's ridiculous," she'd said. "I'm not stressed. I'm fine."

"Well, is there anything that might be causing you tension? Causing you to feel uptight? When exactly did these pains start?"

Now that was a different question altogether.

When had they started? Well, almost three weeks before. She could remember that the first one had occurred the night of her 41st birthday. She'd woken with a slight fuzzy feeling and an aching jaw and had only taken two painkillers as she'd felt that at least they would serve her well for the potential hangover in the morning too.

Not that it had been that wild a night.

She hadn't wanted to go at all actually. She wasn't into birthdays, and it wasn't to do with the fact that they now had a '4' in them – she just wasn't into any social occasion at which she might find herself the centre of attention. She hadn't had a 21st birthday party for that exact reason. She couldn't have coped with all those people, all there on her behalf. And she definitely couldn't have coped with the stress of worrying that all those people mightn't turn up at all.

She even found other people's parties stressful at the best of times. She was not one of those people that bounced into the room, scanning it gleefully for someone interesting to talk to, flitting from group to group, working the room, making new friends. No, she was far more likely to wait until the last minute to arrive, knowing exactly who'd be there by then and hoping that she'd be able to find them straight away. The relief when she'd spot someone she knew across the crowded room was sometimes dizzying. Seconded only by the relief of that first crisp, confidence-giving glass of white sliding down her throat.

So no, parties were not her thing. For her 40th birthday, rather than go through the trauma of having to explain why she didn't want a party, she'd booked a trip to Connecticut for two weeks, a week safely either side of the big event.

And for this birthday? She'd wanted to do nothing. Seriously. It didn't interest her, it was just another day. But no. Three of her friends had insisted on booking a table in the local Italian and she'd have looked churlish to refuse.

Even more churlish than normal, and that was saying something.

Sandra, Toni and Angela were all old school friends. They'd stayed in touch despite the fact that in recent years Mary definitely felt that the amount they had in common was becoming increasingly less.

Sandra was married to her childhood sweetheart and had four

children ranging in ages from fourteen down to seven. Also married, Angela had started her family later in life and as a result had only two children – each after a protracted battle with infertility. She had then removed herself from any further heartbreak by deciding that two was definitely enough and frankly, infertility or no, Mary could see where she was coming from. Sandra on the other hand was definitely prone to the 'easy for you' comments but, in fairness to Angela, it was like water off a duck's back to her.

And then there was Toni. Toni had been Mary's ally for years as they'd remained steadfastly single and apparently quite happy with that status. But now, Toni was about to ruin it all. Not only was she about to marry the dishy-in-a-nerdy-way Arthur but was also going to obtain two teenage stepchildren in the process.

Yes, churlish.

Was it any wonder that it was the first word to spring to Mary's mind every time she anticipated these nights out? *She mustn't be churlish*. It wasn't their fault that they all had relationships and family stories in common. Would she prefer that they talk about the new demands of the Central Bank for the evening?

Did she really expect them to listen to her talk about Olivia and the ins and outs of that whole horrible situation yet again? At one point she did consider bringing it up but, looking around the table, it was just wasn't the time nor the place.

So she'd sat there for the evening, sipping her wine, waiting for topics to arise that would mean she could join in. They were few and far between. Sandra was a stay-at-home mother, and her children were the centre of her universe. The last film she'd seen was some Disney monstrosity. And the last book she read? Well, didn't that question make her fling her hands in the air with a shriek of "*Books? Sure where would I get the time?*"

To be fair to Angela, having children later in life had meant that she had a pretty good grounding in the 'world outside' before they'd come along. Their battles with conceiving both Dylan and Connie had been so all-consuming at the time that she'd made a conscious effort to claw back some of her life since Connie's birth some five years ago. She worked three days a week in her local Bank of Ireland and as such was usually a good bet for non-child-related conversation.

But not on this occasion. The minute Toni tentatively suggested that she might be thinking of going down the IVF route, all chances of non-child-related conversation bit the dust.

Toni & her eggs: One.

Mary & her banking stories: Nil.

Yes, that had been the first night of the pains. The funny thing was that after a year of nightly agony they'd stopped last Friday night. The same day Olivia had said she was leaving. Mary had woken up next morning and wondered what felt so different. Then she realised she'd had a full night's sleep. And again on Saturday and Sunday … so unusual for a Sunday …

Funny that.

She thought of today's developments at the office and rubbed her jaw automatically as she took the turn down Mount Anville Road towards her mother's.

Best to take a few painkillers before bed tonight maybe.

Chapter 12

LEONA

Sender: LSharpe@DKB.com
To: JPattenson@DKB.com

I am fully aware of the complexities, tight timeframes, and demands on your department. Indeed they are no more than we in Finance are witnessing ourselves and endeavour to deal with on a daily basis (with less staff).

To this end, I have on several occasions communicated the difficulties we at DKB are experiencing to our Central Bank supervisor Mr Patrick Feehey but he has informed me that there is very little he can do to alleviate this onerous situation at the current time.

The Central Bank Reform Act of 2010, which I'm quite sure I don't need to quote to you, has meant stringent deadlines are a feature of our lives now and whilst in the past I have tried to help you meet your deadlines by letting my staff help on various projects that were definitely of a Risk as opposed to a Finance nature, recent changes to our team mean that this simply won't be possible any more and that you really need to look within your own ranks to find the resources you need.

So it would be more in your line to actually do some work instead of composing ridiculous lengthy emails that are not only taking up my time but indeed the time of the seventeen people you insist on CC-ing every time you send them.

Leona sighed and hit backspace. What she *wanted* to say and what she *could* say were sometimes two completely different things.

Sometimes? Usually.

The Risk Department were on her back again and frankly she'd had enough. Jennifer Pattenson was not even that high on the Risk pecking order but she was like a thorn in Leona's side. Every day there was an email bemoaning the fact that they were up to their tonsils and pushing some work or other back on the Finance team. And every day Leona had to step out of what she was doing, try and calm her own team who were starting to crack under Jennifer's demands, and bat her back like the really annoying gnat that she was.

Her rapidly shrinking team, that was, though at least now Mary had some help which should stop her complaining for a while.

Well, if she knew what was good for her Jennifer would back off. Leona was rapidly losing patience with her demands and, one thing for sure, Jennifer Pattenson would not like her if she was angry.

She lifted the draft board papers from her printer and walked out of her office. The open-plan area was empty. It was after nine and no one ever really worked later than that on a Monday evening. In fact, the whole building was probably empty by now, bar the security guard who would sit downstairs in reception until she left.

Which wouldn't be for a while yet.

She walked over to Mary's desk but, halfway across the room, she noticed the sky through the huge windows. Despite the fact that the sun had long since sunk behind the Ulster Bank buildings across the river it was still streaked with a beautiful pattern of pinks and oranges.

Dropping the sheaf of papers on Mary's desk, she went over to the window.

Rachel would love that sky.

The view from the huge window stretched out across the Liffey as it flowed slowly past the distinctive neon-lit barrel of the new Convention Centre and down towards Dublin Bay beyond. She could see the two regal red-and-white-striped Poolbeg Chimneys like two tall twins above the distant buildings and then, in front, the beautiful Samuel Beckett Bridge that spanned the pink-reflected surface of the river, its vast curved pylon rising like a giant fin from the water.

Rising like a giant fin from the water.

Well, didn't that bring back memories.

The sun had been setting that time too. Slowly but just as beautifully above the Californian hills that sat high over Monterey Bay. To one side was the distant sight of Santa Cruz and to the other the picturesque Carmel seashore. The sea was smooth, lapping gently against the side of the boat. She wished she could lean down and trail her hands in the water but the side of the yacht was too high. So instead she leaned her bronzed arms against the rail and looked out towards the ocean, the white fringe of her kaftan floating gently in the cool breeze.

She could hear him behind her, chatting to all the other guests on board. Some of them he knew from other work trips but most he'd never met before. Not that you'd notice – he'd had a way of being the life and soul of every party; he was the one that everyone wanted to talk to, to be around.

He was the total opposite of her. She knew she was too quiet, that she needed to network more, to put herself out there. But she hated that kind of thing, she just wanted to do her job and come home and just couldn't be bothered with all that came with constantly appraising your position, of always being on the lookout for the next big step in your career. Whereas he, he was Mr Linked-In, always networking, always wheeling and dealing, always on the go ...

"Having fun?"

Two strong arms slipped around her slim waist and she felt his warm breath on her neck. She wound her long dark hair over her other shoulder and, leaning back into him, nodded.

"It's so beautiful here. I don't think I want to ever go home."

He squeezed her tighter.

"If we didn't go home we couldn't ever go on holidays again. And that, young lady, would be a crying shame."

"I suppose," she whispered, blushing with a silly delight that already, this early in the relationship, he expected there to be more holidays.

"What do you want to do this evening? Shrimp and cocktails at the Shack again or would you like something more exotic?"

She blushed again. "I don't mind. This is all pretty exotic to me already."

The boat tipped slightly then and she squealed as she lost her balance, falling into him even more.

"Hey – easy there now!" He laughed as he righted her.

She was laughing too but then grabbed his arm.

"Oh wow – look!" She was pointing out towards the sea. A huge black form just breaking the surface not too far beyond their boat. "I think it's a whale!"

Several others joined them now at their side of the boat as word spread.

"Oh my God, I think it really is!" She was so excited. They'd been told that there was a possibility of seeing whales or dolphins out here in Monterey Bay but the actual sight of the gigantic black form so close was unbelievably exciting.

Then, as she looked, a huge fin rose up out of the water. It was the turn of everyone on the boat to shriek now. It was so big and tall, and rivulets of water flowed from its tip back down into the water.

"A real whale!" she gasped. "I just can't believe it!"

He held her close as they watched the giant tail rise from the water and then slam back down into the sea with a massive slap. The whole boat cheered and laughed as the water splashed over their faces. Within minutes the giant tail had risen again, black and dripping against the peach sky. She felt him turn her to face him.

She smiled up at him. He was tall, not that it was hard to be taller than her. Tall, broad and handsome. She had to pinch herself that he was here, with her. Despite him telling her constantly that she was the most beautiful woman he'd ever seen, she still felt like this was a dream and that she would soon wake up.

"Marry me," he whispered into her ear.

She gasped. "What did you just say?"

He laughed at the shock in her wide green eyes. "Come on. We have good fun, don't we? Marry me and let's do this every year – twice a year – three times if you include a skiing trip."

"You're crazy, it's only been a few months!" She shoved him gently, trying to pretend that his question had not just knocked her for six. Yes, it had been only a few months and while he was right in that they did have such fun together, someone had to exercise caution here. "Marriage is about more than just fun times, you know!" was the best she could manage.

"Ah, but it doesn't have to be. Come on, what do you say?"

"I still say you're mad."

"Let's see what everyone else thinks!"

Before she could say another word he'd spun around to the rest of the boat.

"Ladies and gentlemen, I've just asked this lovely lady to marry me – what do you all think she should say?"

There was a rousing cheer from the other guests and she was enveloped in a tide of goodwill.

"Okay, okay," she laughed. "I'll say yes if it means we can all go back to looking at that beautiful creature."

There was a huge whoop and he kissed her victoriously before dashing off to check with the crew if there was enough champagne on board for everyone. That was him all over. It was why she loved him really; he was everything she wasn't.

She smiled and turned back to look at the sea but it was still and calm. It was too late, the moment had passed and it seemed that the show was over for today.

Well, the show was definitely over now.

She leaned against the window ledge, resting her head against the cold glass. The automated lights that were installed in every building in the IFSC went out suddenly, drowning the whole floor in darkness. The motion sensor to restart them was at the far side of the room but still she stood, lost in thought.

Just then there was a noise behind her and she jumped and turned. Her breath caught with fright as she saw a figure framed in the door at the far side that led to the bright hall beyond.

"I'm sorry – I was in the loo and didn't realise anyone was still here – I didn't know – well, I thought everyone was gone – you know, with the lights off and everything."

She knew from his voice that it was Rob from Olivia's team but she couldn't really see his face as he was just a silhouette against the bright doorframe.

"What are you doing still here?" she asked without moving.

"I'm working on some of the back-up for the budgets. It has to be ready for Group by the end of the month."

"The budgets, of course. I can't believe it's October already." She sighed. "It just gets better and better, doesn't it?"

"It will all be fine. They'll get done."

"I admire your confidence." She turned back towards the window. "I have a million things I should be doing and here I am. Looking at a streaky sky." She laughed an almost choked, bitter laugh. "You must think I'm mad."

He didn't answer and, embarrassed, she turned from the window and made her way back to her own office, the lights blinking back on as she reached her door.

She went in and sat at her desk looking at the unfinished email on her screen. The fight was gone out of her now so she just signed it off and pressed send wearily. Jennifer was going to ignore it anyway; she was just wasting her time.

Now what was next?

There was a noise at her door and she jumped again.

"I'm sorry! That's twice I've tried not to scare you and twice I've managed to fail miserably."

Rob was standing at her door, with a steaming mug in his hand.

"It's coffee. I'm pretty sure it's what modern armies march on."

"Why, thank you," she managed, trying to hide her surprise.

"No problem. And just to let you know, I'm probably going to go now – you should think about it yourself."

She nodded and looked at him as he turned to leave the room, then smiling to herself she got back to work.

ROB

I don't care what else you say happened either before that day, or since then – that's what I remember most. Not Kate starting or Mary being a bitch.

I just remember her.

And I'm not going to lie, it was as if I saw her for the first time that night. Her slight frame against the backdrop of that streaky pink sky, the blinking lights of Dublin City spread like a carpet under her feet. It was like the whole city was waiting for her, was depending on her. And she had no one. There was just her.

Everyone hated her, you know, but for me, well, there was no going back for me from that point.

No going back.

Extract from interview with Robert Kiniron
Recorded 12 November 2011
3:00pm

Chapter 13

MARY

The glorious streaks in the October sky had well vanished by the time Mary got back into her car. In fact she had watched them fade through the window behind her mother's chair as she sat captive in the front sitting room listening to her go on and on and on.

Every now and again her mother would pause her monologue and shoot a question at Mary's poor father sitting opposite and when he didn't answer straight away she would look knowingly back at Mary, as if to say 'There, I told you, he's losing it'.

Oh, he was losing something alright, Mary thought, but no more than the rest of us – it was probably just the will to live.

Her intended half-hour visit had dragged on to over an hour and when she finally managed to escape, she was so cross.

Her whole evening was ruined.

It was too late now to go for a run along the sea front. Yes, it would be well lit with street lighting but she knew of old that with the dusk came the groups of teenagers and winos that hung around the seafront benches and she just wasn't in the mood for heckling tonight.

She looked at her watch. It was now half past nine.

Damn Dympna anyway.

She really hadn't wanted to miss tonight's run. She'd found the last few hard and could not figure out what she was doing wrong. Even worse, the last time out she'd felt like just stopping and walking back to her car and she was afraid that if this happened too often then she'd simply give up altogether.

She was almost home when she thought of the athletics ground just around the corner from her estate. It was where she'd started running all those years ago, back when she'd been too busy struggling to keep going to worry about the scenery. Running laps would be boring but at least she'd be safe and only two minutes from her house – and, better still, only a short walk to her car if at any stage she felt like throwing in the towel.

But hopefully that wouldn't happen. Hopefully tonight she'd relive one of those nights where she felt like she could stride on forever.

And that would mean a victory despite them all.

She parked her car in the dilapidated car park to the right of the club, surprised by how many cars were already there. It wouldn't have been an unusual sight years ago but then most people had moved on to expensive gyms and personal trainers and the lowly athletics track had become a ghost-town.

She locked her car and slipped her car key and her phone into the tiny pocket in the waistband of her running leggings. She didn't use earphones when running, preferring to listen to the drumming of her footsteps banishing the thoughts from her head.

Because, apart from any weight loss or fitness benefits, that was what she used to love running for – therapy. It had been especially useful for nights like tonight when her shoulders cracked with tension. She used to be able to run and run until the tension had seeped from her shoulders right down to her calves and her head was clear and free from worries.

'*Worries?*' she could almost hear her mother shriek, '*Worries?*'

Yes, Mother, you might think I do nothing but sit at a desk all day filing my nails and waiting for my massive pay check to arrive but, yes, I have worries. And not ones that are all in my head like yours.

She tightened her laces one last time and pushed open the gate to the track. Her lips pursed slightly when she saw a gaggle of people all in matching T-shirts down at the start. Squinting slightly she read '*Ronan's Runners*' blazoned across their fronts as they all jogged on the spot waving their arms in giant circles, appearing to be following the example of a tall man with a beard.

She rolled her eyes. Only beginners did that kind of enthusiastic warm-up. Well, she just hoped they'd stay out of her way.

She slipped onto the track on the bend and started to walk briskly, preparing herself mentally and physically for the endeavour ahead.

She felt good so far. Maybe this would be the night to get her back on track after all. She slipped her phone out of her pocket and hit 'New Workout' on her running app. The app told no lies. Her distances had decreased over the last few weeks while her times had done precisely the opposite.

But every night was a fresh start, right? She started to jog, trying to pay attention to the fall of her feet and her posture before deliberately moving her thoughts to matters outside running.

Matters outside of running. Well, let's see, there was work and there was, well, work. The good thing was, she actually really liked her job.

Sad but true. She actually did like it.

She liked the orderly nature of the bank. She liked being a cog in such a large wheel and she liked knowing that she was well thought of and appreciated. She liked that she knew exactly what she was doing, that she never felt out of her depth, that whilst she spent a lot of time under severe deadline pressure that she always got there in the end.

Thud thud. Thud thud.

So far so good, three laps down which brought her over the kilometre. She was still feeling light on her feet, nothing was sore, her breathing was still nice and calm.

She'd started there almost fifteen years ago now. It was crazy really when you thought about it. She and Olivia had started at the same time.

Olivia.

She wondered would she miss her.

It came as somewhat of a shock to realise that she probably would. There was a massive gap in the room since her colleague had walked out the previous Friday. Her desk still sat there, not a single thing had been moved. Her pens were still in her holder and, despite the usual shortage, no one had even swiped her stapler.

Even her photograph of the boys was still sitting there in its lollipop-stick handmade frame. Three cherubic faces with blonde curls and chocolate-brown eyes. Whereas before the sight of it had irritated Mary to the point of distraction, now every time it caught her eye she felt uncomfortable. Uneasy. Like as if they were staring at her, their accusatory eyes boring into her as she worked. She must stick it into the desk drawer out of sight. Though really someone should pack it up and send it on to Olivia. But not her. It couldn't be her. Not after what happened that last day. She winced as she remembered that last afternoon.

It was hard to remember that they'd worked side by side for so long and that it had been only in later years that there'd been any problems.

Well, as far as she was concerned.

Thud thud. Thud thud.

Fuck it.

She reached behind for her phone as she'd lost track of the laps. But she knew without checking that it wasn't that many.

And it had started already. The pain. The effort.

It had started and it was way, way too early.

The app said 3.5km – for God's sake, she used to be able to do three times that amount! What was happening to her? Her pace had started to slow and become laboured. Sweat was breaking out on her forehead, fuelled by a rising heat that felt like her whole brain might explode.

She couldn't do it. She was going to have to stop. And to make matters worse she could hear footfall behind her which meant those bloody beginners were about to pass her out.

The utter humiliation of it.

They were so close she could hear their chatter now.

"So, Ronan, how are the girls adjusting?"

"Ah grand – they were a bit unsettled at first, but I collect them from Dolores every day for a while, and whatever I can manage at the weekend."

"Ah that's good. What ages are they now?"

"Esther is five, and Monica is going on seven now."

"Ah lovely!"

Nearer and nearer came the voices and then even nearer again came the footsteps.

"Stop thinking about it," came a male voice at her shoulder.

She went to look sideways but only managed to see that it was the tall instructor with the beard before he spoke again.

"Look straight ahead. Straighten up your back, pull your shoulders back, open up your rib cage and pull in those breaths."

She opened her mouth to tell him to fuck right off and mind his own business but he was still speaking.

"Unclench those hands – you can't run with fists like that. Unclench them and shake them out."

Again she was about to stop and berate him but as he spoke she realised she was doing what he was saying – her back had straightened, her shoulders were looser and she'd unravelled her hands so they hung limply.

"Now slow down while you're at it. Slow right down and breathe. Breathe in through your mouth and out through your mouth."

"I know how to fucking breathe," she managed to mutter.

"Of course you do, but you're not doing it right. You're breathing in through your nose, and that won't get enough air in. And the main thing is, if you're thinking about breathing you're not thinking about whatever to hell else has you running like a mad ball of stress – no wonder you were about to pull up."

"I wasn't."

"Oh right. Forgive me, I've been running this club a long time but my mistake. You feel better now, though, right?"

Mary nodded. She did feel better. She found that she could match his stride, now that she was bouncing as opposed to dragging her feet off the ground for each step.

He was talking again now, but she was only half listening. Instead she was marvelling at the new lightness in her step, the sensation of her head cooling, the complete absence of tension in her shoulders.

"Now keep thinking about your feet, keep them in your head until you find a rhythm, and then keep that rhythm. Don't think about anything else."

She nodded.

"Don't think about work, don't think about the government, don't think about the kids, just think about your body and how easy this is now."

She nodded again.

It was nice to be running alongside someone. She never ran with anyone and had never had any interest in races or charity runs.

But this was nice.

"Right so, I'd better go back to the others. Well done, you've a nice way of running when you relax."

And then he was gone, jogging backwards to his group.

Thank God for that, she muttered to herself, trying to ignore any disappointment that she felt to be back to her own devices.

Yes, the help had been nice, she told herself, but she was back in control now and that was even nicer. Who'd have thought the day would end on such a positive note after all? She straightened her shoulders even more, conscious that the eyes of that bossy instructor were probably still on her. Not that she cared of course. Beards were so not her thing.

OLIVIA

So I left Bank of Ireland in 2002. It was all very strategic. You see, we got engaged in 2001 and started looking for a house straight away. There was a lull in the economy then, you see. Well, actually I hadn't really realised that there was any lull, but Danny had. He's good about stuff like that. Do you know he must be one of the only people in Ireland that made money from Eircom shares? It was shortly after we met. I remember all the kerfuffle about those shares. But Danny, well, he bought them one afternoon and sold them next morning, and never said a word till the following Saturday night and sure by then he'd the money all tied up in some really safe deposit account. He's clever like that, is my Danny.

But anyhow, nearly from the minute we met he'd been saying that I should move jobs, that I was too good for somewhere like Bank of Ireland. That I was never going to go places (he obviously didn't know about Goggins and his path from lowly bank clerk to Chief Executive Officer then either). But anyhow, when we got engaged he kind of changed his mind, said that if we were buying a house it'd be better if I'd been in a job for a while, and sure we could get a good rate with them. Oh, he was the clever one alright, always two steps ahead of everyone.

So I waited until the following autumn before making the move.

It was a big step for me to leave Bank of Ireland, I'm not going to lie. My dad thought I was mad. Forty-odd years he worked for the same crowd. Jobs were for life in his eyes and you didn't leave a good one. To him though, good was 'steady', dependable, and that was definitely what I had in Bank of Ireland. But, well, Danny thought I could be earning more. What with the exams and all that. And he was right.

But I guess Dad was never going to agree with anything Danny said. Not after Saipan anyway; it was nearly Christmas before the two of them could be in a room together after that bloody World Cup. Danny is a big Man U supporter and, well, sure, Dad said that there was no way Keane should have walked out. He said you never walk out like that, that letting people down is no way of getting revenge.

I thought he was right back then. Now, well, sure now I know it's not that easy.

But Roy Keane or no, he should have given Danny more credit. Because he's going places, you know. I mean he will be. He's working in Blanchardstown, in that big pharmaceutical plant, but someday he wants his own business. We're not sure what yet, but he'll be great. I never met anyone with such knowledge. I'm not even sure where he gets it from – the internet mostly, I think. He loves the internet. He spends hours every evening on places like boards.ie, helping out people, advising them. I mean you'd pay for that kind of advice really, wouldn't you?

Anyhow, going to the recruitment agent was his idea. He even arranged it all, not that there were that many agents to choose from back in those days. Not like during the boom, recruitment agents on every corner – back then only the proper guys were doing it. Though maybe it's gone back to that now, maybe only the ones that were ever any good at it are still there. The fly-by-nights vanished off back to wherever they came from. Kind of the way it should be really.

That's mostly why I'm glad Danny didn't decide to be a plumber, or an electrician like his brothers. Sure everyone wanted to be their own boss then, set up their own company. Oh they were the big men for those few years, with their huge jeeps and expense accounts. We were only in the ha'penny place, me and Dan, the poor relations. But, do you know, Danny always said it would never last. And he was right. Sure when it all went belly up, they couldn't even get the dole. They weren't so big then.

So, between the jigs and the reels, a month later I had done three different interviews for three different companies and then one evening I got the phone call. I had been offered a placement with DKB, a German merchant bank with an office in Dublin.

International Financial Services Centre, here I come!

Chapter 14

GAVIN

"Daddy, hold this!"

The pink, slightly grubby Barbie bag was thrust into Gavin's hand and then his daughter was gone. He soon lost sight of her as she blended into the slipstream of navy blue that was hurtling down the path only to split delta-like on reaching the playground. The boys, and braver girls, headed for the climbing frame while the remainder rushed to get first dibs on the swings.

Another Friday at the playground.

Another Friday that didn't involve a liquid lunch or after-work drinks in Searson's. Ties and tongues loose, cracking old jokes about targets and clients before moving on to the heavier topics like who was going to win the Triple Crown, or if Sexton could ever really replace O'Gara.

Another Friday that had nothing about it to suggest that it wasn't Monday, Tuesday, Wednesday or Thursday.

He fell in line with the other left-behind adults and made his way over to his spot. Only then did he look up. The usual cluster were occupying the benches beside him. The nannies with their high cheekbones and Slavic, sloe-like eyes were sitting huddled together, looking cold even on this mild September afternoon.

Beside them, a rotund Polish man was regaling his gathering of buddies with a story. Ruddy-faced and laughing, it was clear that unemployment had not gripped *his* spirit with its icy hands, squeezing it until every vestige of self-respect had left, draining it dry. An equally rotund lady sat beside him. Gavin wondered was she his wife. She was hanging onto his every jovial word.

Imagine.

The only thing Leona hung onto these days was the purse-strings. And the power.

He glanced around. Nothing but women as far as the eye could see, bar him and the storytelling Polish man.

There was no point in looking at his watch; they'd only been there barely five minutes and no way was he getting away with it that easy. When he found himself searching for a cloud in the sky in the hope that it might rain he really had to tell himself to cop on and just have patience until all of the others started to go home and he might have some chance of escape.

It didn't look likely just yet though. The place was mayhem. There were children everywhere. How anyone knew which were theirs was beyond him – he certainly couldn't see Rachel anywhere but just had to presume she was in the melée somewhere. He was glad she seemed to be mixing well. The potential trauma of changing schools had seemed to pass her by and now, not for the first time, he made a note to remind himself to bring something bright to tie in her ponytail so that she might be easier to spot. He'd already tried the High Viz idea but it hadn't gone down well.

He smiled as he remembered the indignation on her face when he'd suggested it.

"Daddy, you really have no sense, do you?"

She could do insulting just as competently as her mother.

"Watch out!"

He swung around just in time to see a small red-haired boy hurtle into him, but not in time to save himself from being knocked backwards by the impact. He landed flat on his backside and looked up in shock.

"What the hell?" he muttered.

"Oh Jesus, I'm so sorry – I'll kill him – well, when I catch him I'll kill him – honestly, I'm so sorry!"

Still in shock, he allowed himself be helped up by the girl who had rushed over to him and obviously had been the shouter of the earlier-but-too-late warning shout of 'Watch out!'.

"I'm so, so sorry!"

He couldn't get a word in with her apologies and to his horror she started to brush him down to remove the little stones of tarmac that were now all over him from the fall.

"I'm grand – honestly, I'm grand!" he tried to interrupt her before her brushing hand moved around to his arse where the real damage was done.

"He's a divil – I swear to God, I'll kill him!"

He had to take a step back to stop her patting him and, when he did so, she finally looked up enough for him to see her face. She was small, blonde and so slight that he doubted that she'd be able to kill anyone, let alone the blocky young lad that had just knocked him over.

"Honestly, it's fine." He smiled ruefully. "Once I get over the embarrassment, sure I'll be grand."

"You did go down pretty easily all the same." She suddenly giggled, her up-to-now serious face looking prettier with the shy smile.

"He caught me off balance."

"Yeah. Sure he did." She looked around her. "I've no control over him – it's terrible. He walloped one of the PTA last week with a stick – I swear to fuck, he'll be flung out of the place."

"PTA?" Gavin had no clue what she was talking about. "Are they some kind of paramilitary group or something?"

"Ha, kind of, that's them over there –" She gestured to a very serious-looking group of women standing over the far side of the playground. "Parent Teacher Association – they run the school, or at least they think they do. They're the ones that send out all those letters. Always looking for something, they are. Money for this, money for that – remember that note about the Bag Pack we got last week?"

Gavin shook his head. This was all like double Dutch to him.

"Well, check the school bag – it'll be in the bottom of it. Though I don't see you as being the bag-packing type."

"Well, as I don't even know what a 'bag pack' is, you could be right. You sound enthusiastic though – take it you'll be partaking in this magical bag-packing experience?"

She shook her head furiously. "No way. Sure there's only me at home and I can hardly bring that little shit with me to a supermarket to pack someone else's shopping bags – we'd be asked to leave," she rolled her eyes, "and not for the first time either."

"Ah, so that's what it involves – I see," he said. No daddy at home so – unless she just meant the daddy was out at work? He wondered if she would ask about his situation. And if she did, what would he say? He started to panic as he tried to formulate an answer in his head.

"So which one is yours?" she asked eventually.

"Ehm …" He scanned the swirling vortex of kids in front of him and luckily spotted Rachel's swinging ponytail streaming in the air from one of the swings. "That one – on the swings. With the dark hair."

"Ah, I see. She's pretty."

"She is."

Like her mother, he should have said, but funnily enough the words got stuck in his throat.

"You're lucky having a girl – boys are a bleeding nightmare." The girl had moved on anyway. "They want to have Adam assessed but I don't think there's anything wrong with him bar he's just like his father. I tried telling them that but sure they want to assess him anyway. They say he could get extra help and stuff but I bet it just means I'll feel extra guilt when I'm trying to clobber him."

"Extra help?"

"Yeah, in the classroom like. Well for them, I said – any chance of extra help for me at home? They don't think of that, do they?"

No, Gavin thought to himself, they don't.

The playground was finally starting to thin out. Mothers right and left were shrieking at their children and brandishing coats like matadors at a bull fight.

It was finally time to go. But still he stood. It was nice to have someone to talk to and this would possibly be the only adult conversation he would have for another what, eight, nine hours?

It wasn't like it being Friday meant anything different to Leona either, it certainly didn't mean she came home any earlier, that was for sure.

Soon they were the only two left and still they stood there watching the blocky red-haired child, who Gavin now knew as

Adam, slide backwards down the slide, over and over.

Then Gavin felt a tug at his top. He looked down.

"Daddy, I'm hungry."

It was time to go. He looked at his new friend and rolled his eyes conspiratorially. "Never ends, does it?"

"Never. Sure I'll see you again. I'll stay here for a while now that he's occupied. It'll be a long day once we get home."

"I know what you mean," Gavin smiled. "Yes, I'll see you again. Bye, Adam!" The child ignored him. "Bye, eh …"

"Trish," she said, "and sorry again for him knocking you over."

"No problem," he said. "Sure I'll get him next time."

Chapter 15

KATE

"Look, if you get into the group stages, you're made – anything after that is a bonus …"

The boys in Strategy were talking football again. Their youthful exuberance meant they either didn't realise the whole Finance Department could hear them, or they simply didn't care. Every morning was the same: football, rugby, the odd golf analysis. For some reason Rob seemed to know a lot about horse-racing – old Éamonn from Treasury was forever asking him for tips but Rob always just smiled politely and changed the subject. Cian talked a lot about sport, but it was clear from looking at him that he didn't actually play any. He seemed to spend his entire weekends 'in town' having drinks with an endless stream of crazily named females and, despite his arrogance, his stories were all quite funny. Kate didn't mind listening to all the chat; it was entertaining and it wasn't like the work she was doing had her on the edge of her seat with excitement.

However, judging from the amount of eye-rolling and sighing, it seemed to really annoy Mary. But then Mary was, Kate imagined, easily annoyed. She could go from perfectly fine to frosty quicker than anyone else she knew.

"Eh, lads, less *Off the Wall* and more of those quarter-four forecasting reports I'm waiting on, if you don't mind."

Kate jumped in her seat. She hadn't heard Leona come out of the office behind her and found herself blushing and staring even more intently at her screen, as though she'd been caught napping herself instead of sorting through the invoices for the month of September. It was actually a job that she should have finished the previous day but she'd learned the hard way to stretch out anything Mary gave her to do as the tasks given out by the other girl were generally pretty simple and completed in no time. She thought she'd enjoy being given little jobs to do, without all the responsibility of being in charge. But then she realised that mostly what Mary was giving her were silly little tasks that Mary just didn't want to do herself. Still, she hated sitting with nothing at all to do so any menial task Mary did throw her way she tended to try and make it last. And of course she didn't want to get caught by Leona sitting there doing nothing either, another reason to stretch everything out.

The senior manager terrified her and had done from that very first morning when Geraldine, the nice HR lady, had eventually introduced them. Kate had held out her hand but Leona had just looked up and said, "Oh yes, I saw you earlier. Let me guess, you're the girl they hired when my back was turned?" She'd said it so simply that Kate had smiled, expecting that any minute the extraordinarily pretty Leona would also burst into a warm smile and say 'Just kidding – welcome to the company!' but she didn't, and both Kate's smile and hand had retreated together in confusion. As she said to Michael later that evening, "She's fierce and I don't mean in the Beyoncé sense …"

"*Off the Ball*," drawled Cian, not moving from where he was sprawled, snaky hips jutting provocatively at Leona's back as she went back into her office.

"I beg your pardon?" The finance manager spun on one tiny heel and glared at him.

"I said '*Off the Ball*'. That's what it's called. Assuming it's the radio sports show you're referring to?" He didn't bat a ridiculously long eyelash as he matched Leona stare for stare.

"And *I* said get back to work, Cian." Her voice was cold and quiet, but every word resonated with a threatening undertone, and it was clear that she meant business. She turned again to go into her room, calling over one shoulder, "Rob, could I see you for a moment, please?"

Cian smirked at Rob and dragged himself around to face his desk.

"*'Rob, could I see you for a moment, please?'*" he mimicked, following it with a slightly less audible "Cow" under his breath.

Kate still wasn't sure what to make of Cian. He was very good-looking, that was for sure, but almost intimidating in his looks, like some of those pretty boys you'd see in men's magazines with cheekbones that could slice bread. And yet, despite the obvious fact that he spent longer in front of the bathroom mirror than most women she knew, his lazy aggressiveness and smouldering sexuality meant no one would ever suspect him of being gay. Maybe what disturbed her most was that he was definitely the kind of boy she'd have lost sleep over ten years ago but now, well, it irked her that he probably didn't even see her as female. She wasn't in her early twenties, she was married, and the fact that little humans had grown inside her and now puked daily on her shoulder just meant she was invisible to a boy like him.

Not that she wanted him to fancy her – but, well, it would have been nice to have some impact. She still had a great figure, her highlighted hair showed not a speck of grey and she was well able to swing her hips as she walked by him.

But no. He never even looked up.

She felt silly for even thinking about it. She needed to be more like Leona Blake who obviously cared very little what someone like Cian viewed her as, as long as it was as someone who should be obeyed.

Kate sighed and wondered what poor Rob had done to be summoned so brutally to the office. Kate liked Rob. In his late twenties too, that was where any resemblance to Cian ended. While Cian was sharp and intimidating, Rob was easygoing and popular with everyone in the office. He was good-looking in a different way from Cian. Tall, gangly and slightly awkward, even the gravel-toned Jacinta had a soft spot for his brown eyes and soft Tipperary accent. And he was funny, gosh, he was so funny. Not in a smart-aleck way, and never at anyone's expense, but sometimes he'd say something and she'd look quickly at him to see if he was joking and his expression would be bland, but then he'd wink at her and she'd smile, feeling part of some special private club.

Yes, Rob was nice and if only for the fact that he'd been the only person to be nice to her on that first morning, she didn't think he deserved the hair-dryer treatment from Leona, and God love him but he was in and out of her office a lot these days. It was funny, though – he never seemed to give out about her, and generally tried to change the subject when someone else did. As a result he did come in for some teasing and Cian was forever calling him Teacher's Pet.

Even Mary looked up now and said to no one in particular: "He's in with her again?"

Kate stayed staring at her computer; it was highly unlikely that Mary was addressing the question to her.

"Seems so," said Cian. "Rather him than me."

Mary shrugged. "You say that now, Cian, but wait until he's running the bank and we're all left behind like eejits."

And everyone laughed.

Chapter 16

MARY

Mary smoothed down the skirt of her dress and stood back from the full-length mirror in the ladies' of the Lighthouse restaurant in Dalkey. She could not have been more pleased with herself. She'd decided to go for a slightly different look for Toni's wedding and the 1940's swing to her dress made her feel young and vibrant. She'd had her long black hair pulled into a neat knot at the back of her neck and she'd even bought a new pink lip gloss instead of her usual neutral.

She'd been nervous getting ready that morning but, as she walked back out of the toilet towards the restaurant, she could feel herself starting to relax. Maybe, just maybe, this wedding might actually be fun.

Mary had never really been too fond of weddings but she blamed Pinterest for the recent evolution of the Irish wedding into something that had exploded out of all control. Actually she blamed the latest social networking craze for a lot of things. It was just so goddamn smug. Now, Facebook was bad enough – every evening she scowled as she scrolled down through numerous pictures of people's babies, pictures of people's dogs, and worst of all, pictures of people's dinners. And then there were the wine pictures – every Friday was the bloody same. "**Wine O'Clock!**" would screech the caption and below would be a picture of a glass of wine, the only variation being whatever seasonal scene made up the backdrop: a sunny back garden in summer and a roaring log fire in winter.

Cheers!

But then along came Pinterest, which went a step further. Now you didn't have to have a fancy dinner to 'share' – you could just share a picture of someone else's fancy dinner and piggy-back on their success.

The **'Bacon Done Seven Ways'** picture that was beautifully shot and filtered to death by some other eejit became yours for the taking by merely adding the line: **'Oh – Saturday night supper sorted!'** You didn't even have to make the goddamn thing – your pin just convinced everyone that you were at least contemplating it.

Like, take that whole Mason jar thing. **'Delicious Everyday Lunches in a Jar'** – seriously? Who in god's name brought lunch in a goddamn jar – was there ever anything more impractical? Firstly they were just clunky and clumsy to carry, secondly there was the very great chance you'd smash the bloody thing on the journey in to the office, and thirdly if your hipster jar contained organic, paleo, vegan-friendly sustenance like soup, sure you couldn't even stick the jar in the office microwave because of all the metal fiddly fasteners. Like seriously?

But that was the glory of Pinterest: you really only had to *pretend* you were bringing your lunch in a jar. It was like taking candy from a baby.

But jars and recipes aside, it was the Pinterest wedding that really took the biscuit, Mary thought. What was so wrong with a hotel, where the bride turned up to find the flowers already on the table and all she had to do was hand over some Lily O'Brien chocolates for the staff to set out at every place setting? Back when Dympna had married Phil they'd used the local hotel in Rathfarnham and everything had been relatively simple. But nowadays weddings had exploded to so much more than a Mass, a dinner and a dance. In fact they no longer were over in just twenty-four hours – now there were rehearsal dinners, the day itself and some other bloody event to go to the next day no matter how hung over you were. That's three days in the company of the same people, three new outfits and three days of good-to-presentable hair.

For God's sake.

In fact, one of the nicer days of the past working week involved a conversation at coffee break about this exact topic – with Kate of all people. She'd had them all in stitches telling them about her cousin Vicky and her recent nuptials and how the new wave for all things 'alternative' had taken a turn for the ridiculous.

Apparently, not for Vicky a wedding in the local hotel, oh no. Vicky had decided she was getting married in a forest with everyone barefoot.

"Barefoot?" said Kate, rolling her eyes. "Did you ever hear the like?"

Thankfully the barefoot idea was short-lived due to a remarkable number of people not too keen on stepping on broken beer bottles and nettles just so that Cousin Vicky's filtered-to-the-hilt photographs could be Instagram-ed to the world at large. She'd settled instead for barefoot bridesmaids and flower girls and a sea of handmade kitschy decorations adorning the trees. Everything was hand-tied: hand-tied bouquets, hand-tied sprays of hand-dyed willow branches ...

"Seriously," Kate shook her head in disbelief as her audience almost wept with laughter, "is there any other way to tie something? Robot-tied? Computer-tied? Please!"

But that's the way it was heading these days and, as Kate said, even the guests weren't safe. If you stood still long enough at a modern wedding these days you were in severe danger of having bunting hung on you or being asked to hold a scratchy hand-painted sign that said '*Happiness this Way*'.

Yes, they'd had a good laugh that day.

But thankfully, when she arrived at Toni's wedding several hours ago there was no sign of any '*Happiness this Way*' signs. They weren't needed. It was quite clear to see that there was happiness as far as the eye could see. In fact, unlike her usual solo wedding attendances, Mary had a calm, relaxed feeling from the start.

There was something utterly romantic about a couple who'd found each other 'later in life'. For Arthur it was a second chance at happiness. His wife Aisling had died of breast cancer some four years previously but any tinge of sadness was counter-balanced by the fact that Toni had met Mr Right at last.

At last.

Because she was the wrong side of forty now, you know ...

At any other wedding it would have been written in bunting and hung from the restaurant ceiling. Little phrases on each pastel or multi-coloured flag, like:

"At last!"

"Phew!"

"Nick of Time!"

"Cutting it fine!"

But it wasn't. Well, for starters there wasn't any bunting. No bunting, no frothy meringue-style frock, no sweet cart, no plethora of bridesmaids.

It actually looked like it was going to be the perfect wedding.

Two people coming together, deciding that they'd had enough of being alone and that they loved each other enough to risk this whole 'rest of our lives' thing. They didn't need the trappings; they just wanted thirty of their nearest and dearest to celebrate their decision and to wish them well.

It was beautiful.

So beautiful that the ever-present cynic in Mary was silenced. There was nothing she could sneer at, nothing she would change.

Beautiful.

And it was nice too to meet a few people that she hadn't seen in years and Toni had taken care to seat her at a table with Sandra and Angela and their respective partners and another nice couple, Bernie and Tom, from Toni's college days. The wine flowed during the meal and the chat got very lively. Mary was really relaxed by the time the speeches started, and more than a little emotional at all the love in the room for her lovely friend.

So emotional that when Arthur started his speech, it was understandable that she should find herself wiping a tear from her eye.

At which time she felt a soft pat on her arm and Bernie's sweet, reassuring voice in her ear:

"See? There's always hope ..."

Bernie was speaking to her.

Always hope ...

It took her a minute to realise what exactly she meant.

But before she could open her mouth they were all on their feet to toast the happy couple. There was no way then to escape turning to Bernie, who winked as she raised her glass to Mary's with the immortal words: "*Cheers!*"

"Always hope? *Always fucking hope?*"

Mary was by now very, very drunk and the very second the lovely Bernie and the slightly-chubby-and-rather-messy-at-eating Tom had moved to say hi to friends at the far side of the room, she'd exploded.

"Always hope," Angela nodded sagely, patting her on her knee. "So don't give up yet."

Both Sandra and Angela could not help but dissolve in convulsions of laughter.

"Well, I'm glad you pair think it's so funny!" Mary snapped.

"Oh Mary!" Angela grabbed her napkin to wipe the tears from her eyes. "You know it's not you we're laughing at! I'm laughing that she somehow thought that that was an appropriate thing to say!"

"And I'm laughing," Sandra could barely breathe at this stage, "at the fact that she's still alive after saying it!"

They were now laughing so much they couldn't even speak anymore but Mary still sat there with a mournful look on her face.

"Like 'always hope'? Of what – that some other poor wife will die and donate me her husband? So, what she's really saying is that maybe all married women should carry a card and their husbands could be told at their hospital bedside, just before they flick the switch: 'The good news at this sad time is that we have a recipient for her heart, her kidneys – oh and you – so get your bag packed and let's get the transplants underway as soon as possible.'"

By now Mary's two married friends had given up all hope of their make-up making it through this conversation. The angrier Mary got the more they tried to stop laughing, and the more they tried, the worse they got.

"Always hope. I'll give her 'always hope'!" Mary was not for letting this go. "And did you see the state of her own husband? The dashing Tom? I tell you one thing, even if she carried one of those cards no one would want him. He's had food in his teeth for the last hour and he eats with his mouth open. Always hope, my arse!"

"Oh Mary, don't mind her." Angela had calmed down sufficiently to realise that Mary, who was downing the wine in giant gulps at this stage, needed to be calmed down. "She probably didn't mean it the way it sounded."

"What other way is there to mean it?" Mary scowled. "You'd swear I was sitting crying into my pan-fried fucking seabass at having no husband. I'm perfectly happy with my life. Perfectly happy."

"Of course you are." Angela now looked dolefully at her glass. "In fact I often bloody wished I'd chosen the career route myself."

Sandra looked in horror at Angela but it was too late.

"*The career route?*" Mary almost screeched across the table. "The career route? Jesus Christ, Ang – that's nearly bloody worse!"

Angela looked blankly back at her, not really sure what she'd said wrong. "All I'm saying is – all I'm saying is that maybe I often wish I'd done as well as you, you know, work-wise, instead of spending every day covered in vomit and dried yoghurt."

"No, what you're saying is that I *chose* to not have a family so that I could have a fancy career. You can have both, you know! I didn't *choose* one over the other."

"It's very hard to have both," said Angela, still hopeful of getting this conversation back on track. She looked to Sandra for help but Sandra was conveniently rooting in her handbag for something and would not look up. "I mean, look at poor Olivia in your office."

"Poor Olivia?" Mary's voice was low and cold now, all drunken hysteria evaporated. "Please explain how that works?"

"*No! That's enough!*"

They both jumped as Sandra cut in, using a voice that meant she was not to be messed with.

"Enough," she said again. "And I mean it. We are *not* doing this here. This is Toni's night and she has paid for all this lovely wine so that we can get happily drunk instead of fish-wifey drunk which is exactly where this conversation is heading. Mary – that woman was silly, and our Angie is just trying to say she thinks you have a great life – albeit not that well – but don't start taking meanings from things that aren't there."

Mary blushed. Sandra was right. She resolved to say no more tonight but at the same time, as the wine continued to flow, she couldn't stop the earlier conversation going round and round in her head.

Career route.

Was that what everyone thought? She hadn't chosen to be unmarried at forty-one but neither was she deeply unhappy with her current situation. She had a great life, a lovely house that she'd bought way before things went crazy and, to be quite honest, she didn't look with jealousy on people like Sandra and her four children, because, frankly, she wasn't sure that kind of life was for her. She couldn't imagine what it would be like to have to consider five other people every time she left the house, or to have to clean up after five other people, or cook for five other people.

No, what bothered her more was the 'Poor Olivia' comment. Because being single might not have bothered Mary at all – and it really didn't – but what did bother her was the fact that anyone might have sympathy for her former colleague. There had been nothing 'poor' about Olivia.

For someone who hadn't chosen the 'career route'.

Poor Olivia.

Poor Olivia, my arse, she thought. Poor Olivia had landed the job that Mary wanted, and had managed to do it with very little inconvenience to herself.

Poor Olivia had the dream job but had just walked away without a backwards glance.

Mary stopped suddenly. Poor Olivia was gone. But the job was still there. For someone who *had* chosen the career route and could do it justice.

Poor Olivia?

Fuck poor Olivia. Now it was Mary's turn at the job she should have got years ago. It was time to stop walking on eggshells around that bloody office and go in and tell them exactly what she wanted. Let them see that more than 'poor Olivia' could make demands.

Chapter 17

LEONA

"I can see why you like working early on a Saturday morning," Rob said as he crossed the large office towards her open door. "It's so quiet."

"It's not just the quiet – it's the lack of interruptions – no one phones me, there are no emails, no knocks at the door – I'd say I get four times the normal amount of work done in here at this hour on a Saturday."

"Do you do this often then?"

She shrugged. "I try not to, but sometimes yes."

"Have you nothing you'd rather be doing?"

She looked at him but he didn't look like he was trying to be smart so she decided to answer. "No, I don't. My daughter has swimming lessons on a Saturday morning so I find if I get in here, get a few bits done then I'm home by lunchtime and available to her for the afternoon. Why, have you nothing better to be doing yourself?"

"Not this morning, no. The lads in the house were out drinking last night so there'll not be much happening there till later and, besides, they'd a bit of a party when they got back and I'm damned if I'm scraping cold pizza off the couch when I'd nothing to do with putting it there."

"You didn't go out yourself then?"

"Oh, I did. I came home ahead of that lot though."

She looked at his brown eyes curiously for some trace of hangover

105

but they were as bright as always, not a trace of the awful red puffiness of a night on the beer.

"Well, you don't look like you were out."

"Ah, I don't drink, so bar a slight touch of sleep deprivation from listening to that lot playing Jenga at 4am, I'm grand."

"Oh." She was surprised. She thought everyone drank like it was going out of fashion these days. "I'm sorry."

He laughed.

"For what?"

"For assuming you drank. It was a bit presumptuous."

"So now you think I'm a recovering alcoholic or something."

"I didn't say that."

"You didn't have to. Everyone thinks I've some deep dark secret but the honest truth is I don't. I just never really developed the habit as I was always up too early in the mornings to have much of a head on me from the night before. Besides, where I lived in Tipp was fairly remote so you either drove or stayed at home. No self-respecting taxi would be too keen to drop you home, and if they did they'd be looking to be well compensated."

"Fair enough. But for the record, I didn't think you were an alcoholic."

He shrugged. "Makes no odds to me if you did. I'm in on a Saturday morning to work. I'd imagine that's all you're interested in really, when it comes down to it."

"How very astute of you. Now that you are here, I suppose we could get started by reviewing the latest budget figures?"

"We'll get started when that kettle has boiled and I have a rather large mug of tea in my hand. Would you like one?"

"No, thank you." She indicated the takeaway cup on her desk. "I got a coffee on the way in."

"Fair enough, back in a tick."

She watched him go back out and across to the door that led to the canteen. She didn't know what to make of him really and she really wasn't used to being spoken to in such a casual manner in here at all. And to be honest, she wasn't sure if she was comfortable with it. What was it about the way he spoke to her that was so different from everyone else?

Fear. That was it, there was no fear.

She looked up again as he walked in, a mug of steaming tea in one hand and a small stack of biscuits balancing precariously on a saucer in the other. "Breakfast," he said, through a mouth that was clearly already full of biscuit.

"You're not afraid of me at all, are you?"

He almost choked trying to swallow the biscuit then hastily wiped the crumbs from around his mouth.

"Ehm, no, I'm not." He gave another wipe. "Should I be?"

"Well, yes, actually – everyone else is!"

"That is true, but I come in, I work hard, I do a good job, I don't do anything deliberately wrong so I feel I've no reason to be afraid of you."

"Oh." She was quite stunned at his answer. "What is it with you boys in the Strategy Department? Does Geraldine deliberately pick candidates that are brimful of self-confidence or what?"

"What's wrong with confidence?" He looked at her from under a shock of curly hair.

"Nothing apart from the fact that it should really be me, not you, that decides whether or not you're doing a good job."

"And am I?"

"You're doing okay."

"Well, then? Why can I not be confidently unafraid of you?"

"Because you've only been working with me for a short while and frankly anything could happen yet?"

He smiled. "You say that like you're almost wishing something would go wrong."

"I'm not wishing it but, trust me, I've been here longer than you. It's never plain sailing for long."

"And if I do mess up? What would happen then?"

"Oh, I'm afraid I'm not very nice when I'm cross."

"But that's just silly really. Why can't you just be nice? What does being mean achieve?"

"Now, come on, exactly how far do you think being nice would get me in here? If I'm not 'being mean' as you so eloquently put it, then nothing would get done and everyone would walk all over me."

"I wouldn't walk all over you. I'd treat you the exact same as I'm treating you now. In fact I'd probably like you more – nobody likes a mean girl now really, do they?"

"I think you're mistaking me for someone who cares whether people like me or not. The only thing I care about is getting this job done as well as I can."

"Really, this place is actually the only thing you care about?"

"At the moment it has to be top of my list of priorities, yes."

"Fair enough." He shrugged again. "That's your business. You can choose to be a mean girl if you want to be, but I'll tell you now I can equally choose whether or not to be afraid of you. And I've chosen not to be. I've watched someone live in fear of a complete prick and, to be honest, that's not for me. You just end up doing stupid things out of fear and it's not healthy."

"Right, well, you'd better keep working hard – then you'll have nothing to be afraid of."

He laughed. "I suppose I should – move over there now and let's get started."

OLIVIA

The night I told my dad that I'd got the new job could easily have gone either way. Not so much in relation to the job itself – he'd come around to the idea that it was time to move on – but more so where my new office was going to be. Because unlike most of my new colleagues who only knew the IFSC to be the big shiny, fancy array of buildings it was now, well, to us, it was different.

There's a story Declan loves to tell about a mother he met once at the Yacht Club. According to him she said, "Oh, my son told me this morning he wants to be a doctor when he grows up" so just to annoy her he replied at the top of his voice "A docker, you say? He wants to be a docker?" That was Declan's way of putting a posh mother down, by insinuating her son wanted to work on the docks.

Well, my dad was a third-generation docker, and the first of his family to move from the East Wall further out to the suburbs when he got married. His brothers still live there – well, one got moved the time they tore down the Ringsend flats but he got a house nearby as part of the scheme they had to introduce when all the locals went mental. His father, my grandfather, had the button, you see, and on the day my dad turned sixteen he was frog-marched down to the docks to sign up. The main man would have known my grandad, and that meant that Dad got picked that first day, but he still had to prove himself. He still had to work. It was the same with each of my uncles – they all started at the age of sixteen and would head off

109

every morning. My granny used to tell fierce funny stories about the rows they'd have over dinner in the evening because Grandad would be criticising the way they did things but you didn't argue with a button man. I suppose I should explain that the button men were the dockers who had joined the Union way back and been given a button as a kind of identity tag. They were always chosen first for work by the ganger and only after that would any of the other men be chosen.

As a result, the old Dublin Docklands was a place very familiar to me. But if you think this is where I'm going to tell you about the idyllic times we used to spend there as children then you'd be wrong. My dad remembers the good old days alright, when giant American ships would glide in and the sailors would fling sweets and bananas to the children on the quays, when ships carrying tea and Guinness were a daily sight, when the area was heaving with ruddy-faced welders and carpenters, mechanics and farriers all on hand to tend to ship after ship that rolled in to dock at the bustling port.

But by the time I came along things had started to change. Most of the North Wall had turned into huge expanses of warehouses and then, in time, row after row after row of shipping containers. The numbers employed on the docks dropped at that time at a ferocious rate. My dad was one of the few to keep his job. He says it was because he showed from the word go that he was adaptable and willing to roll with whatever changes they threw at him. But others weren't either so clever or so lucky. The whole area suffered massive unemployment and became an area to avoid; the freight yards were deserted and the dank, grotty laneways crawled with criminals and drug users. In the end he wouldn't bring us anymore and that made us sad.

And yet, when word on the street had it that big plans were afoot, I'm not sure how happy my dad was, or indeed any of the locals for that matter. The government had tried to clean the place up before and memories were long enough to remember earlier regeneration attempts where locals got shipped out to the suburbs without any consultation. But before long the whole area between the Custom House and the North Wall seemed to mushroom overnight into what my dad started to call The Emerald City. Now, there were the doubters, of course, and sure everyone was full of gossip about how none of the companies housed in these giant green-glassed buildings were paying any tax – and how some of them had only one member of staff in the whole building to man the phones and that the rest of the building was simply used for its address – but there was no taking from the fact that the place looked better. And in time, the naysayers softened again when further development in the late 90s coincided with a huge drive to involve the local communities and provide more social housing and amenities.

Still though, I wasn't quite sure how Dad would react when he heard I was 'going over to the Dark Side' but the night I told him, he surprised me. His face broke into a broad smile and for a second I thought I might see a tear start to slide down his weathered cheek.

"Begorrah," he said, "I watched them build that place. I watched them clear that big old warehouse, level the carpark and tear the old days asunder. And then I watched the new ways rise and rise. And now, now you're going to be part of it. Isn't that just grand?"

And I laughed at him getting all emotional but, do you know what, I know Danny was all about the money, but Dad? Dad was just pure proud.

And yes, indeed, that was just grand.

PART TWO

Paradigm Shift
noun
a fundamental change in approach or underlying assumptions.
"Geophysical evidence supporting Wegener's theory led to a rapid
paradigm shift in the earth sciences."

ARIANNE

I don't know why I'm being dragged into this to be honest. No, I didn't notice anything. Was there a bad atmosphere? Of course there was, but there's been a bad atmosphere in here since I started three years ago.

Look, there's no point in me pretending that I don't know what this is all about. It's the talk of the building now. I'm not saying I knew about it, but I'm saying it doesn't surprise me.

Nothing would surprise me about this place.

Extract from interview with Arianne Phillips
Recorded 11 November 2011
9.30am

Chapter 18

GAVIN

"What's for tea?" For the seventeenth time that hour, seven-year-old Rachel Blake raised her head from her homework.

"Never mind what's for tea, Rachel, just finish that sentence!"

"But I'm starving – how am I meant to do homework when I'm starving?"

"Tea won't be for an hour – you'll be lucky to have that sentence finished by then at this rate."

"Well, can I have a snack then?"

Gavin sighed and slid off the high stool at the breakfast bar. Going to the counter he took a slice of bread and buttered it and brought it over, along with a glass of milk and put it on the granite worktop beside his daughter.

"There's a snack, now finish your homework."

"Lucy Grogan brings vegetable men for her lunch," said Rachel, gazing into space, with no acknowledgement of the snack whatsoever.

"Vegetable men? What in God's name are vegetable men?"

"Little men made out of vegetables. Like you know, carrot heads, cucumber arms, I think the faces are, ehm … I don't know … liquorice maybe?"

"Unlikely." Gavin was pretty sure that a woman militant enough to get up and make men hewn out of vegetables was not going to fall at the final hurdle and put liquorice faces on them.

"Well, maybe not, maybe they're ... oh, I don't know. But they're pretty cool."

"Well, isn't Lucy Grogan's mammy great making those," said Gavin.

"Yeah. I guess. Our mammy just makes money."

Gavin nearly choked. "Rachel – for the last time – homework!"

"Mammy does know about tonight, doesn't she?"

"She does, Rach."

"Did you remind her?"

"I did. I phoned a while ago and left her a message."

"Do you think she'll be there?"

"I don't know, Rachel. I know she'll do her best."

"I know." Rachel chewed her lip thinking for a second, "She always does, I guess. But, Dad?"

"What, Rachel?"

"Do you ever wish she wasn't so important? Like it's good for the bank, but it's a bit not very good for us really."

"Jesus, Rach, give me that sentence and I'll just finish it myself!"

Gavin Blake spent sixty per cent of every day in complete shock that this was his life now. That he didn't get up at six thirty every morning, put on an already-ironed-shirt and tie and go to work. That he didn't have twenty minutes on the DART in from Dun Laoghaire to read the sports pages and then work a day where what he did actually achieved something and was of value. That he didn't come home to see Rachel dressed for bed, kiss Leona on the cheek and sit down to his dinner before going to bed to get up the next morning and do it all again.

"Do you ever wish she wasn't so important?"

'Out of the mouths of babes, eh?' he'd almost answered. "No, Rach, but I often wish she didn't *think* she was that important."

Let's face it, Leona had spent years coming home reasonably on time. He realised she'd been promoted but, still, a bit of a happy coincidence that now that he was at home doing it all she had to stay late.

He wasn't stupid. She might think he was, but he wasn't.

He'd never rushed home either when he hadn't had to. And risk being home in that mad hour between six and seven? No thanks! He'd witnessed too often the craziness of that hour after Rachel was picked up from crèche – shovelling her dinner into her and checking her homework, while simultaneously attempting to get her into her pyjamas for bed.

He never got that checking-the-homework thing. "Are we not paying someone to do that already, Lee?" he'd asked.

"We are, Gavin, but no matter what we pay them, she's not theirs. They're never going to be as vigilant as us, are they? They don't *really* care how well it's done, once it's done."

Well, by Jesus, after six months of this mind-numbing craic, he could relate to them entirely.

Six months.

Christ.

The longest Gavin had ever taken off work before that had been the three weeks they'd spent in Florida in 2007 – and even at that he hadn't minded going back. He hadn't minded going back then because he knew he was about to hand in his notice. Fourteen years he'd been with Alliance & Ulster and he'd left to be a big shot in E-Corporate.

A company that no longer existed and he'd been one of the first to be let go.

Last in. First out.

Without a penny.

Some decisions were hard to reconcile when you looked back at them. And he knew he wasn't alone in this – he was hardly the only one who'd made an unfortunate career move, who'd bought a house that was only just affordable on current salary, who thought things would continue to get better and better ...

Florida, eh? Florida had cost them six thousand euro.

Six fucking thousand euro.

Nearly as bad as the TV in the front room that had cost four and a half. The TV that now had Saorview as they couldn't afford the Sky subscription anymore. Well, okay, they could probably afford a basic package but, well, it wasn't worth a curse without the Sports, was it?

But sure didn't *Scooby Doo* look great on a 52" high-def screen?

Speaking of screens, he took out his iPhone – again bought before the crash. He needed to clear some of the storage so that he could video Rachel's drama recital this evening.

Because, as he knew and she knew, Mammy was going to be way too important to make it.

Chapter 19

LEONA

"So what is the takeaway from this?" Declan Donegan asked the four people around the table.

Leona looked at him, one dark eye closing slightly. "I beg your pardon?"

"The takeaway, you know, the learnings ..."

"You mean – what's the conclusion after this last hour of waffling and talking around the problem rather than solving it?"

"Well, yes."

Well, then say that, you fool.

Leona had had enough. They had been sitting in the boardroom for some seventy-five minutes now and had got nowhere. It didn't help that her boss, Declan, liked to use seven words where one would do and that his unfaltering addiction to the most cringe-worthy business lingo caused more confusion than it cured.

Having said that, there was very little about Declan that didn't irritate her. His propensity for monogrammed shirts and the infernal ever-present red braces – both a throwback to his time in London City – were just the start of it.

"Well, in the City, we'd have done ..."

"Well, during my time in the City ..."

"Oh, we'd never have done that in the City ..."

And, every time, Leona said, *"Back in Saint Olaf ..."* under her breath, reminded of the old TV show *The Golden Girls* and how the character Rose would look back wistfully at her formative years in her hometown of St Olaf and bore everyone to tears with some longwinded story about them.

Leona always wished she could share the joke but the younger members of staff wouldn't even get the reference and, besides, she couldn't make jokes in her position. That was an occupational hazard. There could be no sharing jokes. Sharing jokes would be a seriously bad idea.

Nice people shared jokes. Nice people didn't get results.

"Well," she sighed instead, "here's a novel idea, Declan. Why don't we sit here until we do actually reach a conclusion? If we leave this now we'll end up meeting again in two days' time and another two days after that – and, frankly, I'm just too busy for that. I'm short-staffed and, really, if we could just set a date for this system to roll out, our collective minds might find it easier to focus on what exactly needs to be done, and when."

"I think that's not a bad idea," Sheila, manager of Commercial Banking said, using a calm, quiet voice – poles apart from the stinging tones of Leona. In fact pretty much everything about Sheila was infinitely different to Leona. She was in her late fifties, a maternal figure, her years in one of the larger commercial banks giving her wisdom and a calmness that often settled the room. Especially when the fieriness of Leona was about to clash with the incessant verbal diarrhoea of Declan. "Leona does have a point in that this is already the fourth time we've met about this subject and really we don't seem to be making any headway. Realistically we are never going to find a timescale that suits everyone so why don't we spend the next ten minutes working one out that works for most?"

"Well, there is another issue that really needs discussion too, and I may as well bring it up as it seems no one else is going to." Frank Newcombe was the Chief Risk Officer. Technically both he and Declan worked at the same level in the bank but in the game of Risk versus Finance there was generally only one winner – and when Frank spoke, he rightfully expected people to listen.

"What issue would that be?" Leona asked, a cool edge to her voice.

"Well, I think it's pretty obvious that we're missing a key member of staff and really we need to know the implications of this before we start anything."

"If the member of staff you're referring to is Olivia, then let me assure you that there are no implications," Leona said quietly.

"I appreciate your reassurance, Leona, but there most definitely are implications. There are risk implications."

"'*Key man risk*', we used to call it back in the City," Declan added helpfully.

Leona glared at him.

"Not that I'm saying there is a key-man dependency gap," he added, trying to backtrack.

"Because there isn't," she snapped, wishing he'd stop making things worse.

"Olivia was the Finance person embedded in this project," said Frank. "She's been involved since its inception. How are there no implications now that she's gone?"

"All her work is being covered by me," said Leona, "and in recent days I've enlisted Rob Kinirons from Olivia's team to assist me with her duties. He has great knowledge of everything they were working on and is willing to put in the hours. There is no cause for you to be concerned."

"I disagree," said Frank. "The arrangement you have in place is surely only temporary – there is no way you can cover her absence long-term – you have your day-to-day work – how can you possibly fit in this project also?"

"We will cope for as long as we have to."

"But what if you need time off? What if you end up sick?"

"I appreciate your concern but I don't need time off and I'm never sick."

"I think you misunderstand me – my concern is for the bank, not for you."

"Touching."

"Okay – if I might interrupt?" After the previous looks that Leona had shot him, Declan felt he should ask for permission to speak. "Steps are underway to formulate a more long-term solution to Olivia's departure – this will however take some time and if Leona is happy enough to bridge the gap for now, then I can't see how this is a problem."

"Well, it also concerns me greatly that no one seems willing to tell me *why* Olivia left?" Frank was clearly not ready to leave this issue.

"She left because she wanted to leave." Leona was doubly clear about not wanting to discuss it.

"With no notice period? I find that very unorthodox."

"If she wanted to go, was there any point in making her work out her notice?"

"Every point, I would have thought? At least it would have bought us some time to find her replacement?"

"A month was never going to be enough time to replace her. We need to have another look at her position – there needs to be changes."

"What kind of changes?" Frank's eyes narrowed.

"It wasn't working." Leona didn't seem a bit fazed.

"Seemed to be working fine to me – but then, of course, what would I know given that no one seems willing to let me know exactly what happened?"

Leona stared at him unflinchingly and, in the awkward silence that ensued, Declan spoke up again.

"Look – this is all counterproductive. Olivia is gone and no matter whose fault it is, nothing is going to change that."

"What do you mean 'whose fault it is'?" Now it was Leona's turn for eye-narrowing.

"I'm just saying, there was obviously some reason for her departure, but whatever the optics, we clearly need to recruit for Olivia's backfill to alleviate Leona's bandwith, but today is not the day for that deep dive."

Now everyone looked at Declan openmouthed, united in awe at the manner in which he had just surpassed even himself with business gobbledy-gook.

"I think, Declan, you are possibly right. Today is not the day for this." Frank looked at Leona, his sudden sympathy for her softening his expression. "Leona, I'm willing to run with this situation for now if you could pull together a report showing how you plan to resource this whole project – showing contingencies for time off and unexpected issues that may pull you back into your normal job."

"I appreciate your acquiescence, Frank, but is a report really necessary?" The thought of yet more work on her desk did not appeal to Leona.

"Yes, it is, and it needs to include both a scheduling plan and a resourcing plan. When Jeremy Taylor from Group Finance gets here next week he is going to be all over this, not to mention the Central Bank. This is one of the biggest projects we've ever rolled out – we need to know all the assessed risks and our response to them – I want every 'i' dotted and every 't' crossed – there can be no shortcuts – not on my watch."

Leona nodded. "Right. I'll get working on it. When do you need it?"

"Well, the sooner the better really – he's due early next week. Tomorrow afternoon?"

Leona looked at him openmouthed.

"Look, Leona, if you feel you don't have time to get that done, can I repeat again how concerned I am at you taking on Olivia's duties?"

"Did I say I didn't have time?" Leona snapped. "You'll have it in the morning."

He smiled. "Thanks."

"Smashing!" Declan clapped his hands together before leaning back and slapping his ridiculous red braces off his barrel-like chest. "You can inbox me with that too, Leona."

For a second Leona could have sworn that Frank had snorted but when she looked at him he seemed to be engrossed in his sheaf of papers.

"I think that's enough for today," Sheila interrupted hastily. "Maybe we could reconvene in a day or two, once Frank is happy with the contingency plan, and actually pick a date for the rollout?"

"Yes, we should diarise that now," said Declan.

"Diarise away and let me know." Leona stood up.

"You're leaving?" Declan looked at her.

"Yes, I'm leaving, Declan. I've tabled a session with Cian Casey, one of the Strategy juniors – I feel he needs his nurture-bubble burst – but let's take it offline and touch base later, yeah?"

She turned to leave the room, this time to a very definite snort from Frank.

Chapter 20

LEONA

Leona sat at her desk and, as was her habit, scanned it for documents that should be turned to lie face down before anyone sat opposite her. It was amazing how some people, who seemed incapable of reading what they should be reading, had an uncanny knack of reading upside-down information that did not concern them. Only one set of bound pages were left unturned with the title page beaming up at her.

Cian Casey

Quarterly Review

She didn't need to open them again; she knew exactly what they contained and what needed to be said, so instead she pulled her diary closer and updated her to-do list with the reports that were now required for Frank.

She hand-wrote her to-do list every evening before she left for the night. No matter how late it was, she turned the page in her diary and wrote her list of things that had to be done the next day. That way she could come in in the morning and not waste any time procrastinating. In fact, she'd also learnt over the years to get at least one task from the list done before she even opened her emails and got distracted by the new wave of requests.

Leona hated to be distracted.

For that same reason, her work phone spent 80% of its time diverted to her answering machine. That way it was under her control if and when to deal with a call and she was not at the beck

125

and call of the twenty-odd people that tried to get in touch with her every hour. If it was urgent, people would send her an email, and anyway she preferred this as it gave her time to consider her answer and avoided any chance of being put on the spot for some issue or request. Looking at her phone now she could see the light flashing and 'one new message' showing on the display. She looked at the small alarm clock on her desk – another one of her control tools – and saw she had four minutes left. She hit the message button on her telephone.

'Lee, it's Gavin. Just checking that you haven't forgotten Rachel's drama thing this evening. 8pm at the school. You'll hardly be home first so we'll just meet you there, I guess. See you then.'

Leona looked at the calendar. Drama thing? What on earth was he talking about? She picked up the phone to call her husband to ask him exactly that but just as she punched the last number her door opened.

The fact that there had been no knock first meant it could only be one person.

"Cian, you're early,"

"Is that a problem?"

"Well, you're here now, aren't you? Take a seat while I finish this off and I'll be with you in a moment."

She had nothing to finish off, but this was all about control. He had tried to annoy her by barging in early, now he could cool his jets and sit there until she decided she was ready to start the meeting.

She turned to her computer and the spreadsheet that was still open on the screen. Scrolling down through the pages she made a few small changes, moved around a few figures and then pressed save.

She turned back to him. "Right, so where do we start?"

"Well, as I'm here for my appraisal, it might be an idea to start with the document that you were meant to fill out and return to me last week?"

"I'm aware why you're here, Cian, and yes, there is an option for me to return the appraisal form to you once I've completed my side, but I find – in these particular kinds of situations – that this way works better."

"These particular kinds of situations?"

"That's what I said."

"Well, doesn't that sound ominous!"

For such a good-looking guy he had a very ugly sneer when he wanted to.

Stay pleasant, Leona reminded herself. "Well, that's why I think we should start with how you think the last six months went. What do you feel your achievements were?"

"I think the last six months went pretty well actually. I'm quite happy with both my performance and, eh, my achievements. But then you know that because I actually *did* follow the proper procedure and, as a result, you have my part of the appraisal in front of you."

"You're right, I do," said Leona, smiling, "and if my memory serves me right, you've given yourself very positive scores indeed. Let's have a look at a few." She opened the sheaf of papers on her desk. "*Mmm* ... has the last year been bad or good for you ... yes, I see ... what do you consider to be your most important achievements of the past year ... interesting ... what do you like and dislike about working for this organization ... again some interesting points ... But here we go: the scores section."

She paused for a second to see if she could detect even the smallest shift of discomfort from Cian in front of her, but he didn't so much as blink.

"Let's see ... Score your own capability or knowledge in the following areas in terms of your current role requirements where one to three is poor, *blah blah blah*, and ten is excellent. I take it you understood the requirements when filling this out?" She looked up at him.

"Implicitly," he answered. Again not a blink.

"I see." She looked back at the form, saying almost under her breath as she did so, "Well, clearly, we can leave 'steadiness under pressure' at a 10." She cleared her throat. "Creativity is rarely an issue either from what I can see. Communication Skills again we can leave at a 10 as I don't think that ambiguity is ever a problem with you either, Cian, is it?"

There was a flicker of a smile on his lips now and, with that small sign of him relaxing, she pounced.

"However, meeting deadlines and commitments, team working, energy, determination and work rate ... I'm not going to lie, I'm having difficulty with those tens."

"Really? I'm afraid I don't agree."

"And I didn't really expect you to." Leona closed the sheaf of papers and sat back. "Nor do I need you to, really." She was ready for this now. "Look, Cian, I'm going to cut to the chase here. The gap between what you think you should be doing, and what we think you should be doing, is not getting any narrower."

"Again I don't agree."

"Whether you agree or not is not the issue. I'm not saying that you are not a good worker. And Olivia's notes confirm that anything you produce is certainly up to the level required –"

"I fail to see what the issue is then."

"The issue is that it's up to the level, but never exceeds it. We need more, Cian, *I* need more. You are at the bottom of the ladder here in Finance – you should be showing how much you want this – how much you want to progress."

"And doing my job well doesn't show that already?"

"No, frankly, it doesn't. We're all doing our jobs well, Cian, but some of us are doing more than that."

"Nobody should have to do 'more than' their job."

"In an ideal world, no, they shouldn't. But we are currently in a period of great change here – the demands on us are increasing at a pace that our staffing levels can't keep up with. No one is more aware than I am that we need more personnel, but it would be counter-productive long-term to rush into getting the wrong people. So for now, we all need to do a little bit extra – if everyone did a little more then no one would have to do a lot."

"Leona, I don't know the last time I walked out of here at 5pm."

"I understand that, Cian, but it's not about the hours. I need you to give me more, I need you to anticipate what needs to be done and do it, not wait to be asked – or begged."

"I don't understand what you mean."

"Well, for example, last week I asked you to pull together the information for the quarterly board packs."

"Which I did."

"Which you did. But you've been doing this how long now? You know the extra bits that I need, you know how to pull it to a conclusion, but yet you still didn't give me any context, any resolution – you could have anticipated the questions we were going to be asked – there's always a question about the loan books comparing them quarter on quarter – where was your narrative about the number paying, the number in arrears?"

"Correct me if I'm wrong – but that's your job?"

"Well, you should be aiming for my job! You know that there are promotions coming up next week but right now, Cian, you are not the person we have in mind. I need someone who gives me more. Do you understand?"

"Oh, I understand all right. Loud and clear ..."

"Right. Good. Well, why don't we leave it for today and meet again tomorrow to talk about your goals for the year?"

"Well, why can't we do that now?"

"Because I'd like you to go away and think about them for a while, and take into consideration everything I've just said." She looked at her watch. "Look, Cian, why don't you just head home and we'll meet up again tomorrow morning at..." She clicked onto her diary on screen and scanned the page for a blank slot. "Typical. Tomorrow is pretty full. I have to meet the credit committee at eight thirty but I'd have a bit of time after that?"

"I'd still prefer to do it now."

"Well, we're not doing it now, Cian. Apart from the fact that I think you need to put a bit of thought into it, I have stuff here myself that has to be off my desk this evening – I've papers to review for tomorrow – I've still to finish these projections that Olivia was working on. Look, I won't bore you, I'll see you in the morning. And, Cian, remember – to get anywhere in here, you need to give me something extra, something special. Understand?"

Cian didn't answer but just got up and snatched his own papers from the desk. In a couple of long strides he'd left her office, slamming her door shut behind him. Such was the force of the blow that Leona jumped.

So immature. She shook her head in disgust before pulling her diary with the to-do list in front of her. Ignoring how long it now was, she started to number what still had to be done, trying to put some order on her evening. So engrossed did she become that she didn't hear the soft knock at the door and it open gently afterwards.

OLIVIA

It's hard to pinpoint where it all went wrong really. It wasn't like one day I went in and everything was going swimmingly and went in the next and they were so horrible I had to leave. But it was definitely all fine at the start.

Danny has a theory that Mary was always jealous of me because, well, I had him and then later the kids. He could have a point but, in all honesty, it's not like I didn't try to set her up with his cousin Tommy at our wedding and, do you know what, I wouldn't be bothering to try that again. It was a bit embarrassing actually – she could have made some effort.

I always wondered why she bought her house so early. Like she owned hers since before she even started in DKB. Danny reckons she must have got a fairly hefty help-out from her parents to be able to buy in Rathfarnham – though as Danny says it's really more like the posh end of Tallaght. I think he did say that to her once too, on one of our nights out. Do you know, she could be such a bitch, even back then? Danny also reckons that she only bought her house way back then because she knew there was no point in waiting for someone to buy one with her. But I don't know – I think Mary just always loved being one step ahead of everyone else and definitely she had a chip on her shoulder about a man not being the be-all and end-all of life.

I was in her house once. I was picking her up to go to one of those team-building events in Kildare. She had it gorgeous in fairness. I mean it was smaller than ours even though we both have three bedrooms but she gutted hers when she got it. Ripped out the kitchen and put blonde wooden floors throughout the whole downstairs. All the walls were painted white and she had beautiful artwork on the walls from those exhibitions they have round Stephen's Green. When Ikea opened up North she drove up and bought a carload of furniture and every room looked like it was straight out of an Ikea catalogue. You know, in that way that only some people really manage to pull off? Like you can't just get a few bits of Ikea and expect to get that effect – you need to go all out. Well, she did and to be fair to her it looked amazing. Not very kiddie-friendly, all those angles and that sparseness but then that's not an issue for her really, is it?

But sure look, I could analyse her all day. It's not going to get me anywhere. The truth of the matter is her problem with me started when I had the kids.

And trust me, when it started, it started.

Chapter 21

LEONA

"Leona, would you have a minute?"

Leona looked up in surprise as she hadn't heard any knock at the door. She sighed in relief when she saw it was just Mary.

"Yes, Mary, of course. What can I do for you?"

She scanned the older girl's face but couldn't see any nerves. But then that was the thing that Leona liked most about her dark-haired accountant, that she was virtually unshakable. It wasn't that she didn't have a healthy respect for Leona – she certainly did, but it took a lot to un-nerve her. In fairness, Mary had never had much reason to be afraid of her really. She came in, she did her job, and she never panicked no matter what kind of deadline was put in front of her. Having said that, she looked slightly different today. She had confidently pulled out a chair and sat down without waiting for invitation which was definitely an action Leona would associate more with Cian than Mary.

"Okay, so here it is," Mary said, surprising Leona yet further by getting straight to the point. "It's about Olivia's job. Or what I mean is that I've been thinking about Olivia's job."

"Olivia's job?" Leona sighed. "Oh. Well, I'm glad one of us has been thinking about it. I don't know what I'm going to do, though it hasn't even made it onto my list of things to worry about yet."

"Well, that's the thing. *I'd* like it."

Mary looked her square in the eye but Leona was confused.

132

"You'd like what exactly?"

"Olivia's job." Mary seemed to take a deep breath before continuing. "I'd like to put myself forward for Olivia's job."

"*Olivia's* job?" Even as Leona repeated the phrase her words rang stupidly in her ear but she really was at loss as to what Mary was talking about.

"Well, yes. It's a direction I've often thought I'd like to go in and, well, now's my chance, I suppose."

"Direction? What do you mean 'direction'? Or, more to the point, what's wrong with the direction you're already going in?"

"I've been in Finance for some ten years now, Leona –"

Mary seemed to be well prepared but Leona didn't care. This was silly talk. "And for good reason, Mary. That's what you're best at. That's where your strengths lie. You're not a Strategy person. That's just ridiculous."

"Ridiculous?" Mary's face paled slightly as it became apparent that this conversation was not quite going in the direction she'd planned.

"Well, maybe ridiculous is the wrong word but – well, yes, you have to admit that it is just a bit ridiculous? I mean, it's just not the job for you, Mary. Strategy requires vision, imagination. Especially now. Things are so volatile these days and this is a role that we have to take great care to fill – we need to find the absolute right person this time. I'm sorry, but you are not that person."

She looked at Mary's face as she sat there and just couldn't understand the devastation on her face.

"Mary, I can see this is not the answer you wanted. But if you think about this, you'll see I'm right."

"I don't need to think about it. You're not right and I don't understand. I thought you valued me as an employee, I thought after all my hard work –"

"But Mary, can't you see? It's *because* I value you as an employee! I need you exactly where you are at the moment. When everything settles down here I will look into a promotion for you, maybe even expand your role, especially now that you have Kate to offer you support with some of the more basic stuff – but it won't be expanding in the direction you've just requested. I'm sorry, but it won't. It just wouldn't make any sense."

"So there is no point in me even applying? Even though I know I could do the job, even though I've done plenty of it over the years filling in every time Olivia took a day off, or went home early, or –"

"Mary, I am well aware of the ways in which the last person in that role was found lacking – no one knows them more than me. But you more than anyone should be able to understand that that is why I won't be making that mistake again."

"But how would you be making that mistake with me? I mean, that's a preposterous thing to say."

"Mary, that's my final word on the subject. As I said, I'm aware your role is due some kind of review and in a few months hopefully we'll get around to that, but I need you to be aware that it's here I see your future, in Finance."

"Well, there certainly doesn't seem any point in discussing this further then." Mary's voice was cold and it was with a murderous face that she stood up then turned to leave the room.

At the door she almost collided with Rob on his way in but, when he apologised and stepped back, she just kept walking and didn't answer.

Rob stared after her and then turned to Leona. "Ehm, I have those figures for you."

Leona looked at him blankly. "Figures?"

"The figures Olivia was working on – you'd said you wanted to pull that stuff together – now, they may not be right, but it's a starting place."

She continued to look blankly at him for a moment before realising what he was talking about. She'd almost forgotten about that report.

"I'm sorry," she said. "Yes, of course. Thanks."

Great. Something else to put on the list.

"I'll just leave them here then," said Rob, walking towards her desk and placing the figures in front of her.

"Thanks," she said again, her mind already on her list, mentally lining up the mess in front of her into some kind of order. There were things she could do tomorrow, but she'd really rather get them done this evening.

Then she realised Rob was still there, standing at her desk.

"Sorry, Rob, was there something else? You'd like to be Vice

President maybe? Chief Executive? A spot on the board?"

Now it was his turn to look confused.

"Ehm, no. Well, I didn't realise there were opportunities like that in the offing."

"Well, it seems to be the day for bizarre requests so you may as well." She shook her head. "I'm sorry – don't mind me. Shoot."

"Well, it's just that I thought if we went over that wages budget I just gave you, well, there's not that much more to it really – we could, you know, get it finished and that'd be one thing done. Then if you liked, I could give you a hand with that report for Frank. If that suited, that's all ..."

Leona looked at Rob, and for a moment wondered was she in some kind of parallel universe where everyone had been subsumed by aliens and that this blushing, mumbling Rob was another imposter. Or else he was just being nice, in which case did she need to wonder where the catch was? But the look on his face was genuine and she felt a strange calm come over her. Rob was not like the others. He seemed to be genuinely on her side and not for the first time in recent weeks she almost had to remind herself that he was ten years younger than her and not someone she should be leaning on so much.

And she would stop soon. But not today.

"Thank you," she said, "that would be great. I appreciate it."

"Okay then," he said, pulling a chair over. "Let's get started."

"Yes, show me what you have – what I was thinking earlier was –"

With that the door sprang open.

"Oh," said Declan, on seeing Rob sitting there. "I thought you'd be done with him."

Rob looked at Leona with a raised eyebrow.

"Oh no – sorry." Leona realised who he was talking about. "I am. This is a different 'him'. Why? Did you need to see me?"

"Yes, yes, I do."

Rob got up from his chair. "I'll leave you to it."

"Thanks, Rob, I'm sure it won't take long."

"So who's he then?" asked Declan when Rob had barely left the room.

"That's Robert Kinirons. I mentioned him to you in the meeting earlier today? It was Cian Casey who was getting his review. More's the pity – there's a fair gap between the two of them."

"Oh." Declan shrugged, already losing interest. "Anyway, look, there's something we really need to get our ducks in a row on. I was hoping that it'd not come to anything but Frank requested a little man-to-man after that last meeting and it seems that whatever rumbles I've been hearing are becoming more than just rumbles."

"Rumbles?" Leona did not like the sound of this.

"Look, Leona, don't take this personally. I've seen many a restructure during my time in the City and whilst it always seems a big deal at the time –"

"Restructure? What restructure?"

Declan sighed. "It's all coming from Frankfurt. There are some issues around the current situation and they're even less happy with – with Dublin. I think they've lost confidence in us and, well, let's just say we need to start impressing them or I'm afraid they're going to make me drink the Kool-Aid on this one."

"Declan, what on earth are you talking about?"

"I just think it's time that we took stock, you know? Head Office are not happy so we need to, you know, jazz up the optics, circle the wagons and all start singing from the same hymn sheet, you know? Impress them."

"Impress them?" Leona snapped. "Impress them? And what exactly would do that if nothing we're doing already is achieving it?"

"Oh, it's all smoke and mirrors, you know what they're like."

Leona shook her head in disbelief.

You know what they're like …

"Yes, yes, I do."

"But of course, and obviously I told them that we were completely committed to improving and sure we can shoot the breeze with the team when they're over next week – which reminds me – you have all those notes to the accounts up to date? That's the first thing they're going to want on Tuesday when they get here."

"Of course I do," she snapped but as soon as he was gone out the door her head sank into her hands.

She didn't have them up to date. She'd forgotten. What was happening to her? She never forgot anything.

Shit. Shit. Shit.

She heard a noise and looked up to see Rob's head around her door.

"For *fuck's* sake – *what*?"

"You said to come back," he said quietly.

"For what?"

"To run over the wages budget again?"

"Oh, Jesus Christ, Rob, just finish it yourself, will you? I can't be holding everyone's hand in here."

As soon as the words were out of her mouth she remembered what he'd said to her that Saturday morning:

'*No one really likes a mean girl, do they?*'

But it was too late. He'd nodded, his mouth set in a grim line. And just then she noticed the two mugs in his hands.

Coffee. He'd been bringing her coffee.

ROB

Look, she could be an absolute tyrant, right? I'm not going to deny that. I'd be lying if I said there was never an occasion where she was completely in the wrong. There were loads of them.

That evening when she practically threw me out of the office? I was so mad. I just thought 'Fuck you, you absolute bitch'. I might have even used a different word – in fact, I'm quite sure I did. I just turned around and went straight home. Actually I went out with the lads that night. I even hooked up with my ex, Marnie. I was that mad.

So, I suppose what I'm saying is that you're wrong to say there was preferential treatment for anyone. Or that she treated anyone worse than anyone else.

When she was in bad form, everyone got it. And anyone who says differently is a liar.

Extract from interview with Robert Kinirons
Recorded 12 November 2011
2.55pm

Chapter 22

LEONA

When Leona pulled up outside the giant automatic gates at the entrance to her estate, she could see her sitting-room light on through the bars. As the gate rolled across, she eased her navy Audi forward and drove slowly down the avenue. Two of the nine houses were empty now and she noticed a new *For Sale* sign on one of the other five-bed houses this evening.

So the Dunnes were selling now. Not that she knew them – there wasn't much socialising between the houses anymore. Or maybe there was but she just wasn't around to see it. That first Christmas when Rachel was only a baby they'd started a tradition of having a drinks party inviting the whole road for mince pies and a tipple of their choice, but that hadn't happened since Gavin had lost his job.

She swung her car up the giant cobble-locked driveway and rolled to a stop next to Gavin's BMW. There'd been no point in selling either car and getting something cheaper. The value had gone out of the luxury vehicles and it would have cost more to get something smaller like the Golf she used to have. The Golf that Gavin had made her trade in for this giant gas-guzzler.

She got out of the car and clicked her buzzer. The car gave a quiet 'beep' to indicate the alarm was on but even it seemed loud in the desolate estate. She hoped it wouldn't wake him, assuming that Gavin had just accidentally left on the light when he'd gone upstairs to bed.

She slipped her shoes off on the marble tiles inside the hall door and, padding past the sitting room, slipped her hand round the door to turn off the light.

"Eh, leave that on, please," came a voice from inside the room.

"Oh!" She looked round the door to see Gavin sitting on the giant leather couch, laptop on his lap and an open beer bottle on the floor beside him. He was wearing an old T-shirt and sweatpants. But still looked as gorgeous as the first night she met him.

"I'm sorry – when the TV wasn't on I assumed you'd be in bed."

"Sure, a Friday night, where else would I be?"

She rolled her eyes – he might be gorgeous but he definitely did petulant better than his seven-year-old daughter.

"You're right, Gavin. And there was me out partying."

"Oh, partying, was it? You can tell that to Rachel – she'll be glad there was a good reason that you missed her show."

"Her show?" What in God's name was he on about now? Then with a sinking heart she remembered, "Oh *shit*. Shit shit shit."

"I phoned you. I left a message."

"I know. I got it but ..." Her voice trailed off. She couldn't believe this. Of course *she* knew why she'd forgotten but there was no way he was going to understand, especially given the belligerent look on his face now. "I'm sorry. I couldn't make it but that's no excuse."

"It's not even that you didn't make it – trust me, we're used to that now – but the fact that you didn't even bother to phone is a new one."

"Christ, Gav, I said I'm sorry. I had an insane evening. I'm sorry."

He shrugged and went back to his laptop and clearly the conversation was over as far as he was concerned. God forbid he'd ask her what had made her evening so mental. Used she be more supportive when he was the one coming in late? She actually couldn't remember. Maybe? She sighed and sat down on the armchair next to him.

"What's the laptop out for?"

"I need to tweak my CV."

"Oh really? Why's that?"

"Jim Boylan rang today – he thinks he might have something."

She sat up straight in the chair. "Really? Where? Doing what?"

"Eh, doing what I do? I used to actually have a job, remember?

Now, mind you, this one sounds a little bit different. There'll be less travel for a start."

"Whoa, wait! Travel? What kind of travel?"

He shrugged again. "I don't know – London a few days a week maybe – but, as I was saying, not as much as I used to do before."

"Gav, you'll have to tell him no."

He looked at her over the top of his laptop screen.

"Why would I do that?"

"Because one of us has to be here in the evenings."

"And it needs to be me?" He laughed. "Try again, Lee."

"Gavin, I'm serious. I can't guarantee to be here. It's insane in there at the moment. I'm not saying it'll always be like that but it is for now and there's nothing I can do about it."

"Well, you'll have to find something you can do about it … I've had it, Lee – I can't take another day of this shite. I need to get out of here."

"And it's always about what you need, isn't it, Gav?" Leona had sprung to her feet. "What about what Rachel needs? Do you want her in childcare around the clock?"

"Don't you *dare* lecture me about what Rachel needs! You've some cheek! You're not the one that had to console her for an hour when you didn't show up tonight. You're not the one that had to scrape gravel from her fucking knee when she fell in school today!" Now he was on his feet, having flung down the laptop in temper. "You're not the one that did any of that. You just stroll back in here at eleven o'clock at night from that stupid job –"

"The stupid job that's paying for this stupid mortgage? That's paying for those stupid cars? That's paying for –"

"Oh, go on – rub it in, you're dying to!"

"No, I'm fucking not dying to – but I only took this stupid bloody promotion when –" She stopped. This was dangerous territory.

"When what, Leona?"

His eyes had narrowed and she hated the way he was looking at her.

"Look, Gav, I'm just saying. The timing is wrong for you taking on anything like that. Give me six months."

"I won't last six months. I'm telling you, I'm going out of my tree."

"Gavin, I asked you before to be patient about something. And now I'm asking you again." She looked him straight in the eye and, as she did, both of them knew exactly what she was talking about.

He opened his mouth to speak and then shut it again. He then turned from her and sat down, picking up the television remote.

She didn't bother sitting back down beside him. She'd lost interest. Instead she went out the door and down the long hall to the kitchen. She went to the huge double-sized American fridge and filled a glass with ice, then splashed in some vodka from the cabinet and took a Diet Coke from the larder press.

There were two other reception rooms she could sit in but she'd no interest in any of them. The giant games room with its ridiculous television just made her feel ill and the sun room would be cold at this hour of the night as they could no longer afford to have the heat on out there.

They could barely afford any of this anymore.

So instead she took her glass up the stairs and around the high banisters towards Rachel's bedroom. The thick cream carpet underfoot felt warm between her toes after the icy cold of the marble hall. She put her drink down on a small table in the corridor and opened the bedroom door. There she was, fast asleep, her dark hair fanned out on her pillow. She sighed. She would talk to her tomorrow. Make it up to her. She placed a soft kiss on her forehead and pulled the quilt up over her tiny shoulders and, sighing, went back out and into her own room.

Of all the rooms in her house she loved her bedroom best. The high window at the far end looked out over the rooftops to the Malahide coast beyond. If she stood on her tippy-toes on a clear day she could see the sea but not tonight. She'd grown up down in the little coastal town of Enniscrone in Sligo and it killed her not to hear the crashing of the waves from her bedroom. She'd told Gavin she wanted to live near the sea but when, bursting with excitement, he showed her this gated estate in Malahide, she hadn't the heart to tell him this wasn't quite what she wanted.

None of this was what she wanted.

OLIVIA

Anyhow, like I said, we got married in 2004. It was a simple enough wedding by today's standards. It's not like we cut corners or anything but we'd saved for it from the minute we'd bought the house and Danny had worked a whole budget out so that between the savings and what he reckoned we'd get in presents we wouldn't have to borrow anything.

I'm not sorry we didn't borrow. It's just one day – I far rather have nice furniture that we use every day. A nice solid family car. We owed nobody anything apart from our mortgage and that was well doable. At least when the shit hit the fan we weren't afraid to open our post, you know?

Do you know, I read lately that in July 2004, the same month we had our wedding, some property developer guy and his socialite wife got married too. They didn't use a three-star hotel on the Navan Road like we did though – they opted for some 17th century villa on the Italian Riviera. Bertie Ahern and all was meant to be there but he didn't go in the end – he said it was in case he was more trouble than he was worth. I'd say he was raging though – imagine missing a party that cost 1.5 million euro.

1.5 million for a party.

And it didn't stop there. They went on honeymoon then. Normal enough you say, and it sure is. We went to Thailand for a couple of weeks, which I'm not going to lie cost a few bob. Well, it was cheap enough when we got there in fairness. We stayed in beach huts and stuff but, still, it was a holiday of a lifetime for us.

But no beach huts for this pair! No, they decided to hire Aristotle Onassis's old yacht and brought a load of guests with them. Lovely. The yacht cost 65,000 euro a day to charter.

I'll say that again – 65,000 euro a day.

Oh and that didn't include food, drink or fuel. The fuel alone cost €575 an hour.

But do you know what? That's all grand. People should be able to spend whatever money they want and sure maybe their two million or whatever they spent on their wedding was the same to them as our ten grand was to us.

See, I'd be okay with that. But when I was reading about the wedding I also read that this same fella was the same guy who then tried to buy half of Dublin the following year and turn it into some posher version of London. He paid 53.7 million per acre for this land – breaking whatever per-acre record had been there before.

Sorry, did I say 'paid'? My mistake. He didn't actually pay anything as those loans were never paid back. They're lying now in some kind of toxic-loan purgatory and it'll be you and me that'll end up paying for them no doubt.

So maybe, because of him and his bloody wedding and greedy need for grandeur, I'll end up being afraid to open my post yet. That makes me really mad. I've had it with paying for other people's mistakes. I'm done with it.

Chapter 23

KATE

It was Monday morning and, before Kate's computer had even warmed up and her first cup of tea been made, she knew something was wrong. The first sign she'd noticed on arrival was Mary's thunderous face and at that her heart had sunk. Things had been good between them for the last few weeks and she racked her brain to try and think of what she might have done wrong. She came in, she took whatever awful boring load of crap Mary didn't feel like doing, she did it as well as she could, then she handed it back. It was a mind-numbingly depressing format but it seemed to work. For one of them at least. But Happy Mary was much easier to live with than Grumpy Mary so it was a win-win.

So what she had done to deserve Grumpy Mary today was anyone's guess.

When she noticed Rob being uncharacteristically quiet she started to relax a bit and, finally, when Leona crashed out of her office and slammed some report slashed with pencil in front of Cian, she really started to calm down.

Whatever had happened, it appeared to be nothing to do with her.

Thank goodness for that. Clearly, it was definitely going to be what she used to call in her old job 'a head-down day'. She'd some recollection of Leona and Rob being due at the Irish Bankers' Federation at ten for some kind of presentation by the Central Bank so with any luck they'd take at least some of the atmosphere with them.

She sighed as someone slammed a door for the fifth time in the hour since she'd been in. She opened her inbox and selected something long and laborious to get stuck into. She'd dealt with enough childish behaviour at the weekend, at yet another neighbourhood gathering, and that had been just from her neighbour.

Yes, Siobhán, I am enjoying being back at work.

No, Siobhán, the children are not in therapy yet.

Yes, Siobhán, it is worth my while after crèche fees.

No, Siobhán, I don't feel like I'm missing out.

What was wrong with people? Her being back at work did not affect Siobhán's life in the slightest so why could she not keep her passive-aggressive questioning to herself?

She was sick of trying to convince everyone that she was happy to be back at work. Why did no one believe her?

She sighed again.

Truth be known, right now she was finding it difficult to believe herself. She'd been here two weeks now and was already starting to have grave doubts that it was all she'd expected. And it wasn't the early starts, or the late evenings, or even the fact that she'd spent all day yesterday making dinners for the week.

Truth be known, she was a bit, well, bored.

In her old job she'd never had a chance to be bored. She'd been so busy. It had been so full of meetings and different projects. Hardly a day ever passed that seemed the same as the days that had passed before.

What was it about this job? Had she, after all her deliberations and research actually chosen badly?

Oh stop it!

She felt like shaking herself. It had only been two weeks, it was far too early to judge. She needed to give it a chance.

She looked at Mary again. Imagine, she had been here for over ten years. Would she herself still be here in ten years? Would she still be pulling together spreadsheets and inserting data in power-point presentations for the next level up? She'd wanted a job with no responsibility and no stress – but, Christ, had she ever expected it to be this boring?

Yet then when she looked at Leona, she instantly knew that she didn't want that deal either. When she'd brought the brownies into

146

work on Friday Leona had come into the tea room and spotted them.

"Who's the baker?" she'd asked and Kate had tentatively put her hand up.

"Well, aren't you the right little Martha Stewart?" Leona reached over to pick up one of the little chocolate squares.

"Yes, well, it's my daughter's birthday on Saturday – I was baking anyway." Kate tried to smile in spite of her nervousness at speaking directly to the great-but-incredibly-frightening Leona.

"Saturday? It's my daughter's on Sunday!"

"Oh lovely, are you having a party too?" Kate asked.

"Eh no, thank you very much." Leona looked at Kate like she might just be slightly crazy. "We'll go for dinner. I could think of nothing worse than a houseful of crazy children and their needy parents."

You have one child, Kate remembered thinking, that's one party, one day a year. How in God's name could that be too much to ask? Dinner with her parents? The poor child! How boring.

So no, she didn't want to be Leona either. But was there no in-between?

She sighed again. Talk about a shit morning.

Chapter 24

MARY

Mary heard Kate sigh as she opened her files and knew that it was probably to do with her. She hadn't raised her head since Kate had come in that morning and, had she not still felt so cross, she'd have felt guilty. They'd been getting on okay lately. Kate was quite funny and they had discovered that they shared a common dislike of stupid people and, really, it was good to have someone that she could have a bit of a laugh with, especially after the tension of the last few months. Plus, she had to admit that having a bit of help was great. Kate was good and, more to the point, did exactly what she asked, as soon as she was asked to do it. No, it definitely wasn't her she was mad at.

And, boy, was she mad!

When she'd left Leona's office on Friday evening she had hardly even noticed that she'd almost crashed into Rob at the door. By the time she'd got back to her desk there were tears fighting their way out of her eyes and she had to fight just as hard to keep them back. She was not going to cry, or as they used to call it 'do an Olivia'. She'd managed to keep it together until she got out to her car and then she'd flung her high heels into the foot-well of the passenger seat and practically screeched *"Bitch!"* into the echoes of the underground car park. *"Bitch! Bitch! Bitch!"* Leona had actually laughed at her. Laughed! Why was it such a laughable idea that she do Olivia's job? She was just as qualified, just as capable and far, far,

148

far more hardworking.

It was so fucking unfair.

"I'm aware your role is due some kind of review and in a few months hopefully we'll get around to that."

In a few months' time.

Hopefully.

For the first time ever Mary felt a giant clock ticking in her ear. For someone who'd chosen the 'career route', how had she got her corporate climb so horribly wrong?

In a few months' time? Some kind of review?

Why had she sat so still for so long and just observed Olivia rise and rise? Why had she presumed that just doing your job as best as you possibly could would be enough?

She'd been a fool. She should have known that being good at your job was never going to be enough. She should have shoved herself forward earlier. Why had she not? Why had she not demanded a promotion years ago?

As she sat there in her car, angry thoughts swirling in her head, she'd wished she had Toni to call but that lucky bitch – who seemed to have managed to choose a far nicer route in life – was on honeymoon still in South America. There was no point in phoning any of the others. Toni would have understood. She'd have told her to calm down, put on her runners and go for a run. But she hadn't felt like being alone with her own thoughts.

Fuck you, Leona, for making me feel like this, she'd cursed to herself, fuck you.

Now, she looked across at Rob. There was clearly something wrong with him too but she had no idea what it was. He'd smiled when she'd almost crashed into him on Friday evening but he definitely wasn't smiling now. Obviously something had happened in the office afterwards to put him in this mood. Which was unusual in itself. Rob usually let everything go over his head and whenever Leona had had a go at him before, it hadn't seemed to take a jot out of him. Whatever could have happened? Not that it mattered really. Whatever had caused it, she was glad Rob was pissed off – the more people that Leona annoyed these days the better. After Leona's reaction to her question on Friday, she felt more than just annoyed herself, she felt embarrassed, underappreciated and very, very angry.

Her weekend hadn't improved after Friday night either. She'd spent most of Saturday trying to show her mother how to send an email.

And not for the first time.

Jesus Christ, why did it always have to be her?

Press what?

Which button?

Wait! What did you do there?

What do I do now? Why are you going so fast?

And of course this would be peppered with:

Would you believe I haven't seen Dympna all week?

You do realise your father isn't well, don't you?

What are you doing tomorrow, I need to get an outfit for x or y or z or whatever ...

Why did it always have to be her?

Chosen the career route? My arse, she thought. Chosen the route to insanity more like. The more she did for people the more they expected.

Well, it wouldn't be happening again. They'd soon notice the difference.

"Robert?"

At Jacinta's voice, Mary looked up. Jacinta was approaching Rob's desk with a sheaf of bound documents.

"Will you tell Leona that your taxi is booked for ten twenty? Here are your papers, one for you and one for Leona."

"Thanks, Jacinta," said Rob, "but maybe tell her yourself, will you? Last time I went into that office it didn't go so well, but I doubt she'd throw *you* out."

"She certainly would not," Jacinta snorted. "However, Robert, not only is that uncharacteristically childish behaviour, which, might I say, won't get you very far in this establishment but it implies that I have nothing better to do than act as a go-between between you and your superior. So kindly do as I ask and stop acting the pup."

Cian sniggered.

"And as for you, Mr Casey, you'd do better to concentrate on your own difficulties instead of laughing at others. Another pup." She shook her head as she turned to go back to her own desk. "I remember a time when the only people they let work in banks were professionals."

Mary saw Cian make a face at Jacinta's retreating back but even that didn't seem to get a smile from Rob. He just sat there with a face like thunder, idly scrolling up and down whatever spreadsheet he was working on. Eventually he cursed under his breath and got up and walked over to Leona's office.

He went in and, to her disappointment, closed the door.

Chapter 25

LEONA

"Yes?"

Leona didn't look up when Rob came into the room and shut the door.

"I was told to tell you the taxi will be here at twenty past ten," he said.

"What time is it now?" she asked, not taking her eyes from the screen, her fingers still keying in figures on her laptop.

"It's just ten."

"Mmmm?"

She knew he was talking but she just couldn't listen at the moment. She had to find out what was – "Got it!" She banged her hands on her desk.

"I beg your pardon?"

"Forget it. Wait – shit, what time did you say it was again?"

"Ten o'clock."

"Damn – right – I need one of the data modellers to take a look at this – could you get Simon Devaney to come in to me?"

She looked back at her screen, not even noticing Rob leave the room, her train of thought almost lost. Dammit anyway, she would love just one day with no interruptions. Just one hour would do.

She looked at her watch, 10.13am – where the hell was Simon? She reached for her phone and slammed in some numbers.

You could have cut the atmosphere in the taxi with a knife. Rob was

152

uncharacteristically quiet and Leona's mind was miles away. She was vaguely aware that her assistant was quieter than normal, but to Leona this meant nothing.

Her husband wasn't speaking to her either.

Well, they could all form a queue – she had quite enough to be worrying about.

She watched Dublin City slide by her window in an attempt to calm herself down. It was truly beautiful at this time of the morning. The early-morning traffic had subsided and the streets were clear and bright. As they travelled down the docks the light bounced off the roofs of the Grand Canal complex and made the acres of glass seem like sheets of pure sunshine. The car swung around by Trinity College and travelled the last stretch to Nassau Street to where the Institute of Bankers had their office.

Just as they pulled up, her phone rang. She looked at the display.

For God's sake, it was Gavin. She stabbed at the answer button with her finger.

"What, Gavin?" she snapped.

She could see Rob look at her but his displeasure at her tone was the least of her worries. Gavin started to talk but she cut him dead straight away.

"I am not having this discussion now! I told you this last night. What is it about now not being a good time that you don't understand?"

He tried again but, aware that Rob was sitting looking at her as they were already running late, she stopped him again.

"I'm well aware that there's a cut-off time – but I fail to see how that changes anything? We discussed this. I've told you what I think – I don't understand why you're even asking me again. Actually I don't care why. End of discussion, Gav, now I'm hanging up!" She snapped her phone cover closed and hissed, "Arsehole!" before looking at Rob. "And you can take that face off you too. Are we going in here or not?"

She didn't wait for an answer but got out of the cab and marched into the building.

James Gallagher from the Central Bank had been talking for some thirty-five minutes now and no one around the table had had any chance to get a word in. DKB was only one of some ten or more banks represented around the table, and not only was Rob the youngest in the room, but Leona was the only female.

They were not the angriest there though. This presentation was about yet another new reporting requirement that the Central Bank was meting out and frankly the room had had enough.

Gallagher had all the pomp of someone who knew that he held all the power though. For every objection flung his way he had an answer. He'd sigh and shake his head and try and look like he cared about the work load this whole new obligation meant but it was quite clear he didn't feel that it was his problem. Rob could not understand why they were even there. This could all have been done by letter, or even email.

It wasn't like Leona was even contributing. She was just sitting there doodling and every now and again she'd punch something into her phone.

Probably still fighting with her husband, only via text this time.

On and on Gallagher went.

Mistakes of the past ...

Debt ratios ...

Responsibility not recklessness ...

On and on and on.

Then Rob noticed Leona elbow a man sitting to her right and whisper furiously in his ear. The man looked down at her doodles and hissed something back.

Gallagher looked down crossly.

"Have we yet another objection?"

Leona looked up. "Nope. No objection from me once what you're asking is possible, that's all."

"I beg your pardon?"

"Your requirement – what you're asking for – it's not possible."

There was a murmur around the room and several people shifted uncomfortably in their seats.

"I'm sorry – who are you anyway?"

"Leona Blake – DKB."

"Ah, I see, one of our smaller brethren. So you object to this new requirement?"

"No, not at all, Mr Gallagher, I'm all for regulation. We love regulation, in DKB, don't we, Rob?"

Rob looked at her, unsure of what to say so said nothing.

"I'm sure you do, Ms Blake, but I fail to see where your problem is then?"

"Well, I've spent the last two days trying to figure out why something about this smelled and just before I came out I called in one of my modellers and he's just emailed. I was right."

"You were right?"

"Yes, I was right – which means – no offence – but you guys are wrong."

"I very much doubt that, Ms Blake."

"Well, I very much don't, Mr. Gallagher. I've been over your pre-briefing notice and there are fundamental flaws in your spreadsheet – in fact at least three of your ratios are contradicting each other so until you get that little problem sorted out, there really is no point in rolling out any of this."

"I find what you're saying preposterous, frankly!" Mr Gallagher looked like he was about to call security but then the man to Leona's right spoke.

"I think she could be right actually. I'm just looking at this email on her phone and, to be honest, we couldn't work through it either last week but just didn't have the time to look further into it. What her guy has come up with here seems to be hitting the nail on the head alright."

Someone else at the back of the room muttered something similar so at that Leona stood up.

"Well, that's that then? Get your technical guys to have a look at it and revert to us. And sure once you've got your house in order, send us all a Version 2 and we'll give it another go."

"But where are you going now?"

"Mr. Gallagher, I really appreciate the vast amount of work that's on your to-do list on a daily basis. I am also well aware that the banking system in this country screwed up and that it's your job to pull us all into line but right now I have my own to-do list and it's as long as the street outside and most of it relates to items that you require – which is absolutely fine – as I said, I can understand your position but I'd like you to show me the same courtesy and make some attempt to understand mine."

A couple of others seized the opportunity to stand up too and with that the meeting ended and everyone filed out of the room.

"So sometimes there's an advantage to you fighting with the whole world?" Rob said as soon as they got outside the front door.

"Do you think? Well, that's good, I guess, because I get up every morning in the hope that I'll get to fight with more people every day."

"I don't doubt it."

"Thanks for the vote of support, Rob. Now what time is the taxi coming back?"

"I don't know – what time did you tell it to come back?"

"Me?" She looked at him in surprise. "I told him nothing."

"Oh yes, that's right, you didn't. Sure how could you when you were on the phone bawling out your fourth person today?"

"That's right, Rob, I was. How very observant of you. Now will you kindly ring the office and tell them to send a cab?"

"There's no need." He gestured behind her. "Here it is now."

"Right, good."

The cab passed her and pulled up. She opened the door.

"Right, well, I'll see you back at the office," said Rob, walking past her.

She looked at him in shock. "What do you mean?"

"The meeting's over early, it's a twenty-minute walk back, so I'm walking."

"Oh for God's sake!" she cried. "What is your *problem*?"

"I've had enough, Leona."

For a moment she thought he might be joking, but no there was no sign of any joviality in his expression. He did, however, look very angry. His dark brown eyes were cold and for some reason he looked older, like the stress of working with her had aged him. She didn't know what to say but in any case he was on a roll and didn't seem too interested in waiting for her to say anything.

"You don't get to speak to me the way you have been lately," he continued. "I've been sticking up for you this last couple of weeks, you know that? And I know they talk about me back in the office. They think I don't hear them, or notice the looks that they exchange every time I go into your office, but I do. And up to now I didn't care. They could say whatever they liked and I'd have still stuck up for you."

156

"Well, you needn't bother. I'm well able to stick up for myself, you know."

"Good," he said, looking tired all of a sudden. "See you later, then."

"Oh fuck you!" she shouted at his back as he turned away. She saw him shake his head and for some reason this stopped her from getting into the cab. "You think it's so easy, Rob – you think you can just choose to be like this. Well, it's *not* that easy. It's *not* a choice."

He turned back. "I think it is."

"It's not. Do you think I would *choose* to be this person?" she said hoarsely at his rapidly retreating back. "Do you think *I* don't get tired of it?"

He stopped and turned again.

"Sometimes it's very hard to tell," he said, "but I'd like to think you do."

"Nobody understands," she half-whispered.

"You'd be surprised."

"I don't even know where to start."

He looked down at her feet. "They look like shoes that could withstand a twenty-minute walk," he said. "Let's start with that."

She laughed. "Shoes? What would you know about shoes?"

"I have six older sisters," he said. "Trust me, I know shoes."

Chapter 26

KATE

A certain lull had descended over the office once Leona and Rob finally left. Even knowing Leona wasn't in the building seemed to lower everyone's blood pressure and Kate hoped that the meeting would turn out to be a long one. It was clear that Mary was still in a bad mood. She was working away silently, but then, to Kate's surprise, at eleven o'clock an email pinged into her inbox from Mary that simply said '**Coffee?**'

She nodded over to her colleague and they made their way out to the tea room.

"Are you busy?" Mary asked as she slipped a pod into the Nespresso.

"Kept going," said Kate. "Mostly just trying to stay awake though. Invoicing is not exactly setting me alight with exhilaration."

"Ha, be careful what you wish for – excitement around here generally doesn't result from pleasant circumstances."

"I guess not. Did you have a nice weekend?" It was such a clichéd question but Kate was determined to keep the conversation going.

"Nope, you?"

"Nope."

The two women laughed.

The door swung open then and there was Alice, looking – even for her – unusually wide-eyed and anxious.

"Jacinta wants ye – Declan's on the rampage – he's going mad!"

Mary rolled her eyes at Kate.

"See? Never pleasant."

They went back out to the open-plan area to see Declan pacing up and down at Jacinta's desk.

"What do you mean her phone is turned off?"

Jacinta looked at him. "I mean exactly that, Mr Donegan. Her phone is turned off. As it should be when she is in a meeting."

"Well, try it again."

"I will try it again. Oh, here's the girls – they might be able to help you."

"What girls? Oh those – about time!" he said when he saw them.

"Eh, Declan, we were gone for about two minutes," said Mary.

"Oh never mind that, you're here now." He looked from Mary to Kate, "No, wait – you're not who I want." He turned to Jacinta "Where is Olivia?"

"Olivia?" She raised one eyebrow.

"Yes – oh shit! I forgot. Right, Mary, you'll do. I need projections."

"Projections?" Mary frowned, "For what? Who wants them?"

"Head Office," Jacinta answered as Declan had by now grabbed her phone and was typing in Leona's number.

"Well, I'm afraid that wouldn't be my department. Where's Cian? He's part of the Strategy team – I'm not, *remember*?" There was an iciness to her tone that was just barely distinguishable, but there all the same.

"Cian, apparently, has gone out to put some cash in the parking meter," Jacinta sighed.

"Well, he'll be back shortly surely, or Rob will be back, or Leona." Mary strolled over to her desk. "So they'll just have to wait."

"They can't wait – Frankfurt is on the verge of collapse and Head Office are on their way here!" Alice could not contain herself any longer.

"Frankfurt is what?"

"Collapsing," Alice said solemnly.

Jacinta was by now trying to wrestle her phone back off Declan.

"The whole city?" Mary looked at Alice in amusement. "I very much doubt it."

"I'm telling you – Dirk just rang Declan and it's all gone mental."

Mary looked from Alice to Kate who just shrugged and sat back at her own computer.

"Alice, get back to work!" Jacinta swatted her assistant with a manila folder as she finally got Declan from behind her desk. "Frankfurt is not going under. Sicher Deutsche Kompanie has announced a massive hole in its balance sheet. Apparent GIMV, another insurance company that they took over last month, was slightly overegging its *own* balance sheet which means SDK now has a massive hole in theirs. Which would be fine if Head Office had not funded the takeover and are now massively exposed. They need our Capital Ratios to make sure the depositors are looked after if it all goes belly-up." She turned to Declan. "You need to calm down, Declan – all this panic is not getting us anywhere."

"I won't calm down!" Declan spluttered like a frustrated, spoilt child. "The Finance team from Head Office are on their way here in a plane. We are already on their fucking radar as having a complete lack of synergy. They've been in the air for the last hour and quite likely know nothing about this. However, when they do find out, the first thing they are going to demand to see are our figures and here we are, not a Strategy person in the fucking building to pull together a ratios report. They're not coming here to fuck spiders, you know – we're toast!"

"But Leona said they weren't coming until tomorrow," said Mary.

"That was my previous information, yes, but apparently no, it's today."

"Oh," she shrugged, turning to her own monitor. "Well, I'm sure your Strategy team will be back shortly."

Mary knew she was taking a risk but at the same time couldn't help smirking to herself. Let them see now that she was the only dependable one here and why that job should be hers. She picked up the file she'd been working on before her break and started to type. She was still smirking when, from behind her, she heard Kate's voice pipe up.

"Could I help? I did a lot of that kind of work in my old job?"

And, at that moment, Mary knew she'd just made a big mistake. Huge.

ROB

I know the day you're talking about. I still don't see what any of this has to do with anything but if you want to know, then I'll tell you.

We were walking back from that meeting in the Irish Bankers' Federation. I was surprised that she agreed to my suggestion to walk, but I think she wanted to talk. So I waited till we'd walked a bit. It was too hard to hear each other on the footpath around Trinity, too crowded. Students and tourists, all either clamouring for buses or just standing there talking. So I waited till we got around the corner and were on Westmoreland Street. And then I asked her could she deny that she had enjoyed every second of that meeting.

"That back there?" She looked at me while gesturing behind her to the Bankers' Federation. "Oh, I'm not going to deny that I enjoyed that alright. That Gallagher is an awful prick."

Sure what could I do but laugh. "You're unreal," I said. And I meant it.

But she just looked at me and said, "Rob, there is no point in me lying. Yes, I enjoyed being right and socking it to him. But if you're asking did I enjoy the sixty hours' work I put into proving I was right – well, then, no, I didn't. I didn't enjoy being here until 11pm on Friday night, I didn't enjoy the row when I got home and discovered I had completely forgotten my daughter's drama show, I didn't enjoy having to then tell Gavin that I had to come in Sunday to finish off the four other things I didn't get to because I was trying to work out Gallagher's stupid ratios and I didn't," she paused, "I didn't enjoy fighting with you."

And that's exactly what she said. And we just kind of looked at each other. I couldn't figure out if she was apologising or just simply stating a fact.

I still don't know actually.

"I didn't enjoy fighting with you."

I mean, this woman fights for fun – this was quite the statement.

I didn't know what to say, so I just said, "Sure don't worry about me. I have to do what I'm told."

But she just shrugged. So I changed the subject.

"So you missed a play, huh? Was your daughter upset?"

There was another shrug at that.

"A bit. She wasn't too bad. But then I guess she's getting used to it." She kind of bit her lip then and for an awful second I thought she was going to cry.

"You'll make the next one," I said quickly. I didn't know what else to say.

She nodded at that.

"Her dad took a video. We watched that a few times."

"Oh. Good man, Dad. He made it then." I was glad that there'd been a happy ending.

But she just rolled her eyes. "Oh he did. Sure Daddy can do no wrong."

No happy ending after all then. Dad was clearly persona non grata and I only remembered then that it was probably the same guy she'd bawled out on the phone earlier.

"You're very hard on yourself, you know," I said then. "You do a fair bit right too – no one else in that room was able to point out what you did today. So stop it."

Now that felt weird, I can tell you. Who was I to be telling her to stop being hard on herself? But, Jesus, I mean she was hard on herself. She was so hard on herself all the time.

But she just smiled a kind of even more bitter smile then

and said, "Anyone who put the same time into that," she nodded again back towards the Federation offices, "could have done exactly the same job."

"But they didn't," I said.

"But don't you see, Rob?" And she turned to me just as we reached the busy O'Connell Street junction, saying "That just makes me the biggest fucking eejit of them all."

And so I said it to her. "You're very bitter all of a sudden."

But she just laughed. Again it was a pathetic attempt at a laugh and I remember thinking that someday I was going to get her to laugh properly.

But then she stopped that silly half laugh and said, kind of sadly, I thought, "Some would say I'm bitter all the time these days."

"Not to your face, they wouldn't," I said, laughing myself at that point.

"Ha," she nodded, "you know, you're probably right – though I think that might just be in the office. No one else is as afraid of me, more's the pity."

"Oh I don't know, that last phone call I overheard frightened the crap out of me and I wasn't even at the other end."

It wasn't a word of a lie, let me tell you.

"Well, trust me," she said, in a kind of sneery tone, "he'll do what he wants. He always does."

And at that we both stopped pretending to laugh. But it didn't matter as the lights had changed and it was time to cross.

"Christ, I'd forgotten how busy this junction is," she said. "Must be years since I've walked anywhere around here."

"Really? Sure that's what's wrong with you, so," I said. "No fresh air."

"Note to self: factor fresh air into eighteen-hour day."

She stopped as we got across the first junction and, instead of continuing over O'Connell Bridge and to the other side of the river, I turned instead down the side of the river and started walking along the southside of George's Quay.

"Should we not cross to the other side?" she said. "It's shorter surely?"

"This is nicer," I answered. "Why, are you in a hurry? What's the point in cutting that meeting short if we can't take the scenic route home?"

And she looked at me. And I knew that this was a big thing for her. She knew she should be back in the office. Hell, I knew she should be back in the office. And I could see the struggle in her face as her mind ran back and forward between the two options.

"Come on," I said, "I want to show you something. I promise it'll be worth it."

And that seemed to do it. She kind of shook her head, not in a negative way, but as if she was trying to shake off the 'you know this is the wrong thing to do' thoughts.

And so we walked. And it definitely got worse before it got better. Burgh Quay is kind of dirty and noisy and then the DART screeched overhead as we walked under Tara Street Bridge and it all kind of shook and rattled and she put her hands over her ears as if to block it out.

"*So how is this a nicer way to go?*" she screeched, her voice fighting with the rattling, whining train.

"Have patience, woman," I said and just kept walking.

And sure then we were beyond the junction and the bridge and the traffic and the sky opened out and river rolled beside us. Down that side of the quays is so nice these days with all the regeneration – there are little trees and it's quiet – you'd swear you were in a different town, a different country even. And eventually I could actually see her visibly start to relax.

The beautiful long low lines of the Custom House ran alongside the other side of the river and on our side everything seemed to widen out. The road was wider and quieter, even the footpath was wider and a hush seemed to descend on the world.

And we just walked.

And we kept walking, even when we reached the Talbot Memorial Bridge which leads across almost to the front door of our building. She did look at me as if to say 'This one, no?' but there was none of the hesitation of before. When I didn't turn, she didn't either. It was that simple.

"Right, here we are," I said, when a few hundred metres down the path we reached the pedestrian Seán O'Casey Bridge.

"What do you mean, here we are? This is it? This is what you wanted to show me – a bridge?"

"Yep."

"But sure, Rob, I've seen this bridge a thousand times. We work right over there, remember?" She looked puzzled and, more than that, nearly annoyed.

"But have you ever crossed it?" I asked.

"Crossed it?" She looked at me. "Well, no, but I can't see how different it'll be from crossing that one twenty feet back."

"Oh come on! Stop being such a cynic."

And I took her hand.

I know I shouldn't have. I didn't mean to. But I did it the same way I'd grab Marnie, or Claire or any of the gang – hell, I'd nearly grab Paulie's hand to cross the road sometimes.

I just grabbed it and we stepped onto the bridge and we kept walking until we got to the middle. And I turned her and made her look down towards the mouth of the Liffey. Towards the big beautiful arc of the Samuel Beckett Bridge.

And then, out of nowhere she said, "I've never smelt the sea here before. I drive in every day and I park in the basement and go to my office. I don't leave my office all day, I go back to my car and I drive home. But now, out here, I can actually smell the sea."

And for some reason she started to cry, and I put my arm around her and we just stood.

So you can say what you like about anything that happened. I can only tell you what *I* know. And it's not like what they're saying. Not in my mind. And after that, do you know what? You can believe what you like.

And on that note, I think I'd like to take a break now.

I need a cigarette.

Extract from interview with Robert Kinirons
Recorded 12 November 2011
3.50pm

Chapter 27

KATE

"Could I help? I did a lot of that kind of work in my old job?"

The words were out before Kate even realised she'd spoken them.

But by the time she'd spoken them it was too late to take them back as Declan had clapped his hands together in glee and shouted "Result!"

Then without pausing to ask how she proposed to do any of this or even let her know in detail what he needed he strode from the room shouting, "Get those into me A-SAP!"

And then there was silence as Kate tried to get to grips with what had just happened.

What on earth had she done? Head Office were on their way, from Frankfurt, there was a crisis and reports were needed.

Reports that she'd never done for this bank before.

Reports that no one at her level should be even attempting.

Everyone was looking at her.

"Kate, are you sure you can –" started Jacinta.

"*Sssh!*" She put up her hand to cut Jacinta off. "I need to think."

And then, even as the words of authority left her lips she felt a calm descend over her. She could do this. She used to do this kind of thing with her eyes closed and, whilst fashions might have changed since she last worked in a bank, ratios definitely hadn't.

She stood up.

"Okay, I'll need the spreadsheets Olivia used to use. I don't think

I have access to that drive on my own PC – does anyone have her password?"

She looked at Mary who just shrugged and looked away and then at Alice who was still standing open-mouthed.

"Eh, hello? I need some help here – anyone?"

Her voice was sharp now and, if they weren't looking at her funny before, they certainly were now.

"I'll call IT," Jacinta called from her desk. "They should be able to override her password and get you access to whatever you need."

"Thanks, Jacinta." Kate turned to Mary. "I'll need her paper files too – I'm sure the back-up for previous periods is in there. Mary, you must know where they are?"

Mary was clearly pretending not to hear but this new assertive Kate was not taking any nonsense.

"Mary?" she repeated.

"Yes?"

"Can you show me where Olivia kept her paper files, please?"

Mary rolled back her chair reluctantly and walked, not too quickly, over to the cabinets on the far wall. "I think they're in here," she said. "I've no idea what order anything is in though."

"That's fine, I'll take it from here."

She didn't look to see what kind of dirty look she was getting for that remark as, to be honest, she didn't have time to care.

She had a job to do.

Less than an hour later, Kate raised her hand to knock on Declan's door then paused to take a deep breath. She was pretty confident that the file in her hand contained all the information he needed and, whilst her heart was pounding in her chest, she knew that it wasn't nerves, it was excitement.

This was the feeling she'd missed.

She'd been midway through wading her way through the various formulas when Cian had returned. He didn't seem one bit perturbed that all hell had broken loose while he was away and, if possible, was in an even more laidback and laconic mood than usual. He'd been helpful though, she had to hand him that. He'd been able to show her where one or two of Olivia's old figures had come from and had pulled whatever reports she needed from the system promptly.

Which was more than she could say about Mary. Whatever crisis the rest of the bank seemed to be having did not appear to be of any concern whatsoever to Mary. She was tapping away vigorously on her own computer as if her life depended on it. Or at the very least, as if she were afraid that if she didn't she'd be asked to help someone else.

Well, anyhow, she could get stuffed. Kate didn't need her help. Between her own knowledge, Cian's help and Olivia's pretty ample audit trail she was ready to go in.

Ready to prove that she was more than just a data-entry clerk.

She knocked on Declan's door and went in.

He had his back to her and was on his mobile at the window. When he eventually noticed she was in the room he gestured to the chair in front of his desk and continued to talk.

"Yes, Dirk, I am in agreement with you. Yes, I understand how important. Yes. I said yes. Yes, I understand, Dirk. Yes."

Kate felt uncomfortable to be witnessing such a conversation so she deliberately zoned out and started looking around her. She'd never even been in this office before. It was huge, at least twice the size of Leona's. There was a couch with a coffee table down one end with the usual finance magazines and a fresh, untouched *Financial Times*. But it was the windows that caught her eye the most. Like in the rest of the building they stretched from floor to ceiling but, unlike the view from the open plan, the windows here looked out over the IFSC itself and the myriad waterways and bridges that always made Kate think of her honeymoon in Venice. She really did love working down in this part of the city.

With a start she realised Declan was off the phone and striding back towards his desk.

"Those goddam Europeans," he said angrily. "They just have no patience and no idea of the stress and pressure we're under here. Do this, do that, why have you not got this done, why have you not got that done? It is absolutely coming between them and their sleep that Olivia is not here – they're all about the plans and budgets – if we don't get a goddam replacement for her soon they'll come over and put in one of their own and that is the last goddam thing I need – another bloody German under my nose."

He sat down and she handed him her papers.

As he read down through the figures she could see him visibly start to relax.

"The results don't look too bad actually," he said, almost to himself.

"No, we would appear to be well covered in most areas alright."

"Yes. Now you're sure these are right? Jeremy is famous for his hypervising so these need to pass muster."

"I am sure," she said confidently.

"Excellent." He kept scrolling down and then paused.

"Is there something wrong?" she asked, feeling suddenly anxious.

"No – quite the contrary actually. You did all this kind of work before?"

"Yes, quite a lot of it, in my old job. Why? Is that not the way you'd do it here? It was the best I could –"

He put up his hands to stop her. "That's not where I'm going with this, Kate. I'm having a bit of a thought-shower here …"

"I beg your pardon?"

"A thought-shower – you know, a 'Come to Jesus' moment."

Kate looked at him blankly.

"I've something to run up your flagpole …"

She couldn't help another "I beg your pardon?" at this.

"Look, you know we're having a personnel crisis here and I'm not going to lie to you, Leona doesn't have the bandwidth to cover for much longer. Add to that her insistence that we boil the ocean on this one and, I'm telling you, I'm left with a lot of pain points. So what do you think?"

"I really don't know what to think," she replied quite truthfully as she had absolutely no idea what he was talking about.

"Olivia's job. You know, we could waste time looking across the piece on this but maybe you're the answer? You're here, you're ready and you can hit the ground running. So are you in?"

"Am I in?" She looked at him in confusion, and then she realised what he was talking about. "You mean for Olivia's job?"

"Well, yes, of course that's what I mean. Are you interested in the job? Now obviously there'd be a bit of catching up to do but I'm quite confident that would all be like double-loop learning to someone like you."

Kate opened her mouth in horror. Olivia's job? Was he nuts? Of

Margaret Scott

course she couldn't even consider it!

And then a voice somewhere in the recess of her brain said, 'Why not? Are *you* nuts?' And she thought about the excitement of the last hour and the voice said again, 'At least don't say no straight away,' and so it happened that for the second time in an hour she heard words come out of her mouth that she might later regret.

"Thank you very much, Mr Donegan. I'll certainly consider putting my hat in the ring."

Just then his phone buzzed and he picked it up absently while still scrolling down through the schedules.

"They're here? Jesus. That was close. Right so, I'll be out."

He stood up and straightened his comical red braces.

"They're here," he said.

She got up quickly and made her way to the door but, just as she was leaving, it opened and a tall, good-looking man stood back when he saw her.

"Ah Jeremy!" said Declan, arriving over at her side. "Great to see you again."

"And you, Declan, and," he looked at Kate, "I'm sorry – I don't recognise this face?"

Kate held out her hand. "Nice to meet you, Jeremy. Kate O'Brien. I'm not here that long. A newbie."

"Yes," said Declan, and then a strange look came over his face. "Actually Kate is our new Olivia – a strategy genius if ever I saw one. We're both delighted and relieved to have her on board. Isn't that right, Kate?"

Kate looked from Declan to Jeremy in horror and then, glancing over Jeremy's shoulder, caught sight of Mary at her desk in the open-plan area. And she didn't need to wonder had Mary heard Declan's ridiculous announcement, because, for once, Mary's face said it all.

OLIVIA

You know, when I joined DKB I was fairly down the pecking order in the Finance Department, but I'd known I would be. The Finance Department of a commercial bank is very different to that of branch banking. I needed to learn the ropes and I was happy to do that from the ground up. So, I started off in Creditors. The biggest change was their system. I hadn't used it before so I'd come in early every morning to double check what I'd done the day before. Again, I didn't mind. I wanted to make a good impression and the sooner I got up to speed the better. I didn't really stay late. It's hard to believe but no one did really, back then.

No one.

So eventually I got to grips with the work end of things. Now, I'm not going to lie – even at that, I did often wonder what I'd got myself into. It was so different. There was none of the chat and gossip of the bigger banks – everyone seemed a bit older, more sedate – isn't that the word? And, of course, there was only the staff there. No members of the public and I suppose I kind of missed that.

I've always got on with people, you see. Always. I like meeting people and I never had any problems with anyone before. I feel you should know that, in case you think, well, that it was me.

It wasn't.

I always got on with everyone.

I settled in soon enough really, like I said. It helped that I wasn't

171

the only new person. Another girl started the same day as me. They'd had two vacancies and at the start our jobs were pretty similar. We were both Accounts Assistants and we did whatever was thrown our way. I may not have had a Finance degree like her but, to be honest, I'm not sure what kind of advantage it would have been anyway. She never seemed to be finding it any easier than I was.

I liked it though. We were part of a nice team. And it was a good place to work. Hard work was rewarding and within a couple of years I was asked to assist Michael Hughes with the Strategy role in advance of his retirement. Mary, the other girl that started the same time as me, then moved up a grade in Finance and even got a junior as an assistant. Again, there was a bit of a face when my duties changed, but she was so good in Finance, they only moved me because I could be spared. I'm not sure what her problem was anyway – it wasn't like I got any more money, it was a just a different role, all budgets and projections which back then were pretty run-of-the-mill and boring. She had some mad notion that it was a more 'visible' role and that before I could say Jack Robinson I'd be at board meetings on the ninth floor with the big lads.

Imagine me. On the ninth floor.

We weren't even allowed on that floor. That's where all the big noises were. The only person allowed up there was Jacinta, and I'm not even so sure she was actually allowed or whether she just went up regardless because she didn't trust the secretaries up there to do a good enough job. Jacinta had been with DKB since the days when their office was on Merrion Square and, by God, did she know the right way and the wrong way to do stuff! Back then the big noises had hung out on the third floor of the much smaller, though rather ornate Georgian Building and, for the third floor, it had to be the right way. She organised the catering for all their functions. They had their own dining room up there and chefs used to come from the posh restaurant on nearby Fitzwilliam Square to cook luncheons just for them. I saw one of their lunch bills once – we weren't meant to but one got mixed up in the general creditors. That bill was an absolute sin – my Danny said he wouldn't pay that amount of money for a car, let alone a meal.

So, no, I'd no ambition in that direction. The biggest advantage for me with moving to the Strategy team was that Matthew, my boss then, agreed to me having a four-day week when I returned after having my first baby. It was Danny's idea to ask. He'd worked it all out and with the tax and travel costs and everything, my actual money wouldn't be down that much and it meant that one day a week he didn't have to rush home to get the kids from my mam.

So I reckoned there'd be no harm in asking, nothing ventured nothing gained, and when Matthew said yes, it was great. Well, it was great until Mary found out. She was not impressed. Which was childish really – it's not like she'd kids to be at home with herself.

Anyway, none of it was my decision. As I said, Matthew Boyce was in charge of us then. He was pretty easygoing, when he was in, that is. He golfed a lot, all part of the job we were told. Golf and various junkets – sorry, business trips – in Europe. He spent a fair while in Frankfurt and Brussels – you know, fancy cities in Europe, but again, I'm not sure how much of it was work-related.

To be honest we all had it pretty good back then. Once a year we went away to some European city or other on an all-expenses-paid trip. The year before I had Sam we all went to Paris – that was the most amazing experience. Limo from the airport, the poshest hotel, dinner in a swanky boat on the river – honestly, I don't think we put our hands in our pocket once. And it wasn't just our office either – several of the European offices were there too, and a few from Head Office.

Magical.

Actually more miraculous than magical as whatever effect Paris had on Mary, she was like a different person for that whole trip. We were meant to be sharing a room but sure I barely saw her. She went to bed after me and was up before me. Or so she said. I wondered a few nights had she come up to our room at all but sure it was none of my business.

It was worth it to see her smiling.

That was nearly eight years ago now. Imagine. Sam was born in 2006. I didn't go on the trip that year. To Madrid it was. I believe it was out of this world. I find it hard to believe that it could have topped Paris but I heard it did. I would have loved to have gone but, well, Sam was only a small baby and Danny didn't think it was right. I did consider it given that it was only for a few days but Danny said I'd only miss the baby – he said to wait till the following year.

But there wasn't one the following year.

Madrid was the last one.

That was in 2007.

And after that everything started to change. When I got back from my maternity leave after having my second child Max, Michael Hughes and Matthew Boyce had both moved on. Michael retired to farm pedigree cows in County Mayo and Matthew went to head up Commercial Lending in Ulster Bank though I'd say the pedigree cows might well have turned out to be the easier option.

So instead of Matthew, we got Declan.

And then eventually, Leona, who'd been working in the Lending Department, was promoted to head up our team.

And that was the beginning of the end.

It all went downhill from there.

Chapter 28

MARY

"I am livid. I'm just livid." Mary could barely spit the words out.

"You may have mentioned that alright," her bearded running companion, who she now knew as Ronan, replied.

"Livid. She's only in the place a wet week and, to add insult to injury, she's meant to be my number two!"

"So I believe."

"I'm not letting this go, you know."

"You've certainly given me that impression alright. Even if it wasn't your third time to mention it in the last eight kilometres."

"Eight kilometres? We're not at that much already, are we?"

Ronan looked at his running watch. "Eight point five actually."

"God, that's great, isn't it?"

"Time certainly flies when you're having fun alright."

"Oh shut up!" She shoved him with one bobbing elbow. "I can't believe you once told me not to think about work while running – sure look how well I'm doing tonight and it's all I can think about!"

"You're right. You should start your own club. You could call it The Bitter Bitches Running Club. Now, seeing as you're feeling so smugly invincible, let's up the pace – you can go faster than this."

"You're such a smartarse. Must be great to live such a stress-free life – nothing to worry about other than where your next pair of runners is coming from."

"Do you think that's by accident? Or do you think it's a decision

175

I made?"

"Well, obviously you decided that this was going to be your job. So not quite by accident ..."

"Oh, so you think I left school and just started running?"

"Well, no, to be honest, I never thought about what you did at all."

"Clearly. I was an actuary, you know. I had a big job like yours," he elbowed her playfully, "so I know a fair bit more than just about runners."

"And what happened? Did you lose your job? My boss's husband was in Insurance and he lost his too. It's not meant to be public knowledge but I heard it all the same."

"No. I didn't lose my job. I feel kind of left out of this whole recession business actually. I had the option of a super redundancy package, paid off my not-that-excessive mortgage and had enough left over to try something else for a while. I always thought I might go back to Finance but you know what? I'm not so sure I'll bother."

"Really?"

"Yep, turns out I prefer to help Bitter Bitches to run better than spend my life manipulating spreadsheets. Go figure. Now, speaking of same – get a move on, we haven't all night for this kind of dawdling. I'm in a hurry, I've to collect the girls on the way home."

And with that he was gone, long legs striding ahead and she cursed her big mouth as she tried to find the energy to go after him.

An hour later she was sitting in her mother's kitchen having received a phone call stating that her presence was required at a moving-photos-from-phone-to-computer emergency. Stephen, of course, was nowhere to be found though funnily enough he'd had his dinner there earlier and would, no doubt, be back to sleep in the warmed-up bed later on.

"Mum, can I not just do it for you, please?"

"No. Sure then how will I ever learn how to do it myself?"

"Mum, there are very few certainties in life but one of them is that you are definitely never going to do this yourself."

"You just think I'm a thick."

"There's a lot of that going around," said her father drily from his chair by the fire.

"I didn't say you were thick, Séamus – I said there was something wrong with your brain," her mother clarified.

"There is," he answered back. "It's sore from listening to your voice."

"It's spiralling out of control, you know," Mary's mother hissed in her ear. "He's forgetting things right, left and centre."

"He's just getting older, Mum, we all are ..."

"It's not that – you're as bad as him, in complete denial. You know he forgot about *Prime Time* tonight and he hasn't missed a programme since the nineties when it was *Today Tonight* ... though I think it's more Miriam that keeps him watching these days, it's all that depressing. Wouldn't mind but I wanted to watch it myself tonight – there was to be a bit about the fluoride in the water and what it's doing to us all ..."

"Well, Jesus, Mum, I'm glad you missed it so – you've enough imaginary symptoms to be keeping you busy these days without adding fluoride reactions to the list."

"It's mass medication, you know. It's a complete sin – they're just doing it to numb us all, to keep us quiet."

"By the hokey, get your mother a glass of water there so, love, will you?" winked her father and Mary burst out laughing.

"O ye of little faith!" her mother stood up. "The laugh will be on the other side of your faces when I'm the only one left functioning and you're all like zombies."

Mary laughed again. Her mother was a complete nutter.

"So what's so funny?" Stephen walked into the room, and went straight to the fridge.

"The idea of a forty-year-old man back living with his parents," Mary answered drily.

"Oh, you're such a comedian, Mary." Stephen made a face at his older sister and she promptly made one back. "I hope you never fall on rough times."

"Stephen, the only thing you've fallen on lately was your feet when you moved back in here."

"Now, Mary, leave him alone. Sure isn't it great having him around? A bit of company for your poor dad and him in his condition."

Mary rolled her eyes but she grudgingly had to admit to herself that one advantage of having Stephen around was that waiting on him hand and foot might just distract her mother from the rest of them.

She was still thinking about them all as she drove home. Her poor dad, how he put up with her mother at all she'd never know. She turned up her driveway and was at the front door putting her key in the lock when she heard a voice behind her.

"I thought you'd moved house or something."

She swung around.

"Well, look what the cat dragged in," she said, folding her arms and leaning against her front porch.

"Meaning I can come in?"

"Meaning it's a bit cheeky to just turn up."

"Well, you didn't look in the best of moods in the office earlier so I thought it better to let you calm down for a while."

"Really? And what makes you think that's happened?"

"Nothing, but I couldn't wait much longer."

She said nothing but just stood there.

"So can I come in?" he asked again.

"I haven't had my shower yet."

"Fine by me. Sure I could join you."

She shook her head, smiling, and turning to put her key in the door said, "Jeremy Taylor, you really haven't changed a bit, have you?"

OLIVIA

They say having your first baby changes everything. Well, I was quite happy to let that change happen. We wanted a baby, we had a baby – I mean, what part of that are people not ready for? Yes, there were sleepless nights but, to be honest, I just slept next day when Sam was sleeping. Okay, the house became a bit of a mess but how could it not? I had a baby. That meant other things had to slide. It really is that simple, is it not? Yes, my life changed but for the better really. I embraced it. Even during my pregnancy I was quite happy to take things easy. I see people who are so keen to tell you they kept running up until they could practically feel the baby making an appearance but I think they're just not taking advantage of a situation that, let's face it, is not going to come their way very often in their lifetime.

I put my feet up a lot. I watched a lot of TV and I read a lot of books. They tell you to take it easy and, I'm not going to lie to you, they didn't need to tell me twice. I had to be careful anyway, my blood pressure was slightly high one day when I went in so I couldn't risk that happening again. I probably ate a lot too but, again, I was careful all the same. A friend of mine was pregnant at the same time and used to go out of her way to pick prawns, soft cheese and nuts every time we were out for dinner. It was like she was trying to prove that pregnancy wouldn't change her. But sure that was ridiculous. It does change you. And the sooner you accept those changes, the happier you'll be. Same goes for babies. Why would you torture yourself with trying to prove a baby doesn't change your life? Madness.

I tell you what it did change while we're on the subject – for some reason it definitely changed Mary's attitude to me. Up to me having the kids we were grand. I think I told you before that her nose got a bit out of joint when I moved to the Strategy division and got the four-day week. Again, Danny said she was just jealous but what I tried to tell her was that I was also getting paid less. One fifth less. It wasn't like I just didn't bother my backside coming in one day a week and got paid anyway. And, to be honest, I got a lot of work done those other days, probably five days' work in four days if a proper analysis was done.

But anyhow, back in those early days it was grand. We weren't very busy in the bank at that stage and Mam was minding Sam for me so things didn't really change a whole lot, I guess. No, it wasn't until I came back from my second maternity leave in 2007 that the shit really hit the fan.

Chapter 29

LEONA

"Okay, so pick a story then," Leona said as she pulled the curtains in Rachel's bedroom.

"What do you mean? I have my book?" came the voice from the bed behind her.

She turned. "Oh. Well, give it to me then."

"But, Mammy, I just read myself. I don't need anyone to read to me anymore. Daddy hasn't read to me in *aaaaages*!"

Leona looked at the bemused look on her seven-year-old daughter's face and something twisted deep inside her.

How did she not know this?

She should know this.

She decided to lie. "I know that, Rachel. I just want to see what you're reading, that's all."

But she knew the child wasn't buying it.

Pathetic.

She was surprised when she saw the size of the book. It was a proper book, with chapters, and not too many pictures either.

"David Walliams, eh?" She was surprised again by the author. "Are you sure this is suitable for you?" Anytime she'd seen him on TV he'd been doing rather risqué humour for adults.

"Yes, Mammy." Rachel looked at her with a 'you're so lame' look on her face. "It's a children's book. I've loads of his. This is the new one. Daddy got it for me."

Ah, did he now? Good old Daddy. Then she instantly felt slightly ashamed of her bitterness.

Slightly ashamed of herself overall.

Gavin's jaw had dropped when he saw her come in the door an hour earlier at six o'clock.

He'd opened his mouth, presumably to say something sarcastic, but she had just looked at him and he'd known that it wasn't a good time. Before either of them had a chance to speak she'd been bowled over by an extremely excited Rachel who'd flung herself at her mother with joy at the unexpected surprise of having her home. And Leona had been glad of the distraction. She didn't want him to ask her why she was home so early, mostly because she really didn't know why herself.

But one thing was for sure, she could not have stayed in that office for a minute longer.

Getting back to the office to find the mayhem that had broken out in her absence had been a massive shock. She was already reeling from what had happened out on the bridge. She hadn't been expecting those tears, she wasn't a crier, but when they'd spilled up from behind her eyes and poured in rivulets down her cheeks she'd had no choice but to let them. And then when Rob had put his arm around her she turned into him and sobbed like her heart would break. She didn't know why she was crying but the release had been intoxicating. As the tears flowed she'd wondered what on earth she was going to say if he asked her what was wrong but he never did, so when they stopped she'd felt no pressure to explain what she couldn't explain.

Instead he'd gone and got them two takeaway coffees from the Harbourmaster pub and brought them back out to the bridge and they'd drunk them in silence. When she'd managed to pull herself together completely they'd walked across the bridge and back to the office.

And she'd known before the glass doors had opened in front of her that something was wrong. Jacinta had quickly taken her by the arm and ushered her away from Rob and into her office where she filled her in.

"Head Office are here? Jeremy is here? How the hell did Declan get that one wrong?" Leona asked, her blood literally running cold at the thought of the hour she'd just wasted.

"God only knows, but the problem is, he did. And yes, there was a bit of upheaval when you were gone but it's all fixed now. Himself and Kate are in with them now and everything seems to be going okay."

"Himself and who?"

"Kate."

"Kate? Our Kate as in New Kate?"

"Yes."

"Jesus, why in God's name is she in there?"

"Well now, Leona, only for her we'd all be in a much more precarious situation than we currently find ourselves in. She was able to pull together all of the figures that Declan needed – otherwise he was about to launch himself from an upstairs window."

"*Kate* did? But sure Mary could have done all that – or Cian?"

"Cian wasn't here, he'd popped out, and Mary, I'm afraid, was being less than co-operative, God knows why."

"Oh right." She turned to go to her desk and, trying to sound casual, asked, "Did Declan say anything about me not being here?"

"Well, obviously he hates when you're not at his right arm but what could you do? You were at a meeting, weren't you?"

Leona looked sideways at Jacinta but her face was blank, not a sign of suspicion.

"Yes. Of course. I know that. It's just … well anyway, it all seems to be fine now."

"Yes, it is. I suppose he was just doubly frustrated as he couldn't get you on your phone either."

"My phone?" She looked at Jacinta and then remembered Rob had turned it off. "Oh yes, it ran out of power actually. Just after the meeting."

"I see." Again Jacinta's expression was inscrutable.

Leona just wanted to change the subject. "So, what's the agenda for today then, Jacinta? Do they have plans?"

"Yes, well, I think they already had meetings booked in with Frank and the rest of the Risk team at –" she looked at her watch, "actually in five minutes. And then at four o'clock they have that big meeting with the Chief Executive and the rest of the board. So technically Declan was right – they still won't really be meeting with us until tomorrow – but I think the GIMV drama threw the whole thing off kilter."

"Oh right," Leona sat down. "There's no point in me going in to them now then. I'll see them tomorrow as per the original schedule. Can you tell everyone else I'm not to be disturbed? I've quite a lot to get through here."

"Yes," said Jacinta as she turned to leave the room. At the door she stopped and looking back said, "Oh, do you need my charger?"

"For what?" Leona looked at her blankly.

"For your phone? You usually borrow mine when you forget to bring in your own."

"Oh," Leona blushed. "Ehm no, I didn't forget it. I have it somewhere. I just forgot ..." Her words trailed off as she cursed herself for telling such a stupid lie to begin with.

"Right so." Jacinta looked like she was about to say something else, but then didn't and when she was gone Leona sat down at her desk, her head in her hands.

Leona blushed again even just thinking about it. The day had not improved after that and she'd had a thumping headache all afternoon. Eventually at five o'clock she'd told Jacinta she wasn't feeling great and had left. And now here she was. Her head was still throbbing though it did occur to her that it was probably dehydration.

After all, there had been a lot of tears.

She went back downstairs once Rachel was asleep and into the kitchen. Gavin was there looking into the fridge.

"I'm sorry – I've nothing ready for you, I wasn't expecting –" he started.

"It's okay. I wasn't expecting you to have anything."

"Is everything okay?"

"You mean have I been fired? Not yet."

"That's not even funny and definitely not what I meant. You just look awful, that's all. Bad day?"

"Something like that."

"But yet you're home so early?"

"I know." She went to the fridge and poured herself a very large glass of white wine. "Head Office are over and I'd say I'll be late the next few days so I just wanted to get out of there this evening while they were busy with someone else."

"So would you like a bit of steak or an omelette or something?"

"No, honestly, I'm fine. I was thinking I might just head up to bed if that's okay. Rachel's asleep."

"Okay, well, I'm just going to get myself something then I'll be up, okay?"

She nodded.

Once up in her room she slipped out of her work clothes and into a vest top and soft lounge pants. Then, taking her wine, she went into her cream marble en suite and stood in front of her mirror. Gavin was right, she did look pretty bad. Her eyes were rimmed in red and underneath hung huge circles of darkness. She took up a cotton pad and dabbed it with her cleanser. She started to wipe her face clean and when every scrap of make-up was gone she looked at her reflection again.

For the first time ever she wondered did she look her age. Her forehead was clear of wrinkles and there were no lines or creases around the dark-green eyes that were a gift from her French grandmother. Nor were there any laughter lines around her mouth. She looked okay for her thirty-nine years, she concluded, and for some reason this was a relief. And as she wondered why this was something she should suddenly be worrying about, she took her glass of wine and drank long and deeply.

Rob had knocked softly at her door just before five.

"I was waiting for Jacinta to go to the post room," he'd whispered smiling, but Leona hadn't smiled back.

"Rob, go back to your desk," she said quietly.

"I wanted to check you were okay."

"I'm fine."

"Not beating yourself up with guilt over not rushing back this morning?"

"Rob, please go back to your desk." She'd looked back down at her work at that point and waited for him to leave. Shortly after that she'd gone out and told Jacinta she was going home herself and she'd left the office without looking right or left.

She took another drink and closed her eyes at the sensation of the ice-cold wine sliding down her throat and at that she heard a noise behind her and felt another sensation, that of a kiss on the back of her neck. She stiffened but then two arms crept around her waist and she thought again of the giant fin rising from the water.

And the fin made her think of the bridge.

And the bridge made her think of being in someone else's arms and the feeling of someone else's lips brushing the top of her forehead as tears flowed down her cheeks.

And so, keeping her eyes closed, she turned around.

Chapter 30

KATE

Of all nights, Michael was at a work function and wasn't due home until nine. Kate had managed to leave early enough to collect the children, but on the way home had popped into the supermarket and picked up some nice steaks for dinner. Her hand had hovered over a bottle of wine too and after only moments of deliberation she'd picked a different one. A better one.

This was a big night.

She was buzzing with a kind of excitement that she hadn't felt in some time and she couldn't wait to give him the news.

Selected for a promotion already. After just a few weeks? She just couldn't believe it and even the fact that Jess was in a foul mood and David was slightly more trouble than normal to get to bed couldn't dent her mood.

Up and down the stairs she went to him, in the end resorting to something she never did – a spoon of Calpol. He had two rosy-red cheeks and in a way the fact that he was starting to get the first of his teeth only served to make her feel slightly more excited. Teeth signalled yet another way that her baby was growing up – she nearly felt like telling them to hurry up so that yet another awful stage would be over. But, even if he was still only small, it was okay for her to step up her career a bit, wasn't it? She'd tried taking the lower job and, God, it hadn't turned out like she'd imagined at all. She was bored, she wanted to be challenged and, above all, she was sick and tired of being everyone else's dogsbody. She was there full-time anyway – what difference would it make if the job she was doing was more senior? What difference at all only probably more money and definitely more job satisfaction?

She skipped around the kitchen as she tidied up all signs of children and set the table for just two. She actually felt like the past three years had faded into the darkest recesses of her memory and that there were the first signs of a glimpse of light in the future. By the time Michael got home she had the wine warming by the fire and the first glass almost gone.

"Hang on, you've been asked to do what?" Michael looked mildly amused at the sight of his beaming wife, spotless house and a table set with the good silver including two of the wedding-present-steak-knives.

"Go for Olivia's job."

"And remind me again who Olivia is?"

"She's the girl that left the week before I started – she headed up the Strategy team."

"Oh. So it's not a little job then."

"No, it's not, Michael, why?"

"Why? I'm just asking, that's all."

"I'd be well able for it – it's nothing that I haven't done before, you know."

"Kate, I didn't say that it was. Christ, this is kind of a big deal, that's all – why are you so defensive?"

"Well, why are you so *negative*?"

"I'm not being negative – for God's sake, am I allowed ask what we're letting ourselves in for here?"

"See there you go again –'letting ourselves in for' – more negativity!"

She slammed down his plate in front of him so hard that his steak bounced off its bed of onions and onto the chair.

She looked blankly at the plate where the steak used to be and then looked at Michael's shocked face and they both burst into laughter.

"Ehm, sorry about that," she said, fishing the offending piece of meat from his chair back onto his plate.

"No problem," he said, trying very hard to keep a straight face.

"Good," she said flippantly, though she had the good grace to look slightly sheepish at the same time.

He took this as a good sign. "Katie pet, I'm not being negative. I was just asking – this is all a bit out of the blue, that's all."

She sat down opposite him and sighed. "I know. I guess I just thought you'd be prouder of me, that's all. It was kind of a big deal being asked to go forward for it and I just thought you'd be delighted."

"Ah Kate," Michael got up from his seat and went around to her, "I am already so proud of you – if you were to sit in there and answer the phones all day I'd be just as proud."

"Well, I wouldn't," said Kate with vehemence. "I hate being down the pecking order in there, I really do. I thought I could put up with it, just do the bare minimum but it's so boring. I miss being part of the cut-and-thrust of it all. I know I can do it, Michael, I just know I can!"

Michael looked at her and saw the excitement shining in her eyes and he had to smile. Even though she hadn't aged much in the seven or eight years that he'd known her, in recent years she'd seemed tense, and tired. Whereas tonight? This was more like the old Kate and, while he had his reservations about the pressure she was about to put herself under, this evening wasn't the time to voice them. He picked up his glass.

"A toast then?" he said, "To my ambitious, talented, hardworking wife, Kate O'Brien, getting her career on track and letting nothing get in her way?"

"I'll drink to that alright!" She held up her glass. "To me!"

When she woke two hours later it took her a minute to find her way out of the foggy sleep that too much nice red wine induces. But she was certain she'd heard something. She listened again and then there it was.

The sound of retching and coughing followed by a wail, all coming from the bedroom across the hall.

"*Shit.*"

She flung back the duvet and jumped out of the bed and in a few long strides was in at David's cot.

Too late. He was rolling around in the bed and all around him was a pool of vomit. At the sight and smell of it she felt her own stomach turn over.

"*Michael!*" she hissed over her shoulder. "I need a hand here!"

Within seconds Michael was beside her and he took charge of stripping the bed and finding new sheets while she removed the poor wailing child to the bathroom to clean him up. He did not appreciate having his head dunked under a tap at that hour of the morning but there was vomit in his hair, behind his ears and all down his front.

She was seriously mere seconds from throwing back up a half-bottle of red wine herself.

"How are you doing?" she heard Michael's voice behind her.

"Nearly there." She sprinkled talcum powder on the poor crying baby before wrestling him into a fresh Babygro.

Michael looked at her worried face and said, "Hey, he'll be okay, you know – you're not to be worried."

"Well, I am worried, Michael! How could I not be worried?"

"It's just a bit of puke – we've had pukers before, come on!" He put an arm around her but she shrugged him off.

"You really don't see, do you?" she snapped, her eyes flashing.

"See what?"

"The difference between this and all the other times we've mopped up puke at this hour?"

"Kate, are you okay? You're making no sense."

"Michael, it's 3am and my child has just thrown up all over his bedroom – and I'm expected to be at my desk in less than five hours showing them that I'm capable of taking the most important promotion of my career? Am I making sense now?"

And with that she burst into tears.

OLIVIA

We were a laughing stock for years, you know. Me and Danny. We only owned one house in Ireland and none abroad. And then a group of Danny's friends decided they were only going and buying a feckin' racehorse between them. A racehorse? Danny had never heard such madness but, do you know what, there was some hullabaloo when he said no. Oh, we'd be the only ones not in the Winner's Enclosure in Punchestown, but sure that didn't bother Danny – he'd rather go to the odd Manchester United match. You were nearly guaranteed the win in the Ferguson days, and if the worst-case scenario happened and they lost, at least you weren't paying trainers' fees, vet bills and buying ridiculously expensive shoes for them.

We were the only one of our friends that stayed in the house we'd bought before we got married. It was in Artane, nothing fancy, but sure my mam was still in Coolock and the kids had to be dropped there each day so it was grand.

My friend Suzannah used to live near Mam in Coolock, but when she got married in 2006 nothing would do them only to up sticks and move to Dunboyne. More bang for your buck, they said, and in fairness they did get a lot of bang. It's a huge house. Five bedrooms, a games room and a sunroom. Now I only saw the plans, we never did manage to get up there – it's a fair trip, you know, to Dunboyne. Danny didn't see why he should use his petrol on a trek just to see her fancy pad, and sure then we'd have to drive home so it's not like

191

we could even have a drink up there. She never asks us up anymore though I think, to be honest, she's a bit embarrassed that the view from the sunroom is onto an unfinished green and that four of the houses in her cul de sac are now boarded up. It's silly to be embarrassed really – it's not like Danny would say he'd told her so, even though he did, didn't he?

I do often wonder where it all went wrong. I know what they say, that we all went mental and spent too much, but I don't buy that really. Disasters like that don't happen overnight and I think just to say we all need to take responsibility for our actions is a bit unfair. We never bought anything we couldn't afford so no, I don't buy it for a minute.

Neither does my dad. Dad would be into this kind of thing. He was a great man for the politics, he'd a good head on him and I'd say if things were different in his time, he could have had a career in economics, or social commentary. Instead he'd come home from a long day at the docks and we'd have to sit and listen to him over dinner as he opined the greatness of Fianna Fáil on one hand, but bemoaned long-drawn-out prophecies of doom on the other.

So, his theory is that it all started back in the sixties when they decided to pass some act or other allowing local authority tenants in urban areas to buy their homes. I mean, don't get me wrong, he bought our house under this scheme in the late seventies, a great bargain he said it was. But he says that while Blaney's original idea was that there'd be a 'home for every family', in reality all that really happened with privatisation of housing was that the old need for a house was replaced by a whole new need – a need for a mortgage. Oh, there were all these grants and stuff for buying houses, he said, but sure who was paying for them only us too?

Anyhow that's where the banks came in. Slowly, he says, and at first with no interest in the little man, but surely in time they took over – out went the Building Societies and definitely out went Local Authority lending …

Full of schemes my dad says they were in those days, like that one in the eighties where his brother Paddy got that grant to sell his council house in Bayview back to the council so they could pass it on to someone who needed it. But sure Dad says that all that did was make Bayview, a previously respectable housing estate, into a ghetto and sure now no one worth their salt would want to live there. Paddy ended up buying out on the Navan road instead, in one of the new developments at the time. And sure that was what it was all about really, according to Dad, making sure that all the developers had an endless stream of customers.

There I go, rambling again, but I guess what I'm saying is that it had all gone wrong long before I came along. So I don't see why I should be the one to be punished, tormenting myself about it for the rest of my life.

So I guess that's why I've decided to do something about it now.

You know, I never really had much luck with maternity leaves. When I was having Sam the statutory amount was 18 weeks and it went up the following year to 22. But it was even worse with Max. I had him on 1 February 2007 and had he been born on or after the 1 March 2007 we would have got the new statutory leave of 26 weeks. I mean how unlucky is that?

But then we had no luck at all with Max really. From the time he was two weeks old I knew there was something different, something wrong. Both my boys were big babies and from the second he was born Sam loved his bottles so I fully expected Max to be the same. But they couldn't have been more different. After a week or so it was obvious that nothing I was doing was right. He didn't settle like Sam did, he didn't feed like Sam and he sure as hell didn't sleep like Sam. My mother told me to relax and stop comparing them, that all children were different but sure I couldn't stop wondering what the hell I was doing wrong?

I waited and waited for things to settle down. I just kept thinking that if I could get him to finish his bottles then the rest of the problems, the crying and the lack of sleeping, would just sort themselves out. But while he seemed hungry, he'd take a few sips then bash the bottle from my hand and then look for it again. So I tried a different formula and when this didn't work I tried different teats for the bottles. I spent a fortune but for once I didn't even care that Danny was going mad about the cost. I just wanted my baby to settle down but it just kept getting worse and worse. He would cry and cry and the odd time that I did manage to get a decent amount of milk into him, no sooner would it be down than he would projectile-vomit the whole thing back up at me. Sometimes he even looked like he was drowning and his stomach would make mad gurgling noises as he choked and spat. It got to the stage where I dreaded every feed.

And the worst thing was that everyone thought I was mad. If one more person had told me to 'relax' I would have stabbed them and I am not a violent person. 'Babies cry,' I was told, 'that's what babies do.' I wanted to scream back that 'Babies don't arch their back in agony every time you try to feed them, or claw at your arms or chest as if to beg you to stop torturing them!' It got to the point that I wouldn't meet anyone or let anyone visit me in the house lest it clash with feeding time. So then the unwanted advice came rolling in. 'But he's still so young – you need to give him time,' my neighbor Bernie said. And yes, at that stage he was barely six weeks old – but six weeks of this seemed like six years to be honest.

Pretty soon not only was I avoiding meeting people but when I did actually meet them I was avoiding eye contact. I didn't know what to say. I had nothing in common with all the other mothers whose children sucked away happily and started to last longer and longer gaps between feeds. I remember one morning a friend of mine asking in a cautious but concerned manner did I think I should 'talk to someone' and she gave me this look that clearly said 'and I don't mean about the baby'. She thought I was depressed. I wanted to scream at her, 'Of course I'm bloody depressed but there's a reason for it!'

Soon the only people that would visit our house were my parents. Looking back now, I think they too were concerned as they would often just arrive and sit for a few hours and drink tea and just be there.

Then one such evening they called around eight o'clock. At nine o'clock he needed to be fed and I just couldn't face struggling with him in front of them so I went upstairs to my room to feed him in peace. Anyhow the news was coming on and I knew the last thing my father would need was Max bellowing and roaring while he was trying to hear it. Eventually, after the usual forty-minute fight to feed him, he fell asleep and the tears started to roll down my face. I was sick and tired of it. Absolutely sick and tired and fed up and, do you know what, I'd just had enough. As I leaned over to put him in his Moses basket I caught sight of Danny's laptop on the bedside locker. I opened it and clicked on the internet icon, bringing up Google.

Somebody somewhere had to have had this problem before? I started to type.

Within twenty minutes I had my answer. For the first time in almost three months I felt like a normal human. It was as if a giant load was lifted off my head and I flung down Danny's precious laptop and ran downstairs and then burst into the sitting room.

"I know what's wrong with him!" I shouted.

They turned from the TV to look at me.

"Who?" asked Danny.

"Max! It's called reflux – he has reflux!" I was almost crying again with the mix of relief and excitement. "And it's not quite curable but there's stuff we can do."

I looked at their faces but something was clearly after happening while I was gone. My mother was pale and both my dad and Danny were looking at me blankly while clearly wanting me to stop talking so they could go back to the TV.

"That's great, love," my mother said in a hushed voice and I could tell she was trying to be nice while at the same time trying very definitely to shut me up. "Maybe you could tell us all about it when this is over."

I looked at the TV and then at the three heads that had simultaneously swivelled back to look at it.

"What is it? What's on TV, what's after happening?" I asked.

"It's some documentary," my mother hissed. "Called Future Shock. *And yer man is saying awful things. There'll be war on* Joe Duffy *tomorrow …"*

"What kind of things?" I hissed back, thinking, what kind of things can be more important than the fact that I'm not a lunatic after all?

"He's saying it's all coming to an end, that the bubble is about to burst. But sure that's lunacy. He's just scaremongering …"

"Women! Would ye shush, for Jesus' sake!" My father didn't even turn around as he berated us.

I made a face at him behind his back and sat down on the couch beside my mother and we all watched the rest of the programme in silence.

To ominous music and a gloomy backdrop of gathering clouds, a journalist, Richard Curran, was outlining the dangers of a steep drop in property prices to Ireland's economy in a creepy, futuristic style documentary. He spoke of rising interest rates and the fact that we were too dependent on the construction industry while the rest of the world was facing its own economic storm, in particular the USA and its weakening dollar.

In the final part of the programme he did a mock-up of what a crash might look like, going through each of the next few years and the implication of various scenarios. It made for very alarming viewing: 400,000 jobs in danger, house prices down, banks not lending, mounting credit-card debt leading to a drop in national spending. House values dropping by as much as 30%, multinationals moving out of the country. I lost track.

As the final credits rolled there was still silence in the room.

"I bloody knew it," said Danny.

"You did," said my dad.

"In for a bumpy ride is right," said Danny.

"This country is fucked," said Dad.

And even now, looking back on that surreal evening, the thing I remember most is thinking to myself that this was probably the first, and only, time they'd ever agreed on anything.

Chapter 31

MARY

When Mary woke next morning it was well before her alarm was due to go off. Which wasn't in itself unusual. She was the kind of person that never had any problem getting out of bed and at the sound of her alarm – the radio set to *Newstalk* – was always out of bed in seconds.

What was unusual was that on this particular morning Mary was not alone in her bed. And this in itself meant she hadn't slept great, unaccustomed as she was to the sound of someone else breathing just inches away. And now it was morning and, like so many mornings on various occasions before, she lay there assessing exactly what had just happened. And like so many times before, the previous night had been such good fun.

Jeremy's and Mary's relationship was completely devoid of the usual events that normal couples enjoyed – no family weddings, birthday or anniversary parties. Instead a lot of their time together revolved around eating in lovely restaurants, just the two of them.

And she absolutely loved it.

Ever since that first night in Paris when they'd crept away from the rest of the banking crowd, they'd met in Dublin several times a year and sometimes she even travelled to London or Frankfurt to enjoy a European mini break. They'd even once spent a romantic weekend up in Inverness and she'd been thrilled to finally visit his home country but, again, it had been just the two of them and there had been no mention of a visit to his hometown of Glasgow.

After all these years they had a favourite restaurant in many of the major cities across Europe but last night, given the hour of Jeremy's visit, they'd had to go to a tiny little Chinese restaurant just off Camden Street. It was dark and secluded which was very important, as their relationship was still very much a secret.

Okay maybe 'secret' sounded too mysterious, but definitely no one in the bank knew that she was sleeping with the Head of Group Finance.

And waking with the Head of Group Finance.

She looked over and watched the rise and fall of his breathing.

Not for the first time she wondered if this was what it was like all the time for people like Leona and Olivia? Waking up and instantly being so aware of someone else? Not being able to stretch out lest you interrupt someone else's sleep. Normally now she'd throw on Sky News or the radio and grab the early morning headlines but this was clearly not an option. And yes, the previous night had been nice – but it was this, the interruption in her normal routine – could she really cope with this on a regular basis? Definitely years ago when they'd met first it might have been something she could have got used to, but now?

Who was she kidding, of course she could.

So lost in her thoughts was she that she didn't notice that he'd awoken and was now watching her watch him.

"What's up?" he asked.

"Oh. Good morning. Nothing."

"Och, don't make me ask you again."

"How long are you over for this time?"

"You asked me that last night."

"Did I?" she yawned. "Remind me then, what was the answer?"

"The answer was, just a few days, probably flying back on Thursday."

"Oh," she sighed and lay back. Try as she might to pretend the short durations of their meetings didn't bother her, they always did when the next morning arrived.

"However," he reached out and tucked a strand of long dark hair behind her ear, "between you and me, it's looking like I'll be back in a couple of weeks. Probably for quite a wee while."

"Oh really?" She rose on one elbow. "Why's that?"

"Och, Frankfurt just want to keep a better eye on Dublin, or so I hear. But then you know how these things can change so say nothing."

"Jeremy, have I ever mentioned anything you've ever said to me, to anyone?"

"Aye, I know, I know." He patted her shoulder and lay back. "It's just all getting a bit complicated. I'm not sure who has the most headless chickens in their org structures these days – Germany or Ireland. It's such a fucking mess."

"How?"

"Oh look, it doesn't matter. Let's just focus on the positive that I'll be around more."

"Yes," she said and then, before really thinking added, "You know, that'll be weird."

"Well, it won't be any weirder than the way we are now." He smiled as he spoke.

"Well, it will because we'll be working in the same building and then seeing each other a lot more at night time."

"Well, not necessarily."

She looked at him, her eyes narrowing slightly.

"What do you mean?"

"Oh come on, Mary, I'm not sure either of us would benefit from starting to live in one another's pockets, do you?"

"I didn't mention anything about living in each other's pockets, Jeremy, but I don't think it's that 'out there' to suggest that if you are based in Dublin that we would see a lot more of each other."

"Mary, I'm over here to sort out a mess – I'm going to be busy."

"I think you're forgetting, Jeremy, that I tend to be fairly busy myself."

"I know that," he sighed, "I suppose I just mean we'll have to be discreet, you know, more than normal."

"Discreet?"

"Oh come on, you know what I mean. The last thing I need is Head Office thinking my mind is not on the job and that instead I'm screwing one of the people I'm meant to be monitoring!"

Mary sat up in bed.

"Jesus, Jeremy, relax! All I said was that we'd probably be seeing more of each other – I didn't suggest that we announce our relationship to the Board. Get over yourself!"

She flung back the duvet and stomped to the ensuite, slamming the door behind her.

But as the hot jets of water rained down on her, she wasn't sure who she was more angry with: Jeremy or herself. What the hell was wrong with her? She didn't want all her free time tied up with someone else either so what was the big fuss about? What was with all this boat-rocking these days? If she didn't watch herself she'd have neither a job nor a boyfriend.

It was Toni's fault, putting ideas in her head.

Ideas that she'd no interest in.

Sighing, she started to rinse the shampoo from her hair and thought carefully about how she was going to undo the damage she'd just done.

Chapter 32

LEONA

Leona had left her house slightly earlier than usual. She'd wanted to be in well before anyone else and knew that if she was, the unusual occasion of her leaving early yesterday would be quickly forgotten. There was a lot about yesterday she wanted forgotten, she thought as she pulled into the garage on the Malahide Road, and a good coffee and painkillers were going to help kick-start that process right now.

As she drove towards the city she tried to compose her thoughts and focus on what the day ahead might hold for her. As the painkillers started to do their job, she could feel herself relax. By the time she reached her parking spot she felt calm and collected and ready to work but, just as she clicked the door-lock on her key, her mobile rang in her pocket. She looked down at the unfamiliar number and pressed answer.

"I just think the reports are pathetic." Leona looked at the printouts Mary had just handed her, shaking her head in disgust.

"I agree," said Mary. "I mean, this is the fourth time we've gone back to them and they still can't supply us with a proper spend report."

"We may as well stick to the old system if this is the best they can do!"

"I wish we could. This bloody changeover has already been more trouble than it's worth."

Leona looked at Mary and wondered if the slightly pale, pinched look on her face was really as a result of her concerns about the new system or if there was something else. Either way, she was happy enough that Mary had something on her mind as it meant she wouldn't be worrying too much about the shadows under Leona's own eyes.

"Look, Mary, I'm going to leave this with you. What time is it now?" She looked at her watch. "Wait till nine o'clock and then would you liaise with Frank in OPI and see if this is the best they can come up with? Tell him you're concerned that this spend report is just not adequate and that at the very least you'd like them to be able to run it by department and be able to extract the figures in whatever grouping we need."

"Yes, I'll look after that."

"Thank you, and Mary, I really appreciate that I can leave this with you. I know I can rely on you."

Mary blushed as she got up to leave.

Then Leona remembered the phone call from earlier. "Oh, I nearly forgot – Kate phoned, one of the kids spent the night puking so she won't be in until eleven – her mother-in-law is taking over then or something – but could you just process that payment run she was hoping to do and then she'll get it all signed when she comes in?"

For a second she thought Mary couldn't have heard her properly as she simply stood there, mouth open, whilst her face went from a pleasant blushed hue to a curious shade of puce.

"Well, isn't that just fucking fantastic!" Mary spat eventually.

"I beg your pardon?" Now Leona wondered was *she* hearing correctly.

"Less than twenty-four hours since she lined herself up for the job and she's become Olivia Mark Two already? Well, I am telling you right now that I am not going through this shit again."

"Mary!" Leona exclaimed in shock. "I'm going to have to ask you to calm down – and then, when you've calmed yourself, could you please tell me what on earth you're talking about?"

"*Ha!*" Mary flung her hands in the air, looking slightly deranged. "I had a feeling you didn't know. Some things round here never change, do they?"

"Know what? What things?" Leona was now looking at Mary in

confusion. What in God's name was she talking about?

"Declan told Kate yesterday that he'd give her Olivia's job. She's only in the place a wet week and gets offered a position that a loyal hardworking member of staff who's been here nearly ten years was refused."

"He *what*?"

"Oh yes," she sneered. "And then, to top it all off, the very next goddamn morning she pulls the sick-child card. Where's the justice in that, eh? I'm telling you now, Leona, I won't be standing for this shit again. I spent the last five years being a mug and it's just not happening again."

Leona sat looking at Mary in total shock.

Declan had offered Kate Olivia's job. She'd only been out of the building for two hours. What in God's name was he thinking?

But, more urgently, how was she going to calm this raging lunatic in front of her down?

"Mary," she started calmly, "I can see why you're upset. But I can guarantee you that I knew nothing of this. And I have been so busy I never even got around to discussing the fact that you showed any interest in the role with Declan, so it's not that he's chosen her over you." She stopped. "I don't even know why I'm defending him – I'm sorry, Mary, I should be talking to him. This is just –" she tried to pick her words carefully but all she could do was repeat, "I should be talking to him."

"Well, talk away, but I'm not putting up with it, I tell you I'm not."

"Now, Mary, I'm afraid you will have to cover for her this morning." Volatile and all as Mary seemed to be, Leona needed to call some order on this meeting and she couldn't have anyone, mad or not, dictating to her what they would or wouldn't do. "It won't take you long to print off that run and just leave it on Kate's desk. I'll make sure she looks after the rest of it."

Mary flung her eyes up to heaven and flounced out of the room.

Jesus fucking Christ, what was she going to do? Reaching for two more painkillers, Leona dialled Declan's extension.

"We need to talk. Now."

ROB

What killed me most was the feeling that I'd made things worse for her. That wasn't the plan. Okay, I didn't have a plan, but it was never my intention to make things worse.

And knowing that I had made me feel sick. And, well, I just couldn't leave it at that.

Look, maybe that was my excuse but by now she was all I could think of.

I just wanted to put everything right.

I just wanted to make her laugh.

Extract from interview with Robert Kinirons
Recorded 12 November 2011
4.30pm

Chapter 33

GAVIN

Gavin often thought about what he'd miss the least if he went back to work – *when* he went back to work. And really, hanging up the washing had got to be one of those things. Especially on a rainy day like this, when every single tiny pink knickers and a multitude of socks had to be hung individually on a series of clothes horses on their grandiose balcony.

Because putting loads in the tumble dryer cost money.

And you aren't earning any.

Okay, so she'd never actually said that second bit, but she didn't need to. It was implied in every single conversation they ever had these days. Which was why he was so surprised at her responding to him at all last night.

He'd been completely chancing his arm. Things in 'that department' had been pretty non-existent for the last while but just something about her when she'd come home last night had reminded him of the old Leona.

Back when she was nice.

Back when she didn't think he was a completely useless arsehole.

Back when she was the Leona he'd met and fallen in love with, not the woman he lived with now. It was hard to remember that far back, hard to remember that very first night. Because so much had changed since then. She wasn't the same girl, and he was quite sure that he was a long way from the same man.

He always said he'd fallen in love with Leona the very first second he'd laid eyes on her. That always sounded far more romantic than the reality. The reality was that he saw Leona from across a room and decided there and then that she would be his. The exact same way he decided the Lexus would be his, the Rolex watch he still wore would be his and that white elephant of a TV would be his. That was how he rolled back then: he wanted something and he got it.

They'd met a party. It was one of those situations where really it might not have happened at all. She was there with a girlfriend who in turn was drunkenly chasing someone else, and he was only there as he'd heard a business contact that *he'd* been chasing was possibly going to be in attendance.

Held in a luxurious, split-level penthouse apartment on Aston Quay, it was a typical party of its time. Teeming with movers and shakers. He wasn't even sure who the host was. But he didn't seem to be alone in that – the champagne was flowing and no one he spoke to seemed to know, or even care, who was paying for it. He tried his usual 'work the room' game but it was hard. Everyone was very drunk and that, coupled with the music ringing in his ears, made him wonder if he should just head on to somewhere quieter. When the embarrassing grinding to 'Golddigger' started he decided he would have one more drink and then leave. Going to the bucket of ice in the corner he took another bottle of beer and started to look for the colleague he'd come with.

But absurd and all as it sounded, this being a city-centre apartment, not a twelve-bedroomed mansion in Cavan, Ben, his colleague, seemed to have disappeared. He was almost at the top of the stairs leading to the upper level when he saw her there. She was standing with a group of men who all seemed to be watching a boxing match that was projected onto the giant white double-height wall. Slim with a cloud of black hair and the smokiest feline-like eyes he'd ever seen, he thought for a moment she was one of the Corr sisters – but no, at second glance she didn't look Irish at all. She had the sharpest cheekbones and her perfectly formed mouth was pursed in a sullen pout. Her eyes were ringed in kohl and the eyes themselves that were watching the fight intently were a dark grey or green.

She was beautiful and, better again, she was standing there on her own.

A lesser man might have made enquiries, thought about maybe approaching her later but not Gavin. Gavin had no reservations whatsoever about bounding up the last few steps and going to her side.

"You seem to be on your own?" He got straight to the point.

She looked around. "I seem to be on my own at the moment, alright."

She was definitely Irish, he decided – he would find out later that her grandmother was French but she herself had moved from Sligo fairly recently which explained the soft accent that at the time he couldn't place.

"Have you been abandoned?"

"It would appear so." A blush rose on her porcelain-white cheeks.

"Who did you come with?"

"My friend. I think she's doing coke with some boy in the toilet."

He looked at her, slightly shocked at the matter-of-fact way that she'd relayed this piece of information to him.

"Don't you mind?"

She shrugged. "I don't want to do coke in the toilet, so it's fine. I wanted to see this match anyway."

He looked at the screen.

"Who's fighting?"

"It's that new guy, Bernard Dunne. He's won all his fourteen matches in America, now he's home. This is some kind of title fight."

"You don't strike me as the boxing-fan type?"

She shrugged again. "I'm not usually but he's easy to watch."

He looked at the screen and could see what she meant. It was only the second round and the wiry Irishman's opponent's legs were already visibly shaking. Round and round the two of them went and, more than anything, it was the glint of determination he noticed most about the Irish boxer. Then, as they watched, Dunne landed a right hook square on his opponent's chin and instantly the Englishman's legs buckled. Dunne followed it up with a left then a right and then the referee had to intervene.

"It's all over now," she said, folding her arms.

"Yes, you were right. He's very impressive."

"And so confident. I think that's what I like the most about him."

"That's how you like your men then?" He turned up the volume of his flirting. "Confident?"

She smiled shyly, but at the same time looked at him with a glint in her green eyes. "Yes. But preferably taller."

He looked at her and she looked back and that was it: he knew his mission was accomplished.

"Come on," he said. "Your friend can find her own way home."

The memory of that evening still made him smile. Even if here he was, some eight years later, on a balcony hanging up socks on a clothes airer. He looked at his watch: today was the 15th of October – last night was their anniversary – well, the anniversary of that very meeting.

How apt.

He thought of how she'd been last night. How she'd responded to his touch, the arch of her back and the curve of her neck as he'd kissed her. The way she'd turned around then and melted into his arms. He'd expected rejection but it was like the last two years had never happened. Maybe this could be a new start for them? She obviously still loved him in some way. Maybe last night was all they'd needed?

He wondered what time she'd be home tonight. Tonight he would be waiting for her, he'd have dinner made and Rachel in bed.

He smiled again and reached for another sock.

Chapter 34

LEONA

"Declan, we need to speak."

All four heads in the room shot up but Leona didn't care.

"Can't it wait?" Declan looked up from the report he'd been going over with Cian and Rob.

"I've been waiting all day, Declan, and either you've been in meetings or I've been in meetings and now it's getting late and, as I'd like to go home at some stage today, no, it actually can't wait any longer."

"Well, Leona, technically I'm still in a meeting."

"I need to speak to you, today."

"Well, Rob was just about to –"

"I can come back," Rob interrupted quickly. "I'll pop back in to you later. I – we – we've all enough to be going on with here."

He shot a warning glance at Cian who took the hint and started to gather up their papers.

"So what's the problem?" Declan asked but Leona pointedly kept her lips closed until the others had left the room.

"What's the problem?" she said then. "The problem? What in God's name did you think you were doing offering that job to Kate?"

"Oh that!" He all but heaved a sigh of relief before continuing, "I didn't exactly offer it to her. I simply said that she should throw her hat in the ring when the time comes."

"Well, you'd no business doing that!"

"With all due respect, Leona, I think you might need to –"

"With all due respect, Declan, I've just spent the best part of a year trying to get to the point where I could fill this position with a suitable candidate and now you go and muddy the waters by suggesting it to someone who is, yet again, not suitable."

"Well, what's so unsuitable about her? She did a perfectly good job for me here yesterday."

"She handed you a few reports, Declan. Given the right access to the system, bloody Jacinta could have done the same thing."

"Well, now I doubt –"

"Oh for God's sake – what is wrong with you people? We need someone in that job with drive, ambition and a kind of dedication that that role has never been given. We do not need another L-driver that I need to spend my life supervising and picking up the slack for!"

Declan looked at her. "So what you're really saying is that this is about you?"

"It's about the bank primarily, but yes, there's a bit that's about me," Leona answered.

"Well, what you don't seem to understand is that it's you I'm really thinking of!"

Leona looked at Declan suspiciously.

"You're thinking of me? What on earth are you talking about now?"

"Leona, I don't think you realise how perilous the situation is here in the bank. Do you think Jeremy is over here for the good of his health? They are worried about us, and them being worried about *us* worries *me*. Frankfurt are coming under a lot of pressure to move out of the IFSC, and you know that. For the last year the Germans have been conducting a wholesale clean-up of their banks – Merkel is insisting on it – and do you realise that they call us, the IFSC, the 'Liechtenstein on the Liffey'? This whole bloody country is a laughing stock and they really don't want to be part of it."

"But DKB has never done anything corrupt! We're as straight as a die."

"We're straight from an Irish perspective, yes, but you're talking about a country in which the hardest banking job is the one where you're responsible for trying to persuade people to take up a credit card. Hardly an Irish problem."

"But, Declan, that's ridiculous – the Germans are up to their neck in banking difficulties too – sure they were as heavily dependent on the US as any of us?"

"Leona, you know as well as I do that that will never come to light. It will all be kept under some big carpet somewhere until some kind of deal can be done with the IMF and their tax payers will pay for it over decades. Not for them the public humiliation that Ireland had to go through – they just don't do that kind of thing. They don't do scandal. They are known as the financial bedrock of Europe and they will do anything to uphold that reputation."

"I still don't understand what any of this has to do with me?"

"We need to be seen to be in control here. And right now we have a staffing gap that we don't seem capable of filling. I know exactly what will happen if that gap remains – it'll be filled by Frankfurt and instead of nice malleable Kate we'll get some stony-faced Hans or Jurgen who'll see into all our systems, have an input into every single report and result that we send to Head Office, and I for one do not want that. Having them fill the role, I'm telling you, will become a way worse problem for us. I'm not saying give her the bloody job, but let's just try and look like our ducks are all in a row and the situation is firmly under control. We don't need their scrutiny – *you* don't need their scrutiny – do you hear what I'm saying?"

"So I let her think she's getting the job and then don't give it to her?" Leona could feel her headache coming back. "That's going to go down like the proverbial lead balloon."

"Lots of people go for jobs and don't get them, Leona – she's only here a few weeks – surely she won't be all that surprised?"

"It's going to cause murder in there, Declan. I hadn't told you as I didn't think it was going to be an issue, but Mary already asked for a transfer to Strategy and now she's going bloody mental that Kate is being considered and not her."

"Well, won't she be delighted then when Kate doesn't get it? See? Win-win."

Leona looked at him in disbelief. "Easy knowing it's not you that has to clean up the messes after the cat-fights in here, Declan."

"Well, now the last one was hardly my fault, was it?"

"Are you saying it was mine?"

"What I'm saying is that neither of us need any more negative publicity, Leona, and whatever you need to do to sort that out is fine by me. Just like the last time."

Leona could think of nothing else to say to that. She was beaten and he knew it.

As she left the office she felt even smaller than she had when she went in. Who'd have thought, after everything she did, that her position was in that much danger? She'd risked everything for this job for the last few years, she'd had to risk everything, and all because Gavin had risked everything and lost.

Well, fuck them all.

She went back to her office and sat down.

Before she had time to think about what she should pick next from her list, there was a ping to say she'd got an email.

Sender: RKinirons@DKB.com
To: LBlake@DKB.com

I am unsure as to whether or not my ban from your office still stands, so I am enquiring virtually as to whether you need anything this evening. I have just completed those figures for Declan but he appears to be gone home.

Sender: LBlake@DKB.com
To: RKinirons@DKB.com

The ban still stands. And the only thing I need right now is a drink so off you go and I'll see you tomorrow.

She pressed send but then found herself watching to see what his reply would be. But there was nothing. She waited and waited and finally had to face facts. He was gone home. Home, where she should be. She sighed and minimised her email to see the screen behind it.

Then there was a noise at her door and it swung open.

"Right, are you ready?" came a voice from outside it.

It was Rob. She couldn't see him, but it was him.

"I'm sorry? Ready for what?"

"For that drink. Come on, there's nothing can't wait till tomorrow."

"And pray tell, how exactly would you know that?"

"No cheek. Come on, I'm in a hurry."

"Oh. Well, okay then."

She reached under the table, grabbed her bag and switched off her monitor. He was right. Everything else could wait until tomorrow.

OLIVIA

Where was I? Oh yes, I went back to work in June of that year and, to be honest, it was a nightmare. Max still wasn't sleeping at night and used to howl the house down. Of course it helped that I now knew the reason for all this crying, but knowing what it was and trying to keep it at bay were two completely different things. I absolutely hated leaving him with my mother who, in turn, did not hide the fact that she hated having him in equal measure. I knew that despite his diagnosis she still felt that I was mollycoddling him and that the whole thing was more of a reflection on my parenting than an actual illness. And there was definitely no one in the bank that really understood. I'd have thought Leona would have had some sympathy given that she had her own child but she seemed distracted and, to be honest, was a lot more unfriendly than before I'd left. As for Mary, she might have thought she was doing it behind my back but I knew she was rolling her eyes every time I mentioned one of the kids. So I tried not to, but it wasn't easy, you know?

So as best I could I tried to put my head down and do my work, but it meant that some things went under my radar – I mean, I couldn't be taking on the whole bloody world's troubles, could I? On three hours sleep a night? Which is why I think that I never really saw it all coming – the whole crash thing – despite the warnings. Danny did, of course – he was on morning, noon and night about sub-prime problems in the States and how it was only a matter of

214

time but, to be honest, I had to tell him to stop. That I had bigger things on my mind besides whatever woes the American banks were facing.

When McCreevy announced the SSIAs as part of the 2001 budget, Danny became like a man possessed. As soon as it started we both put in the full amount every month and he'd watch interest rates nearly on a daily basis. He had a spreadsheet and at the start I thought it was funny, that really he should have been working in a bank himself, but eventually I had to tell him to put it away. Honestly, I'd enough of that kind of thing in work. Anyhow, fair play to him, when the whole thing finished in early 2007 we ended up with quite a lot of money but sure he'd another spreadsheet for that. Half of it we spent putting a small extension on our little house, just enough to make the kitchen bigger and a bit of a decking and that, and then the rest he wanted to invest in some kind of savings account. Jesus, if he didn't drive me mad altogether about that. But sure at that stage I was in the middle of puke and tears with Max and I wasn't long telling him to get himself off to boards.ie where he usually got all his advice and stop annoying me about it. So he did and I never asked him any more about it.

So when he phoned me that Friday morning in September, it took me a few minutes to figure out what he was roaring about. Danny would never phone me in work, well, he'd usually be in work himself and they're not allowed use their phones on the factory floor, so when I saw his number coming up, the first thing I thought of was Max. That something was after happening to him – or worse still after happening to my mother and Max because why else would it be Danny on the phone to me and not her? Max had put in a particularly bad night the night before – we were introducing solids, you see, in the hope they would agree with him better than the milk but things had gone from bad to worse. They weren't agreeing with him and to be honest I was at the end of my tether with the whole thing.

"Danny, what is it? Slow down and tell me? Is it Max?" I roared down the phone, not caring who in the huge open-plan office could hear me.

"I am telling you – it's the money – I have to go and get our money!" He sounded like a man demented.

"What money? What in God's name are you on about?" I asked, momentarily relieved that at least my mother wasn't run over by a truck and the baby with her.

"The fucking money, Olivia!" he roared again. "The Northern Rock money! I can't get through on the phone and the fucking website is down! I have to go there!"

"Danny, you're going to have to calm down. I have no idea what you're on about."

"Of course you don't, because you didn't want to know, did you? All those times I tried to talk to you about whether to put it in there or in the post office and you didn't want to know. Well, now it's all gone. Those fuckers, those careless, lying, con-artist banking bastards!"

"What do you mean it's all gone?" My original calm on ascertaining this had nothing to do with Max was swiftly starting to fade.

"Jesus Christ, Olivia, do you work in a bank at all? Northern Rock is about to go under, everyone's queueing on Harcourt Street to try and get their money out – but it's not looking good – how do you not know any of this?"

I felt like screaming at him, 'Because I got two hours' sleep last night and to be honest am too busy trying to concentrate on not making any mistakes here!' But needless to say, I didn't.

"Danny, we're busy here – we don't have radios, you know!" I found myself making excuses instead.

"Oh yeah, right. They just don't want you to know. They're all in cahoots. I've seen this coming for months. How did I not just pick the post office?"

Eventually I got him off the phone. I went into Leona's office and herself and Declan were both engrossed in a news bulletin on the small flat screen there.

There were no prizes for guessing what they were watching and seeing the reality of the situation as it played out on the screen was actually frightening. People were literally queueing round the block in Harcourt Street, angrily shouting that they wanted their money back.

"This is insane," Declan was muttering. "All those fucking morons are going to cause a complete panic."

"Still though, there's 2.4bn of Irish money in there?" asked Leona.

"Yes, but they're covered under the Deposit Protection Scheme."

"But is that not just the UK?"

"No, sure Kavanagh has said the Irish funds are covered. Haven't they assets of 130 billion? It's all nonsense, I'm telling you, scaremongering of the highest order. Frankfurt are going to have a fucking fit."

"Our money is there," I said. *"Danny is on his way there."*

Declan looked at me.

"Oh. Right," he said, *not having the good grace to even look embarrassed. "It will all be fine, they're not going to let it go under like that. Tell him not to bother."*

"I don't think he'd listen. It's everything we have – he's been saving for years." For *an awful moment I thought I was going to burst into tears.*

"Olivia," Leona interrupted, *"try not to worry. I'm sure it will all be sorted out shortly. Now go and get yourself a cup of tea, or –"* she looked at her watch, *"maybe go on your lunch."*

I went to make some tea.

Three hours later Danny still hadn't reached the top of the queue. And sure I got no work done fielding phone call after phone call to try and calm him down. I even tried telling him what I'd overheard between Declan and Leona but that had sent him into overdrive altogether.

"You want me to believe a banker, about lies from another shower of bankers? Are you for real, Olivia?"

Pointing out that technically I was also a banker would have just propelled him into orbit altogether so I didn't bother. The situation was bad enough as it was.

However, that situation got worse anyway when at three thirty it became apparent that he was going to be there for at least another few hours.

Which meant he wasn't going to be able to collect the kids. When I tentatively asked him what his plans in this regard were, he nearly lost his reason.

"Olivia – every penny we own is in this kip – and you want me to go to your ma's? Are you for real?" he screeched.

"Danny, for starters, stop asking me am I for real, and secondly she's had them all day – she'll be going nuts."

"Well then, you go get them. I'm kind of busy here!"

I thought about picking up the phone to my mother, I really did. But I knew that all I'd hear was Max crying in the background. I never rang her anymore for that exact reason. I just texted instead. The first time I'd heard him roaring over the phone, in my mind I could see his little back arching and the agony and terror on his little face and I'd cried for the whole rest of the day. He was due a solids feed at five thirty and I just didn't want her doing it. I wanted him at home, where he should be.

I went into Leona's office.

"I need to go home," I said.

"Why? Are you not well?"

I think she'd forgotten all about Danny at that stage.

"No, but I need to collect the boys. Danny is still in Harcourt Street. He says he's not going home until he has every last penny of our money out of that place."

"But it's only four o'clock, Olivia, and Frankfurt want a conference call with us at five thirty. They want to know that everything here is okay. They'll need to speak to you."

"Can't Mary do it?" I asked. And I didn't feel bad about asking that – sure Mary was always still there at six, she'd be only too delighted to be in on a call to Germany.

"Olivia, you really should be here for this. It's part of your job."

"I have to go, Leona, I'm sorry. I've never asked to go early before, but I'm asking today."

And I knew right there and then that something changed between us. I knew that she was disappointed, that I was letting her down. But I also knew that up in my ma's house in Coolock was a little baby screeching for his mother and it was a no-brainer.

So I went home.

Later that evening Danny rang to say that he'd got our money out and that he was stopping off for a quick pint on his way home to destress. I was kind of hoping he'd be home in time to get us a few bags of chips for the tea, but sure with the day he had he was right really. Bless.

Chapter 35

LEONA

The evening was well drawn in by the time they went downstairs and out the front door. The security man looked up briefly from his station but Leona just called over one shoulder "We'll be back!" and kept walking.

"You even feel you need to tell *him* what you're doing?"

"It's the right thing to do. What if – actually I don't know what if – but I guess he needs to know."

"Do you always do the right thing?"

"Hardly. I've just left a mountain of work on my desk and instead I'm heading out the front door with you in search of an alcoholic beverage."

She looked so rueful that Rob smiled.

"Good woman. It'll be the making of you. Now where did you have in mind to acquire this beverage?"

She shrugged. "If I'd put that much thought into it I'd have talked my way out of it."

"True that. Sometimes it's better not to think."

And with that his arm brushed slightly off hers and she jumped as a shock of electricity ran up her arm. She sprang back from his touch.

"Jesus Christ, Rob!"

"What?" He looked at her, confused.

"Nothing, sorry." Her hand rubbed her arm where only seconds earlier his arm had brushed hers.

He turned and started to walk again but she didn't move.

"Rob, I think I should go back."

He stopped, and without turning said, "Please don't."

"I think I should." Her voice was quiet, almost sad. "I think I need to do the right thing here."

He turned now and started to walk back the few steps towards her.

"It's just a drink, Leona."

"I should be at home."

"But you wouldn't have been though, would you? You'd have been up at that desk, just looking for things to do."

"That's a terrible thing to say."

"But it's true. I've seen you."

She looked down.

"So yes, you probably should be at home. You probably should have gone home two hours ago but you didn't. You were going to stay up there until after ten o'clock like you always do. Well, it's just eight o'clock now. We'll go for one drink and you'll still be at home earlier than you would normally be."

She still looked down, knowing exactly what she should do but not able to say the words.

"Do you know what, Leona, sometimes there's more than one right thing to do. There's the right thing to do for you, and the right thing to do for others. And it's hard to choose, I get that, trust me I get it. My whole family think I'm the most selfish bastard in Ireland right now because their version of the right thing is different to mine."

He was standing right in front of her now, and gently took both her hands in his.

"That place is killing you. I know it is, and you know it is. And I don't know why you're letting it. You say you've no choice but we always have a choice. Let's go for a drink, have a bit of a laugh and in a short while you can go home and go right back to putting everyone and everything else first except you."

She looked up at him now and at the kindness in his eyes and she felt herself falter.

"But for the next two hours just choose you, Leona. That's all I'm asking. Choose you."

"You make it sound so simple."

"It is that simple."

She sighed. She knew this was wrong. Every vestige of her being was telling her to go back into the building but yet she found herself nodding.

"Okay," she whispered, "let's go, but I'm having a coke and I'm going home in one hour."

Chapter 36

GAVIN

"I absolutely cannot believe you talked me into this!" Gavin pulled the high-viz bib over his head. He took a furtive look towards the entrance of the shopping centre in the hope that he wouldn't see anyone he knew. Luckily it all seemed quiet enough but that was scant comfort really.

"Oh relax, will ya?" Trish tried not to laugh at the sight of his thunderous face vanishing under the gaudy fabric. "It's only for two hours, the kids are at school, and sure what else would ya be doing?"

"Jesus Christ," he said in mock horror, "if a man said that to a woman he'd be shot – I've loads I could be doing thanks. What do you think? I sit on my arse all day every day?" He shuddered then before adding, "Christ, I'm starting to sound like my mother!"

"Are you trying to tell me you don't sit on it sometimes?" Trish smiled and not for the first time he found himself thinking how pretty she was.

"And do what exactly? Have you any idea what kind of shite is on the TV during the day? I'd go out of my mind watching it."

"Oh for Jesus' sake!" She threw her hands up in the air. "Do you ever do anything but *moan*?"

"*Whatever!*"

"Do you know what, you're like a big sulky child! And, believe me, I know all there is to know about sulky children."

"Are you quite finished? I believe we have a job to do here?" He

222

pulled at the hem of his vest.

"Ooooh, get *you*! *'I believe we have a job to do here'*," she mimicked and he had to laugh.

Even though this morning laughing really was the last thing he felt like doing.

"Oh, you two know each other then? How lovely!"

They both jumped as their giggle was interrupted by Caitríona Hannigan, Bag Pack Liaison Officer of St Wolstan's PTA.

Her official title.

"Oh. Only sort of," stuttered Gavin, completely intimidated by the bespectacled woman wielding a clipboard in one hand and two collecting buckets in the other.

"Just from the playground," added Trish helpfully.

"I see," Caitriona said a little too brightly. "Well, thank you both for coming – it's great to get people to fill these morning slots when so many of the parents are at work."

Gavin could see Trish try to catch his eye and so avoided her glance.

But Caitriona, Bag Pack Liaison Officer, wasn't finished.

"And especially great to see a dad take part – well done, Dad!"

You patronising wagon ...

"Relax for the love of God, would you?" Trish hissed in his ear as, after taking a bucket each, they followed Caitriona towards the row of check-outs, "You look like you want to stab someone."

"No," Gavin snapped, "I look exactly like someone who'd rather be gnawing off their own leg than doing what they're doing. And there's a very good reason for that – I've never packed someone else's shopping bags in my life – actually, if I can at all avoid packing my own shopping bags, I do. I think I'll just go home." He stopped and put down his bucket and started to rip open the Velcro fastener of his vest.

"And leave me here with Attila the Hun? You will in your arse!" Trish picked up his bucket and shoved it back into his arms, "Now stop your complaining – the feckin' two hours are nearly up already and we haven't even started yet."

Gavin followed her grudgingly and let Attila set him up at a checkout next door. He was in an absolutely foul mood and he knew he was coming across as childish, a bit of an arsehole, but he didn't care. Leona had been gone when he woke this morning, which had annoyed him even more. Given the mood she'd come home in last night, the very least she could have done was have the good grace to apologise this morning..

Yes, it was the very least she could do after her humiliating coldness last night. And after he'd planned the evening as a celebration of the night they'd met? The irony ...

"Ehm, could you *not* put the washing powder in with the bread?"

He looked up to where the voice was coming from. It was a little round woman with a very earnest look on her face.

"What?"

"The bread. It'll get smelly." The lady looked like she was trying really hard to be nice given that he was just a 'poor man' and sure what would they know, but at the same time her hand was hovering protectively over her bread as if terrified that it was about to get shoehorned into a bag with her rather large box of Daz Ultra.

"Oh. Right. Sorry."

Gavin looked from the bread he had in one hand to the bag with the washing powder he was holding in the other.

"I tell you what, if you want to stick all the fruit and veg into that big bag," the lady suggested, clearly trying her absolute hardest not to shout 'Back away from my goddamn shopping, you absolute ignoramus!', "I'll do the other few bits – I've a bit of a system – painful, I know!" She gave a kind of self-deprecating grimace, as if to say 'Honestly, this is all me'.

"Oh, okay. Yes, I can manage that, I guess."

A *system*? Who had a fucking system to packing their groceries? He wondered did Leona have a system. He doubted it. Anyhow, he didn't even want to think about her. He started to load the bag.

"Oh – ehm," came the voice over his head again, "actually, would you mind not putting the tomatoes on the bottom?"

For *fuck's* sake.

An hour later he'd settled into a system of his own. Wait for the customer to approach the checkout, step forward and helpfully ask, 'Would you like a hand with your bags?' If the answer was yes, step forward another step and try and not mess it up. If the answer is a no – and, man, there were a lot of people who just did not want him near their stuff – then he'd instantly take a step back and try not to let them see him heaving a massive sigh of relief.

What he did find was that as the time ticked on he was developing quite an obsession with looking at what everyone else had in their trolleys. Even now, months after this whole debacle had started, he still wasn't into the big weekly shop. Instead he did a bit of a shop here and another bit there and if he ran out of anything he went to the Centra up at the roundabout. Once he stayed within budget then no one (i.e. Leona the Financial Controller), said anything. But these people? Were they shopping to stock bunkers or what? Trolleys full of cakes, biscuits, and yoghurts – what kind of family got through 12 multi-packs of Müller yoghurt in one week? He actually nearly smiled at one point when after helping lift seven bottles of wine into one lady's trolley along with two fillet steaks, an organic chicken and four packets of Serrano ham he found himself muttering to himself, "Ah, no recession in this house, I see."

It was also slightly scary just how much crap people were buying. Just as he helped load 9 cartons of psychedelic orange juice into that same trolley, there was a tap on his shoulder.

"Gavin? Oh gosh, it *is* you!"

He froze, half recognising the voice but hoping against hope he was wrong. But there was nothing for it but to turn. He looked at the owner of the posh trolley.

"Vivienne? Ehm, wow – I was thinking I knew your voice."

"Oh my gosh, Gav, this is so funny – what on earth are you doing?"

If there was a Michelin Star type award for Passive-Aggressive Bitches, Vivienne Hewson would win it every year hands down. Married to Doug Hewson, they were part of a circle Gavin and Leona had once socialised in. Doug was the business partner of Geoffrey, one of their neighbours, and they'd clashed over dinner and at the legendary Christmas drinks parties on many occasions.

"I'm collecting for the school actually."

"Collecting for the school? Bartley College doesn't do collections, does it? Ohhh!" Her hand flew to her lips as her eyes flew open. "I totally forgot. You moved schools, didn't you? Oh wow, how embarrassed am I?"

Definitely not as embarrassed as you'd like *me* to be, guessed Gavin.

225

"Oh, no need to be embarrassed, Viv. I'm sure you've more on your mind these days than keeping up with our business."

"Oh well, I mean I heard about – well, you know – but then –" She stopped again and, putting a very well-manicured hand on his arm, said, "So how *are* you, Gavin?"

"I'm fine, Vivienne, honestly."

"Really?" She didn't look like she believed a bit of it. "Because Doug often thought about phoning you, not that there's a lot he could do, mind you, but you know, to even just offer some support."

"Honestly, there's no need." Gavin actually thought that he might vomit into his bucket so torturous was he finding this conversation. "We're absolutely fine."

"Well, he didn't feel too bad when he heard that Leona got that big job – that'll keep the wolf from the door, he said, buy them a bit of time. But then," she sighed, "I'm not sure any of us ever thought that it would take quite *this* much time ..."

Gavin had his mouth open to tell her that he'd had offers, that it wasn't his fault that it was taking *this* much time but before he could get the words out Attila was back brandishing her buckets and Vivienne had to make her excuses and leave.

Tearing off his high-viz, Gavin turned on his heel and started to stride out of the shopping centre. This was fucking it, the straw that had broken the proverbial camel's back. He just wasn't standing for this kind of shit anymore. One mistake. One mistake he'd made ...

"*Oi, wait up!*"

There was the sound of running feet behind him.

"Gavin! What the fuck is wrong with you? Wait!"

A hand grabbed his arm but he shook it away angrily.

"Leave me alone," he muttered, "I'm going home."

"Wait. Was it to do with that woman? What did she say to you?"

"It doesn't matter. I don't want to talk about it."

"Well then, don't fucking talk about it. Suit yourself, but I did fucking nothing wrong to you so don't bloody take it out on me! You think you're the only one with problems, Gavin? You're a stupid selfish prick, that's what you are! You don't know how good you have it! Well, let me tell you, you know nothing about fucking problems." Trish was clearly really trying to keep her voice down, but her anger was very apparent as she continued. "Darren's da beat me black and blue before I threw him out last October, he doesn't give me a fucking bean now and last night he rocked up to tell me that if I don't find a grand to give him then some fucker from Blanchardstown is going to kneecap him! And God forgive me, but I'm sure as fuck not giving him a grand! Even if I had it, my car insurance is up tomorrow and, to be honest, them screwing me is a much bigger problem. So you fuck off home to your big house and your rich wife and I'll just go home and figure out what to fuck I'm going to do with my problems, okay?"

She turned on her heel and stormed off and a wave of shame swept over him. He hardly knew this woman, but she'd summed him up pretty well in her angrily spat speech.

"Trish! Come back! I'm sorry."

"No, fuck off! I'm sick of you."

"Yeah? Well, I'm sick of me too. So we're quits."

She stopped walking, so he continued.

"And there's not a whole lot I know about preventing a kneecapping but if there's one thing I do know about it's insurance, so let's go grab a coffee and figure out what you can do."

OLIVIA

Things seemed to settle down a bit after that. The country was falling down around us alright, but for some reason it didn't really seem to be affecting us. It was like it was all happening to someone else. We were busier in work alright, Frankfurt had turned into a massive pain in our neck, constantly on to us for some kind of reassurance or other, and it seemed that the budgets and projections I'd been working on for years without anyone really paying them much attention, were now the be-all and end-all of everyone's working day.

Well, I did my best to keep up. But I wasn't prepared to stay there until midnight every night. My hours were nine to five, I was already coming in at eight so the latest I could stay was until six, and even at that I could only do that a couple of times a week.

It drove Danny mad that they expected me to work so many hours without getting paid for them. He didn't work a minute extra in the factory without putting in for it and he didn't see why working in the bank should be any different. In fact, he hated the banks so much by this stage he felt they should nearly be compensating us for dragging the whole country into such a mess let alone pay me for whatever work I was doing.

As 2008 rolled on, Danny's obsession with the banks grew and grew. He reckoned they were all in denial that it was just a minor slump and that their 'economic fundamentals remained sound'. He could tell you on any given day what all the share prices were and

228

when Anglo slumped to an all-time low on Patrick's weekend of that year, sure it was like his birthday. It seemed to give him some kind of strange satisfaction that while the Irish banks thought they were pulling the wool over our eyes, the global markets knew differently. Around that time Morgan Chase took over Bear Stearns and before long Danny was ranting about Fannie Mae and Freddie Mac and I really had to tell him to shut up.

And it wasn't that I was in complete denial of what was going on in the world – after all, I was the one actually working in the bank, not that you'd know that to hear Danny take ownership of the crisis. But really, and I'm aware of how stupid it sounds, I just had other things to be worrying about. There was no point in the two of us going up the wall with anxiety about something that, essentially, neither of us could do anything about.

Max was a little bit better by then. He still had the odd bout of reflux-related sickness but, thank God, he seemed to have almost come out the far side of it all. Which was just as well as work was getting more and more demanding and that whole summer went by in a haze of meetings and deadlines.

And then it was September and the financial shit really hit the fan. On 15th September – and I remember it as it was a Monday and we'd all just come in when we heard the news – the fourth biggest investment house in the world, Lehman Brothers, went under. They'd been trying to broker deals with numerous potential rescuers, including the American government, but to no avail. No one could quite believe it and it was very hard now to ignore the smug smiles of people like Danny who had said it was all coming crashing down. A week later talks started with Congress about a possible 700-billion bailout and everyone felt that if this package was agreed, the worst would be over.

There were similar problems in the UK with HBOS needing a 15-billion-pounds sterling rescue from Lloyds TSB. So obviously all this merger madness started to become the talk of Dublin too. There was a different rumour every hour at one point, though the biggest one was about Anglo and Nationwide.

Then one day my mother rang me just after lunch to tell us to put on the Liveline show on the radio. Apparently they were all going nuts about the uncertainty and wondering should they move their *savings. We listened to it in work, with Declan going nuts about all the scaremongering. I mean, everything had been getting scary for some time but this definitely brought the tension up a notch.*

Two days later Lenihan announced an increase in the state guarantee on savings to 100,000 in a bid to keep people like Danny from organising another run on the banks. But Danny said it was too little too late and that people were already moving their savings from the banks to the Post Office where the guarantee was uncapped. I couldn't help thinking that there must be more money in the country than I thought if there were that many people for whom a 100,000 euro guarantee wasn't enough.

And then on Monday 29th September, it all came to a head. Apparently in the US, the House of Representatives 700 billion bank package had been defeated and the Irish banks were terrified that this would have a knock-on effect on their own shares.

I first heard the news the next morning. I was in the bathroom when Danny started to hammer at the door. At some stage the previous night, the Government had decided to create a guarantee of all the liabilities, customer and interbank deposits and the majority of bonds, of the six major banks.

I looked at Danny howling and cursing and I just couldn't focus on what he was saying at all. I had my own news.

I'd just found out I was pregnant again.

PART THREE

The Burning Platform
 colloq. (orig. *U.S.*). ***burning platform*** : a business lexicon that emphasises the need for immediate and radical change due to dire circumstances

JACINTA

No, I will *not* stick to the point. The pressure everyone is under in here leads people to do all kinds of awful things. I've warned you all that something like this was coming. She is a good girl, a good girl that this place took and broke. In all my forty years working in this company I've never seen anyone used in such an atrocious manner only to be thrown on a scrapheap now that she is of no use to you anymore. Yes, of course what she did is wrong. Do you think she doesn't know that herself? This has severe repercussions for her too, you know. She has already been punished enough without this ridiculous witch hunt.

And I won't have any part in it, I tell you, no part at all. I'm going to tell you what she should have told you years ago, and that's to go and do your own dirty work yourselves.

Extract from interview with Jacinta Fitzmaurice
Recorded 11 November 2011
11.30am

Chapter 37

LEONA

"What the?" Leona was looking at an email that had just zinged into her inbox. She read its contents and was just about to groan when Jacinta burst into her room.

"Why did no one run that past me?"

"Good morning, Jacinta," Leona sighed. "Trust me, no one ran it past me either. Declan did mention something about marking the occasion a number of weeks ago but, no offense, I presumed he meant some kind of presentation at tea break, not a night out ..."

"Well, there is just no need for all this fuss!"

"Jacinta, his intentions are probably good. Forty years is a long time to be with the same company, and it also being your birthday ... well ..."

"Well," Jacinta sniffed, "I don't mind marking it in some way, but I think a meal out and drinks is taking it a bit far. Why could we all not just go for lunch?"

"Declan doesn't like staff lunches. He says that no one can relax because they've got to go back to work, then either no one actually does go back to work or they do and just do nothing. So it's either this or nothing, I'd imagine."

"Well, I think it's a load of rubbish. I'll be going home after the meal."

Leona laughed. "Well, as I'm quite sure I'll be going back to work after the meal then that's fine by me, Jacinta. Now, it's not for another week yet, so why don't you stop worrying and enjoy the last week of your 39th year at Deutsche Kommerzielle Bank?"

Jacinta snorted.

"Forty years and they still haven't learnt a thing," she sniffed as she left the room. "The big eejits!"

Leona smiled at her retreating back. She knew that secretly Jacinta was chuffed that Declan had decided to make such a big deal of it, but still, a night out was the last thing she herself needed. She looked at the email again and rolled her eyes. The bloody restaurant wasn't even local – it was way across town on Merrion Square, which was a lovely idea – bringing Jacinta back to where the old building was – but bloody inconsiderate for those that had to go back to do a few hours work afterwards.

But there was no point in worrying about it now. She looked at the time on her PC: 10:20. She had a meeting with Frank Newcombe, Declan and Jeremy shortly that she had to prepare for.

But hopefully that was all going to go okay. Things had calmed down a bit. Herself and Rob, with the assistance of Kate, had been working hard to bring all the Strategy work up to date, and she hoped Frank would be not be as anxious about the Department at today's meeting.

Just as she was about to stand up, there was a knock at her door. This time it was a nervous Kate that appeared with a printout in her hand.

"Declan asked me to drop these in to you – he said you'd need them for the meeting."

Leona looked at Kate and cursed Declan yet again. Kate was nice, she was reasonably good at her job, she was hardworking. Was she exactly what she needed to solve the huge problem that was the Strategy Department? No.

And it wasn't fair to lead her on like this. To have her think the job was hers. Leona had tried saying this to Declan but as far as he was concerned Kate was a sticking plaster for a wound that could wait.

"Thank you, Kate." Leona took the information from her and waited until she left the room before checking what it was. To be fair it was a computation that neither she nor Rob had had time to do last night, so yes, it was a help. She was quite impressed actually. It must have taken Kate some time to pull it all together.

She put it with the rest of her papers and reached to grab a pen to take with her.

"Leona, can I speak with you for a second?"

Mary had come into the room. There had been no knock this time.

"Mary, I'm on my way to a meeting. Is it urgent?"

"Well, yes. I have a cheque for signing."

"Oh. Well, that can wait surely?" Leona looked in annoyance at Mary, who reddened slightly.

"I suppose it can, yes."

"I'll do it the minute I come back." Leona turned to lock her computer then stopped, "Wait – why are you doing the cheques?"

"Ha. Funny you should ask that."

Leona's heart sank. Mary had that wild-eyed look on her face that meant she clearly had something to say. The cheques were Kate's job, which obviously she hadn't time to do as she'd been doing that Strategy report.

And what was now clear was that getting that cheque signed wasn't what was urgent, but rather the fact that Mary very clearly wanted Leona to know that she was doing Kate's work.

"I see." Leona knew she'd have to pick her words carefully here. "Right, well, I appreciate you taking that on this morning, Mary. I realise you were probably very busy with work of your own."

"It's happening again, Leona." Now that Mary knew that Leona realised she'd had to do yet more of Kate's work, the wild look left her eyes, but it was still very clear that she wasn't happy.

"Mary, I understand that this is not ideal, but I need you to trust me on this. It's not happening again. I won't let it – will you just trust me on that?"

"Just tell me this – is the job really hers? Because I just don't think it's fair to tell her to apply for it when I've been told not to."

"Mary, I didn't tell you not to. I just said that my plans for you were not in Strategy. And no, nothing is definite about anything at the moment. The only thing I have on my desk recruitment-wise is the allocation of the Grade 2 officers and not until all that is over will I even be thinking about anything else. Thank you again for covering today, that's all I can really say."

Mary left and Leona stood up quickly before anyone else could come in. She really had to speak to Declan before this situation put her in an early grave.

"So does that wrap us up for today?" Declan sat back, sliding his thumbs under his red braces as he spoke. "Why don't we all circle back in a few days and see if there are any changes to any of those issues?"

Frank nodded and Leona heaved a sigh of relief that yet another meeting was over.

But Jeremy put up his hand.

"Sorry – if I might just delay you all one minute?"

Leona had to stop herself from rolling her eyes. She liked Jeremy, he was very good at his job and quite pleasant, but there was no way he lacked confidence and he had a tendency to try to make her feel that the mere fact that he was a man automatically meant he was better than her.

"Of course, Jeremy! Of all people, you don't need to apologise. We love to hear from you!" Declan was petrified of Jeremy and it constantly showed in the way he gushed all over him.

"I've been speaking to Hans and they want to come over. They expect to be here for two days. What they're proposing is arriving on the afternoon of Thursday 30th October and then on Friday 31st they want to hold a Team Briefing Day – you know, touch base with everyone and reacquaint the branch with all the latest from Head Office. Make sure we're all singing from the same hymn sheet."

Leona could see the blood drain from Declan's face.

"Frankfurt? Coming here?"

"Yes," said Jeremy. "I've obviously been keeping them updated and they're actually reasonably happy with the way things are going here now. Your staff issues appear to be resolving themselves and they just feel that, with the various changes and new people coming on board, it would be nice to touch base and have a kind of Team Briefing Day. Nothing to worry about."

But Leona's heart sank as she looked at the panic on Declan's face. One thing for sure, this was all going to get worse before it got better.

OLIVIA

I'm not going to lie, it felt good to be on maternity leave again. Of course we had a third boy, Daniel Jnr, but I didn't care. I loved him so much that even when it turned out that he had the same reflux problem that Max had had, I just thought to myself 'We can get through this'.

And then when I had only a month to go, I got a letter from Geraldine, asking me how I would feel about working five days instead of four when I came back. How would I feel? I felt like saying, I don't know, and I'll never know because it's not happening. The whole tone of the letter made me feel a bit sick actually so I talked to Danny that night whose response was 'Tell that miserable shower of bastards that you'll do a five-day week for an extra twenty grand' which wasn't really all that constructive. So I rang Geraldine the next day and again she just sounded a bit funny. In the end I actually had to ask her was this really a question or an order and she just laughed nervously and said 'Just a question ... at the moment ...' So that didn't exactly help my nerves. I had a think about it over that weekend and then first thing Monday morning I contacted Geraldine to tell her I was going to take unpaid leave at the end of my official maternity leave and therefore wouldn't be back for two extra months. You could do that by then, you see, the option of taking unpaid leave had just been made law, and, I felt, it had the added advantage of indicating to them that they could take their five-day *week and stuff it wherever they wanted. Danny wasn't sure if we could afford for me to take any unpaid time off but I told him that I was not going back yet and that was that.*

It didn't solve the problem but it definitely put off the fight.

And, boy, did it end up in a fight.

Chapter 38

LEONA

"Declan, you need to relax. They're not coming to check up on us, they're coming to plan the way forward."

"I need to relax? Maybe you need to un-relax! I do not understand why you are so calm – can't you see? This is the beginning of the end. It might as well be the Troika rolling in." Declan was being most un-Declan like. He was red in the face and waving his arms around like some kind of deranged air-traffic controller.

"Well, it's not the Troika, it's Head Office – Declan, we talk to these people every week – they've been here before – we've been to them." Leona did not like the idea of them coming either but she knew she needed to calm him down or else he was going to make her next two weeks nothing but pure hell.

"It's all that Jeremy's doing – God only knows what he's doing here – do you know he's asked for an office? An office? Well, I'm telling you what I told Geraldine – she can find him one on the fifth floor because he's sure as hell not sitting on this floor listening in to everything that goes on! And what's all this rubbish about giving us two weeks' notice? Two weeks' notice? That's preposterous – how are we meant to be ready in two weeks?"

"We're not meant to be ready. We've nothing to get ready for, Declan – *they're* coming to us. *They're* giving the talk. It's not an audit or an inspection, it's a friendly visit."

"Friendly? These are fucking Germans, remember?"

"Jesus, Declan, you can't say things like that. Any dealings we've had with them up to now have been fine. They just want to protect their brand, make sure we're toeing the party line ..."

"Oh, they'll have us toeing that alright! But you're right. I need to calm down. I need to talk about something else. Give me something else to talk about ..."

"Well, if you really want something else to talk about," Leona spoke quickly, "I need to talk to you about Kate."

"Which one is Kate?" Declan looked blankly at Leona who rolled her eyes.

"Oh for God's sake, Declan, she's only the one who you've just given Olivia's job to!"

"Oh yes, actually that's all working out rather well, isn't it?" he said, looking pleased with himself.

"Well actually, Declan, no, it bloody well isn't!"

"Oh," he looked surprised, "how come?"

"How come? Well, I'll tell you how come, will I? While she's running around trying to impress you and show you how she can pull together any report ever designed, she's leaving the work she's actually being paid to do to Mary – who is getting less and less impressed as the days go by. This can't go on – we need to do something about it."

"So that's what this is about? Mary complaining? It was Mary complaining that got us into this mess, remember?"

"Now, Declan, that's not fair!"

"For crying out loud, Leona, I'll tell you what's not fair. I am doing my best to keep all our jobs here. My absolute best. And if that means putting someone's nose out of joint for a few weeks then, really, I couldn't care less. I really couldn't. It's just not something I need to be worrying about right now."

"I appreciate that, but it's still not fair, Declan. It's not fair on Mary who's doing her work, it's not fair on me because I can't set in motion what I need to fill that job and, above all, it's not fair on Kate who thinks she has it in the bag!"

"Who gives a shit about Kate? Who is she, Leona? She's only been here five minutes. She means nothing to me! As for you – I understand you have a different plan for this job – but it will just have to wait until Frankfurt have been and gone. That's only a week or two – it can surely wait that long?"

Leona looked at him and knew this battle had been lost for now. "It doesn't sound like I've much choice but to park that for now, then, does it?"

"It would really help me out if you could do that."

"Right, well then, there's one other thing." She was going to get something out of this conversation if it killed her. "The Grade 2 promotion. I want to give it to Rob Kinirons."

"Rob who? Which one is he?"

She shook her head in disbelief. Did he know who any of his fucking staff were?

"He's the hardworking one, Declan."

"Oh. Right, yes, knock yourself out there. Great stuff."

Leona relaxed slightly. At least that was something positive to come out of today, because she had an awful feeling the next two weeks were going to be very hard work.

Chapter 39

KATE

"They are just the oddest bunch of people," Kate said later that evening, fork in mid-air.

"Kate, I don't like to interrupt you mid-flow, but I feel I should remind you that it's nine thirty, and you're not even halfway through that, eh –" Michael looked down at the congealed mess of breaded fish, beans and waffles on Kate's plate, "dinner."

"Right, right, sorry." Kate absentmindedly stabbed a piece of fish and prodded it into the beans. "But seriously, Michael, I've worked in offices before, it's not like I'm a complete novice – I've seriously never met any staff with as many neuroses as this lot."

"And coming from you, my dear, that's really saying something," Michael grinned.

"Ha, ha, very funny!" Kate made a face at him before continuing, "But still, there's Jacinta – I mean she's a complete powerhouse – if I could be half as amazing as her when I'm sixty-odd then I'd be delighted – but, man, she thinks we're all back in the time of *Mad Men* or something – she seriously berated poor Alice the other day for wearing a sleeveless top. *'If I wanted to see armpits, Alice, I'd be working on a building site! Now cover up!'*" Kate tried to emulate the deep gravelly tone of Jacinta. "Poor Alice, she nearly died. But then she is an awful eejit, pretty but seriously nothing between the ears."

"Eat, Kate."

"I am, I am." She finally put the forkful of fish and beans in her

242

mouth, and gulped them down before continuing, "And then there's Mary – seriously, Michael – I just can't figure her out at all."

"You may have mentioned that alright, possibly every night since you started?"

"Well, she's like an absolute lunatic these days," Kate continued, ignoring his sarcasm. "Would you believe she waited until four o'clock to give me that reconciliation today to do, even though I know for a fact she knew it needed to be done since first thing yesterday morning."

"She hardly does that on purpose though, Kate."

"I'm telling you, she does. Aside from the fact that she seems intent on tripping me up whenever she can. She also seems to have a morbid fear of anyone getting out of that place on time and do you know what? Leona is as bad. She has a seven-year-old child but I'm pretty sure she comes into work at seven and there's no way she leaves before nine most nights, later sometimes. Sure that's madness."

"Says the girl who's now leaving the house at seven thirty and isn't back until after seven again," Michael mocked her gently.

"Look, it will all settle down. I just want to show them I can do this!"

"Of course you can do it," Michael looked down at his plate, "but I'm just sad that it's to the detriment of our health – I mean, I don't like to point it out, but this is the third time this week that we've had beans – I'm starting to forget that some vegetables don't come out of tins –"

"For the love of God, Michael, cut me a bit of slack!" Kate banged her hand down on the kitchen table. "It's only been two weeks and would it kill you to pull something together for dinner yourself?"

"Eh, there's no need to take the head off me, you know. I'm just worried that it all might be a bit much, that's all."

"Well, it's not, so you can stop worrying."

"Right, I will."

"Good," she sighed. "And I'm sorry about the goddamn dinner, but as soon as I get Jess's party over on Saturday, things will be better."

"Look, that party is another thing – do we really need to do the whole invite-everyone-from-the-village-to-the-house party? Can't we do a play centre given you'll be in work until 7pm Friday evening?"

"No, we bloody can't! Jess is dying for her party and there's been enough change around here without having to tell her that it's not happening either."

"She would be just as happy to head off to Party Central or whatever that hellhole is called – you know she would."

"Michael," Kate shot him a warning glance, "Lynn Crosby did Abigail's party last year even though she had a broken wrist and Leo was in Abu Dhabi for a month so how you think I can't cope with doing Jess's, when all we've to drum up is a few buns and a bouncy castle, is beyond me."

Michael sighed. "Right, fine, I just thought I'd throw it out there, that's all. But you might bear in mind that Lynn has three sisters who all rowed in that time – she didn't achieve all that as single-handedly as you're making out."

"Michael, we're doing the party. And then on Sunday I'll cook up a heap of stuff for the freezer so that at least you'll eat like a king next week and can stop your whinging."

"I think wondering if we could have a proper dinner at a proper time once in a while hardly constitutes whinging!"

"Well, it sounds like bloody whinging to me!" Kate snapped.

"Kate, relax, I'm just kidding. You're not to get stressed about this."

"I am not stressed, Michael, I'm fine. You're the one that's getting stressed about a few shagging fish fingers!"

"Whassa shaggin fish finger?" a little voice asked at the kitchen door.

They both spun around to see Jess standing there bleary-eyed, one little arm hooked around Jingo her toy dog.

"Jess, what are you doing up? I thought you were asleep ages ago!" Kate slid her chair back from the table, wiping her mouth with a sheet of kitchen towel as she did so.

"I was, but I was dweaming about my pawty and I wanna tell you what I was dreaming, so you'd know."

"I know all about your party, Jess, but it's not until Saturday and there'll be a bouncy castle and cake and it will be super fun. Now back up to bed, come on – I'll tuck you in." Kate took the little girl by the hand to shepherd her back up the stairs.

"*Nooo* … my *other* pawty?" The little girl wasn't for shepherding and stood firm at the kitchen door.

"What other party?"

"My Happy Hands pawty – Happy Hands Caroline said I have one on Fwiday, with my new fwiends an' you just give me stuff."

"What stuff?" Kate felt her blood run cold.

"You know, buns 'n' cake 'n' stuff." Jess looked up at Kate with big blue eyes and an expression that said: 'This is not a problem, just do it.'

"Yep, right okay," Kate sighed. "We'll talk about it in the morning."

She eventually got the almost-three-year-old back into bed and tucked her in. Within minutes she was asleep and Kate could eventually make her way back down to the remains of her meal.

Michael had finished his and was starting to clear up.

"Buns and a cake for Friday then?" he smiled. "Don't worry, I'll fly into the supermarket on the way home and get some."

"Don't bother," retorted Kate. "I'll make them when I get home tomorrow evening."

"Eh, when exactly? You won't be home until after seven – don't be ridiculous, I'll get them."

"Michael, I have never given them shop-bought buns for parties before. I'm not starting now!"

"Kate, that's just ridiculous – it's a party in a crèche – there won't even be any parents there. You are not going to start baking when you get home! You can barely eat your own dinner you're so tired – you'll make yourself sick if you don't cut yourself some slack."

Kate looked down at her dinner.

"I said I'd make them," she said quietly, "so just drop it, okay?"

And as her husband looked at her she pretended she didn't see the first flicker of concern in his eyes and instead chased the last remaining bean round her plate.

By the time Kate got on the Luas on Friday morning she was almost sorry she hadn't just let Michael buy the goddamn buns.

She'd been up until midnight and now it was seven and she was exhausted. But she knew it was her own fault. Yes, she could have just let Michael buy the goodies, but she also could have just made a dozen Rice Krispie buns and not spent two hours putting dots of popping candy in the shape of '3' on fairy cakes iced with chocolate ganache.

And deciding to make brownies to bring into work with the leftover chocolate definitely could have been omitted for the sake of her sanity.

She sighed. She was fully aware of the fact that she was her own worst enemy. The buns were not for the kids – well, obviously they were but there was no point in denying that the fact that each child would go home that evening and tell their mother that Jess O'Brien had had a party and her mammy had made her buns with popping candy '3's on top, had a lot to do with it.

Because some of those mothers were people she knew, and people that she knew had smirked when they'd heard she was going back to work.

"That'll soften her cough," they'd said as they'd shook their heads in glee. Now, she'd no actual evidence that any of them had ever said anything remotely like this but she was pretty sure she was right. Well, sure enough.

The truth was that the making of said buns was something familiar. Every other birthday she'd made buns; this one could not be any different. Making buns was something within her control and as much as she didn't want to admit it to her husband, she was really starting to feel like very little else was.

She was really struggling to get out of the office at any kind of decent time every day. Most days it was half five, once or twice it had been closer to six and there were another couple of seven o'clocks. And because of this, from three o'clock every day her heart started to thump as her brain automatically began to calculate what work was on her desk and what Mary, Leona or now Declan, was likely to hand her to do.

And then there were the meetings. Meetings were a sort of mixed blessing. She was rarely actually called into one herself which meant a few hours' peace while Leona was otherwise occupied. However, late afternoon meetings were risky. Unless you managed to escape off home before they concluded there was the very real chance that when everyone spilled out of the boardroom, you could find yourself given something to do, and usually with a very tight deadline.

Kate lived on her nerves every afternoon, there was no doubt about that, but mostly because her every day was so out of her control.

And Kate O'Brien did not like to be out of control.

But even though it might be nine thirty before she sat down to sometimes nothing more elaborate than breaded fish and mashed potatoes, it didn't quell the new-found spark in her eyes. Sitting face to face with her husband, at least she had something to talk about. They were having real live adult conversation. The fact that her colleagues were all slightly mad didn't matter – she had colleagues to discuss. The fact that she'd left three tasks uncompleted on her desk did not take away from the fact that she'd completed four other tasks and none of them were laundry. Yes, she mightn't be the boss, but she was already clawing her way up ...

She'd just have to find a way to make it work. There could be no going back.

She hugged her tub of brownies to her chest.

No, there could be no going back.

OLIVIA

From the minute I came back, it was very obvious that I wasn't wanted. I couldn't do the overtime they wanted which meant Mary had to do a lot of that after-hours work but yet all my requests that we get someone else in to help fell on deaf ears. It was so unfair. They were horrible to me. Leona picked up on every single mistake I made, roaring and shouting at me like I was some kind of thick, when in reality there were days in there where I just shouldn't have come in because I'd had maybe only two hours of sleep the night before.

So what do you do in that kind of circumstance? Do you come in and try your best or do you just not come in? In hindsight I think I should have just phoned in sick every time I felt I couldn't give a day's work my full attention but then hindsight is great really, isn't it? And to be honest, they didn't look too kindly on you not coming in either so it was hard to win.

I was doing the best I could. What I hadn't realised was that while I was on Maternity Leave a new Act had been passed called the Central Bank Reform Act 2010. If I'd known the impact it would have on my life I might have paid more attention but essentially what it meant was that the Financial Regulator had finally woken up and decided that there needed to be a better eye kept on the banks. And guess who all that fell on? Staff like me. People like me, who'd done nothing wrong in the whole stupid debacle were now working under the most awful pressure. And I know that Leona was the same – I'm not completely unfair. She wasn't asking me to do any hours that she wasn't prepared to do herself but, as Danny kept saying, that was why she was on the big bucks. At one stage I did say to him that maybe I should give in, tell them that I'd work for the five days for a few months until they got over the backlog that was rapidly building but Danny said no. He said if I gave them an inch they'd take a mile but I still couldn't help thinking that maybe my life would be easier if I just gave in.

Sometimes it's hard to keep everyone happy.

Chapter 40

KATE

"So it's all going well?" Lynn settled into her seat beside Kate in their local branch of CoffeeCo.

It was a Saturday morning and for once Lynn's husband was in the country, enabling her to escape with just one child, the cherubic Charlie, who was asleep in his buggy beside them.

"It is." Kate hesitated slightly before repeating, "It is."

"It is?" Lynn smiled.

"Look, Lynn, this is you and me. I'm not going to lie. It's not easy and if this promotion comes through, it's not going to get any easier."

Lynn looked at her friend in amazement.

"Promotion? What promotion? You're only there a few weeks?"

"Well, it's the position that's been vacant since before I came. Remember I told you someone left just before I started?"

"Mmm … I don't, to be honest. But tell me again. This is the girl who did your job before you?"

"No. My position seems to have been a new one. I was brought in to help Mary but, to be honest, any eejit could do what I'm doing. In fact, I can't see how she couldn't cope perfectly well without me – it's not like she's flat out herself. Not that she'd be caught dead telling me if she was. Olivia was the girl who ran the Strategy Department before I joined but just left the Friday before. That's the job that they're filling now and have asked me to apply for."

"Wow! That's amazing. Go, you!"

"Well, we'll see. There's been a definite change in atmosphere in there since I was asked so I'm guessing it hasn't gone down well with some of them."

"Like who?"

"Well, Mary for starters. She's made it painfully obvious that my doing the few bits of forecasting is vastly impinging on all these wonderful things she was 'just about' to give me to do but you know I begged her for more work over the last few weeks but she swore she had nothing for me – now my presence at her elbow, available for her every beck and call, seems to have become paramount to her existence ..."

"So it's just her that's funny about it?"

"Well, it's just her who's making it obvious. It's too hard to tell with Leona. I didn't think she was too enthusiastic at the start but now she seems to be in better form so I just don't know. I can't figure any of them out at all to be honest."

"It does sound slightly weird alright."

"Oh look, we'll see. Since they said it to me I've been doing a few bits and pieces for them but only because they're under so much pressure."

"Pressure? Because she's gone? Why didn't they get someone before she left? Surely someone at that level would have to give long notice?"

"I guess." Kate paused to think. "I never thought about that actually. No one really talks about her. She doesn't seem to have given much notice – in fact, some of the stuff I'm doing is work she started before she resigned but seems to have been just left in mid-air. I never wondered why she left – maybe there were personal reasons?"

"Would you leave stuff you were working on in that kind of state? Even for personal reasons?"

"I guess you would if you left in a hurry. Though actually, even at that, I don't think I could – but then I'm a control freak, remember?"

"This is true," Lynn smiled. "So how is being a control freak working with all the hours you're doing? Though I should add, you look like this is all suiting you very much."

"It is, to be honest. I actually love being back at work, Lynn. I really do and I especially love it now that I'm doing work I'm actually interested in. It felt wrong to be leaving the children all day just to punch in figures to try – and fail – to appease some stupid notion of being 'me' again. But lately? Lately I feel I can justify it."

"So you'll take the job if they offer it to you?"

"I'd say I will, yes. I want to, Lynn – it's the type of job I'd have chewed my right arm off for four years ago so why shouldn't I? I'm still the same person, I still have the same ambitions and skills. Only difference is I have two children – why should that stop me?"

"You're right, it shouldn't."

"Oh now, that's not a dig at you – I totally admire anyone who stays at home. It's as hard a job as any. It's just not for me, that's all."

"Kate, I think I know you well enough by now that you're not having a dig. And, to be honest, if you were I'd just tell you to get stuffed. I chose to stay at home. And it is a choice. I don't feel a bit hard done by. I love being at home and it works for us. Do I miss adult company? Yes. Do I get sick of picking up socks and putting on washes? Yes."

"Ehm, I pick up socks and put on washes too, remember – I don't have servants!"

"No, you don't. But when you all leave the house at eight in the morning and come home at six – for those eight or more hours, someone else is giving your child drinks, blowing their nose, answering their questions, and tidying up in their wake. Now, I'm not saying that for those eight hours you're sitting on your bum with your feet up – I realise you're working. Each role is difficult in its own way but, as I said to you, you do look better for this whole going back to work lark. I was worried about you there for a while …" She paused as if she had something else to say, but then just said, "It's great. I'm delighted for you."

"I can sense a 'but'?" Kate looked at her, not fooled for a moment by all the positivity.

Lynn sighed. "It's not really a 'but' and it might not be any of my business but do a bit of research before you take that other job. You're only there a while and, yes, I know you don't like to be bored but don't take on too much too soon. Have a good think about it, that's all. And yes, I know it's a job you'd have leapt at four years ago and I know that having the kids shouldn't be an issue – but they do exist, Kate, and they ain't going anywhere anytime soon."

Kate sighed. Lynn was right. In her head she kept wondering if this promotion could solve all her problems – it was exciting, it made her feel worthwhile – but the downside was that already, even before she'd been offered the job, the attitude of various people had changed towards her and this did raise the question of whether it was going to be worth all that extra grief.

"I know you're right. I can see plusses and negatives for taking it. Did I tell you we have a night out on Thursday? Apparently staff nights out are pretty rare but Declan has decided we all need to go for dinner to celebrate the secretary's forty years with the company."

"Forty years? Christ!"

"I know. Imagine. Anyway, no one wants to go but everyone is afraid not to … should be a super night …" She rolled her eyes and Lynn laughed.

"Well, if it gets too bad get Michael to play the helpless father and issue an SOS for your return home. Tell him to mention teeth or something, that'll do it."

Kate laughed. "I might have to – God only knows what happens to that lot with a few drinks on them."

Chapter 41

KATE

"And so, on that note, I would like you all to raise your glasses and join me in a very special toast to the backbone of DKB and a very, very special lady – Ms Jacinta Fitzmaurice!"

Kate raised her glass to Alice beside her and murmured "To Jacinta" along with everyone else. It was so obvious that of the twenty or so people around the table no one really wanted to be there. Least of all the woman of the moment, poor Jacinta, who was sitting at the head of the table sandwiched between Declan and Frank Newcombe.

The atmosphere in the office had been strained all day. Alice and Arianne had been in a huddle since early morning discussing outfit choices and how to achieve the best contured day-to-night look for the evening's festivities, which had got them into trouble on several occasions, whereas everyone else seemed determined to show that the night out was the least of their problems and they couldn't even think that far ahead until X, Y or Z meeting was over and, even at that, they weren't even sure if they could make it. This contrasted greatly with the obvious care that everyone – including the boys – had gone to with their outfit choices and, for that reason alone, there seemed to be no doubt that there was going to be a full attendance at L'Epoch that evening.

Kate herself wasn't in great mood either. She'd had an awful day. Mary was still ignoring her except to hand her the most mundane, clearly non-urgent tasks as if trying to prove some very obvious but totally spurious point.

Then the crèche had phoned earlier. Kate's heart had plummeted when she saw the number show up – her first thought being that one of them was sick and that she'd have to go and collect them. But no, they were phoning to ask could they have a chat with her when she was picking up. Which was bad enough, but not quite as bad as having to try and figure out how she was going to explain having to leave in the middle of the day. Still though, it *would* happen the one day that she wasn't actually collecting them herself because of the stupid night out.

Then, at six o'clock, just as she was wondering was anyone ever going to acknowledge the fact that they were all meant to be in a restaurant on the far side of town in twenty minutes, Michael had phoned. It was "nothing to worry about" just a "couple of issues" with Jess that were "probably normal" for a child new to a "childcare regime".

Like what in God's name was that all meant to mean?

She'd wanted to go straight home there and then but Michael had insisted that everything was okay and anyway, even at that stage she'd barely have been home before bedtime. And there'd been a very definite 'be there' undertone to this evening's proceedings so she'd decided that for the sake of a few hours, she really should just stay. Someone else was talking now and it was time for yet another toast.

"To Jacinta!" She turned to click glasses with Rob beside her, but was surprised to see him looking even more distracted than she did.

"Sorry, what?" He looked at her as she faced him with her glass raised.

"To Jacinta!" she said again before hissing, "We're meant to be toasting Jacinta!"

He looked blankly at her and then at Jacinta sitting with a face like granite at the top of the table. "That woman looks like the only toast she needs is of the hot buttered variety and if someone could get her a hot cup of tea to go with it, that'd be great." He picked up his glass of water and half-heartedly clinked it with Kate's.

Kate burst out laughing at the forlorn look on his face.

"Water? At least the rest of us are having the decency to pretend we're out for the night."

"Arrah sure – the night is young, eh?"

Kate followed his gaze down towards the head of the table where Jacinta, Frank, Declan and Leona sat.

"Really? You're out for the night? I'm off the minute this bloody food is eaten and I thought –" She was interrupted by the sound a mobile ringing.

Rob straightened immediately and reached into his pocket, looking at the screen. "Shit – sorry, Kate – I – I have to take this," and he pushed his chair back, nodding apologies to the people around him at the table.

"What's up with him?" Cian, who'd been sitting on the far side of Rob, asked.

"Phone call." Kate shrugged.

"Must be his ma."

"Cian, don't be such a sneer – it could well be a girlfriend we don't know about."

"It could," said Cian. "But I bet it's not."

"I doubt he tells us everything," Kate answered.

"Now, you can bet your hat on that alright."

They were interrupted by Rob's return. He looked at the faces looking up at him expectantly and said, "Geez, sorry – have I disturbed ye this much?"

"Who was it?" asked Cian.

"Me mam, why?"

Cian and those around erupted into laughter.

Kate patted the seat next to her. "Sit down, don't mind them."

But Rob didn't seem to have even noticed that he was now the butt of one of Cian's jokes.

"Everything okay?" Kate asked.

He shook his head. "As okay as it ever is," he answered, his mouth set in a grim line.

"Trust me," Kate said, "I've taken a call a bit like that today too. The sooner I get out of this place the better I can tell you."

Rob nodded. "You too, then?" He turned to look down the table. "I mean seriously, this is shit, isn't it? Like is there anywhere else in the world that you wouldn't rather be?"

Now Kate was getting worried.

"Rob! This isn't like you. Even at tea break you act like you're at a party, and now, well, you're at a party and you're acting like you're at a funeral. Do you want to talk about it?"

"Not really, no. Maybe another day, eh?"

Kate looked at him in surprise. "Ah Rob, I'm sorry to hear things are that bad. But why don't you have a drink and try and forget about whatever's bothering you."

"Have a drink? Not quite sure that'd solve it."

"Yes, have a drink!"

They both turned to see Jeremy standing behind them.

"Oh, hi," said Kate.

"Never mind hi – what is wrong with everyone? I thought you Irish were like us Scots, always up for a good party?"

"Eh, we are, but this doesn't count as a good party, Jeremy, old pal," said Cian with his usual sarcasm.

"Cian!" Kate turned back to Jeremy. "Don't mind him, this is all lovely."

"Eh, if you're an ould wan that likes wine," Cian said with a sneer.

"God, someone give him a beer and a smelly sock," Kate snapped back. "They don't do beer here, remember?"

Kate turned again to apologise to Jeremy but he was gone.

"Cian can be such an arsehole," she muttered to Rob, but he wasn't listening.

He seemed to be miles away and Kate was just wondering how this night could get any worse when she was interrupted by a waiter to her right.

"Pardon, madam. If I might just make some room for the champagne?"

She watched in amazement as the waiter parted some of the crockery on the table in front of her to make room for a rather large ice bucket.

"Champagne?" she said, looking down to table to see numerous other ice buckets being placed with equal ceremony.

"Yes, courtesy of the very generous Mr Taylor," answered the waiter.

There was a whoop from Cian and for a moment Kate thought about how she'd intended to be home early. Thought about it, and swiftly abandoned that thought.

Whatever Jess's issues were, they could wait another hour. She looked at Alice beside her eying her glass suspiciously and an idea popped into her head.

"Come on, Alice," she hissed conspiratorially, "drink up. I think it's time you told me all the office gossip, I want to know all about everyone, even those that have left ..."

Chapter 42

MARY

Mary looked around the table at her colleagues and marvelled at how the noise level had risen since Jeremy's champagne had made an appearance.

Good old Jeremy, eh?

Flashing the cash – everyone's favourite now.

Well, he could get stuffed – him, his cash and his fucking champagne.

Mary, unlike the others, had been quite looking forward to this evening. She'd heard them all giving out, moaning and groaning about it being 'the far side of town' and 'only serving wine' but none of that bothered her. She was aware that it was possible that her own social life could be found wanting but, really, what excited her most was to be out with Jeremy again in a social setting. Not since Paris had they both been out together in the company of their peers and she was curious to see how he was going to act.

Going out straight after work was such a tricky one though. She didn't want to be seen to be the only one 'making an effort' and yet, she really wanted to look her best for this occasion. As a result she got her hair cut into a mid-length bob at the weekend and also got her very first colour put in. She was lucky to have got away without colouring it up to now, but the very first strands of grey were starting to show and she felt it best to nip them in the bud before it became obvious they'd been taken care of. So with the cut and colour already done it was just a matter of getting up an hour earlier that morning to blow-dry it herself, and though she was never going to be as good as Heather, her hairdresser, she'd done a surprisingly good job and was quite pleased with the results.

What she was also very pleased with was her shape. Okay, so she'd always been slim but lately she just felt so much leaner and stronger. She'd joined Ronan's middle-distance running group and even the fact that they now ran together on a Saturday morning at eight meant an end to her Friday-night bottle of Riesling and that omission in itself was making itself known in her waistband. She'd also started in one of the group's 'Core Strength for Runners' classes and despite her moaning and groaning was really rather enjoying the fact that she could now hold a lunge for longer than some of the younger girls.

Which just left picking something to wear. Mary wasn't sure if the reason she'd started buying more expensive clothes was because of her age, or the fact that she had the money. There was a day when she could have shoehorned herself into a little cheap something or other but in the last couple of years she'd become much more discerning and tonight she was wearing a beautifully cut black Diane von Furstenberg wrap dress. She'd put a lot of thought into her choice and had hidden her slim frame in a loosely cut jacket for the whole day, not unveiling the full effect of the dress until she'd walked into the restaurant slightly behind everyone else.

She'd wondered all day if Jeremy would engineer a way to sit beside her, maybe touching her leg sexily below the table while talking business to someone sitting the other side. Or would he sit opposite her so that he could catch her eye without anyone noticing, waiting for the right moment to signal her that he was going out on the balconied smoking area, hoping to catch a quick kiss. Either way, a frisson of excitement ran through her every time she thought about the evening ahead.

The reality had brought her down to earth with a thud.

She'd entered the room and approached the end of the table where Jeremy was standing and without even casting a look in her direction he'd signalled her down to the other end of the table. With a jolt she realised that she was being put down with the 'plebs' and that only those people that were 'someone' were sitting up at the top.

Jeremy, Leona, Declan, Jacinta and Frank Newcombe.

The only minor consolation was that Kate appeared to be opposite her in between Rob and Alice – had she been up at the top with the glitterati she'd have lost her reason altogether.

Still there were angry tears stinging the back of her eyes as she'd taken her seat beside Geraldine, and even the sound of Geraldine whispering, "You look amazing, Mary" wasn't enough to cheer her up.

The absolute injustice of it.

The humiliation.

She should be sitting up there with him. If Olivia had been still here there's no way she'd be down the far end of the table with the commoners. If she, Mary, were publicly Jeremy's girlfriend she'd be up there with him. She thought of Toni and what would happen if Arthur had thought of banishing her to the far end of the table. Or rather she tried to think what would happen and couldn't. The whole idea was just too preposterous. So then what made her, Mary, deserve less than Toni?

She picked up her glass of wine. Well, he could shove his goddamn champagne. When did it become so important to be popular with everyone except her? Christ, she was so annoyed. What kind of an eejit was she? How had she thought for even a minute that this evening would be any different? She could see him from here chatting easily to Leona, and her gut twisted with jealousy. Not that he might be romantically drawn to Leona – though God knows she was looking pretty attractive tonight – but more that he viewed her as his equal. That he thought it was okay to be seen chatting to her.

He would see it as perfectly fine to share Mary's bed later though.

"You really do look very beautiful tonight, Mary."

It was Geraldine again. Mary nodded her thanks.

"For all the good it does me, Ger," she mumbled without thinking.

"Oh, I don't know. I'd say you could have your pick of Dublin's men this evening in that dress," Geraldine smiled. "Just make sure that when you're picking one, you pick the right one …"

"Yes, because I'm spoilt for choice as you can see." Mary was torn between not particularly wanting to continue the conversation but also strangely feeling the need to vent some of her fury.

"Did you ever think that you might have already chosen?"

"I beg your pardon?" Mary nearly spat out her soup. Did Geraldine know about Jeremy? She couldn't know surely?

"Well, you've chosen not to be in the wrong relationship, haven't you?"

She definitely didn't know.

Mary grunted. "That's hardly a choice, Geraldine."

"But of course it is, Mary, love. I could be in a relationship now if I really wanted. I've had my offers over the years, and I don't doubt you have too. But none of them were the right man. So I chose to say no, because, and I firmly believe this, the wrong man would be a million times worse than none at all."

Mary shrugged.

"You know I'm right. Of course a bit of company would be nice, but you know, my life is pretty sewn up these days – there's work, my house, my social life, my second house, my social life in Waterford. Would it be nice to share it all with someone? Yes, I guess. Is it nice not to have to worry about anyone else? Not having to think about someone else's timetable when I'm making plans for my downtime? Not waiting for someone to call to see when they can fit me into their downtime? Of course it's nice. I find being single quite liberating actually. I have friends who have been in bad marriages almost as long as I haven't and I've often thought to myself, isn't it an awful curse to be with the wrong man? A life wasted, waiting for an improvement that never happens."

Mary looked down the table at Jeremy chatting to Leona.

A life wasted waiting for an improvement that never happens.

She'd never seen it like that before. She'd never really felt like she was waiting for him to do something, like make some big gesture, some pronouncement on their future. The relaxed format of their relationship had suited her, hadn't it? He would definitely say that it had.

Well, he would say that, wouldn't he?

She could almost hear Toni already.

But they'd never actually discussed it. Okay, she'd alluded to seeing more of each other on that morning a few weeks ago, but she'd never really seriously suggested that they go public.

So why not just suggest it to him tonight? What was she making such a big deal about? Imagine if, after all this worrying and analysing, he just said yes? It was a work night out after all – it could be the ideal time – everyone would think it was a drunken encounter and then the look on their faces when they'd tell them it had, in fact, been going on for years ...

She reached for the untouched champagne glass.

For some reason, despite all this optimism, she felt a bit of Dutch courage might do no harm at all.

Chapter 43

LEONA

By the time the meal was over, the noise level in the room was vastly higher than it had been when it started and, thanks to Jeremy's champagne, there was very little sign of anyone wanting to go home.

Leona knew that she had probably drunk more than was advisable in a work social situation but for once she didn't care. She was up to her elbows in work back at the office. Declan had been like an annoying gnat in her ear for the last week, piling ridiculous task after ridiculous task on her lap, but yet when she'd suggested that she give the evening a miss he'd recoiled in horror. Apparently he really wanted to show Jeremy what an amazingly "synergized" company they were and that the team had depth and history that equalled no other branch of DKB.

So Leona had decided that if she wasn't going to be allowed work, then she wasn't going to be in working mode full stop. She'd managed to avoid having to sit beside Declan at all at the 'executive' end of the table and if Jeremy had spotted what she was at, he certainly hadn't interfered. In fact, she was nearly certain that he'd winked at her when she'd swiftly sidestepped the empty chair between Declan and Frank and slipped neatly into the chair between Jeremy and Sheila instead.

On a professional level she'd always found Jeremy to be a bit of an arsehole. He, rightfully or not, assumed he was on a different level to all the rest of them and he could be very arrogant in meetings.

However, on a social level he could be quite entertaining and she'd much rather sit beside someone who was verging on the 'can't be shut up' rather than the 'blood from a stone' side of chatty at a work do.

He could be quite flirtatious too and, whilst she wasn't drunk enough to imagine that he'd be any nicer to her at their planned meeting next morning, she still enjoyed being able to meet his thinly veiled digs with thinly veiled digs and watch his eyes darken with appreciation at each well-directed barb she managed to shoot back at him.

Yes, it was a slightly surreal work-do experience, not helped by the fact that she was very aware that the person she really would have loved to sit beside was at the other end of table with an uncharacteristic face like thunder.

She, like everyone else, had heard his phone ring after Declan's speech and had wondered who it might be that would be so important as to make him actually leave the table and take the call. When he'd come back and seemed impervious to whatever teasing Cian was levelling at him she'd almost pushed her chair back to go to him. To ask him what was wrong in the way that she knew he would ask her.

Then she'd felt Jacinta's hand on her arm and heard her whisper sotto voce, "I think Declan wants you for something."

But the funny thing was when Leona leaned over to Declan he appeared to be in the middle of a conversation with Frank. She turned back to Jacinta to see what she'd meant but she was turned in the other direction chatting to someone else. The moment had passed by then and, looking one last time, she'd just gone back to chatting to Jeremy.

By now the meal was over and, whilst no one seemed to be giving even the remotest impression that they might be thinking of going home, the vast majority of them had moved from the tiny private dining room out to the bar. She looked around the table to see what Rob was doing but his seat was already empty.

To her surprise this concerned her more than it really should have. She waited for several moments to see if he'd return but eventually it became apparent he'd left the table for good.

Jeremy turned to her.

"More wine, Ms Blake?"

"No, thank you. I think I should be going really ..." She touched her napkin to her chin and made as if to move her chair back.

"Och no, will ya stop! Sure the night is young!" Jeremy was having none of it. "Have another glass of wine. Or more champagne?"

"Ehm ... hi ..."

They both turned to see a slightly unsteady Mary standing behind them.

"Oh Mary," said Leona, "did you enjoy your meal?"

"I did, thank you."

"Oh, good." Leona didn't know what else to say but Mary showed no sign of moving on.

"Was there something else, Mary?" Jeremy asked, smiling.

"Well, just thought I'd do a bit of networking, chat to everyone, always the right thing to do at these things, isn't that right, Jeremy?"

"Oh aye, of course, super idea ... sorry," he said, looking slightly taken aback. "Ehm, sure pull over a chair there."

"Actually," Leona seized her chance, "why don't you take mine for now, Mary? I ... I, ehm, need to find the ladies' actually. Anyone have any clues?"

"Through the bar and down to the left – near the door to the smoking area, I believe," Jeremy smiled, before adding in a whisper, "I've just found out for Jacinta – I think she may have over-imbibed the champers too."

Leona smiled back at him, resisting the urge to tell him she had over-imbibed nothing thank you very much, and pushed her chair back. She rose to her feet and for a second steadied herself – the last thing she wanted to do was stagger out of the room in front of him.

"Arsehole," she muttered to herself as she strode as confidently as she could from the table.

The bar was surprisingly full, albeit mostly with the overflow from their party but she still couldn't see Rob anywhere. Then she remembered that Jeremy had mentioned a smoking area so she went in search of it.

She eventually found the smoking area out through a door that led onto a flat roof, ringed with decorative balustrades with a view out over Merrion Square below. Despite the fact that it was by now officially late autumn, it wasn't a cold night which was just as well as she'd left the table in such a hurry she'd left her jacket behind and the thin silk sleeves of her shirt didn't offer much in the line of protection against the elements.

"I didn't know you smoked!" She walked up to Rob who was hunched over the far end of the balcony, pulling on a cigarette with all his might.

"I don't," he answered.

"Oh," she smiled, "my mistake."

He didn't smile back. Instead he exhaled slowly then asked, "What has you out here?"

"Oh. Well, I can't get my emails in there, coverage is awful." She surprised herself with how quickly she'd thought of the lie given the bottle of wine she'd just drunk. She even took out her phone for good effect, and gave it a half-hearted shake. "Hans in Frankfurt is meant to be sending me over something."

"Oh, show me?"

She handed the phone to him and he promptly put it in his pocket saying, "It's midnight. Hans can fucking wait until the morning."

"Wow. What's rattled your cage? And don't say 'nothing'."

"Not a thing."

"Well, who was on the phone then?"

"You don't miss much, do you?"

"I miss nothing, Rob, and now that we've established that maybe you'd like to let me know what's wrong?"

"I don't want to talk it about it here."

"Well, let's go somewhere else then."

"No. I won't want to talk about it there either."

This was a Rob she hadn't seen before and it was hard to know from the look in his eye if he needed a hug or a good shake. One thing was for sure though – if he didn't want to talk to her then there was not a whole lot she could do about it.

"I'm going to go in and get a drink, Rob," she said softly, deciding to make one last attempt to get him to tell her what was wrong, "and then I'm going to come back and ask you again, so it might be an idea to think of something to tell me. And don't bother lying. I'm a mother, remember? I can spot a lie a mile off ..."

She went back inside and threaded her way to the bar where she ordered a vodka and Diet Coke. Then, making eye contact with no one else, she went back outside and placed her glass on top of the balustrade and leaned over, standing inches from Rob.

Neither spoke for a minute but then Rob started to talk.

"My father is Henry Kinirons."

She frowned. "I know that name – how do I know that name?"

Rob gave a slightly bitter laugh. "Well, you might know it from a virtually unparalleled National Hunt training career that spanned sixty years or you might know it from reading in the newspapers over the last six months about how he is about to stand trial for using performance-enhancing drugs on his horses over the last three years."

"Christ. I didn't realise that was your dad."

"Well, it is. The stupid prick."

"Ah Rob, don't talk about your dad like that!"

"Let me tell you, that's mild to the way I want to talk about him."

"Is that what the call was about then?"

He nodded. "It was my mum. He got his date. His case. It's going ahead. Monday fortnight."

"Oh, shit. Is there any chance that he'll get off?"

"None."

"That's awful. You must be so worried."

"I'm not worried. I'm just so unbelievably annoyed. Why was he such a fucking eejit?" His head sank into his hands. "He's putting us through all this and for what?" He sighed then as he stubbed the cigarette butt into the wall. "And, yes, I'm worried too. The stress of this could kill him. But it will probably just kill my mother instead. And then I'll have to kill him anyway."

"What possessed him?"

"Greed. Stupidity. Fear. His main owner for the last few years was Tony Bailey, the builder. Slowly but surely he ended up being our biggest owner, took over most of our yard and all he wanted was winners and plenty of them. It was perfectly clear that if Dad hadn't done what he wanted he'd have taken every last horse somewhere else. Well, he should have let him."

"Sounds like his intentions were good … but he didn't think it through, I guess," she said. "Didn't think and lost everything. Don't I have a man at home who bought the same T-shirt?"

"Really? Who?"

"Who do you think?"

"Your husband?

"The very man. And sorry, I didn't mean to change the subject."

"Jesus, change away – I'd much rather talk about someone else's problems." He hung his head in his hands again. "It's such a fucking mess."

She wanted to reach over and touch his arm, she wanted to pull him into her arms as he'd done once for her but she couldn't. They weren't alone and she wasn't even sure if it was the right thing to do. But, without doubt had they been alone, she mightn't have cared about doing the right thing.

"He wants me to go back. To take over his license."

She froze at these words.

"Back?"

"Back to Tipp. Leave Dublin. Leave my job. Leave everything."

"Oh." Her voice was barely audible as she tried to take this last piece of news in.

"Yep. Because that's what I should do because he's fucked up. Take over, take up the reins, drop all my own hopes and dreams."

"That's what I did," she said quietly, almost to herself. "I didn't want this fucking job. I loved my old job. I said no at first, but when I got home that evening he was there with his news: his job was gone, no redundancy, no pension, no nothing but the debts he'd run up during the good times. So all my plans had to change and, well, here I am."

"What were your other plans?"

"I wanted another baby," she said quietly.

"Oh. I don't really know what to say to that."

"Ha, I didn't expect you to. There's nothing *to* say really."

"Could you not just have one anyway? Sure at least he's at home to mind it."

She laughed at the simplicity of his suggestion. "Now? It's too late. Besides, hard to have a baby with someone who hates the sight of you."

He shook his head slowly. "I bet he doesn't, you know."

"Oh trust me, he does. He thinks I'm a selfish bitch who won't let him take a stupid job just because I want to keep him at home as some kind of punishment for ruining our lives."

"And is he right? Do you want to punish him?"

"I probably do. But that's not why I don't want him to take the job. We have a seven-year-old, a gorgeous child who we simply cannot put through any more change. At the moment she has one of us, and she adores him. She'd die if he went whereas she's used to me not being there." Her voice cracked as her sentence tailed off. "I think we really need to start talking about you again."

He laughed. "There's nowt to say about me. It's shit but there's nothing I can do about that."

"You *could* go back," she said, looking straight ahead.

"I don't want to. And definitely not now."

She knew without turning that he was looking directly at her.

"I don't want you to either," she whispered.

Neither of them said anything for a while.

"Do you want to hear something funny?" she whispered, half laughing but still not meeting his eye. "I dreamed about you last night." She nodded. "I dreamed about you and then I woke up and I felt sick. I felt sick and yet more wonderful than I've felt in a very, very long time. And I don't know what to do about that."

"Jesus!" His weight shifted imperceptibly until the full length of the side of his body was against hers and she could feel his strong lean arm through the thin fabric of her silk shirt, and it burned and scorched her skin until she felt she might faint.

"I think we should go," he said.

"I don't think we should," she answered. "I don't think we should."

Chapter 44

MARY

"3 The Grove, Bannon Drive, Rathfarnham, please." Mary opened the taxi door and sat into it bum first, then twisted, tucking her legs, ankles together like the respectable celebrities did. For some reason it felt of utmost importance to her that she maintain a level of composure, at the very least until she got in her own front door.

Even though 'composed' was the last thing she felt.

She wasn't quite sure how she felt actually. She was very calm granted, and weirdly excited.

She'd felt quite brave interrupting Leona and Jeremy. She'd watched them chatting as the meal neared its end and she'd told herself that when people started moving around she would walk up to them and just start chatting, like she had every right to do. She had every right to do it as a well-thought-of employee of the company, and as the person who had been sleeping with Jeremy for the past eight years.

She was going to start treating herself like she wanted others to treat her, she told herself as she rose to her feet and walked down to their end of the table. She hadn't been expecting Leona to jump up and leave so quickly but it suited her perfectly that she did. Jeremy had just looked at her with an amused look on his face once Leona had gone.

"So you're working the room then?" he smiled at her.

"I am. That's what one is meant to do at these shindigs, isn't it?"

271

"I guess it is," he smiled.

"Well, anyway," Mary looked around to see if Leona was out of earshot, "now that she's gone, I guess me and you can just have a chat."

"I guess we can," Jeremy said. "But you better not delay if you want to talk to everyone one by one before they leave."

"But I don't. In fact, Jeremy, it was really just you I wanted to talk to."

"That sounds ominous."

"Does it?" Mary asked. "And if it does, why? Why would you be worried it was about something bad?"

"Because if it was something good, there is no doubt that you would wait until later on, when we can talk in peace."

"Why? What's later on?" Mary kept her voice level and cool but there was no escaping the fact that there was an edge to her tone.

"Oh, playing hard to get! I like it!" He smiled, waiting for her to soften and smile, but she acted like she hadn't even heard him.

"I think we should go public, Jeremy," she said instead.

He nearly spat out his wine.

"Jesus Christ, Mary! Keep your voice down."

"Why? What would be so bad about anyone hearing me? People get together at work functions all the time. Neither of us is married – to the best of my knowledge – so what's the problem?"

"Mary, exactly how much have you had to drink? Can we talk about this maybe in the morning?"

"No. Or yes, I mean, of course we could, but I've had very little to drink and very little is going to change by the morning."

"Mary, I'm not discussing this now. This is a business occasion. If you don't want to discuss it later then fine, but I don't want to discuss it now."

"Why are you so afraid that anyone will find out about me?"

"I'm not afraid. I'm – it's – I'm not afraid but it's not appropriate. I've told you before, I'm here in a regulatory capacity. It would be frowned upon."

"Then I'm really sorry. But I want more, Jeremy, I want someone who is here for me, not someone who is ashamed of me."

"Och, for Christ's sake, Mary! I'm not ashamed. Everything is fine as it is – what do you want to go messing with it for? The very second other people start interfering, what we have, what we treasure, will be gone. It's no one else's business. What difference is it going to make to what we have if other people know or not?"

"It would make a difference to me, Jeremy."

"But why? You're a private person. What – you just want to be able to tell everyone you've a boyfriend? Is that it?"

Mary looked at him.

Was that it?

"But I don't have a boyfriend, Jeremy, do I?"

He looked furtively around the room but there was no one within earshot nor was anyone looking in their direction.

"What do you not have that you want so badly?" he asked.

"What do I not have that would make you proud to say I was yours?" she asked softly. "I'm not angry, Jeremy, but I'm just not sure that this, us, is enough anymore."

He looked at her. "Is there someone else?"

She laughed. "Because there would have to be?"

"I'm asking you, is there someone else?"

She looked at him, smiling. "Yes, yes, there is, Jeremy. There's me."

That seemed to unnerve him slightly.

"I don't think you mean this," he said. "I think you need to have a think about it. I can see what you're saying, but I can't complicate things in this way at the moment. I just can't. We could talk about it again in a few weeks, when Head Office have been and gone and maybe when I've been here a couple of months and it won't be as big a deal to anyone."

She looked at him, not quite sure what to say.

"Look, we can't talk here," he said. "I promise, we can talk later, or tomorrow even. I'll come over tomorrow night, we can have a bottle of wine, talk about the whole thing ... "

"Tomorrow night doesn't suit," she found herself saying. "I run now on Saturday mornings."

"Oh." He looked taken aback. "Well, can't you miss it?"

"No," she said simply. "I can't."

"Well, I'm flying home on Saturday for a few days, so that doesn't suit either."

Neither of them said anything then so Mary stood up.

"Right, that's that so. Goodnight, Jeremy."

"What do you mean, goodnight? Will I call around later or what?"

She shook her head. "No, don't. I need time to think. Actually, why don't *I* think about it until Head Office are gone?"

And with that she'd gone back to her seat, picked up her coat and handbag and left the restaurant.

Now sitting in the cab she could feel her resolve start to slip. What on earth had she been thinking? She should phone him, tell him that it had been the drink after all. That she'd been having a moment. She reached into her handbag and took out her phone. Looking out the window, she watched the city lights roll by as she held her phone in her hand for a moment.

She was shaking with indecision, but then, taking a deep breath she swiped the lock off and keyed in a number. Only when it answered did the tears come and, with a sob, she said, "Toni, it's Mary. I think I've just broken up with Jeremy."

ROB

Yes, we left together.

Did we go home together? No.

Did I drive her home? No.

I walked her to a taxi. I could have driven her home but my car was back at the office and, whilst I didn't mind walking back across on my own, it probably wasn't safe to walk her with me.

On so many levels.

So I walked her down Merrion Street. To be honest, we could have flagged a cab from anywhere but it was a beautiful night and we were just walking and chatting.

At one point she turned to me and said, "That's where it all started, eh?"

I turned to see we were outside Government Buildings.

"It surely is."

"Another batch of eejits that were probably just trying to do the right thing."

"You think?"

"You don't?"

I shrugged. "All I know is that Bailey at one point was building apartments that were so small he had furniture specially made for the show-houses so that people would think the rooms were bigger than they actually were and go

275

borrowing stupid amounts of money to buy them. Someone should have stopped that happening."

"I'm not so sure anyone would have listened, Rob, I know Gavin wouldn't have. Everyone was drunk on the notion that at last we were as good as everyone else. We wanted it all."

We stopped for a minute to look through the black wrought-iron gates, across the green space and at the lights in the buildings that surrounded it.

"Wonder is there anyone working in there now?" I asked.

"Are you mad?" There was no ignoring the bitter tone of her voice. "Sure 'tis only the eejits picking up the pieces that still work till this hour."

Out of the corner of my eye I could see something move. It was the security man in the hut at the gate.

"Come on." I nudged her shoulder with my hand. "I don't want them thinking this is some kind of two-man protest. Imagine the scandal if we got arrested."

She laughed then and we moved on, and my hand did stay on her shoulder but only for about three steps until she stepped, probably deliberately, out of its reach.

"So what are you going to do?" she asked, just slightly ahead of me, enough that I couldn't see her face.

"I don't know. I'm the boy, you know? I'm the reason my mother had seven children. My arrival after six sisters was like the Second Coming. And now it's the scandal of the century that I'm not stepping up to the plate."

"You know you're getting the Grade 2, don't you?"

I stopped walking.

"I didn't. Sure how would I know that?"

She had to stop too, and she turned, but only slightly.

"Well, all our end is done. Declan agreed to it last week and it's with Geraldine now. But look, I definitely shouldn't be saying anything to you, but it just might help you decide, that's all."

"Oh, I've made my decision," I said then. "But thanks. I appreciate that."

And at that point, yes, I reached out to her again. I reached for her shoulder and, even though she resisted, I pulled her towards me anyway.

"I've decided," I repeated.

We were standing inches from each other. I went to turn her face towards mine but she stepped ever so slightly back again.

"Leona –" I started.

"Don't..." she whispered.

"But –"

"Don't, Rob ... please ..." She couldn't even look at me. "Don't," she repeated again, "because at this point I can still say I've done nothing wrong. I can go home and convince myself that I've done nothing wrong. The very second I can't do that anymore, it's all ruined, it becomes something bad, something to be ashamed of and I've enough to be feeling bad about ..."

She was crying now and I should have done the right thing and just left her alone like she asked but I didn't.

I took a step towards her and I told her to stand still. And I kissed her on each crying eye, I kissed the tears on her cheeks and I hovered for a second at her beautiful mouth, and it was so close, too close, but not close enough.

"Now, you've still done nothing wrong," I whispered.

And we stood like that for what seemed like forever. Cheek to cheek, close, but not close enough.

Then she hailed a taxi and went home.

Make of that what you will.

Extract from interview with Robert Kiniron
Recorded 12 November 2011
5.45pm

OLIVIA

I'd been feeling sick for weeks before that final big row. I wasn't sleeping, I couldn't eat. Thursday nights I cried because the week was over and from Saturday night I cried because the next day was Sunday. I never knew what was ahead of me each week, and it wasn't the work that had me upset. It was the politics. Not a week went by that someone hadn't slyly booked an important meeting for a time that they knew didn't suit me. They planned conference calls for six pm when they knew I'd either be gone, or trying to get out the door. They booked important meetings for Friday mornings which were still my day off, so that every week it looked bad that I couldn't be there. It was a constant stream of tricks and tactics.

And I wasn't stupid. Mary was just as bad as Leona. I knew she was complaining about me all the time. Jacinta tried to warn me. But there was nothing I could do. If I stayed late I had to listen to Danny or my mother complaining about how much work the boys were when I was gone and if I didn't stay late I knew Mary was giving out about me to anyone who would listen. I'd always had a good relationship with Declan but now it seemed that he too was annoyed with me for some reason that I just couldn't fathom.

By the time that final afternoon came, was it any wonder I cracked? I hadn't slept in three nights and I just couldn't take it anymore.

I just couldn't.

Chapter 45

KATE

To say there was a strange atmosphere in the office the morning after Jacinta's Big Night Out was putting it mildly. Like any other office worldwide after a night out it was a mixture of people trying to keep their head down, and people not being able to keep their head up.

Kate was glad she'd left at a reasonably respectable time and, despite the last-minute decision to have a couple of glasses of champagne, the fact that she'd been home, in bed and asleep before midnight was definitely standing to her. However, she couldn't help but be curious about what exactly had gone on after she left.

It was hard to judge what kind of a night it had been. Leona's office door was shut, though she did appear to be in. This in itself was not unusual but Rob, for someone who didn't drink, looked remarkably hungover and was working away quietly, none of his usual jokes or chat. Then she noticed that the usually dapper Cian had an uncharacteristically ruddy complexion and bloodshot eyes. Mary was in but instead of looking thunderous as usual, looked pale and pre-occupied. And of course Declan was nowhere to be seen.

Kate sighed. She'd have to live with not knowing. Her own head was melted and what a group of dysfunctional adults did, in the final hours of a night out that appeared to have only served to make them even more dysfunctional, really was beyond what she should be caring about.

She'd had a chat last night with Michael about Jess. It seemed that

Jess's behavior had deteriorated a lot over the last few days. She had become un-cooperative with the staff and there'd been a couple of high-profile tantrums over seemingly minor issues. The lovely young woman in charge felt that this was all part of settling in and that tiredness had a lot to do with it. There was also the very big chance that the novelty of going to crèche every day might just be starting to wear off which, Michael had been assured, was all perfectly normal. All in all, Michael seemed relatively unconcerned, but then that was Michael all over.

"It'll be grand."

That was what he said about everything but she'd driven the children to the crèche herself that morning and had a word with the young woman who had spoken to Michael the previous day. Assured that the problems were minor and would probably pass, she then drove in to the office. She'd have to pay for the day's parking but one day wouldn't kill her.

She looked across at poor hungover Alice who was definitely in the 'keeping her head down' group this morning. She was sitting at her desk, her bleary eyes on her monitor, afraid to move lest she make a mistake that the not-so-hungover-and-still-vigilant Jacinta might notice.

She wasn't meeting anyone's gaze so it was hard to know how much, if any, she remembered of the conversation with Kate last night. Kate rather hoped she didn't, or at the very least didn't remember the volley of questions that Kate had levelled at her.

Not that she'd managed to find out much. She wasn't really that interested in the fact that Arianne had a thing for Cian but it was Jennifer from Risk that he had gone home with after last year's Christmas party. But on and on Alice had chatted, until Kate had cut across her to ask the question whose answer she really wanted to hear.

"So, tell me all about Olivia."

"Olivia," Alice had repeated blankly.

"Yes, Olivia. I mean I feel like I nearly do know her which is strange given we've never met."

"You do?"

Kate's subtlety was a bit too 'out there' for poor Alice.

"Well, you must have known her very well?"

"Oh no," Alice shook her head quickly, "not really. She was always out."

"Well, she'd three maternity leaves in four years, I guess," Kate had laughed. "Does that count as being always out?"

"Well, I wasn't around for most of that. I mean, in recent times …"

"Oh really? Did she have bad health?"

"No. Nothing like that. Actually, do you know what? I don't want to talk about Olivia. Let's talk about something else," Alice had mumbled then, her head down and voice barely audible lest anyone would hear.

"Ah now, Alice," Kate said smiling, "you're hardly talking about her – well, you are, but you're not saying anything bad. Why was it that she left again?"

"I'm not allowed to say," Alice whispered.

"What do you mean?" Kate had abandoned all attempts at subtlety.

"Kate, please, I told you, I don't want to talk about Olivia. We were warned not to talk about her. I'd get into awful trouble, in fact I'd say I'd be fired – I've probably already said enough to get fired. So can we talk about someone else?"

Kate was shocked at the fear in Alice's voice. What had happened? She'd left it at that though as there was clearly no point in pushing it. So she knew nothing more really, nothing apart from the very clear fact that there was something to know. She hadn't wanted to upset Alice any further so she'd let her prattle on about how she fancied Rob for a few minutes before saying that she needed to go to the loo and then just hadn't gone back.

"Kate?"

She looked up. It was Arianne.

"Yes?"

"A few of us are going to McDonald's for lunch – do you want to come?"

Kate turned to see Rob, Cian and Alice putting on their coats. Mary wasn't at her desk but she didn't see Mary as the McDonald's-Hangover-Cure type.

Nor was she really. Firstly, she didn't actually have a hangover and, secondly, McDonald's with a foursome of 'young folk' didn't really appeal.

"Ah thanks – but I have a few things to do so I might just try and get through them, then maybe get home early instead."

Arianne didn't ask twice – she'd clearly only included Kate in the invitation out of friendliness and seemed happy enough that the double date continue with no elderly add-ons.

The office was now empty. Kate looked at her to-do list to pick what she should do next. Those bloody budgets still weren't finalised. She picked up her file and moved across to Olivia's empty desk. She often sat there now when she was using Olivia's files or her system. She had the password for her PC, she had access to her cabinets and drawers.

She'd access to everything bar the knowledge of what the hell had gone on to make her leave.

While waiting for her computer to load she opened her file and started to sort through the loose pages at the front. Fuck it, she'd forgotten to bring over her hole-punch. Surely there had to be a spare hole-punch here somewhere? She rolled open the drawer of Olivia's desk and started to riffle around under the diary that was sitting on top. She thought she felt the cold hard edge of a desk-punch so she took out the diary. But no, it was actually the edge of a picture frame. With a start she saw the picture was of three small boys of various ages and the frame was made of lollipop sticks, obviously made by one of the little boys. They must be Olivia's kids, she thought. What beautiful children!

And what a peculiar thing to leave behind …

She took out the frame and, looking around to make sure that no one had come into the room, placed it face down on her desk and put her file over it. She reached into the drawer but there was nothing else of a personal nature. Just pens and highlighters, the diary and a few other bits that you'd normally find in someone's desk drawers. The frame had obviously been on Olivia's desk until someone decided it should be stashed in a drawer until someone else decided what to do with it. Knowing this place there'd have to be a board meeting about it and some directive signed in triplicate with the blood of the seventh son of a seventh son.

She put the framed photo back in under the diary and then rolled open the second drawer. Nothing. Just a DKB employee manual and two old issues of *Hello* magazine.

She slid the middle drawer closed again and then opened the last one. At first there appeared to be nothing but analysis books, some blank envelopes, a few empty manila folders and an industrial-sized hole-punch! *Voila!*

But then when she lifted out the punch something fell forward. She reached down and lifted it up. It was a make-up bag, and it was quite heavy. She slid across the zip to see that it was full of very expensive make-up. There were three Mac palettes, a barely used Chanel blusher, numerous expensive-looking lipsticks and a practically brand-new jar of Dior foundation. Olivia had clearly been into her products.

Now, whatever about leaving behind a picture of your children – what kind of girl left a couple of hundred euros worth of make-up in her drawer?

None of this made any sense.

Kate looked at the make-up bag in her hands. She was pretty sure that no one else knew it was there. For one, it wouldn't have been as visible as the photo which had probably been on top of the desk and, secondly, she was pretty sure that if make-up-obsessed Arianne had had wind of its existence there was no way there would still be this amount of product in it.

This bag should be returned to its rightful owner. She should give it in to Jacinta who would put all the proper procedures in place to ensure its return. She would probably post it back.

But what if someone was to hand-deliver it instead? Less chance of it being damaged, or lost, or stolen …

Someone with a car.

Someone who was nice and not connected to whatever the original problem was.

Someone neutral.

Taking one last look around the room, Kate slipped the make-up bag into her folder and brought the whole lot back over to her own desk. She then slid the bag down into her own handbag and shoved it under her desk with her foot.

At the very least Olivia would get her stuff back, she told herself.

Anything else would be a bonus. Now, how was she going to find out where Olivia Sharpe lived?

Chapter 46

MARY

"So it's really all off then?" Toni closed her menu and sat back.

"Well, it's no different than it was when I left last night. He's been in meetings all day – not that that matters – he's not the 'drop by my desk' type anyway."

"So what way did you leave it? You're to have a think about it?"

"That was his last suggestion alright. He suggested I think until tonight. I told him it didn't suit to meet tonight as I was running early tomorrow morning."

"You did not!"

"I did, and why wouldn't I? Sure it's true. So then he told me that he was going back to Scotland tomorrow so I said I'd think about it until the Frankfurt visit was over."

"You're a howl. And have you been thinking about it?"

Mary shrugged and closed her own menu. She didn't feel much like eating even though Ciao Bella's was her favourite place to lunch. Toni had insisted on coming into town to meet her, mostly, Mary guessed, in case her resolve crumbled and she decided to go back to her cad of a boyfriend.

"I'm not sure what I should be thinking about. In fact, I did have a spell this morning where I wondered had I overthought it and that's what the problem was. Everything was fine, you know, we could have gone on forever ..."

"Ah, Mary!"

"No, I don't mean I regret it. I just feel kind of empty really. Like I had something that was 'okay' but now I've – well, I've nothing. And I should feel upset, but, well, I don't. We only saw each other a few times a year anyway, and yes, because of that it suited to keep it private. But I suppose I don't want to go out with someone who lives in Dublin and still wants to keep it private. That's too hard."

"So you're okay then?" Toni looked anxiously at Mary. Her friend looked okay but then with Mary it was always very hard to tell. She was very private, and never good at showing how she really felt. But then maybe in this situation she really didn't know herself?

"I think I'm okay," Mary smiled nervously. "I don't know what it is, but lately I've just felt that really I need to take control of my destiny. Life is passing me by – it's time to sit up and take it by the horns, you know?"

Toni was impressed. This was definitely a side to Mary she'd never seen before.

"I feel I look well, I'm good at my job, I've a lovely house, good friends. Why should I accept second-best for anything?"

"Well, you're definitely busier. Anytime I phone now you're out running."

Mary smiled. "Well, I might be single, but at least I'm skinny eh?"

Chapter 47

KATE

Kate put on her indicator and checked the Google Maps app on her phone one last time. Whitechapel Lawns, Artane. Yes, this was definitely it. She'd had a funny feeling in her stomach since she'd left the office but now it had escalated into 'What in God's name am I doing?'

Just give her the make-up bag, that's all you've got to do.

She'd ended up leaving the office early, just so she could go on this ridiculous fool's errand. She felt justified given that the McDonald's lunch had gone on for an hour and a half and she'd already been in an hour before anyone else that morning.

So when four o'clock came and all the senior people had gone into a meeting on the fourth floor that was scheduled to go on for hours, she decided she'd done quite enough for the day and that she would nip off. And so now, here she was, outside Olivia Sharpe's house.

Kate was surprised at how close Olivia actually lived. She must have had the perfect commute, she thought, as she pulled up on the kerb outside her house. It had taken her no time to get from the office to here.

Kate wondered was she at home. Her cunning plan was going to be foiled if she'd gone on to work somewhere else but the fact that there was a car in the driveway looked promising. A steel-grey people carrier that was so shiny it put Kate's semi-clean Toyota to shame. The little garden reminded her of Lynn's – neat and not a weed or overgrown shrub in sight.

She went up the driveway with the make-up bag in her hand and rehearsed her opening line again before taking a deep breath and ringing the doorbell. Just as the bell rang, there was a movement at the window beside the front door and from behind what she assumed was the sitting-room curtains a small blonde tousled head looked out at her.

She smiled and waved at the child, thinking he was probably about the same age as Jess. He smiled broadly and waved back and as she waved again the front door opened. A blonde young woman stood there, carrying another younger child on her hip.

"Oh – sorry, I was distracted," Kate said, smiling, gesturing to the little boy at the window.

"Oh Ruairí!" the girl sighed. "I've told him not to do that. Sure God knows who'd be at the door and him waving at them."

"He's lovely." Kate smiled at him again then quickly remembered that this poor woman had no idea of who she was. "Oh, I'm sorry, I'm Kate O'Brien – I was hoping to speak to Olivia?"

"Yes, that's me." She smiled whilst frowning slightly. "I'm sorry – but should I know you?"

"No. No, you won't know me. But I work in DKB." Kate smiled broadly back in what she hoped looked like a reassuring manner but, to her horror, the girl's face froze.

"You what?"

"I work in DKB, where you used to work."

"You got my job?" She said it so quietly that Kate could barely hear her.

"Oh no!" Kate said quickly. "I work with Mary, in Finance ... for my sins!" She half laughed but Olivia didn't laugh back.

In fact she looked like she'd just heard that someone close to her had died.

Kate knew she needed to do something drastic here and fast because she had an awful feeling the door was about to be slammed in her face. Luckily she then remembered the make-up bag in her hand and held it up.

"Oh I'm sorry – I nearly forgot why I came. I was wondering was this yours by any chance?"

Olivia looked at the bag and there was a flash of recognition on her face. "Actually it is – I lost it months ago – a long time ago actually." She looked totally bewildered now.

"Well, I found it today," said Kate, again trying a smile. "In the drawer of your desk."

"In DKB? Did you? Oh wow, is that what happened? I hadn't thought I'd left it there …"

Kate handed it to her, almost sighing with relief at the softening in her expression. "I'm delighted it's yours. It sounds bad, but I looked inside when I was trying to figure out whose it was and we share a similar taste in make-up. Expensive!"

"Oh really?" She smiled properly for the first time since she'd opened the front door and Kate felt herself relax.

"Oh yes, but don't worry – I didn't go as far as to actually use any of it. In fact, the only reason I'm returning it is in case it got into the wrong hands – there's a few there that would love some of your lovely products."

"Yes, yes, I suppose there are. Well, thanks, you're very good to drop it over." Her face seemed to change again as she said, "So you've just started with them then?" She looked almost wistful as she said this.

"I have. It's not as handy for me as for you though. I'm commuting to Saggart."

"Oh really? Yes, it was handy for me alright. Not so much when they were based on the other side of town, but for the past few years, yes, I guess it had that going for it."

"Probably good to have a relatively short commute with these guys." Kate gestured to the two faces that were now looking out the front window at her, thinking she'd smile back and that it would coast her nicely up to asking how she'd manage to convince them to give her part-time.

"What's that supposed to mean?" Olivia snapped instead.

"Oh, well, I just mean, I find the commute hard, that's all."

"I can't remember your name but let me tell you I was perfectly able to do my job!"

She practically spat the words at Kate who almost fell off the front step with shock.

"Olivia," she had no idea what she had said wrong, "I've seen your files – I'm under no doubt that you were able to do your –"

"You shouldn't have come here," Olivia interrupted, and to Kate's horror she could see that she was now crying.

"I'm really sorry – I only wanted to –"

"*You shouldn't have come!*" she nearly screamed with a sob, before stepping back and slamming the door in her face.

Chapter 48

LEONA

Leona lay in bed that night and listened to the rise and fall of her husband's breathing. He had clearly decided he wasn't talking to her when she got home earlier, probably because she'd been so late home the previous night. But then it was hard to know if he really wasn't talking to her, or if they had just run out of things to say.

She wasn't sure which was worse.

She wondered were many marriages like this. Marriages that had started off okay, then taken some kind of a wrong turn, ending up in two people lying side by side, not talking to each other.

Not caring enough to talk to each other.

She remembered reading once about a writer who'd reached an impasse in their book, and how they were advised to delete the last ten thousand words and take it back to where it had first started going wrong.

How many words would herself and Gavin have to delete to get it back to before it went wrong? But there was no marriage backspace button, no magic switch to delete without trace all the things that had gone wrong. If there was, how far back would she go? Back to where he lost his job? Were they okay then? Or would she have to go back further? Back to where she was working doing a normal job and he was the high flier. Further back still?

Would she have to delete Rachel?

That was the problem, wasn't it? It would be hard to do a proper cull without deleting the good stuff too. She couldn't remember what the advice had been regarding keeping the good bits. But, in all of this, the one true good thing to have happened was Rachel.

She pushed back her side of the duvet and crept out of her bedroom and across the hall to the door beside Rachel's bedroom. She opened it with a soft click and went in, switching on the light that was fitted with a soft pink bulb.

She hadn't been in here in years but it was exactly how she'd left it when they'd moved Rachel to the bigger middle bedroom. The cot was still in the corner of the room, her nursing chair was still beside it, even her yoga ball was still rolled into the corner. She padded across the thick carpet and sat in the nursing chair, swinging herself gently back and forth. She used to come in here a bit, mostly to tidy or put away little clothes that Rachel had grown out of, to keep them safe for the next one.

The next one.

Why was she thinking so much about this tonight? Was it because of her conversation with Rob last night? She had never admitted it out loud to anyone before.

She remembered lying in this very chair later in her pregnancy, her hands on her softly rounding stomach, feeling her baby move. She'd been one of those women who revelled in every second of being pregnant. She loved people to notice, to comment and to squeal 'Oh, how exciting!'. She loved that she couldn't drink, she loved to pore over books every night in bed and see how big her baby was, and what she should or shouldn't be feeling. She'd loved getting bigger and bigger and getting the room ready for the new baby.

She'd even loved childbirth, which she knew made her sound like a nutter. She'd read all the books beforehand, she knew what was required of her body and she was ready. When her waters had broken that night she'd been the calm one and had insisted on staying at home for as long as she could bear it, laughing at Gavin running around with bags and cases – at one stage she even caught him making sandwiches, for who was anyone's guess. And when they'd reached the hospital she'd managed to remain calm, and had refused all pain relief, preferring instead to listen to her body and work with it. Towards the end she'd wondered had this been such a good idea as everything started to happen so quickly and at that point she'd given in to Gavin's insistence that she at least take some gas and air, but the sensation had made her laugh and Rachel's birth had thrown her into a spasm of euphoric giggles that swept away the memory of all the pain and effort.

She often remembered how it had been so empowering for once to be doing something that Gavin couldn't do for her and she would never forget the way he'd looked at her over the head of their beautiful baby girl after she'd tumbled into the world, a slick squirming bundle of gorgeousness. Like she, Leona, was a hero, the giver of this great and wonderful gift, tears streaming down his face as he'd whispered how he loved her over and over again.

Was it any wonder that all she'd wanted since was to experience it all again? But Gavin had put her off and now she often wondered was it because he'd had an inkling what was coming down the line in work or was it because he was a selfish prick who wasn't mad on having another newborn around the house. Either way, all of a sudden she was flung into a busy demanding job and a baby was no longer an option.

Of course she could have just had another baby. Rob was right. Gavin was now at home so childcare wouldn't have been any extra, but that wasn't what she wanted. When she'd imagined having another baby she'd always thought that this time she'd take a full year off, or maybe even give up altogether. With Rachel, she'd gone back to work after the statutory number of weeks, and having to wean her from her breast at that stage had been a crippling experience emotionally.

How she missed those early days when it had been just her and Rachel, snuggled in bed for hours and hours on end. It had felt like them against the world, like together they could face anything.

And now? She was the one that was faced. She was no longer part of the together.

How she wanted the hopes and dreams that she'd once felt in this room back again. But it could never happen. It had gone too far and she couldn't believe how lonely a person could feel in their own home.

She reached over to the cot and pulled at one of the soft fleece blankets hanging on the side until it covered her arms and up to her chin. Still rocking, she closed her eyes and tried to sleep.

Chapter 49

KATE

It was Monday morning and Declan was on the rampage again. He had bounded across the room shouting "The Germans are coming!" so often at this stage that that all Kate could think of when she saw him was Basil Fawlty, and smirk to herself.

She had to get her laughs from somewhere these days.

The weekends were just going so quickly. Saturday was spent bringing Jess to her usual Saturday activities which now included ballet and swimming. Swimming used to be on Tuesday afternoons but now that wasn't possible anymore so the only slot available was on Saturday afternoons. David was still too small to bring, so they had to divide and conquer, one staying to mind him and the other venturing off to the swimming pool. If Michael asked one more time what the urgency with the swimming lessons was, she was going to throw him in the pool after her.

"She needs to learn to swim!" Kate had snapped at him when he'd asked her, yet again, on Saturday what the big panic was. "It is one of the most important skills she will ever learn, especially from a safety aspect."

"Yes, I get that," Michael had sighed, "and of course everyone should know how to swim. I'm just saying that putting yourself under this kind of pressure at the moment to fit in lessons seems slightly mad. Surely it'll be a while before she's near any body of water without us, and if there is the flood or tsunami you're expecting, then whatever skills she's currently picking up in Plankton or whatever it's called are probably not going to be enough."

"It's Tadpoles, you stupid man," Kate had snarled back at him. "And everyone else's children are doing lessons – I'm not having mine miss out!"

He'd just sighed then and muttered that she should do whatever she wanted as she would anyway and so they'd left it at that.

Well, left it at that until she'd then insisted that they all go to the Zoo the following morning as they'd done nothing as a family in ages. And this was all despite the fact that it was raining and both children had been exhausted and whingey for the entire day.

She'd nearly come to work for a rest this morning.

Which was ironic given the pandemonium that was now going on around her. She just couldn't understand what all the fuss about the visit was for anyway. Surely it couldn't be that big a deal that Head Office were coming for a day or two? From what she'd heard from Jeremy, they were simply coming to have a 'touch base' kind of meeting, impart a few new procedures that they wanted carried out group-wide, and generally make sure that Dublin was aware of the group view on certain issues.

But this morning Declan had taken advantage of the fact that Jeremy had gone home for a few days and was stalking around like a lunatic making sure that no stone was left unturned with regard to preparations for the big visit.

He wanted current figures, he wanted past figures, he wanted current versions of past figures – in fact, Kate was ready to lay a bet that no one in the department had any idea any more of what he really wanted. He was bandying around phrases like "This is how we're going to journey them" (which Kate assumed meant 'This is how we're going to pull the wool over their eyes') and shouting demands about making sure the indicative quarter end numbers were "well sweated" – in other words, no fuck-ups, this has got to be spot on!

It would have been all quite exciting had she not been so mindful of the fact that it was later and later every evening when she was getting home. There were demands for figures coming at her from all angles and, coupled with that, she was still trying to get her old job done lest she incur yet further wrath from Mary the Merciless.

And on top of all this, Jess had become very unsettled over the last few days. She was crying going to bed, talking about how she was going to have bad dreams and, while she seemed happy enough going into the crèche each morning, it still killed Kate that this might all somehow be her fault.

It was getting harder and harder to keep everyone happy and she could feel her stress levels go further and further through the roof.

It will calm down after the visit, she kept telling herself. After the visit she would hopefully be able to apply for the job properly, set down some ground rules about what kind of hours she was willing to work and then, as soon as she was replaced herself, Mary would be happy again and normal life could resume.

It didn't help that it was such a horrible day outside. On a nice day there was no more beautiful view, but today all she could see was sheets of rain lashing against the huge windows and miles and miles of heavy grey sky. She looked at her watch. She couldn't wait for lunchtime. She'd leftover quiche from the ill-fated zoo picnic yesterday and, really, a cup of tea would go a long way towards brightening her mood.

That's if anyone was stopping for lunch. It wouldn't be unusual at the best of times for people to work through, and today was not looking good. She heard the low ping of an email and clicked on her Outlook icon. Two had just popped in together. The first was from Geraldine with the 'news' that Rob had got the Grade 2 promotion, and the address on the second didn't look familiar at all. She looked at the 'Re'. It said 'apology'.

Jesus, what was this? She sighed, thinking if it was a request for payment then they were too late – the run had been sent on Friday and there wasn't going to be another one until after the big visit.

She clicked it open.

Sender: LivvySharpe121@sparkmail.com
To: Kate.O'Brien@DKB.com

Hi,

I don't even know if this will get to you. I'm not even sure if you spell your name with a K or a C like some of those fancy Cates that are on TV. But I'm hoping that they haven't changed the way they do staff emails and that you will get it.

The thing is, I was very rude to you the other day and I haven't slept a wink thinking about it all weekend. You probably think I'm a nutter and if you've asked anyone in there then they've probably agreed. The thing is, I was wondering would you do me a favour? I could ask one of the others but for many reasons there's no one in there that I ever want to speak to again – but well, you, you seem nice.

Anyhow, it's my picture. I left it on my desk – I left in such a hurry, you see, and it's a frame that Sam made me in school, so it's a special one and I'm afraid that they'll bin it. Or maybe they have already. Anyhow I'm in town today – if you could meet me maybe at lunchtime?

Look, I'll understand if you don't want to meet me. In fact, you needn't even answer this and sure I'll never know if you just ignored it or if it never got to you, so don't worry.

But my mobile is 087 2256789 if you had a chance. It's the picture of the three boys.

I need to get them out of there.

Thanks

Olivia

Kate read the email twice. And then a third time. And she looked across to Olivia's desk, to the drawer where she knew the picture lay. And then she took out her mobile and started to text.

Chapter 50

MARY

"What possessed me to come out running on a night like this?" Mary held her exercise jacket out from her chest and watched the rivulets of rain flow down onto the ground. They'd only just arrived at the meeting spot and already she felt she was wet to her underpants. And she'd dashed out of work early for this? She must be mad, she thought to herself.

"Dedication," Ronan answered, rain flowing down his beard, slicking the hair to his chin.

"Or lunacy."

"Arrah sure, what else would you have been doing – sitting in front of your Sky box?" He was mimicking her sister and Mary shoved him.

She'd had quite enough of Dympna lately and had vented a bit to Ronan about her. She'd been on again this evening about how poor Dad had finally given in to poor Mam about going for tests and who was going to drive them to the hospital on Thursday because she'd have the school run and sure Stephen currently had no car insurance.

"Smartarse." She made a face at him, but sure it was wasted given they could hardly see their hands in front of their faces with the rain.

"Anyway, running in the rain is fine – the worst thing that can happen is you get wet. Which has just happened so now the worst is over."

"You're the epitome of optimism, aren't you?" she said. "What happens if, now that I'm wet, I get pneumonia and end up not being able to go into work on the busiest week of the year, and miss the big German visit on Thursday? I'll be fired!"

He looked at her. "Thursday, did you say?"

"Yes, why?"

"Oh, no why. I've a thing on myself on Thursday." He bent down and started messing with his shoelace.

"A 'thing', Ronan Sexton?" she teased, "And what kind of 'a thing', pray tell?"

"Well, I've decided to start that whole networking malarkey and I've joined up with the South Dublin group. Anyhow, the first social thing is on Thursday."

"Well, best of luck with that. Bring your business cards. I'll be thinking of you when I'm entertaining the Frankfurters."

"I'd say that'll be a barrel of laughs," he said. "German bankers. Only marginally more entertaining than the Irish ones."

"Hey, lay off the banker jokes – I'm a banker, remember?"

"It'd be hard to forget when it's all you ever talk about."

Mary made a face at him and started to tie back her sopping hair.

"I'm sure when you were working you talked a fair bit about it too."

He finished with his lace and stood up. "I *am* working, remember? But yes, you're right. When I had my desk job, it did take over a bit. I worked the same kind of stupid hours you do, for the same kind of stupid reasons."

"Well, if I wasn't surrounded by stupid people who won't pull their weight then I could cut out a lot of the stupid hours, couldn't I?"

"Why aren't they pulling their weight? Or more to the point, how come they can say 'no' to the hours and you can't?"

"Because they've bloody children," grumbled Mary. "And I get that they have to be home at a decent hour, I really do, but why I should have to pick up the pieces for them over and over again is beyond me. Like either have the job or have the stupid children." Her hand flew to her mouth, "Shit, I'm sorry, I didn't mean to insult your children."

He threw back his head and laughed. "You must mean my future children?"

"Eh no, I mean your current children. Why, are you planning more?"

He looked at her, frowning. "Mary, I don't have any children. Well, not that I know of."

"Well, what about the girls you're always talking about?" Mary didn't like people laughing at her – she was cross now.

"The girls?" He grinned. "You mean these girls?" He fished deep into his jacket and took out his phone, and shielding it from the rain with his hand showed it to her. On the screen saver were what looked like two Springer Spaniels. "You mean Esther and Amanda?"

"Oh!" Her hand flew to her mouth again. "They're dogs!"

"They are – currently living with my sister Dolores because the useless builders doing my neighbour's extension knocked down our wall. But yes, they're dogs. And I can't believe you thought otherwise. Why didn't you just ask me?" He laughed again.

Mary was scarlet. "I didn't ask because it's actually none of my business or concern and still isn't," she snapped, raging that he was laughing at her. "Now are we running tonight or not?"

OLIVIA

When I look back now at that last afternoon I can't really tell if that final incident was that bad or if it was literally the straw that broke the camel's back. We'd been working on the budgets for weeks. I liked doing the budgets – it was one of my original jobs and one of the tasks I was most proud of doing. But that Thursday my mam had rung to say that Danny Jnr had a roaring temperature. Now what was I supposed to do? Danny couldn't take all three of them to the doctor so of course I had to go home to take him. And the file I was working on only needed two last figures before it was completed, and I was still waiting on those from Mary.

So, rightly or wrongly, I gave her the file and asked her would she put them in herself and then send the whole lot to Declan. I thought that was a fair request. I didn't think it was taking advantage or asking too much. I mean, Jesus, if anyone asked me to do something like that, of course I'd do it.

And then the next day I did something I never did. I decided to go in, even though it was Friday and it was my day off. It was budget time, we'd a deadline and DJ was feeling a lot better.

So I went in.

And what was the first fucking thing that I saw? Only an email from Declan, thanking Mary for all her work on the file and saying things like "I understand this was sprung on you and you had to stay until quite late to get it done."

The stupid gobshite had clearly CC-ed me on it by mistake.

I scrolled down to read the email from Mary to which he was responding and I thought I would actually get sick. It was no wonder he thought she'd had to put in hours of work – she was claiming credit for it all!

Two figures I'd asked her to put in. Two of HER figures? Sure where was the hours of work in that? And then I started to wonder what other emails with this kind of poisonous shite in them had made their way to Declan? Was it any wonder his attitude to me had changed so much over the last few months?

I was absolutely gutted. I thought I might calm down after a while but, to be honest, I just got more and more upset as the hours went on. I didn't mind getting into trouble when I'd actually done something wrong – but I was not taking this. I'd left Danny Jnr with Mam that morning when I really should have been with him myself – on my fucking day off – and for this? This utter bullshit? So I tell you, I just cracked.

I marched up to Mary and I said, "What's all this about hours of work? You had two fucking figures to put in!"

And she looked up at me, calm as calm could be, not seeming to be a bit put out that I'd seen the email and said "I could hardly pass it on to Declan without checking it all first, now could I?"

I said, "I had checked it. There was nothing wrong with it."

And she said, "Olivia, I am not going to forward something to a Director with my name on it without having checked it thoroughly first."

And I knew looking at her that there was going to be no budging her and I thought about just leaving it but then Leona came over to the desk and asked what was going on. I don't even know why she asked – the stupid email had gone to her too and I was not exactly keeping my voice down. But I answered her anyway even though I knew, I just knew from the look on her face that she had no interest in backing me up. And sure enough she said, "Olivia, Mary was following procedure and really you should be thanking her for taking over from you, yet again."

And I tell you I let her have it. I couldn't even repeat to you what I screeched at the pair of them. I told them that I knew exactly what they'd been playing at for the last year. That I knew that there'd been a very definite campaign to get rid of me. All those important meetings scheduled for my days off, important conference calls that for some reason had to take place after five o'clock and now this. And that now they could have their way – that I was giving them what they wanted. I had no other option but to leave my job.

They'd won.

And that was the end of that. I went home to my babies. The stupid fight was over at last, and I lost.

Or at least I felt they had won, but then maybe that's all about to change?

Chapter 51

THE DAY OF . . .

Jacinta was at the office early, even for her. She wanted everything to be 'just so' for when Head Office arrived. The cleaners were in overnight as they always were but she didn't trust them to have it the way she wanted.

She left her handbag at her desk and, taking a small shopping bag that lived under the desk, she took the lift to the 9th floor.

The 9th floor was quiet, but then it always seemed quieter than any other floor in the building. There was never any of the chatter or banter of the open-plan floors and every one talked in hushed tones as they went into the Directors' offices or down to the end of the corridor to the boardroom.

That was where Jacinta made her way now. It was her favourite room in the whole building. Being higher than the Finance Floor the view from the wraparound floor-to-ceiling windows was even more impressive here and stretched so much further. Even now with the early morning light only starting to filter through the clouds she could clearly see the elegant red-and-white chimneys of the Poolbeg power station and the glistening Irish Sea beyond.

But what she loved most about this room wasn't the panoramic views or the thick, luxurious pile of the carpet underfoot but the main feature of the whole room: the gargantuan mahogany table that held pride of place in the centre of the room. This table was one of the only pieces of furniture that had come with them from Merrion

Square and, while it had been almost too big for the room there, here it was perfect.

She walked over and ran one bony hand down along the wood as if stroking it. It was just as she thought. No modern cleaner knew how to treat such a specimen of woodwork. The streaks were barely visible to the naked eye, but they were visible to her. She reached into her shopping bag and took out a well-used tub of beeswax furniture polish and a soft cloth and, slipping on a latex glove to stop the polish seeping into her beautifully manicured hand, she got to work.

As she worked she wondered who would do this kind of thing when she was gone? Alice? Alice wouldn't know her beeswax from her Flash. She supposed the beautiful table would just be left to the mercy of the cleaners. Nobody else would care. It would be let go, getting steadily dustier and streak-ridden like the rest of the old values of this godforsaken company.

She gave herself a mental shake. She needed to stop being so morose. Ever since her party last week it was like she was more and more aware with each day of her mortality. Forty years was a long time to be with a company and, one thing was for sure, she certainly wouldn't be seeing another forty.

But you're still here now, you silly woman, she chided herself. And while you're here, things will be done properly so stop your ridiculous melancholy.

And they would be done properly. She had single-handedly planned the German's visit to the nth degree, taking it all back from Declan who'd been charging around like a demented lunatic ever since the visit had been announced.

He'd come up with all kinds of ridiculous ideas for the first night of their visit, but she'd refused to listen to any of them. There was no way she was running the risk of bringing middle-aged German bankers into the raucous cobbled streets of Temple Bar, or putting them on a bus to ship them out to Powerscourt in County Wicklow. Mostly she didn't trust her own staff not to let her down – the way last Thursday night had descended into debauchery was still very fresh in her head. So, instead, she had arranged for caterers to come here, to the IFSC. Beside the boardroom was a series of smaller rooms with huge sliding doors between them that, when opened out, made up an area the size of a small function room.

She was going to show them that they, the Irish, knew how to do things properly. That they could be trusted to showcase their country whilst at the same time providing a relaxing and comfortable venue for their visitors.

When the table was finally to her satisfaction, she popped her head into the function room to make sure her directions had been followed in there too. Declan had wanted balloons but Jacinta had shrivelled him with a look that Medusa would have been proud of.

Balloons? You're a bloody balloon, she'd felt like saying. Wouldn't balloons look great with the harpist she was paying to come and play soft Irish music in the corner?

Balloons.

She went back down to her desk and did a few last-minute checks with the caterers. They were under strict orders that the canapés were to be made of only the best of Irish ingredients, Irish bacon, sourdough bread, wild salmon. If she saw anything that didn't look like it could be sourced between Dublin Bay and Spanish Point she would not be held responsible for her actions.

The rooms in the Citi Hotel next door had been booked. Frankfurt had suggested that as many staff as possible stay for the overnight. It was all part of the team-building exercise. Leona had been the only one who'd insisted she wasn't staying, which Jacinta found slightly surprising. She'd refused to say what her reservations were and in the end Jacinta had just left it. She had enough to be worrying about without having to start second-guessing the motives of those around her.

Everything at last seemed to be under control. She even thought Declan looked calmer this morning. He'd driven the team mad all week with ridiculous statements about having things "boxed off" or lining up ducks or some such nonsense – but now? Now he finally seemed to have calmed down. God love him but he was an awful eejit but essentially his heart was in the right place. Jacinta knew things about Declan that no one else did – he'd been treated very badly in the City in London and, really, was it any wonder that he just couldn't afford another blip on his CV?

She looked around the open-plan area. Everyone seemed to have followed her neat dress directive, which was good. The lads were all wearing ties, though Cian didn't appear to be even in. No harm, she thought to herself, he was the one mostly likely to indulge in the 12-year-old Jameson that she'd laid on for the 'grown-ups' so his absence might be a blessing in disguise. Everyone else would toe the party line – even Arianne had managed to batten down her cleavage and looked slightly less like one of those awful reality-show women today than usual.

Yes, it was looking good for this visit, she thought. Everything was going to be fine.

And then the post arrived.

Chapter 52

GERALDINE

Geraldine read the letter again and then put it on the desk in front of her.

Jesus, Mary and Holy Saint Joseph.

It was an exclamation her mother used to use – back when you couldn't shout the 'f' word at the drop of a hat. It wasn't one that she herself had heard or used in years and yet for some reason it was the only thing that she could think of right at this moment. Her brain had gone into shock. Her emotions were in such disarray that she didn't know which one to deal with first.

Anger?

Anxiety?

Dread?

Was dread even an emotion? Well, it was this morning, she thought to herself – it was right up there with anger.

What kind of a company was this? She'd heard of toxic banks and DKB had prided itself on not being one of them.

But it *was* toxic. The humans within its walls were toxic. The motives behind sending this letter were what? Revenge? Trying to get even? Whatever happened to taking whatever hand life dealt you on the chin and just getting on with it? Why did everything always have to be somebody else's fault?

And yes, legally, there was fault. Within the letter of the law, this did not sound good.

But seriously. Why take it this far? There was a more humane way to handle this.

Oh Leona, she thought, you are in a difficult spot here.

Chapter 53

KATE

Kate was aware that there'd been a shift in the atmosphere of the office but she no longer cared.

She no longer cared.

It was as if she'd been in some kind of mental car crash and she felt like she was only just about holding it together. She couldn't manage more than two words to anyone and she had a feeling that even Mary had noticed that the lights were on but there was definitely no one at home. But she could go and take a running jump off one the bridges that spanned the Liffey outside.

She no longer cared.

She'd arrived back to the office after lunch on Monday, and it was as if she was now viewing it and everyone in it through some kind of strange filter. And now, after a week of broken sleep and the type of soul-searching that she'd never done before in her entire life, she finally knew what she had to do.

Olivia had cried when Kate had delivered the picture to her. She was crying before Kate had even handed her the picture, but then, clutching it to her chest, she'd sobbed as if her heart would break.

Kate had not known what to do. There was very little she could do except make comforting noises every time Olivia came up for air. They'd arranged to meet again that night and had drunk tea together until late in the evening.

And now she'd heard the whole horrible story about the systematic bullying of Olivia and how she'd been forced out of her job, a job that she had been doing really well, just because she'd had children, and it made her feel sick. But what shook her most was not what had happened to Olivia and how it was affecting her still – how she couldn't eat, couldn't sleep and very obviously couldn't stop crying – but how it was now affecting her, Kate.

She'd left Artane that night and started to drive home and, as she drove, her mind was spinning with all she'd just heard. She felt like she was in a situation that was so vastly beyond her control that it reminded her of only one thing.

Kate hadn't told anyone she had a birthing plan for Jess's birth. Mostly, because to her, it wasn't really a plan. Like she wasn't insisting on bringing in whale music, scented candles or even one of those giant bouncy balls that she was full sure would only end up in the way. No, she hadn't even written anything down, but in her head she knew. She'd read all about birth and what could go wrong and why. So months beforehand she knew that with enough preparation and attitude she could totally get through this with as little intervention as possible.

She believed that, as with everything, preparation was key and that if women had babies in paddy-fields before returning to work with said child strapped to their back, then so could she.

Well, not back to work, but certainly back to the comfort of her own home the next day.

Preparation was key.

And she was prepared. She'd sailed through that first pregnancy, had kept herself fit and healthy and by the time her due date arrived her body (apart from the rather large bump) was as prepared for battle as an athlete heading for the Olympics. She was ready.

She was still ready ten days later when they made her come in to be induced. And they had to 'make her' as induction was not a route she wanted to take. The day before she had walked four miles and succumbed to borrowing one of those stupid balls to bounce on for hours when she got back. But all to no avail. Half seven next morning found her legs akimbo in the hospital, her waters being unceremoniously broken with a rather large skewer-like object.

As she lay there she tried to ignore the sensation of the fluid gushing from her and she waited, breathing, ready for the first pains.

Last intervention, she swore.

She was still waiting an hour later when they decided to place a drip in her arm and within minutes the pains had started and she was breathing away like a pro. With each pain that came Michael watched the graph and told her calmly when they'd peaked and she'd relax again.

Within ten minutes she was interrupting him to ask were they nearly at the peak.

"No, no, not yet," he answered each time, studying the graph like the engineer he was.

Within another ten minutes she'd grabbed his arm mid-pain and hissed in a guttural voice: "It's okay to fucking lie, you know!"

And at that stage she knew she was in trouble. That this shit had barely started and already she had never known pain like it. She suggested to the nurse that she get out and walk but the nurse shook her head, indicating the trace that was by now strapped to her rigid, spasmodic stomach.

The pains, which were coming quicker now, were horrendous and, to her shame, getting the epidural was completely her idea.

"I just can't!" she gasped to Michael, and he nodded, trying not to show the relief he was feeling at her decision to 'cave'.

She'd heard awful stories about the epidural and how, if the needle went in incorrectly she could be paralysed so she lay, still as a curled-up statue as the anaesthetist went to insert the long needle between the knobs of her spine. And even as she felt the needle pierce her skin a pain started but still she lay, trying to pretend that all this horror was happening to someone else.

And it was worth the effort. Within minutes the pain relief was sweeping through her body and she'd have felt ashamed of the euphoria had it not felt so goddamn good.

It was working.

It was really working.

How could something that felt this good be bad?

She should have done it hours ago.

She lay back in the bed and relaxed, the horrors of the previous hour slipping back into the recesses of her memory.

"Feel better?" Michael asked.

She nodded and, just as she thought she might even go asleep, she went to move herself further up onto her pillows.

And couldn't.

Her legs felt heavy, like they were made of stone and the stupid drip in her hand meant she could put no weight on her wrists to lever herself up.

"What's wrong?" Michael asked.

"I'm kind of stuck," she said.

"You're what?"

"I'm stuck. I can't move. My legs are dead."

They laughed as Michael put both arms under her armpits and hoisted her up onto her pillows. Well, he laughed. She tried to laugh but in her mind she could feel the first feelings of unease start to seep up from her dead limbs. And as she lay back trying to focus on the glorious lack of pain, she tried not to focus on the even stronger feeling that her control over this situation was ebbing ever further away.

And to Kate O'Brien, the terror of that was already worse than the pain.

How was she going to push? How was she going to get into any kind of birthing-friendly position? She was like a giant slug, paralysed from the waist down, unable to sit up, unable to roll over, unable to move herself in any way whatsoever. She had never felt so completely helpless in her life and she didn't like it one bit.

Some eight hours later her lifeless body was ceasing to be her main concern. Several mortifying examinations (made only slightly less mortifying by the fact that if she just closed her eyes she could forget that her lifeless flabby legs were akimbo again) later, it seemed there was a problem. Well, two problems actually. One was her baby appeared to be stuck and the other was that the initial epidural was starting to wear off. Wear off in the pain-relief not paralysis sense, that is. Added to that she was by now exhausted and scared and her breathless panic attacks were starting to clash with the renewed contractions.

As everyone around her started to move more quickly, Kate ceased to move at all. It was like she had slipped into a stupor of shame and helplessness. Tears were sliding out of her closed eyes and when at 5am the midwife took her hand and said that their only option was an emergency C-section she just nodded.

She just wanted this over.

She lay there as they attached yet more drips and prepared her for surgery with razors and giant swabs of some stinking yellowy brown substance. And still she cried. She cried for her dignity, she cried for her plans but most of all, she cried for the loss of control over her life that she was now starting to suspect might be worse than any sleepless nights. In just a few short hours, not only had she lost control over her body, but her mind was gone too.

And that had heralded the beginning of the end of Kate's love of motherhood. She was deeply, deeply ashamed that Jess's birth had been such an embarrassing failure. But then to further compound the shame, when the consultant had hinted that David's birth might well go along the same lines she'd stopped him mid-sentence and asked outright for another section. She couldn't do that emergency situation again. She wanted the quickest, easiest way out; this whole business clearly wasn't for her. She needed to get through it and get back to what she was good at.

Work.

And now this was all falling apart too. Late Monday night she'd held Olivia close and told her over and over again that they couldn't get away with what they'd done to her. She'd urged her strongly to take it to court. And now this morning, she'd heard whispers of solicitors' letters and she had a mild kind of satisfaction that some form of justice was about to be served.

But what about her? Had she the courage to do what *she* needed to?

She needed someone to talk to. She'd ring Lynn at lunchtime.

Chapter 54

LEONA

It was four o'clock and Leona had not moved in some time. She was afraid that if she moved then she would keep moving. That she would walk out her office door, across the open-plan area and to the lift. That she would go down in the lift and out the front door, down the quays until she reached the bridge and keep walking until she reached the centre of it. Then she would lever herself up on the side of it, one leg at a time, and sit there looking at the swirling and heaving of the Liffey water below as it joined the Irish Sea.

And she knew what she would do then. She wouldn't jump. Jumping would be too dramatic, too 'look at me'. She would just slip in, unnoticed, and sink into the heaving waters below. She'd sink so quickly and so heavily that no one would be able to grab her. No one would be able to reach her ever again.

She'd had enough. No matter how hard she'd tried to do the right thing over the past year or more, it was no good. She was never going to win.

All Geraldine would say was that there'd be a complaint.

A formal complaint.

A formal complaint made against her.

Her specifically.

And she probably should have been more surprised. But she wasn't. She was strangely calm about it all. Maybe she'd been expecting it. For the last month, ever since Olivia had left, she'd been waiting for something to happen.

And it had to happen today. Today when the spotlight was being shone on the Dublin office.

Declan was going to go fucking nuts. Actually he was probably going nuts about it right now. Frankfurt were due in less than an hour and there were two solicitors' letters in the building that hadn't been there at nine that morning.

Well, he could go as fucking nuts as he liked. He was as much to blame for all this as she was. He would have to shoulder some of the blame. Take some responsibility for how it had all spiralled out of control and become such a mess.

It wasn't like she was denying that she'd done wrong herself either. She wasn't proud of her actions. She could have, and should have handled things differently but, at the time, at the time she'd done whatever she could.

A formal complaint.

It was going to take her a while to work her way back from this one. She'd seen this kind of thing before. She knew what would have to happen now and the whole process could take weeks, months even. There would be endless meetings that didn't include her and all the staff would have to be interviewed. They would pull apart her personality, her way of working. They would examine every single thing she'd done in the last months, years and then, eventually, come to a verdict. And throughout all of this she would still be trying to do her job. She would still be working night and day so that other people's lives didn't have to change at all. And after that they would make a ruling and she wasn't quite sure what would happen then. It would all be 'handled' and then would eventually go away.

If she could find the energy to wait, this would all eventually go away.

An email pinged into her inbox.

Sender: RKinirons@DKB.com
To: LSharpe@DKB.com

Are you okay?

Despite all her heartache, she smiled. In the midst of all of this nightmare, there was Rob. He was the only person now in her whole world that made her feel like she wasn't a failure. He was the first person she thought of every morning and the last person she thought of at night. Every time she thought of that night when he'd kissed her, she felt like she might go on fire with longing. Yes, throughout all of this there was him.

Why was she fighting the feelings that consumed her every time she thought of him, or saw him across a room? What did she let what felt so right, feel so prohibitively wrong.

Well, she was too tired to fight it anymore. Too tired and too fed up. What was the point in trying to do the right thing? They only came after you and beat you down eventually anyway.

She felt the first quivers of excitement rush through her as she turned to her keyboard and sent two quick emails. The first was to Jacinta saying that she'd like a room booked tonight after all, and the second was to Rob, asking him to come into her office.

Chapter 55

GAVIN

Gavin was at the playground again. Sure where else would he be on a Thursday afternoon, he thought bitterly. And he'd just had a text from Leona to say she wouldn't be home at all. That Declan had insisted that she stay in the hotel with the rest of them in the interest of 'solidarity'.

Such fucking bullshit.

He wasn't stupid. There was something else going on and he had a fair idea what it was. Did she think he was stupid? Did she think that he himself hadn't worked in a corporate environment and witnessed what happened when the hours got longer and longer in work and shorter and shorter at home? Last Thursday night had been the start of it, coming home so late and definitely drunk. Then Friday she'd 'accidentally' fallen asleep in the old nursery.

No, he wasn't stupid.

She was slipping from his fingers and he hated her for it.

He wandered over to his usual spot and stood, the Barbie schoolbag hanging off one arm as usual. He looked at his watch: four thirty. Rachel had a party at five in one of those awful indoor play areas but at least she was now old enough to leave there and he could go and get the groceries in.

Oh, the glamour.

He was surprised how many were in the playground this late in the day. Rachel had had her art class for an hour after school but he didn't realise there'd be this many around after it.

The Polish man was even in his usual spot, but then, Gavin thought, maybe he was always there. Sure it beat sitting at home, he supposed.

He glanced around, telling himself that he wasn't looking for anyone in particular. That it was for want of something better to do. But when he couldn't see who he was allegedly not looking for, the disappointment made his shoulders slump just a little bit more.

Rachel was now hanging from the monkey bars, her tongue clenched firmly between her teeth, her eyes almost crossed with concentration. The silly amount of pride he felt at her bravery was bittersweet as it struck him how like her mother she looked. The same set look of determination. The same survival instinct.

"Not moved over to the Full-Timer's patch yet then?"

He jumped at the sound of Trish's voice. He hadn't seen her walk up.

"Not likely," he grunted.

She was talking about the full-time mothers who were standing, as they always were, at the swings. They pushed, and chatted, and pushed and chatted, pausing only to pull out their tissues and wipe the streaming green noses of their children.

After nearly two years of observation Gavin now knew there was a pecking order. These formidable ladies were deemed to be a vastly superior beast to the Part-Timers who tended to stick together with shame-induced shyness, the knowledge that they in turn are superior to the completely absent Full-Time-Working-Mothers was of little benefit to them.

But then it took a lot to make a Full-Time-Working-Mother feel inferior. He could have told them that much.

"Didn't think you were here." He tried to keep his voice casual.

"I'm not usually, but he's started in some Fit Kids thing after school and I thought it might knacker the little fecker for bedtime so said I'd give it a go."

"Ah, I see. I was thinking it wasn't art classes he was at."

"Me arse is he going to Art – Jesus, he'd only want to be practising at home and I'd end up beating him from one end of the house to the other with the mess he'd make."

"True enough." It wasn't funny, but still a smile started to soften

Gavin's jaw and his shoulders began to loosen just a little bit. "So why don't you go over to them?"

He nodded in the direction of the Full-Time-Mothers.

"I think you have to have a husband," she hissed back. "I'd only be a threat to that lot."

The irony of what she was saying was not lost on Gavin.

"So, any chat?" he asked, changing the subject.

"Not a bit. Haven't heard from Adam's father since, the prick ..."

"Well, that's good, isn't it?"

"It is, if I wasn't full sure that he was going to raise his ugly mug as soon as something else is up with him. What's up with that lot over there?"

She was gesticulating towards three women over at the roundabout; the only creatures that could be deemed on a higher plane than the Full-Time-Mothers – the PTA Mothers. Like witches round a cauldron, they huddled together, their beady eyes already on Gavin and Trish as they chatted. Perversely their disapproval made Gavin strangely excited.

"I think they're on to us," Gavin whispered out the side of his mouth.

"The Single Mother and the Stay-at-Home Dad. Jesus, if they get their mitts on us they'll be like a pack of magpies fighting over a couple of dead frogs."

Her voice was low, deadpan, and he had to laugh at the bitter tone. It felt good to let his jaw relax into the smile that had been threatening since she arrived at his shoulder. He stole a look sideways. Wearing jeans, converse and a sweater today, her blonde hair was tied up for a change. It suited her. She had a nice neck.

"Big sweater today? Do you think it's winter or what?" He gently teased her and she poked him back.

"Well, it's not exactly July, now is it?"

"That is true."

"I take it ye didn't reach any agreement on the job then?"

His smile faded at the change in subject.

"No," he said, shaking his head, "and there won't be. Once my wife makes her mind up on something, that's pretty much it."

"Oh well," she shrugged, "Insurance's loss is our gain then, I suppose."

He didn't answer. What did she mean by that? A muscle deep inside his gut contracted slightly. Very slightly, but not un-noticeably.

Insurance's loss is our gain.

Did that mean she liked him? Liked seeing him around?

Well, wasn't that a welcome change? Someone who didn't just expect him to have dinner on the table. To have the homework done. To have the ironing done.

The fucking ironing.

Leona's crumpled shirts had replaced his on the heap. He couldn't remember the last time he'd ironed a shirt for himself. No need to iron T-shirts. No lining-up-the-crease needed for jeans …

Through a gap in the clouds the sun tried to fling down a bit of heat but there were ominous clouds gathering. And the playground had become bathed in a strange glow.

"See, I told you, practically July," he joked.

"Looks like a storm coming if you ask me," she said gloomily.

"You're such an optimist," he laughed.

"Daddy! Watch me!"

He turned, instantly knowing it was his child calling, mostly because he was the only daddy there.

"I'm watching, honey, you're doing great!"

She was now climbing to the top of the frame. A curl of hair stuck to her forehead with exertion, her little blue shirt wriggling freer from the band of her skirt every time she stretched for a higher bar.

Even his seven-year-old daughter was achieving.

He looked at his watch. "We'd best be off, she has a party at five."

Trish looked at him. "Is that Ava Burke's party? Dylan is going to that."

"Is he?"

"Yep – he's friends with her brother or something."

"So you've a free house then?" He instantly blushed. A proper roaring-red blush.

You fucking eejit.

"I sure do."

His senses swarmed over her answer in a frenzy. Was she offended? Was she pleased? Did she realise what he'd asked? What should he say now?

"I see."

They were looking at each other properly now. Face to face. Eye to eye. And there was a look in her eye that he hadn't seen in a woman in a very, very long time. He felt excited. He felt like a man again.

He felt like Gavin Blake circa 2007.

With a boom a clap of thunder rent the air.

And then there was a scream. And a thud. And a chorus of roars and shrieks from the crowd behind his back.

And Trish gripped his arm but he was frozen. And it was like his limbs were too heavy to turn around, but he did and all he could see was the crumpled pile of navy and blue on the ground under the frame. And the dark curls, and the dark pool of red blood getting bigger and bigger on the concrete. And the strange angle ...

For a second he thought he might pass out. Everything started to spin round him in slow motion.

"RACHEL!"

Chapter 56

LEONA

"Leona, Jacinta told me to tell you that they're waiting to start."

Leona looked up to see Alice's head around her door.

"Thanks, Alice, I'll be out now."

She wasn't long back from town where she'd popped down to buy a few bits for her overnight stay, but she was feeling relatively calm now.

In a way.

In a way she felt like she'd reached a point of no return. Tomorrow, when the big team meeting was over and the German team gone home she would have to face the repercussions of the letter, whatever they might be. But for now? For now she wasn't thinking about that.

She looked at her phone where Gavin's number was flashing again. He was obviously annoyed at her text saying that she was staying the night. So annoyed that this was his third time to ring in the last ten minutes.

Well, he could stay annoyed.

He'd keep until tomorrow too.

She put the phone into the top drawer of her desk and took one last look at her reflection in the little compact she kept there. She looked relatively well considering the day she'd had. And that made her very happy indeed.

By the time she got outside the party was underway. Declan was in a fresh pair of red braces and this time his monogrammed shirt seemed to mirror the colours of the German flag which seemed to be a nice touch if a tad OTT.

She stood to one side, accepting a glass of white wine magically handed to her by a member of the catering staff.

Jacinta sidled up alongside her.

"How are you?" she asked.

"I'm fine, Jacinta, thanks."

"Good." Jacinta nodded her approval at her answer. "No point in worrying about it tonight."

"I know."

Suddenly they were interrupted by a flapping Alice.

"Jacinta, Declan wants you straight away."

Jacinta rolled her eyes. "I'm going to kill that imbecile before this evening is over," she muttered. "What in God's name is wrong with him now?"

"It's something to do with the caviar on the canapés. He wants it wiped off, says the Germans will think it's not in the spirit of austerity or something like that."

"*It's not focking caviar!*" Jacinta threw her hands in the air, the expletive sounding completely foreign when roared in her rich Dublin 4 accent. "*It's focking salmon roe!*" and with that she strode off in the direction of the door, leaving Leona giggling in her wake.

God, how was she laughing? Her whole life was tumbling around her shoulders and here she was, giggling. She saw Rob smile over at her and smiled back.

Ah yes, that was why she was laughing.

"Leona? Could I have a word?"

She turned to see Kate at her side.

"Why yes, of course, Kate, what's up?"

Kate seemed uncomfortable but only hesitated for a second before speaking.

"I'm handing in my notice, Leona. And I know this isn't the time or the place but I can't go another minute without saying it to someone."

"Oh!" Leona was taken aback. "I wasn't expecting that."

"You were never going to give me that job, were you?"

Leona looked at her. "Jesus, Kate, where did that come from?"

"Just answer me, Leona, don't make a fool out of me too."

Leona looked at Kate and decided that she'd nothing to lose by being honest. "No. I wasn't, Kate. It's not the job for you."

"I thought as much." Kate seemed almost relieved to have had her suspicions confirmed so quickly. "Well, I've made the right decision so. I can't work somewhere where women are discriminated against, Leona. I tried to, I thought it wouldn't matter, but the cold hard truth is that I have children. There's nothing I can do about that."

"I see." Leona was taken aback by Kate's words. Where on earth was this coming from?

"And I'm sorry," Kate continued, "I know it's probably letting you down, I know you're under pressure, but I need to work somewhere where it doesn't matter if you're a mother and it certainly isn't held against you."

Leona nodded. "I see," she repeated again before continuing, "Do you know, Kate, I could try and tell you that it's not quite as simple as that here but, for what it's worth, I think you're doing the right thing and I wish you all the best in finding the right position. You're a good worker, there's no doubt about that –"

"But?" asked Kate. "I sense a 'but'?"

"Well the 'but' is that I also feel the need to warn you that this idealistic work situation for mothers doesn't really exist. At least not in this industry, at this level, at this time."

"That's a ridiculous thing to say, if you don't mind my saying so," Kate said, not able to keep the incredulity from her tone.

"I would say it's a ridiculously *sad* thing to say, Kate. And it's wrong, it's so, so wrong. But let me tell you something else too: it takes a certain kind of woman, with a certain drive and focus, to be able to maintain the same level of career after she's had children, to the one she had before children."

"Someone like you, you mean?"

"I am the last example you should follow, Kate. I know you hate me, and I could sit here for hours and tell you all the reasons behind anything I've ever done. But you're not interested and I don't have the energy. I wish you all the best though – as I said, you're a great worker and I really do hope you find the right job. But again, for what it's worth, this wasn't it."

"Thank you," Kate muttered. "I might go home now if that's

okay. I'll talk to Geraldine tomorrow."

Leona nodded and Kate walked away quickly, almost colliding with Mary who was talking rapidly into her mobile phone as she left the room too.

For an awful moment Leona really hoped Mary wasn't onto a recruitment consultant. Then that thought made her smile again and she looked up again to see Rob smiling back at her.

It wouldn't be long now, she thought and felt that rush of excitement again.

But first, she really should start working the room. She walked over to where Declan was talking to Frank and Jans Weber, head of Corporate Lending.

"Oh, here she is now," Frank said and Leona winced.

"Talking about me?" She forced a smile. "I hope it's all good."

"Well, more talking about where you live," said Frank.

"Oh really?"

"Yes," said Declan. "You're Malahide, aren't you?"

"I am." Leona was really smiling now as she could see Rob over Frank's shoulder and he was trying to make her laugh by pulling funny faces. "Why?"

"Oh, apparently there was a seven-year-old child killed there this afternoon, in some freak accident in a playground."

And staring straight at Rob, Leona remembered the three calls she'd ignored from Gavin only an hour earlier and her wineglass slid from her hand and crashed to the ground.

Chapter 57

MARY

Mary pressed the 'end call' button on her mobile and looked through the glass window of the door at the busy room beyond.

She didn't want to go in.

Everyone was laughing and chatting and having a good time and she didn't want to go in. She felt sick to the very pit of her stomach and all she wanted to do was go home.

But then there was no one at home. No one to fall onto, sobbing and crying. No one to tell her that everything was going to be okay.

Nothing would ever be okay again. That had been her mother on the phone. She shouldn't have answered. She wasn't even sure why she had, she never usually answered personal calls in work. But then her mother never usually phoned her.

This was a special occasion though, wasn't it? This was her mother phoning to gloat. To tell them that she'd been right all along.

Her father had had it officially confirmed today that he had early-onset Alzheimer's.

Her poor, poor father.

Her only sane parent had dementia. Her mother, who was as mad as a box of frogs, was perfectly healthy but her poor dad, the one member of her family that kept her sane, was going to slowly but steadily slip into some kind of other world, where he no longer knew his family's faces. And what had actually nearly made her laugh about the whole thing? Her mother had also managed to break the

326

good news that Stephen had decided he was going to emigrate. Canada probably.

Of course he was, thought Mary with a bitter laugh. Did anyone for a second think he was going to stay living at home after that diagnosis? Hell no, she'd say Canada wasn't far enough away for him.

God forbid someone might actually be around to give her a hand.

She just couldn't face going back into the room, so she went down the stairs to her own desk instead. She just wanted to be alone for a few minutes – she needed some time to process what she'd just heard.

To her surprise though, Kate was down on their floor too, and seemed to be getting ready to go home.

"You off?" Mary asked, surprised.

"I am." Kate's voice was curt.

"Oh. Well, see you tomorrow so."

"You will." Kate fastened her belt and then just as she turned to go, she seemed to change her mind, and stopped. "I've just handed in my notice, Mary. Thought you might like to know."

"You've what?" Mary was shocked.

"Handed in my notice. So you got what you wanted. Have a nice evening."

Mary looked at Kate, open-mouthed.

"What's that supposed to mean?"

"You never wanted me here. You've made that painfully obvious from the start. And I'm sorry. I thought we could have got on okay. But there you go, I did my best and it wasn't good enough for you. Just like Olivia's best wasn't good enough for you."

Wow – where had that come from?

"It's not the same – you're not the same," Mary managed to respond but Kate put up her hand to stop her.

"Don't, Mary, I'm not interested."

Mary felt sick. She didn't know what to say, but it didn't matter anyway. Kate had turned and left. And anyway, where would she have started? How could she explain that her behaviour over the last few weeks had been nothing personal? Was that even any kind of an excuse? She hadn't behaved well, she knew that. And yes, she'd had her reasons, but now she wasn't so sure whether that was any excuse either.

She sank down into her chair and looked around the empty room. Well, it was all hers now. She'd heard some rumour that Leona was in trouble with HR but she'd no idea what it was about. She presumed Olivia had put in some kind of a complaint that obviously Kate had heard all about now too. That would be Olivia all over. Never happy unless she was crying about something.

And then it struck her: she could probably have Olivia's job now if she wanted. They'd be in an even bigger hurry to fill it now that Kate was gone. Strangely this thought gave her no comfort. Yes, she'd have Olivia's job alright, and when she wasn't working every last hour in here, she'd be at home, nursing her steadily declining dad and listening to her bloody mother going on and on and on.

Be careful what you wish for ...

Well, one thing was for sure, she couldn't face all this on her own. What had ever possessed her to think she could? Jeremy was right, she hadn't thought that whole situation through. She'd rushed into that whole ultimatum. What had possessed her? Surely some part of someone was better than nothing at all? And there was always the chance that he'd change his mind in time and the secret could be gradually phased out. Did it even matter?

He was upstairs now, she thought to herself. She could go up there now and tell him she'd made an awful mistake. They could share a room tonight in the hotel; it would be like Paris all those years ago.

Anything was better than nothing.

She couldn't do this on her own.

She rose to her feet but, as she did so, heard a beep from her phone.

Chapter 58

GAVIN

Gavin still couldn't speak. He'd barely managed to get out the words he wanted to say to Leona on the phone, and now he was spent.

He had no more words.

What had happened in the playground just kept spinning round and round in his head and he felt sick to the pit of this stomach. He would never forget the sight of the crumpled form under the monkey bars.

He'd managed to walk forward but, just as he got there, a woman flung herself in front of him, howling and screaming in the guttural, universal tone of horror.

"Daddy – help! Get me down!"

He turned to look up, hardly able to believe his ears but, sure enough, Rachel's terrified face stared down at him, her knuckles white and clinging to the bars.

He looked back at the ground, but he could no longer see the fallen child amongst the jostling howling small crowd that had gathered around.

But it didn't matter. He was almost horrified at his selfishness as he repeated over and over to himself: *It's not my child, it's not my child, it's not my child.*

And his selfishness shouldn't have horrified him, not given what he'd been about to do.

But none of that mattered. None of it mattered because it wasn't his child.

He reached up for Rachel. But she was frozen with terror. He couldn't remember the last time he'd seen her so scared. But suddenly he was reminded of Leona and that awful day when he'd told her that he'd lost his job.

She'd looked just like Rachel did now.

Scared.

She'd been scared.

But instead of wallowing in self-pity like he had, she'd picked herself up, taken a horrible job she didn't want and had been working night and day ever since to keep their family together with food to eat and a roof to sleep under. He cringed when he thought of how she'd sat one night and spread all their debt out in front of them on the kitchen table. All that stuff that he'd bought to impress everyone, to show everyone that he could give his beautiful wife and family the best of everything. All that stuff that still he'd been waiting to pay for with his next pay rise, his next bonus.

And she had never once said 'I told you so'.

He didn't deserve either of them.

"Take my hand, Rach."

"I can't, Daddy! I'll fall."

"I won't let you fall, baby, I promise."

And then her tongue was between her teeth again and she was tentatively unwinding her little fingers from the bars and then one hand reached out to him.

And then she was in his arms. He held her tight, not able to believe that he had forgotten about her. That he'd turned his back. That he'd looked away.

He moved away from the chaos that was churning in a screaming maelstrom barely feet away from him. Then he turned around one last time to scan the crowd for the blonde hair. She was also standing back now, the other side of the chaos. And she was sucking, hollow-cheeked, on a cigarette like her every breath depended on it.

He hadn't even known that she smoked.

Over the tousled curls of his daughter's head their eyes met. He looked away first.

I won't let you fall, baby, I promise.

That was what he should have said to Leona that night. That's what he should have said to her every day since the day he'd met her instead of trying to impress her with extravagant purchases that meant nothing to her. Well, he was going to say it to her now. He would say it tonight and he would keep saying it.

It couldn't be too late.

Chapter 59

LEONA

"You summoned me, madam?"

Leona turned from the large window that looked out over the Liffey.

"I'm going, Rob," she said quietly.

"You too? Jesus, Mary's just announced to Declan that she's going as well – said something about going networking or something? And did I hear Kate is gone too? He'll have a conniption!"

They both smiled at the thought of how Declan's evening was rapidly sliding down the tubes but then Rob stopped. "Hang on, what do you mean you're going? Going where? You mean the hotel, right?"

"No, I mean home," she said softly. "I'm going home."

He looked at her and nodded slowly as the realization of what she was saying sank in.

"Leona ..." he took a step towards her but she held up her hand.

"Don't!" she whispered quickly, her voice high and cracked. "Please don't."

"You've changed your mind? Why? Why are you doing this? Is it because of him? Why do you care about him? He – he's an arsehole that doesn't deserve you."

"No, Rob, it's not because of him. It's because someone's child got killed today in a freak playground accident. The playground at Rachel's school. It could have been her, Rob, it could have been my little girl and the last time I'd have seen her awake was last Sunday. And for what? For this place?"

"That's hardly your fault."

"Well, it's definitely not hers."

"Leona, please. Think about it ..."

"I have been thinking about it. There's more. There's a complaint against me which is going to do my reputation no good. I did an awful thing, Rob. This place has turned me into the kind of person that does awful things to other people." He looked puzzled so she continued. "I wanted Olivia out of here. The work was piling up and Declan refused to allow me the budget to get someone else. He told me to get rid of Olivia and we could replace her then with someone who could do the job, who could do the hours. A man, preferably one without a family, without any desire to have a life outside these walls. So, yes, I wanted her gone. I wanted her gone so I bullied her and I made her life a living hell because she was never going to be any good to me. I did awful things to her and I ignored it when other people did the same. She could never work the hours I needed her to work in order for *me* to work less hours. So I orchestrated a campaign that made her so miserable that eventually I got my way and she left."

She couldn't look at him now – she was too embarrassed.

"So now, I need to decide if I'm prepared to jeopardise everything I have at home, to stay here and try and explain my actions. Or do I give it all up, let Gavin take that job and just go home. Or just leave here, sell that stupid house and start again somewhere else. Whatever I do though, above all I want to go back to being the kind of person that doesn't do that to another human being."

"Leona, none of this was your fault. Don't punish yourself like this, please!"

"I have to, Rob, I'm sorry."

"You don't have to. You have a choice, just like I had a choice and I chose to stay, for you, remember?"

"Rob, this is not like your situation. And you did not choose to stay for me. You chose to stay in Dublin as it's the right thing to do. You have your whole life ahead of you and you have every right to decide how and where you want to live it. I have a little girl. My life isn't mine anymore, I need to do what's best for her, and –" she stopped and took a short breath, "I want another baby, Rob. Now maybe I've left it too late, but maybe I haven't. There's only one way to find out."

He nodded but, at the sight of all that anger and disappointment on his beautiful young face, she felt that her heart might crack in two.

"Oh Rob, I'm so sorry," she cried and in a single step she took him into her arms against the backdrop of the streaky orange sky behind. Standing on her tippy-toes she then placed a hand either side of his face, and then she kissed him gently, on the forehead, on each cheek, and then lingered for a second, close to his beautiful lips, but not close enough.

So she could still say she'd done nothing wrong.

Chapter 60

KATE

Kate stepped onto the Luas and deliberately chose a seat up behind the driver. The last thing she wanted was to prove Siobhán right and go and get mugged tonight of all nights.

Especially now that the end was in sight.

She wasn't sure how she was feeling about what had just happened. She'd really, really wanted this job to work.

And it hadn't.

But she realised now that the job was just a symptom of what had gone wrong; it wasn't really the cause. She wanted to work and she wanted a career but Leona had been right about one thing: this wasn't the job for her. She would find the right role though, in the right company. It would just take time.

She wondered what would Michael say when she told him she wanted to go to see a counsellor. He'd probably laugh and say that no money in the world would pay a counsellor to listen to her. But she surely wouldn't be the worst case they'd seen?

She wasn't even sure what she wanted to talk about, but she was pretty sure that she hadn't really felt herself ever since Jess was born. She hadn't realised that until earlier this week. When everything had started to slide out of control and she'd started to think more and more about the awful night of Jess's birth. And how she'd pretty much felt like a failure as a parent ever since.

That was why she'd been so keen to go back to work. She'd

wanted to go back to something she knew she was good at. She wanted to feel like a success again.

The funny thing was she'd mentioned some of this to Lynn today on the phone. And Lynn had said that she'd had a similar birthing experience with Sophie, her third child. And she'd insisted that they keep trying with the natural birth – she'd never had a section before and she didn't want to have one then. And so the medical team had kept trying and sure enough Sophie was born two hours later, only she was blue. Eight years later, Lynn said, she often wondered was that why Sophie was different to the others. She was currently undergoing all kinds of assessments and Lynn said she would never forgive herself if it turned out to be all her fault.

And that had shocked Kate to her core. Lynn? Lynn was beating herself up over something? Well, if that hadn't blown the world of parenting right open!

Blackhorse
Bluebell
Kylemore

She was nearly home. She'd miss the ould Luas, she thought to herself. She'd had no trouble really over the last few weeks. Siobhán had been wrong. Turned out the people to avoid weren't the ones in hoodies after all.

Chapter 61

MARY

Mary click-clacked across the concrete floor of the underground to where her car was parked. She flung open her door and sat in, checking the time on the dial that glowed as soon as her door opened.

She'd just make it.

She never drove in heels but she hadn't time to change her shoes. She flung her jacket in the passenger seat and turned her key in the ignition.

She'd warned Ronan that what she was wearing might not be suitable for a business networking social. A bit formal maybe. But he'd said she'd be perfect. That a Bitter Bitch in a suit was exactly what he needed at his side. He'd only texted her to say he hoped the big day was going okay. Imagine he'd remembered! So when she'd answered that she'd had much better days and in fact she felt like shit, he'd replied instantly that she should ditch the Germans and come on a date instead with a lonely Irishman.

A date?

She'd read it three times before flinging her phone into her bag and almost running to the lift, all thoughts of how she didn't go for beards gone clean out of her head.

As she pulled out onto the Quays her sister's number flashed up on her phone. She reached across and hit the power button, turning it off altogether.

Sorry, Dee, I just don't have time tonight.

337

Chapter 62

LEONA

The sky was dark behind the Samuel Beckett Bridge as Leona came out of her office, having shut down her computer and gathered together her few bits. She didn't walk over to the window this time though. She had no interest. She was going home, home to her baby.

Home to her husband.

On the phone he'd sounded like a version of Gavin she'd never met before. He'd been crying and apologising and not really making much sense at all.

But then neither of them had been making any sense lately. Could they get it all back on track? She didn't know. But she knew she had to at least try.

She owed it to Rachel.

She owed it to Gavin.

But, most of all, she owed it to herself.

"I heard you were going home?"

She turned to see Geraldine behind her.

"I am, Geraldine. It's been a long hard day and I suspect the days to come are not going to be get much easier."

"No. I'm afraid it's probably going to get worse before it gets better alright," Geraldine said. "But I just wanted to make sure you're okay before you go home. And mostly, without going into any detail – tonight is not the night for that – I just wanted you to know that we'll do everything we can to support you on this. You're well thought of here, Leona."

Leona smiled. "I appreciate that, Geraldine. And I'm sorry, this whole mess is the last –"

There was a commotion at the door and they turned to see Alice and Rob walk across the far side of the open-plan office, Alice carrying a half-empty bottle of white wine.

Leona watched them leave the room again and then, feeling Geraldine's eyes on her, looked back at her.

"Sorry, I was saying, it's the last thing you needed. It's the last thing Declan needs, what with Head Office right here in the building."

"Don't you worry about Declan," Geraldine said sagely. "I've met men like him before – he's like the proverbial cockroach. This won't ruin him, he's survived worse before – he'll survive this too."

"Anyhow, I know I handled a couple of things badly, and I take full responsibility for any mess I've caused."

Geraldine opened her mouth as if to speak, but then shut it again and seemed to think for a second or two before then saying, "We'll talk tomorrow, Leona. I'm glad you're okay. And I'm glad you're going home."

Leona smiled and there was a flicker of sadness in her eyes as they drifted to the now closed door through which Rob and Alice had just disappeared.

"I think I will be too, Ger, in time."

OLIVIA

So that's the whole story in a nutshell.

The funny thing is I thought I was getting better at thinking about it. Seeing the counsellor every Tuesday night helps. I had to do something. I couldn't stop crying, I felt like nothing I could do was right and, most of all, I felt like I'd let everyone down by making such a mess of it all. Danny, the kids, my dad and them ... Imagine I felt guilty about them.

It had taken weeks to start feeling like I was making any kind of headway, and when Deborah the counsellor got me to start writing everything down I may have even started to feel a bit worse, but then that too started to help and, honestly, I was starting to feel so much better. Anyhow, I guess that's why I was so shocked at the way I reacted when Kate arrived at my door. I can't explain it. Despite all the work I'd done with Deborah, it all came rushing back and I nearly lost my reason. No wonder Kate looked so horrified. When I think of it now it's a bit embarrassing really. But it was like the thing I was learning to forget about had arrived at my front door, into my home, my safe place and I just couldn't cope. I couldn't even tell Danny – he'd have got so angry and might even have phoned the bank and I didn't want that to happen. She'd been trying to do something nice, but it took me hours to be able to see it like that. And then, when I'd calmed down the first thing I thought of was my photo in its frame. Again it was like I'd left my boys in there, in that horrible place, so I sent the email, not even sure if it would reach her or if it did that she'd even respond.

Meeting Kate that Monday was like being right back at that very first counselling session where I just cried and cried. Again I'm sure she thought I was some kind of deranged person but we met again that evening regardless and I was able to stay calm enough to tell her the whole story. But, unlike the counsellor, when I eventually got to the end, Kate was really, really angry. She told me it was all starting to happen again, that they were trying to do the same thing to her and that I should do something, that I should go to my solicitor and let them know that they weren't going to get away with how they had treated me. I told her about my counselling – that it had really helped and she agreed that maybe it would help her too, but she said it wasn't right that either of us should need counselling for trying to do our job, and by the time she left that night I was like a woman possessed. I was going to take them for every penny I could get.

But then next morning, when I said it to my dad, he thought about it for a while and then he said, "Do you know what, Livvy? That would never do you any favours. Let them off would be my advice."

So I was angry with him then. I accused him of taking their side, of not understanding, but he told me a story then about the time they all were on strike on the docks, and how the rows would start between the people keeping the strike and those that were breaking the picket. He said that the strike set brother against brother, neighbour against neighbour and caused decades of pain. Pain that affected no one but themselves.

And he said, "Sometimes you need to be sure you're fighting the right person and, if you take that fight on, that it's the ones at the top, the ones who are happily pitting you all against one another, that are suffering the fallout, not the wee ones at the bottom."

So then I didn't know what to do. All the feelings of helplessness were coming flooding back. Kate wanted me to do one thing, my dad wanted me to do the other. And I couldn't even tell Danny as I knew he'd have just sided with Kate. And by the time I met Deborah that evening, well, I was angry with her too. I felt like she had fooled me. That I wasn't better at all.

So I cried again. And, when I managed to stop, she listened to me *going on and on and then she told me that feeling like this after meeting Kate was all perfectly normal. She said that she'd been expecting this to happen. She hadn't known if it would be the first time I heard the bank mentioned on the news, or the first time I drove past it, or the first time I found one of my old business cards in the bottom of a bag. She said any of those things would have had the same effect. And that these kinds of things were going to happen again and again but that hopefully my reaction would be less each time, and that eventually I could bump into Leona herself and feel nothing.*

I told her then that I wanted to hate Leona and that, while I felt Kate was right and that she deserved to be punished, a funny thing had happened after leaving my dad that morning. I'd remembered the day I found Leona crying in the toilets, not long before I went on my third maternity leave. And that got me thinking that maybe that she was just like the rest of us really. So I asked Deborah then, did she think my dad was right – that maybe we were all fighting the wrong fight? But she wouldn't answer – she just asked me what did I think myself.

Deborah was crafty like that, though, she always turned it back on me.

So I haven't told Kate yet that I'm not going to go down the legal route. Deborah said I had to stop feeling under pressure to answer to everyone. She said Kate's issues were exactly that – Kate's issues – and that I had to decide myself what mine were. That there was just no way of keeping everyone happy and that I had to learn to live with that fact.

And she's right. I already feel better, stronger and from now on I'm going to try and only look forward, not backwards. I'm not sure Danny likes this new me, mind you, but, as Deborah says, if he wants me to be more assertive then he'll have to know I can't pick and choose when to act on it. It's driving him mad that he has to give me money every week but, do you know what, we're not half as broke as he lets on we are. And it's not like we don't still have those feckin' savings.

I tell you, if he's not careful, I might even cheer for Dublin the next time they meet Meath.

Though maybe not. Maybe I'll wait till I've a bit more written down.

CIAN

I saw them.

It was the morning that there was all that hullabaloo with Head Office. The day they needed all those figures and I got into trouble for being out putting money in a parking meter.

Well, when I was dashing up and down the street trying to get to the meter in time, the two of them were on that bridge, kissing and groping like they'd nowhere else to be.

I knew it then. I knew that I wouldn't get the promotion. Sure hadn't she said to me that she wanted 'something extra' – 'something special' – like what Rob was giving her ...

So was I surprised when I got the email to say it was his? Was I fuck!

Well, the two of them can suffer now. Damn straight I went to a solicitor. You can't do something like that and get away with it. My solicitor said I had a great case so of course I gave him the go-ahead to send the two 'Letters before Action' to DKB. The sooner they got them the better as far as I was concerned.

Let's see how smart they are now.

THE END

FOOTNOTE

In November 2014, The Committee of Inquiry into the Banking Crisis, colloquially known as the Banking Inquiry, was established. The purpose of the Inquiry was to investigate the reasons that Ireland experienced a systemic banking crisis, including the political, economic, social, cultural, financial and behavioural factors and policies which impacted on or contributed to the crisis and the preventative reforms implemented in the wake of the crisis.

The panel concluded public hearings in early September 2015, having heard from 128 witnesses over 49 days of sittings. This included hearing evidence from former Taoisigh Bertie Ahern and Brian Cowen – as well as several former and current senior bankers during hours of public sessions,

The inquiry has to agree a final draft report before the Taoiseach can dissolve the Dáil in early spring 2016 or all the work of the committee will be rendered invalid.

At time of going to print, the committee are thought to be nowhere close to reaching agreement on the initial draft report with some members rendering it 'not fit for purpose'. One member even went so far as to say 'we need to write from scratch in a week a report that is balanced and fair and tells people what happened and why it happened. It's impossible.'

This inquiry has cost €4.9 million to date.

Book Club Questions for
The Fallout

1. How did you enjoy this book? Did it take you long to 'get into'? Did it hold your attention throughout?

2. It's set in the IFSC in the early years of the Irish recession – did you find this an interesting backdrop for the novel?

3. The author uses shifting viewpoints to illustrate the story – did you enjoy this or find it confusing?

4. Why do you think the author chose to tell the story in this way?

5. Did you feel any empathy for any particular character, and did this empathy grow or decrease as the book went on?

6. Which characters did you find likeable, or indeed, unlikeable?

7. Do you think Olivia should take any responsibility for what happened her at DKB?

8. Do you agree with Leona when she says that it takes a 'certain type of woman to maintain the same career after she has children'?

9. Do you think Kate has a realistic view of what a working mother can achieve?

10. Who do you think should feel the most remorse for their behaviour – Leona or Gavin?

11. How much responsibility do you think Rob has for his father's dilemma? Do you think he should return to help him in his hour of need?

12. Did you find the ending satisfactory or would you have preferred a different close to the story? Was the ending what you had expected?

13. Do you think Leona made the right decision in the end?

14. What do you think the future holds for Mary?

15. Did this book make you angry at all, and if so, with whom?

16. Whose side – if any – were you on and did you feel your allegiances changed as you neared the end of the book?

17. Do the characters remind you of anyone you know? Or have you ever found yourself in a similar situation in your workplace?

18. Do you think that Leona is right that she can 'still say she did nothing wrong' when it comes to her relationship with Rob?

19. If you could meet one character again to see where their life headed after the closing lines of the book, who would it be?

For a broader discussion on #thefallout join author @mgtscott and other readers on Twitter and don't forget to hashtag your allegiance to your favourite character ie #TeamKate or #TeamMary to really get the conversation going!

ALSO AVAILABLE

Between You and Me

MARGARET SCOTT

Holly Green is an auditor with a New York firm. While working temporarily in the Dublin office, she falls in love with her colleague Oliver Conlon. Fresh out of a disastrous love affair, she now feels she can rebuild her future.

Then she comes up against corrupt businessman Ger Baron and her tough-minded tactics land her in hot water at work. It looks like she must return to New York, leaving Oliver and a lot of unresolved issues behind.

But, suddenly thinking outside the box, she makes a decision that puts her in a very strange situation indeed . . .

A few days later Holly is live-in nanny to two small children – a withdrawn five-year-old and a demon two-year-old – and is wishing she really *did* have the experience she claimed she had on her CV. Then she makes two discoveries: *Supernanny* – and the fact that applying her own business training may be just the thing to whip the household into shape . . .

Whipping Oliver Conlon into shape is another item on her agenda . . .

ISBN 9781842235966

If you enjoyed this book from
Poolbeg why not visit our website:

poolbeg.com

**and get another book delivered straight
to your home or to a friend's home.**

All books despatched within 24 hours.

Why not join our mailing list
at www.poolbeg.com and get some fantastic
offers, competitions, author interviews
and much more?

CHECK US OUT ON TWITTER AND FACEBOOK

FOR OFFERS, UPDATES, NEW RELEASES AND EVENTS!

@PoolbegBooks   www.facebook.com/poolbeg